MASQUERADE

MASQUERADE

THERESA BUTLER

Butler Did It Publishing
PHOENIX, AZ

MASQUERADE
Copyright © 2015 by Theresa Butler.

For information contact:
Butler Did It Publishing, PO Box 22177, Phoenix, Arizona 85028
www.butlerdiditpub.com

Cover design by GSPH/Raffy Ferras Hoylar
Cover image © Sergey Sizov
ISBN-13: 978-0692552636
ISBN-10: 0692552634

First Edition: October 2015

10 9 8 7 6 5 4 3 2 1

For the Phantom, who brought me Joy
and a lifelong obsession
with tortured masked men

CHAPTER 1

I NEEDED AN ESCAPE. There had to be one somewhere else. Some exit other than the one near the oil painting of some ancient Medici prince blocked by a white-faced mime and his audience.

Too many revellers, eager to gawk at the staged sideshows and dancing, had crowded into the small Venetian ballroom already crammed with gaudy set decorations and priceless historical heirlooms. Their pressing interest in the festivities made my skin crawl and any breathing difficult, the latter worsened by the restrictive costume into which I had stuffed myself hours before.

I paused on the edge of the mob, attempting to collect myself with a steadying gulp of perfumed air, but the cloying sweetness made me gag. A woman standing near me, half watching two aerialists hover over the floor on crimson silks, glanced in my direction. Revulsion etched her partially masked features. I wanted to tell her she was safe. I didn't plan to vomit on her, though I couldn't make any promises. After all, I drank too much champagne and ate little food at dinner.

Anything was possible.

I managed, instead, only a weak smile and pushed toward the centre of the dancing mass in the adjacent and even smaller ballroom, until an unexpected, icy tendril curled up my spine. The tiny hairs on my arms and the back of my neck rose in response to my sudden awareness. I froze, rooted to the antique parquet beneath me, searching for the source of my uneasiness, though I recognised the sensation well enough. After years of people staring at me, first as a model and then as Georgina Cavendish's personal assistant, the only explanation for my discomfiture was a pointed stare assessing me from across the room.

Dancers swayed in circles around me to the music of a baroque harpsichord player sitting on the other side of the sweltering candle-lit room. The dancers' shimmering costumes of colourful brocades and velvets and silks brushed and agitated my clothing in a wordless warning to move lest I become an obstacle in their intricate steps. My brain and legs had other ideas, however, and refused to move when I finally located the costumed man staring at me from beneath a gilded mask.

Two swirling women collided with me mid-spin at the same moment my eyes met his, the momentum of the impact knocking me free of my impersonation of one of the marbled statues lining the walls of the ballroom. I wanted nothing more than to disappear completely, if only to avoid the exasperated rolling eyes from the others who stopped to gape at my faux pas. I excused myself in hurried and effusive Italian for impeding the women, hoping the foreign words were correct.

Not for the first time that night, I silently wished I was at a more intimate venue with a crowd size more to my liking. Or, at the very least, with a crowd more welcoming than the raised noses of the world's elite that had converged on Venice for the penultimate celebration of Carnevale.

I felt hopelessly plebeian. These people were not. Sometimes I wondered if they smelled it on me the way I smelled the stench of their thousand Euro-per-ounce perfume hovering in a thick cloud as they brushed by to fawn over their peers. No doubt, I had slighted them all by interrupting the flow of their dancing. They were not shy about cluing me into their condescension, either, as a wave of hushed admonishment filled the room.

What did my boss see in them, anyway? I never understood her fascination.

She craved nothing more than this glamorous lifestyle, making me indispensable to her as she floated around spreading her wit and charm. What wit and charm, exactly, I was still trying to puzzle out after two and a half years as her assistant. I always found any positive quality especially difficult to spot in her when she treated me like another one of the countless and disposable accessories integral to her image and position in this society. She owned me; the title on my résumé may have read "personal assistant," but I needed no confirmation from her to ascertain my true function as a glorified lady's maid—a status symbol meant only to prove to others she was a legitimate member of their circle. She made a point of pushing me away into the periphery until she needed me, and in the periphery I was to stay, invisible and alone lest I find myself listening to another of her nasally lectures on appropriate behaviour at Events Like This.

I grumbled with the thought, excusing myself when I at last found an open doorway.

My salvation came in the shape of a large stone balcony overlooking the Grand Canal. Only marginally less crowded than the inside of the ballroom, the balcony itself gave me more space to move. Space to breathe. And space to cool off my hot, humiliated face without worrying about someone judging me. I wasted no time gulping down the chilled night air, the deep odour of salty sea and the dampness of a waterlogged city relaxing my frayed nerves in an instant.

Leaning over the stone balustrade, I spotted a lonely gondolier rowing through the canal. A loving couple dressed in matching cream and gold kit cuddled in his boat as it glided effortlessly through the dark rippling water. It seemed such a serene tableau compared to the cacophony and revelry inside the palazzo.

I sighed and relaxed against the railing, easing the pressure on my tired legs. My feet ached. Spending my free afternoon moseying the streets and landmarks of Venice had been a mistake. But I refused to leave without a little culture before anybody whisked me straight back to the dreary doldrums of London's early spring and the reality of my life. My life was, without doubt, a far cry from the most glamorous ballroom on the Grand Canal. I deserved one night of enjoyment for the hell Georgina put me through on a daily basis, even if the stilettos I had teetered on all night didn't make the pain in my feet feel any better.

I slipped off one high heel and then the next, each with a contented sigh. The ancient stones beneath my stocking-covered feet were cold but soothing. As I wondered if I could make a break for the hotel without replacing the torturous things, I felt a strong hand on the small of my back and the added warmth from a body close to me. The blue-eyed man with the gilded mask covering his face slipped into the position beside me, resting his elbow on the railing and cocking his head to the side in a thoroughly arrogant manner.

"Why aren't you dancing?" asked he, in halting Italian.

My face burned with embarrassment. The heat crept down my neck. It was unbearable under the heavily decorated half mask itching my cheeks. I grabbed at the attached feather spray to tear the whole thing off, but before I could, the man stopped me with a hand on my arm.

"Leave the mask on," he said, once more in Italian. He wasn't a native speaker, but he spoke with a fluency matching my own. "Don't ruin the mystery and the… possibilities… of the night."

I frowned. The possibilities? It made me want to laugh. Almost. He would end up in bed with a beautiful woman back at his hotel, and I'd be stuck tossing and turning in my tiny single occupancy room. He had no right to tell me to what to do, and yet I listened to him.

I removed my hand from the mask and placed it on the stone railing, gripping to hold myself steady. I was liable to float off or sink to the ground at any minute if he didn't stop trying to read into my soul.

"You didn't answer me. Why aren't you dancing?"

I shrugged and chose the simplest answer. "No one asked."

"Wonderful! That means you're free," he said. "Would you care to dance?"

Darting a furtive glance toward the gathering inside and then back to the tall man leaning on the railing in his trademarked devil-may-care way, I gulped more air, but it didn't seem to soothe the suffocating pressure in my throat. What did I do? Did I find my employer to tell her of my intention to leave, or did I stay and accept a dance from a man who filled out his eighteenth-century breeches and waistcoat too well?

But even I knew those weren't the questions wanting answers. What needed clarification was why he wanted to dance with me.

Even though layers of an ornate taffeta costume covered every inch of my body, there was no way he could mistake how I didn't fit in with the other rail thin celebrities populating most of the masquerade. The men here—the men who had ignored me all night—didn't care for women shaped like me and hadn't given me a second look. They preferred lingerie models and those preferences, without fail, relegated me to being a wallflower at these types of soirées.

His sentiment, however nice, was to me only a thinly veiled effort to disguise his pity.

"Don't you have a girlfriend?" I asked him. *Like my boss?*

He seemed stunned by my response, but it was hard to tell purely from the slight bodily reflex and his unsure eyes. I wanted to see his face, to read him better. But I knew he wouldn't take well to an unmasking considering how he reacted when I tried to remove my own.

He cleared his throat, now recovered, and answered. "Oh… you must mean Signorina Cavendish."

I squinted in incredulity. Had I not been wearing the mask, it would have made a terrible sight, I was sure, so I was thankful it hid my impertinence.

But he knew me. Couldn't he see me? Had we not, just hours before, sat at the same table while I discussed the schedule for the evening's festivities—and helped sort out the costumes—with both of them?

When I didn't say anything, he merely heaved a sigh. He inched closer to me, dropping his voice and whispering conspiratorially, "Just between you and me, bellissima, we aren't serious."

According to Signorina Cavendish, they were all but engaged, with every news source in the world salivating for the first photos of their nuptials. They met at a polo match seven months earlier—I did not attend due to a prior commitment—after which their relationship regularly became front page news. For a supposed casual relationship, the two participants certainly gave every indication to the contrary.

Of course, I'd been wrong before and I spent little time with the man in the daily activities of my job, especially since "Signorina Cavendish" and I travelled alone for the better part of their relationship. Our interactions, instead, were limited to those few short minutes when he came to pick her up for a night on the town or when he lumbered—bleary eyed and barely clothed, scratching at his day-old auburn beard—down the hallway to the bathroom in the morning.

While he had always been pleasant in the former instances, the latter only created a worshipful infatuation in me. As proper, kind, and well dressed as he was in public, he was every bit the man's man in private. He drank whiskey like it was going out of style and scratched himself impolitely and cared too much about which team won a football match. It was all utterly sexy in a way I could never fully comprehend. I wasn't sure if I ever would comprehend it.

Honestly, I was a little in love with him, and he didn't know I existed. Until that moment, at least. I didn't know whether to feel flattered or excited or—as my brain suggested—pathetic. He must have felt so sorry watching me mope around the ball that he asked to dance.

Some small part of me wondered if he hadn't paid more attention to me all along. But no, he didn't even recognise me, even with my stumbling English-accented Italian while I searched for the correct words and verb conjugations in my head.

"It's a night where anything's possible," he repeated as if reading my thoughts.

He reached out, brushing his fingers lightly over my hand clenching the handrail. Long fingers traced over my knuckles and then down the side of the thumb to my wrist. A shiver skittered up my spine, relaxing my hand enough that he turned it over and danced his fingertips up the underside of my arm. He stopped at the lacy edging of my gown's elbow-length sleeves.

"Dance with me?"

I breathed out again, finding my bodice more constricting than ever. "Fine."

"I promise I will make it worth your while," he assured with a wink.

I took a step toward him, but remembered my shoeless feet when I nearly tripped. "Oh, I, uh… hold on."

Then I realised bending over to replace my shoes while wearing a heavy gown, wig, and mask was impossible without falling over. I stuffed my feet into the things as best as I could manage, but only succeeded in jamming the heel down into the shoe. They needed to be fixed.

"I, um," I mumbled, trying to find a quick solution to the dilemma without his help. I lifted the bottom hem of my dress to show him my predicament. Rather than roll his eyes or scoff in irritation, he took the gallant role. He tossed back the tails of his brocaded coat and knelt on one knee. I silently prayed the breeches did not stain—I promised the clothier we retrieved them from that they would be returned in good repair.

The kneeling man looked up at me expectantly and patted one raised knee. I held onto the balustrade to counterbalance the movement. With nimble fingers, he removed the shoe partly, and as though he were Prince Charming gone looking for his Cinderella, he carefully wrapped his fingers around my ankle to slide the shoe into place.

My foot screamed, of course, to be released from its torturous confines again, but it would have to wait. As crazy and quixotic as my situation had become, I was not going to let it pass by. I would savour it. Remember it. And think about the night for the rest of my life.

"Other foot?"

I started, realising my mind had drifted again to thoughts about Alexander Thorne I had no business having. This was my boss' boyfriend. And I definitely wasn't his type, if his long and well chronicled history of ditzy blonde socialites and fellow celebrities were any indication. A small drop of fantasy on a night of frivolity though it may have been, I couldn't allow myself to believe any of it, no matter how it made me feel.

Again thankful for the mask covering the majority of my blush, I set the fully shoed foot on the ground and raised the other. The loose shoe fell off with a clatter. He reached for it and grabbed my bare foot with the other hand. Not wasting the opportunity, he teased his fingers along the arch, drawing a giggle and another shiver from me.

His playful gaze darted up to me. I imagined him biting his lower lip in mirth beneath the mask, the same way he did when he laughed at something on any old day.

"Grazie," he said and slipped his grip to my ankle. I thought he would stop there, but he kept moving northward, squeezing my calf. I was somewhere between letting out a moan of ecstasy and wanting to kick him away. The other people on the balcony didn't seem to care what was going on, but it was still much too public for me.

This was wrong. So, so wrong. He had to know it was me, Emilia Wyck, Georgina Cavendish's assistant. I wondered if he was just pulling my leg... literally. Some cruel joke he and Georgina had concocted. But that wasn't him. He was too kind. Wasn't he?

"Alex—" I began to say his name, deciding then it was best to drop the Italian to make my next point clear, but silenced when he held up a finger to his mask.

"No names. This is a masquerade."

I didn't really have a point to make anyway. There probably should have been one about him being faithful and me not wanting to wreck a relationship because he couldn't keep his hands to himself, but all words died on my lips as he finally, carefully, worked my second shoe into place.

Ever so reverently, he lowered my leg back to the ground. I stood on the thin heels, regaining my balance and praying my lightheadedness would pass as we manoeuvred our way onto the dance floor. He stood and held his arm out at a right angle for me to take. I did so, clenching my fingers in the rich red and gold fabric of the costume I had admired at the shop when we picked it to match Georgina's clothing. It was the only reason I knew it was him from across the ballroom; I still wasn't entirely convinced whether or not he knew it was his girlfriend's assistant that he was playing with, even though he saw my costume long before I put it on my body.

We made it to the dance floor as the song changed over to something a bit slower. Some time since I left the ballroom, a DJ had replaced the strings and harpsichord playing gavottes and minuets. The DJ, however, kept with the theme of the night and chose a dreamy waltz.

My companion turned to me. "Do you know how to waltz, bellissima?"

"I do, actually," I replied. "Amazing what you can learn at university without actually attending lectures."

He seemed delighted at the news, pulling me to his chest. I took no small amount of pleasure feeling the lean muscles of his lithe body through the many layers of fabric between us, and blew a stream of air from my lips in an attempt to slow my racing heart. A strange heat permeated my clothing, making the hot room more unbearable in an entirely different way. From this vantage, I caught a glimpse of his face just under the protruding chin of his mask, but it was too brief a moment to read his expression. Or to ascertain if he was just as uncomfortable as I was.

Without speaking another word, he used his body to move us into the motion of the dance, rocking us slightly on the balls of our feet to feel the rhythm. When the downbeat came around again, his left thigh pushed against my right, and we were off swirling in the mass of dancers.

He was an expert lead and an even better dancer. I didn't know why I was so surprised, but I imagined it had something to do with my focusing on other things, like the strength of his grip on my shoulder blade and how it steadily crept lower down my back. Or the fact that he smelled of the intoxicating cologne I chose for his birthday so Georgina had a tangible gift to give to him in addition to the Grecian yachting holiday she had me plan.

We danced for awhile as my mind wandered and it was an entirely different song when I realised I needed a breather. When I looked up again, the steady blue gaze was watching me.

"I need to rest," I said.

He nodded and moved us toward a wall so as to not interfere with the ring of dancers in the waltz. "Thank you for the dance, bellissima."

I gave him a small, sad smile when it hit me this was likely where he would bow and take his leave, having completed the gentlemanly duty of dancing with me once. However, I didn't notice how close we were to a private alcove partially shielded from view by a tied velvet curtain. He pushed me inside without asking and pulled the sash, closing us away from the party.

I didn't need to see the intensity in his eyes to know what he planned to do next, but I was still surprised as his hard body pressed me against a wall and pushed the mask on his head back to reveal his beautiful face. He took my mouth with an intensity I had not expected, though it was just as heart stopping as I had fantasised. Soft and hard and demanding all at the same time, it was everything I had dreamed about and yet somehow more. His forcefulness seized all the air from my body but begged for me to return his kiss. My thoughts spun wildly. Blood pounded in my head and made my knees tremble with need.

I clutched the front of his coat for dear life, praying the sensuous assault would cease so I could breathe and remain upright. Even though he had me pinned against the wall, and I was very aware I would not fall, the feeling of weakness that pervaded my every sense made me release a gasping moan. It pierced through the relative silence of our stolen privacy.

The thin bubble of fantasy popped. His firm grasp on my bum—how had his hands even made it there?—loosened and he stepped away. Bright eyes stared back at me only for a moment as my skirts fell back into place. I slumped against the wall, struggling to hold myself up on newly gelatinous legs.

Then he was gone. I waited for him to return and explain himself or to finish what he started.

He did not.

"Fuck me," I muttered, lowering onto the chair in the tiny room. My mind refused to make sense. I wasn't sure my night would ever make sense to me. However, it became clear I needed to leave. No way could I go back into that crowd and once more have him immobilise me with nothing more than a stare from across the room.

CHAPTER 2

I COULDN'T BE ARSED to jump out of bed with any of my usual urgency knowing what waited for me once I trudged up to Georgina's lavish suite. Sadly, reality set in with the sunrise, now no longer hidden in the mask of a Carnevale night. Not only would I have to return to work, but I would also have to face Alex. Though his kiss must have been a mistake in some small part, simply judging from his immediate reaction to leave, another part of me wished it wasn't. I wished Alexander Thorne, Hollywood's latest It Boy, purposely sought me out and chose me over the woman he had supposedly dated for seven months.

A foolish and fanciful wish, yes, but it was the only thing propelling me through my morning ablutions. I chose comfort in jeans and a fuzzy jumper before I gathered my things and stuffed them into an oversized tote. I shoved my thick-rimmed eyeglasses on my face in lieu of my usual contacts and completely ignored my cosmetics bag. For the ball, I made myself up in an effort to play along. I refused to do it this morning, particularly when I wanted to avoid my boss' pointed attention. If I actually tried, she would suspect something and quiz me about it.

I arrived at her suite at exactly 10:30, according to the time on my mobile, and knocked lightly on the door. When no one answered, I figured Georgina was still be in bed. It wasn't unlike her to have a lie-in after a particularly eventful night out playing to a crowd.

The sound of squeaking wheels from the end of the hall made me turn. A porter pushed a wheeled cart in front of him, the cart piled high with the room service I ordered before leaving my room. He stopped beside me and stood up straight at attention.

"Buongiorno!" He greeted me with a welcoming smile and straightened his uniform coat as he stood still and waved his white-gloved hands at the food. "I have your brunch."

I smiled and dug the spare room key out of my pocket to open the door. "It's actually for my boss. Set it up in the dining area, please?"

He nodded and disappeared into the small area off the equally tiny sitting room. I opened the shuttered windows, casting bright light into the room and onto the remnants of a vicious tornado which had apparently wrecked the space the previous evening. Bits and pieces of clothing were flung here and there—on the backs of chairs and sofas and on the floor.

And lamps, I thought to myself, pulling at a sheer nude stocking dangling from a lampshade.

It didn't take a genius to figure out the cause of the sudden disarray. However, my awareness didn't make me feel any better. A sour taste filled my mouth as I moved about the room collecting the costumes to be returned later. How could he have done what he did in the ballroom and come back here, as though nothing were wrong, to make love to Georgina?

The answers to all my questions regarding our night became clearer as I worked. The only explanation was that Alex got carried away when he kissed me, realised his folly, and left me sitting alone in that alcove trying to make sense of it all.

I hated him for making me live through this torture. Not only did he leave me unfulfilled, he threw the fact that I could never have him right back in my face, leaving a mess like this for me to find in the morning. This wasn't the first time I had collected scattered clothing the morning after he stayed over with Georgina. He had to have known what would happen when I arrived.

His red and gold coat did not seem as colourful or richly gorgeous as it had in the dimness of a candlelit ballroom as I examined it on the back of the sofa in the morning's harsh light. In fact, it looked dull and tarnished. And yet, I couldn't help but run the luxurious material through my fingers, remembering how I had held onto one arm and clenched the sinew beneath it as he led me across the dance floor. The memory made me cringe and ball my fists in the fabric. I tossed the garment on top of the other parts of the costume I had collected and reached for the waistcoat, snatching it to me in annoyance.

His golden mask fell out of the folds, landing with a resounding *thunk* on the hardwood flooring. I stared down at the thing with no small amount of contempt, wanting to punt it through the far window and never look at it again. I grumbled and instead bent to retrieve it, reverentially sliding my fingers on the curves around the eyeholes and along the sloped nose, imagining it was still on him. Or better yet, that it was Alex himself, and he allowed me full access to caress the smooth planes and ridges of his handsome patrician face.

When hot, stinging tears sprang to my eyes, I knew I'd mucked it all up. How was I ever going to face him if a bloody mask made me tear up and think such things? Seeing him in the flesh would only make it worse.

"Signorina?"

The voice startled me, but then I realised it was only the porter. I glanced behind him to look at the elegantly set dining table.

"Oh, my apologies," I said. "Hold on one second."

I grabbed my handbag from the sofa and dug out a few Euros for the man.

"Grazie, signorina."

He nodded his head and disappeared out the door, leaving me alone with the mask and my vengeful thoughts. If Alex refused to have a care for these things—for me and for the heart he stepped on—then I refused to let the occasion slip away to shove memories of the moment right back under his nose. I placed the mask on the pristine dining table without really thinking it through. It made a wonderful contrast on the stark white table linens. There would be no way for him to miss it.

I went back to my chores, moving through the suite to put things right. At long last, I heard movement in the bedroom. The door cracked open a smidgeon and then opened fully to reveal the object of my loathing. Thankfully, he wore a proper dressing gown over his athletic frame. Though it did not stop my mind from racing, it helped to keep me from staring like I had done countless times before as he ambled down hallways after nights with her.

He stopped for a moment in the powder room and then shuffled a path into the airy dining room. With a huge yawn, he stretched his arms over his head, then scratched his chest and looked at the food-laden table with a glimmer of desire in his eyes. He had looked at me that way, as though he wanted to devour me. Now it was only reserved for the food.

I watched him for any sign of interest, amusement, sadness—anything—which might give me some inkling as to how he felt about the mask on the table. Surely it would jog his memory from the night before and he would remember what had happened.

My pulse thrummed in excitement when his fingers reverently touched the gilded exterior for the briefest of moments. I hoped to see fondness in his eyes, but he revealed nothing, not unlike the most trained of poker players. The inscrutable expression on his face remained as he pulled out a chair and sat down to his breakfast. Adoration finally crossed his face, but only for the sight of his favourite tea packet in the wicker basket on the table.

I sniffed and returned to folding and hanging the costume garments before placing them in the clothier's bags. As though an afterthought, he finally spoke to me.

"Good morning, Emilia." His voice, still gravelly from sleep, felt like a caress against my skin. It was lovely to hear him speaking in English again, but also disappointing. I wanted mysterious Alex back—the one who spoke flawless Italian, who knelt on the ground to help a lady with her shoes, and who thoroughly snogged women in dark alcoves.

"Hello," I said shortly.

I stuffed two powdered wigs into the hat box and at last moved to the pannier cage structure Georgina had worn beneath her gown. This single piece of women's fashion explained exactly why only rich people wore them when they were en vogue. It required a bevy of maids to collapse it down to a less awkward size. Or, as it were, someone not as angry at life as I was at that particular moment.

I struggled with it for a few minutes, but saw no solution. A masculine laugh filled the room. "Come have breakfast, Em. I'll help you with it later."

I fixed him with a vehement look. "I'm doing just fine, thank you."

I struggled some more, aware of his eyes watching me. It made the task a million times more difficult. There was a huff from somewhere and then a warm hand touched my elbow. I froze and looked at him as he rested his other hand on one of mine. The touch made me uncomfortable.

"Let me help you," he insisted. "I helped her dress last night."

I snatched my arm away from him and stepped back. Of course he had helped her dress, just as he helped her undress. I wanted to scream.

"Well, then, don't just stand there! Show me!"

My exasperation wasn't lost on him when one of his auburn brows rose in question. I both hated and loved it when he gave one of those pinched expressions of consternation. Sometimes he looked like a playful spaniel moving its eyebrows as it listened to its owner. Other times, like when he considered some important theoretical topic, it could be the sexiest thing in the world. This time, I wanted to smack him for its utter condescension.

He reached around me, his long body brushing against mine, to push on a small, nearly invisible latch on the side of the structure. The pannier collapsed instantly. I sighed impatiently and held it to my chest, folding down the parts that could be folded. I placed it in the box it had come in and closed the top. When I turned back around, Alex stood nearer to me. I thought, for a brief minute, he would mention something about the previous night. Maybe apologise for what he had done.

"Have a cuppa. You'll feel better," he said.

He turned and marched back to the dining room, unconcerned for the boiling blood in my body. I contemplated throwing something at his head and even grabbed a pillow from the chair beside me, but aborted the shot when Georgina appeared in the hall with her characteristically pinched lips set in a grimace. For as beautiful as she was, she always looked like she had sucked on the sourest of lemons.

Georgina pulled at the hem of her blouse. I never saw the woman out of sorts, but she still fidgeted with her clothing relentlessly on the off chance someone might locate an imperfection. She bent her head to the side and stopped to look at herself in a small circular mirror on the wall, brushing a strand of long golden hair off her cheek.

"What's all the fuss about this morning?" she asked.

"Nothing," I answered.

Her shrewd, assessing eyes turned to Alex for confirmation. "That's not what it sounded like."

Alex cleared his throat. "She had trouble with the underskirt thing from your dress."

"Panniers, dear," Georgina corrected and flounced over to the table, apparently satisfied with his answer. She laid a hand on his chest and slipped her fingertips just under the flap of the dressing gown to touch his skin. Alex set his hand over hers and turned his head up for a kiss.

It made me sick enough that I had to stop myself from dry heaving.

My boss glanced at me again. "Come have tea, Em."

Suspicious of her kindness, but loath to refuse her, I set what was in my hand down and trudged over to them. I took a seat at the square table across from Alex. Maybe not the best idea, considering the circumstances, but I felt safe with his seemingly deep concern for whatever was on his mobile.

Georgina poured a porcelain teacup full of hot water and handed me the basket with the tea bags. I selected one and dropped it into the water to let it steep.

"Are you feeling well? You look a bit peaky," Georgina said.

"I'm fine, thank you, Georgina."

She nodded. "Too much fun at the ball last night?"

I shifted my eyes to Alex. Still no outward sign of recognition. That question at least deserved a slight choking on the tea in his mouth. But he did nothing. No change in respiration from sudden anxiety. No uncomfortable shift in the chair. No slight twitch in any of his facial muscles. Instead, he sat mesmerised with the mobile screen.

I briefly considered the fact that I may have been hallucinating during the ball. I hadn't felt well, after all. Perhaps the woman who collided with me in the middle of the dance floor hit me on the head. What if none of it happened? It was certainly a possibility if Alex couldn't remember. I was convinced he would show some outward sign or acknowledge what happened if it had. For what I knew of him, he was always so very kind to me. He would have apologised if he made a mistake. He wasn't the type of man who went around doing this sort of thing.

But then I wondered if he wasn't like Georgina after all... that he did it all for show. What if there really was a black heart underneath the shining exterior? What if he went around building up and ripping out women's hearts one at a time? It would explain why he stuck it out with Georgina for seven months. She had no heart for him to rip out and was thus a challenge.

They were made for each other.

Still, I refused to believe he was anything but amazing. In doing so, it left me with only one conclusion: Alex convinced me to dance and then snogged me soundly in a dark alcove before he realised the mistake he made. Then he left me cold and wanting and now he wanted to forget about it. It was the most logical explanation.

Fine then, I'd try to forget about it as well. It was a harmless kiss. Nothing more.

"What is my schedule today, Emilia?"

I blinked hard and wrenched my head to look at Georgina. Had she caught me staring at him? If she had, I hoped my expression was one of frustration and not lust.

"You have no plans today." I reached into my purse and withdrew my tablet, scrolling through to the calendar, just to be sure.

"Lovely," she said. "Alex, dear, Donatella invited us out on her yacht this afternoon. Would you care to go?"

Alex looked up from his mobile, pressing his lips together before his tongue slipped out to wet them. "I have a few calls to make about my own business."

"Oh, have Emilia do it," Georgina replied. "Just give her the information."

Alex's eyes finally turned my way, but only for a split second. "It's quite alright. I'll phone them."

Georgina wasn't impressed with that idea. "I employ her for this, Alexander. You should start using her. You're okay with it, aren't you, Emilia?"

Her pointed glower was not lost on me. I was about to answer in the affirmative, but as I opened my mouth to do so, Alex interrupted me. "Georgina, I'll phone them myself. Emilia doesn't know my schedule, my preferences, or anything of the sort. You give her enough to do already."

And suddenly, every little crumb of ill will I had for him evaporated into thin air. My heart swelled in my chest and my face grew warm. He stuck up for me. No one ever stuck up for me.

"Alex, I would be happy to phone whomever you want me to," I said. "It's not an imposition."

He shook his head and slipped the mobile into the front pocket of his dressing gown. "I'll hear no more of it. I'll do it myself. However, Georgina, you're more than welcome to go without me to Donatella's for the afternoon."

"Are you sure?"

Alex nodded.

"All right, but Lucia Fiore invited us to a cocktail party this evening."

He groaned. "Yes, I remember. I planned to go."

That took the edge off Georgina's growing annoyance. I breathed out a sigh of relief as we fell silent and returned to our repast. Only a few minutes passed before Georgina started in on me. "Will you please arrange for a car to take us to Lucia's this evening?"

"It's already done," I said. "I did it earlier, for eight, as you requested."

She nodded. "Good."

"I thought we might take a gondola or a speedboat like everyone else," Alex interjected.

I almost laughed at Georgina's instantaneous response to scrunch her nose in distaste. I'd received it more times than I could count. "Really, Alexander, don't be silly. It takes so long, and it's cold, and there's water, and it smells."

The muscles in Alex's jaw clenched, but he didn't say anything else. Glad that she won, Georgina grinned triumphantly in my direction. I smiled back, ingratiating myself yet again.

"I have that scheduled, as well as the car tomorrow morning to take you to the port to meet the yacht for Greece," I added.

"I'm glad you brought up Greece," Georgina said. "The only job we have over the next few weeks is for Tobias Sinclair. He needs a suit for his premiere Wednesday."

As though I didn't already know, considering I took the call from the man and also ordered the suits. Alex perked up, though, interested in the conversation about one of his closest friends.

"I have a few three pieces from Burberry to be delivered Tuesday," I explained. "He's supposed to stop at the studio on his way to the premiere."

"Fabulous," she replied. She sipped her tea and then looked at me again. "After Wednesday, you may have a holiday until we return from Greece. I will need you to remain near your mobile, however, for any emergency appointments. I doubt we will have much since fashion weeks are over and awards shows are nearly done."

"Thank you, Georgina."

I really hoped she understood how thankful I was for the time off. After two months of endless styling appointments for her clients and travelling with her to every major runway show in the Western world, I was ready for a break. I wanted to go home, sleep in my own bed, and take care of personal business I neglected during that time. And after what happened at the ball, time off would do my frazzled nerves good. Maybe when she came back, I wouldn't have the same urge to throttle her boyfriend.

She smiled. "Now that that's settled, you may go enjoy the rest of your day and night. Donatella is sending her car for us this afternoon, so I won't need you until we leave tomorrow."

My reaction was one of great surprise. The woman could barely use the toilet without me there to do it for her; that she planned to do all of this on her own was mind-boggling. Even more so that she seemed to be in such a pleasant mood. Alex must have done a very good job on her if she was so complacent.

But that only made the sour taste return to my mouth.

"If you need anything, give me a ring," I told her as I stood from my seat.

Alex looked up at me from beneath furrowed eyebrows before his face softened. "Have a good time, Emilia."

His voice saying my name, again, felt like a caress against my cheek.

I shook my head and turned away. I couldn't look at him. So I gathered the bags and boxes of costumes and disappeared out the door without another glance. I planned to enjoy myself. And I wasn't going to think about the oblivious man in the hotel room having brunch with his girlfriend.

He wasn't for me. He was for her. The night before had only been a mistake. I would just have to learn to live with it, like I did with everything else in my life.

CHAPTER 3

AN OBLIGING CAFÉ near the outermost corner of Piazza San Marco became the perfect spot to enjoy my day. I chose a secluded area in the outdoor seating, hidden under a shady awning away from the main drag. Straight ahead of me sat the magisterial Doge's palazzo while the domes of the basilica rose like round white clouds into the clear blue sky a good distance to my left. Nearest to my outdoor paradise lay the glittering aquamarine lagoon. Speedboats heavy with sightseers enjoying the warm sunshine and sea spray skipped along small frothy waves off to their destinations somewhere else on the island. From my perch on a rather comfortable wicker chair, I quickly and gleefully immersed myself in thoughts having nothing to do with work, which—to me—was a treasure beyond compare.

Thousands of bodies of every nationality imaginable had packed the piazza to the gills for the daily Carnevale festivities long before I arrived. Costumed street actors and adventuresome pedestrians roamed through the crowd, stopping for photographers and interested travellers. Masked characters laughed and played with anyone willing to interact with them. Street buskers danced and drummed and wove their magic with sleight of hand—anything a paying tourist wanted to see. Small children ran in and out under the forest of adult legs, chasing, yelling, and adding such joy to the atmosphere it made me wish I was their age again.

A street vendor selling sweets stopped in front of a group and gave them each a tiny hard candy for a few coins before they scurried off chasing each other again. I certainly couldn't yell, laugh, and dance about like the children, but I did share in their penchant for sweet things.

After I consumed a rich chocolate confection and started my second cappuccino, I settled into my seat and withdrew the sketchpad from the bottom of my tote bag. The thick quality drawing paper felt good between my fingers as I opened it and flipped through the first few used pages. When I reached a blank sheet, I folded the cover over and placed it on the table, rummaging once more for my pencils.

Halfway through sketching the scene in front of me and reworking the detail on a column on the palazzo, I heard a familiar voice talking in a one-sided conversation. I looked around for the source, finding Alex skirting around a bottleneck and passing by my café's seating area. He seemed to be involved in a rather deep conversation with the person on the other end of the call, despite the celebratory atmosphere.

The serious nature of his call notwithstanding, he did not mind the people bumping into him or overhearing his conversation. He did not wear a disguise to keep his anonymity. He was just another one of many in his average jeans-and-shirt combination.

Turning Alex into her human Ken doll became Georgina's personal project from the moment they started dating. With her unfettered access to all the latest male fashions from around the world, she often took it to an extreme. If she wanted to construct the image and attitude of her perfect man—the one she saw herself marrying—she did it, regardless of her own tepid feelings. As time marched on and Alex spent more time involved in Georgina's life, he changed so much I barely recognized the man now.

Worse, Alex seemed fairly complicit in his transformation; he never stopped her from pulling the wool over his eyes, which was why finding him in such simple dress surprised me. In choosing his own wardrobe for the walk outside, it meant he must have fought her for this moment of freedom. Georgina, otherwise, would have never let him out of the hotel in unattractive black corduroys, a basic grey tee and a leather jacket, no matter how well he filled out the latter two. He seemed relaxed, yet presentable, and didn't have the look of a man browbeaten and starched into wearing an image someone had created for him. To me, he looked like the carefree man I met months before.

Even so, I didn't want him to catch me staring. Frankly, I didn't want to be noticed at all. I quickly paid my bill while keeping an eye out for him and my head down. He passed around the crowd and into the café without seeing me. I thought I was free after I stepped outside the roped seating area, but he called my name at the last minute.

I did not turn around despite the momentary shudder of disgust that wormed its way through my body. After the way he had ignored me all morning, I absolutely refused to give him the pleasure of see-ing me fall all over myself whenever he deigned to acknowledge me. A uniformed man in a kiosk to my right caught my attention and pointed to the wooden sign above his head.

"Signorina!" he shouted. "Gondola rides €100!"

I smiled at the man and tried to hide myself in the crowd behind the kiosk. It was fruitless. I turned to see if I was out of sight or, per-haps, if Alex gave up, but instead ran straight into a hard body. My bag fell to the ground with a *thump* as my brain began connecting what had happened. I should have been thankful I landed against his chest rather than falling face first onto the pavement. The thought, however, didn't immediately cross my mind when I stepped back from him in mortification.

"Alex!" The name came out as a surprised squeak. I wanted the intricate stone walkway beneath my feet to swallow me whole.

A slow smile crossed his face. What did he find so amusing? Did he get some sort of pleasure giving me grief?

"Emilia."

I huffed. Alex followed me to the ground tp help collect the spilled contents of my bag laying around our feet, but I rushed to do it before he touched anything. I didn't want his help. When we stood back up, I met his steady gaze and wished I hadn't. His uncanny ability to peer into the souls of the people to whom he spoke always threw me off guard.

"I didn't mean to interrupt you." Alex glanced at the man with the black-and-white striped shirt at the kiosk doing his level best to get our attention. "Were you going on a ride?"

I choked and then coughed into my hand. "Oh, I, well, uh… well…"

"Would you mind terribly if you had some company?"

Yes, I would mind, I thought. I didn't want him around me. I couldn't handle such close proximity to him. Not after our dance. Not doing one of the most romantic things two people could do in Venice, no matter how much of a tourist trap it was.

I chewed on my lip fretfully. How could I possibly say no?

"I…" I paused. "I guess."

When his shoulders relaxed and he grinned, I realised he expected me to rebuff him and send him on his way. Was he unsure of himself? Did he fear my rejection? I found it highly unlikely that a man who oozed confidence like him could be so uncertain, but it was a nice thought.

We paid for a private cruise after a squabble about who would fund the expedition. He merely looked at me, squared his body and handed the guy the full amount in crisp Euro notes. Then the attendant directed us to an awaiting gondolier.

"You didn't have to," I said as we walked toward the dock.

"No, I didn't," he echoed. "But I wanted to. I know what your per diem is like on these work trips."

I laughed, hoping he did not mistake my sarcastic tone. "I make enough in my salary to compensate."

He fixed me with a pointed stare. "We both know you don't."

"I'd prefer not to speak ill of my employer," I deflected. "Can we please not talk about it?"

"As you wish," he replied with a wave of his hand.

We made it to the dock's edge and he followed the gondolier into the boat before me. After he found his balance in the bobbing vehicle, he turned and held out his hand.

"May I?"

I gritted my teeth and took his hand. I instantly regretted it, especially when the mere touch sent a warming shiver through my body. Prior to the masquerade, there had hardly been a reason for us to touch—even our first introduction was without a handshake. But in the span of a day in Venice, he touched me more than was strictly welcome and it affected me much more than I cared to admit. This time was no different.

I didn't thank him when I brushed by to curl into the double seat at the back of the passenger cabin. There were other seats—four by my count—aside from the open one beside me. Four safer locations for him to go. Even before I glanced up at him, I knew which space he planned to take. It didn't ease my distress.

He lowered into the seat beside me and stretched his long legs out in front of him. We were in close quarters between my figure and the amount of stringy body and arms he had to account for, so he slid one long arm onto the back of the seat behind me. I shifted, trying to get comfortable. I shoved my bag beneath the empty chair in front of me. When I settled, he gave me a wolfish grin.

I was well and truly stuck, wedged into a little corner with no hope of escape unless I fancied a swim in the freezing, mucky canal.

"It's a beautiful day," he remarked, turning his face up into the sun. His auburn locks ignited in a fire of copper and red.

"Yes," I replied. "Not too cold, either."

He shook his head. "No. We were lucky to come when it wasn't rainy."

"There was a forecast for some rain this evening."

Alex made a slight humming sound in his throat and looked directly into my eyes. "Pity."

I shrugged and crossed my arms over my chest, trying to sink as far back into the corner as possible. I was no small chick and he dominated the area, smothering me with his presence. Of course it was probably my anger and annoyance from the previous evening playing a bigger role, but I needed space and he wasn't giving it to me.

"Are we going to keep talking about the weather?" I asked.

He laughed lightly. "Not if you wouldn't like to. What topic would you like to talk about?"

The last words were low and seductive. He had such a way with his intonation. It amazed me how he could give words such a physicality that they felt like a pleasant tickling touch, when they were primarily auditory in nature.

For a split second, I thought I might summon the courage to mention our kiss at the ball. The second was fleeting, though. The heat of a blush flooded my cheeks and I trained my eyes on his chin instead of meeting his pointed gaze. I couldn't take it at the moment.

"I haven't anything in mind," I said.

I dared flicking my eyes to his and saw a flash of surprise. Had he expected me to mention the masquerade? I shook my head and turned in my seat, training my attention on the buildings and the people on the bridge ahead of us taking photographs.

They would see us. And they would notice a famous actor sitting in the gondola with me. Georgina would see the pictures when they made it online and then she would fire me.

"Why aren't you wearing a hat or something?" I asked.

"I didn't know it was a requirement."

I frowned. "They'll get photographs of you... of us... and they'll be in all the gossip rags."

Alex pursed his lips and shook his head. "They won't realise it's me."

"How can they not?"

One of his dark brows rose in amusement. "Because they're more concerned about the beautiful architecture, not someone in a gondola."

"Yeah, whatever you say."

He laughed lowly and shifted in his seat. "Don't worry about it."

"*Don't worry about it*, he says." I shook my head angrily and lifted my fingers to my mouth, nervously tearing at a piece of dry skin on my thumb.

"It's too late now, so don't think about it," he replied. It was a loaded statement.

I stopped chewing on my nail and turned to look at him. Was he trying to allay my fears of being plastered across every tabloid in the world? Or was it possible he felt bad about his unwarranted attention despite ignoring me at breakfast? Did he want to move on and forget about it?

"It's impossible to ignore."

He reached out for my hands and held them in his. I hated myself for my slight intake of breath at his touch. Alex seemed unaffected. Our gondola floated ever closer to the bridge. The heated clamminess of anxiety broke on my skin. The chill in the air and the cool wind did nothing to make me more comfortable. I might as well have stepped into a boiling pot of water for how uneasy it made me.

"Stop trying to control the situation," he said. "Relax and let it go."

"I'm not trying to control the situation. I don't want the repercussions."

Alex sat steadfast in his confidence that no one would notice us. A maddening hint of arrogance laced his amusement. I wanted to wipe it off his face.

"You can't change it now. Let go," he commanded.

I was about as prepared for him this time as I was when he pushed me into that damned alcove. Except then it had been private and this time it was on display for the whole world to see.

I was powerless to resist him. What was worse, he knew it and took complete advantage of the situation. He pressed his lips to mine, caressing more than kissing. He searched and sought—for what, exactly, I knew not—but he didn't demand as much of me as he had in the rush of the moment at the ball. Alex took his time exploring my mouth with his teeth, his tongue and lips, before they burned a fire across my cheek and stilled at my ear.

"You haven't let go yet," he purred, his breath warm and wet against my skin. The roughness of his beard tickled and scratched my cheek and earlobe. My heart raced and my stomach churned. He smelled of man and light cologne. Of sunshine and leather.

"I'm not—" I stammered.

He responded with a deep chuckle, one low in his chest. Not the polite one he usually used.

"You are," he responded, mouth teasing my ear.

Vaguely, the volume of our surroundings increased and a shadow passed above us, but I couldn't make sense of it as his lips found mine again, this time coaxing and demanding, rushed and needy. I twined my fingers in his short wavy hair for leverage; I desperately needed something to tether me to reality. But as soon as I relaxed into this new assault, he left my mouth burning with fire and moved to nibble on my other earlobe.

My involuntary sigh of pleasure turned into a low, ardent moan at which I felt the curve of his smile against my ear.

"Thank you," his soft voice murmured as he shifted away from me, leaving a cold space where heat had once been. I had so much to say to him. So much to *yell* at him, but I lost all ability to communicate.

He seemed neither concerned nor regretful as he sat back in his seat and ran his hands through his hair in a vain attempt to put it all back into place. The man shifted in his seat and adjusted the leather coat on his shoulders as if uncomfortable. I glanced where I shouldn't have and noticed him attempting to hide his obvious excitement.

That, more than anything, did things to me I could never describe. I figured the man had only kissed me to prove he could—not because he really wanted to do it, more because he needed to feel the power of controlling the situation—but his excitement showed me the opposite. That I created the rather obvious impediment gave me a weird sense of accomplishment. And instead of yelling, I remained silent and stared straight out at the canal ahead of us.

A few minutes later and after more thought, I realised what he had done. He used me to hide his features from any cameras, tasting one earlobe as we passed into the bridge, and switching to the other as we passed out from under the bridge.

We sat in silence until I heard a familiar ringing coming from my bag. I closed my eyes and rested my head back on the cushion.

"Fuck," I breathed and sat up, reaching under the chair. I found my mobile and pressed it to my ear. "Hello, love."

"Hi, Em!" said the exuberant, stumbling voice of my brother on the other side of the phone. I'd been so wrapped up in my own dilemma, I completely forgot he planned to call me after he finished his shift at work. "What are you doing?"

"Nothing, love," I replied. *Everything?* I glanced at Alex, who kept his eyes forward, but attentive to my call nonetheless. "I can't chat right now. How about you try me again in a half hour?"

"Okay!" he chirped. "Lindsay is taking me to the club for my practice soon. But I'll try again."

I sighed. "All right. Don't worry if you can't, I'll be home tomorrow and we can talk then."

"Good bye," he said. "I love you."

My heart swelled. "I love you, too, Sam. See you tomorrow."

I ended the call and stuffed the mobile into my pocket instead of the bag. Trying to forget about everything that happened in the last twenty minutes, I focused on the buildings as we turned off of the Grand Canal into one of the smaller waterways which looped around to the piazza dock. It wasn't until we were out in the open lagoon again that Alex looked at me curiously.

"Your boyfriend?" he asked.

I shot him what I hoped was a withering glare.

"Girlfriend?"

"What about *your* girlfriend?"

The gondolier, unknowing of our problems, seemed to be taking his sweet time circling the dock and mooring the small boat. All I wanted to do was jump from the boat and disappear into the crowd. I didn't need this in my life. I glanced at Alex. But, good heavens, it would have been so easy to fall.

He leaned over to me, his breath tickling my ear. "Don't worry about Georgina."

I pushed him away. "I thought you were supposed to be more of a gentleman."

"I am," he replied.

"No, you're not. This is the antithesis of gentlemanly behaviour."

I grew unreasonably angry at the affront filling his face. "You don't go snogging girls in dark alcoves and leave them to sort it out on their own. And you don't snog girls who are your girlfriend's employees. And you don't snog girls in gondolas when you're already in a bloody relationship! Frankly, you don't look like you do and randomly snog girls at all because they can get fucking confused!"

At last, the gondola moored into its spot at the loading area. I grabbed my bag and scrambled out of the boat. Alex followed behind me, but once on dry land and with the stability of solid earth beneath my feet, I turned on him.

"Don't follow me!" I exclaimed. "Go back to your girlfriend and have a wonderful fucking time in Greece. I planned the bloody thing, so I'm pretty sure you'll have a magnificent time."

I left him there, escaping into the crowded piazza, regretting that I didn't stay to hear his defence, but also relieved I stood my ground. It was up to me to recapture the calm I had lost in what was left of my free afternoon.

ALEXANDER UNMASKED

(SIX MONTHS BEFORE THE MASQUERADE)

I ONCE BELIEVED if I ever met the perfect woman for me, a choir of angels would exalt her arrival into my life. One of my more romantic notions, of course, but I truly thought some heavenly host would point her out as "The One" in a fanfare of trumpets and warm light and perfection. And, I always thought, she would come to me at the right time in my life—when I was ready for her. After I learned all I needed to be a successful person in the world. When I was a free man, capable of exercising my God-given free will.

My case, however, was very different. No angels sang exaltations. It sounded more like banshees screaming in the distance. No warm glow of light beamed down from the heavens illuminating the woman. Nor did a breeze fetchingly blow the soft chocolate curls behind her head like it did Botticelli's *Venus*. I wasn't free, and I certainly wasn't single. All of this, however, did not prohibit me from knowing I had to have her the instant I spied the statuesque woman standing in the middle of my girlfriend's work studio.

I needed to know every part of her. And I would stop short of nothing to have her.

The tall woman had come in from the street with a wiggling dog under each of her arms. A cord from the white earbuds in her ears disappeared into one of her pockets. I still remember those jeans with fondness, because they fit her rounded bum and shapely legs like a glove; my mouth watered at the sight.

It made all the difference in the world that she wasn't anything like my too-thin girlfriend—at least, the woman I supposed I should refer to as my girlfriend. For all intents and purposes, I was sleeping with Georgina and we did go on dates like normal couples, even though those dates were to give us the pretext of a real relationship based on mutual attraction and respect. Such was the extent of our relationship. At least, I quickly tried to convince myself of that after I laid eyes on this beauty.

After I made a lengthy perusal of her healthy form and plentiful décolletage in the slinky silk blouse tucked into the aforementioned jeans, the banshees brought me straight back to reality. A song playing in her ear caught her fancy and she began singing along with it, albeit very poorly. Of course, I was no singer, either, so I didn't have much room to talk. But this… this gave a whole new meaning to tone deafness. Which was odd, because her speaking voice, as I soon found out, was low and soft with a dark richness like a lovely single malt in front of the fire on a snowy winter's night. It curled around me and delighted more than just my ears.

"Hold on, Gucci," she scolded the wiggling pug in her arms. "I know you want to get down."

She dropped a stack of post on the desk in front of her and then set the pug and Pomeranian on the ground before releasing them from their leads. Both animals growled and nipped playfully as they chased each other toward the living portion of the house and their owner, even though their owner already left for the day.

I realised only too late that I stood in their path and the woman watched them go with laughter on her full cupid's bow lips. The laughter completely died away as did the sparkle it imbued in her large hazel eyes; shock replaced mirth and a violent blush rose on her cheeks as she averted her line of sight for the briefest of moments before daring to look again.

Words spilled out of her mouth in a barely comprehensible rush.

"Oh my God, I'm so sorry. I didn't see you standing there..."

She pulled the earbuds from her ears and took her mobile out of her pocket. Her gaze inched down my body until, at last, she looked away. The becoming blush on her cheeks deepened. She took pleasure in what she saw—at least from what I could ascertain—but it absolutely galled me that she felt it necessary to duck away to keep talking. "I didn't bother you, did I?"

"No," I replied. "I was already awake."

"Georgina left for her morning styling appointment," she explained. "She didn't say you were—"

I flustered her. No doubt it was in large part due to my undress, but I couldn't ignore the thrilling sense of power it gave me to elicit such a reaction from the most physically beautiful woman I ever had the privilege to meet.

It was one thing when I could drive my fans wild. It was something completely different when a woman I was interested in seemed to mirror my sentiments. Honestly, anything was better than Georgina's tepidness.

"It's quite all right, trust me," I said. "I heard you coming in and came to see what it was."

She covered her face with her manicured hands. "Oh, God! You heard me singing, didn't you? I'm sorry you had to hear that."

I chuckled and shook my head. I'd listen to a full concert of her caterwauling if it meant watching her flounce around a stage while doing it.

She turned back to her desk and shuffled through the papers upon it, but she did it only to busy her hands. I smiled.

"I'm Alexander, by the way." I stepped into the room from the hall, my bare feet feeling the chill of the hardwoods beneath them.

"I know who you are," she said lightly and glanced at my feet when a floorboard creaked beneath me.

A few beats of silence passed as she stared at me with no little amount of fright on her face. That certainly wasn't the look I wanted to see. I wanted her to look, to gaze at me, and to blush and giggle. So I stopped and placed my hands on my hips, fully aware that Georgina could walk in at any moment. If she saw me in naught but my pants, she would go absolutely mad. I didn't care.

"And you are?" I offered.

"Oh, um, I'm Emilia," she replied. It was a perfect name for her. Beautiful, and just a touch exotic. "Emilia Wyck. Georgina's assistant."

"I'd gathered that." I smiled. "Where's that name from?"

She sighed and leaned over the desk to grab for something, giving me an ample view of her rounded rear. I was in love.

"It's Dutch. From Van Wyck"

"You don't look—"

"My father was Greek." She cut me off as though she explained her pedigree more often than she cared to do it. "Could you please put clothes on?"

"Don't you dress men all the time?" I asked, struggling to pull my attention away from her arse as she stood back to her full height.

She rolled her eyes at me. "I do all the time, but those men aren't also Georgina's boyfriends. So please, if you will, put clothes on."

I nodded my head in agreement, though it was done with a great amount of reluctance. "If I must."

Emilia made a sound in her throat as I left the studio. I wanted to fluster her a bit longer, but I knew better. My mother would have been ashamed at how I conducted myself, and Emilia was correct. Georgina was my girlfriend. I had no business walking around in my underwear with her employees there to witness it.

But that still didn't change the fact that I was undeniably—indelibly—attracted to the banshee singing, Rubens-worthy beauty with legs for days. I wanted to know her. I wanted to fluster her. I simply wanted *her*.

CHAPTER 4

NEITHER GEORGINA NOR ALEX BOTHERED ME again until I finished dressing for my last night out in Venice. After the stress of the afternoon, I couldn't stay in my hotel room and let the thoughts swirling around in my brain eat away at my sanity. So I pulled an amazing dress out of my luggage with the intent of experiencing Carnevale to the best of my ability without the fear of running into Alex again. Should I happen across someone else willing to give me some attention—even if it were only to share a drink—then I would gladly accept it. I was prepared to do pretty much anything to avoid the problems of the last twenty-four hours.

My mobile rang at half seven, playing a tinny rendition of Bach's Toccata and Fugue until I picked it up and put it against my ear with some amount of annoyance. A bolt of fear and anger shot through my body every time I heard the music, associating it with her as I did. The thought that I really ought to change it made me chuckle ruefully as I accepted the call.

"Hello, Georgina."

I sat on my bed to pull on the high heels waiting for me. They were liable to cause the wearer a nasty sprained ankle at any moment, but the black suede and red-soled stilettos screamed "tart" in the best sense of the word. I hoped they lived up to it this night out, above all nights.

"How may I help you?"

"I need help up here. Now!" The vicious urgency in her voice forced an involuntary cringe from me. I prayed I had done nothing to upset her. Or worse, that Alex hadn't told her what happened.

I hung my head. "I'll be up shortly."

She didn't offer anything else and hung up her line, leaving me in a silent room staring at myself in the mirror hanging on the wall on the other side of the room. Fine creases had started to develop at various locations on my face, making me wonder if I skipped from twenty-eight years to fifty in the last month of nonstop travel with Georgina. With the worry of Alexander looming nearby, on top of her ridiculous, inhuman demands, I felt as though I had added another ten years to my body.

At least the wrinkles complimented the dark half moons under my eyes; I had attempted—but failed—to hide them with concealer.

No matter how much I broke my back bending to every single one of Georgina's whims, it never got me anywhere. I never progressed in my career. I enabled her by doing my job with no questions asked. It only made her worse. I was Dr. Frankenstein and she was my monster. I had, unfortunately, dug myself into a hole and I couldn't help but feel as though it were becoming increasingly impossible to climb out of it.

With a final sigh, I hauled my body off the bed and flicked the light switch off. I couldn't wait to send them on their way to Greece. The glorious peace left in their wake would be nothing short of nirvana.

When I arrived at Georgina's, a black mood instantly settled over my head. The front room looked like a bomb exploded, far worse than how it had looked in the morning. Every single one of her twenty pieces of designer luggage lay scattered about the room, their pricey contents carelessly thrown in the centre. I knew exactly what it meant. They needed to be filled with the mounds of dirty dry clean only designer clothes.

"Oh! There you are!" Georgina snapped. The tapping of her tiny heels on the hardwoods drew my attention in the direction of the hall leading to the bedroom. "It took you long enough."

"I'm sorry, Georgina."

I gritted my teeth to keep my mouth shut. My grandmother taught me better than to behave so poorly toward a boss. And this was a business trip. The anger boiling up inside me was useless. She simply wanted me to do my job.

"Doesn't matter anyway." She waved me off and reached up to place the diamond chandelier earrings held between her bony fingers into each ear. "I need you to pack these things for me before you go out tonight."

I breathed in and out, trying to maintain my composure. Of course she would do this to me at the last possible moment. I pondered the efficacy of wiggling my nose to compel the clothes to magically fold themselves into the brown Louis Vuitton bags scattered among the wreckage. Had she purposely thrown everything around to make the task ten times more difficult? I distinctly remembered repacking all of her used clothes before leaving Milan two days prior, separating the clean clothes into other bags. There was no need to empty them all again unless she planned to spite me for some reason I was unaware.

I nodded. "Of course."

Georgina sneered. "What are you wearing anyway?"

I looked down at myself. "One of the dresses they gave me in Milan."

"Let me see it." Georgina's eyes zeroed in on my coat, anxious to see the fashion statement beneath it. The woman always verified my clothing embodied her standards, and I would have been lying if I said I didn't dress to try to get some degree of approval from her. It was the only way she was capable of showing any positive regard for me.

I shook off my coat and tossed it on the back of a nearby chair. Georgina looked at me with a glint of pleasure in her eyes, as though she found a diamond in the rough and cut me out of it. Never mind I had successfully navigated the fashion world long before I started working for her.

She nodded her head as a brief smile passed her lips. "Such a shame it's not in my size or I'd take it from you."

One brief moment of acceptance and approval, followed by a swift kick in the gut. I watched as she tried to swing her negligible hips and arse toward the bedroom with her head held high. I balled my hands into fists at my sides and talked myself down from tackling her to the ground. Why did everyone in the high fashion world insist on resorting to insults aimed at the higher number on my tags? Had I not been, at one time, a model myself? Just like them, just like Georgina?

The low, deep timbre of the male voice I dreaded floated out into the room in the nick of time. Though unintelligible, the unhappiness in his tone was distinguishable mixed with Georgina's shrill whining. I refused to eavesdrop, so I set myself to the task of picking up, hanging and folding clothes.

Stuffing a Chanel skirt into a bag, the hair on the back of my neck prickled with the familiar and unsettling electricity that came from his interested presence. I placed the garment bag in a hard shell trunk and closed the lid with a loud clang in the quiet room. The energy sizzling down my neck to my shoulders slipped lower, turning into a lick against the backs of my knees. I shivered and glanced behind me, noticing the two trouser-clad legs standing at attention. My eyes wandered up the long length of him as he lazily lifted a monochromatic tie on one finger of his right hand. The expensive silk fabric dangled motionless, somehow taunting me all the way from across the room.

"Georgina said I tied it wrong and that you could help me while she finishes getting ready." He tried to be innocent about it, but the mirth in his pale eyes contradicted his words. And then there was that devastatingly handsome smirk again.

I lifted my eyebrows in a wordless question. I'd seen countless photographs of him long before he met Georgina in all manner of suits. Since then, he had worn more. Bowties, Windsors, half-Windsors, four-in-hands… hell, even a cravat or two with his morning suits at Ascot over the summer. This man knew how to tie a tie. "You didn't try."

"How do you know?"

"Because the tie is silk and it isn't wrinkled like you already attempted to do it yourself." I moved on to my next task folding blouses. All of the clothing required laundering when I returned to London, so I didn't fold them meticulously, but they could not return there in crumpled heaps, either.

He didn't move. "Perhaps I'd like it if you helped me?"

"The last thing you need is my help."

"You don't know what sort of help I need."

His words gave me pause, but I quickly shook them off. They were empty words meant to extract some sort of reaction. That was all. After a moment, I stood to my full height and looked over at him. "I think you need quite a lot of help in some areas, considering how daft you've been over the past twenty-four hours, but tying ties is not included in that."

He showed no other emotion as he sauntered over to the small mirror on the wall and quickly—expertly—tied the thing around his neck. He left it off kilter when he turned back around. "So?"

I threw down the blouse in my hand and strode over to him, pulling at his tie and repositioning it all the while attempting to ignore the fact that he stood much too close, he smelled far too lovely, and his warm breath tickled my cheek.

"You're rather tall," he said.

I shifted uncomfortably and frowned. I was tallish, but even with my choice in footwear, I was quite a few solid centimetres shorter than him. "My heels don't help."

His eyes travelled down between us to look at my feet, though he clearly used it as an excuse to catch a glimpse down the plunging neckline of my dress.

"I don't mind it. I can look you in the eyes. You have beautiful hazel eyes."

Strangled laughter bubbled up my throat. Of course he would cover up his lechery with a comment like that. I willed a blush from blossoming on my cheeks, but I was only partially successful, and made a concerted effort to not allow my gaze to stray past his neck where I fumbled with the tie knot. Long fingers, warm and soft, pressed beneath my chin. I resisted. Well, at least I tried, but as I was learning, Alexander Thorne was nothing if not persistent. He wove a web of magic proving to be too deadly to ignore.

I immediately hated the way he made me forget about myself. We stood in the middle of Georgina's hotel room with the woman likely to walk out and catch us at any moment with me struck completely dumbfounded by her boyfriend; I was too dumbfounded to do any-thing about it. The instant my eyes connected with Alex's, however, nothing else mattered. It wasn't a cosmic connection or an *oh-my-God* love at first sight. It was nothing more than a heady moment of unadulterated hunger surging between us when I finally acknowl-edged the purely masculine gleam of interest in his gaze—the same one which rendered me mute and incapable of movement.

What I truly needed was a quick slap across the face to wake me from this dream-turned-nightmare. I required some perspective and clarity and a sound mind telling me what an idiot I allowed the man to make of me.

I needed this job more than anything—there were bills to pay, mouths to feed, and I did not have the skills necessary to be anything but someone's assistant. And if Georgina were ever to find out about any of this, any chance I had continuing in the fashion world would be ruined. She would personally see to that.

I couldn't afford the luxury of relaxing the control I employed in my own life. He tried valiantly to break me in the gondola earlier and, after thinking about it, I realised he'd tried since the masquerade to pull me out of my head. I let him succeed one too many times; I couldn't allow it any more.

With renewed resolve to stand up to him, I worked the tie knot up quickly until it choked him. "Leave me alone."

The surprise on his face was priceless. He coughed and adjusted the tie again when I returned to folding clothes. Just when I thought he would retreat to the bedroom, he paused and looked back at me. "You look lovely tonight, by the way."

And just like that, I melted into a puddle of goo. Well, at least the resolve to stand up to him did.

"Thank you," I replied.

He walked over to a silver tray set up in the dining room. An ice bucket with an open bottle of champagne inside filled the majority of it. Three empty crystal flutes took up the rest of the space. A fourth was already missing, but I didn't need to ask where it went. Georgina liked the finer things in life, including incredibly expensive champagne before she set foot outside the door at night.

I closed up another suitcase and moved on when I felt the heat of him beside me. He held out a half-filled flute of pale golden bubbly. "Sit down and take a break."

"I'm working."

He sighed heavily and pushed the flute further under my nose. "Come take a break and chat with me. Who knows how long Georgina will be."

I snorted and grabbed the glass from him. I downed it in one long gulp, the fizzy bubbles dancing down my throat into my belly. He sat in a chair opposite me; he unbuttoned his coat and lowered into the seat, leaning back as though he owned the place with his long legs spread wide. And then I realised I was staring at his crotch.

For a brief moment, I wished for more champagne. Anything to occupy my wandering mind and burning cheeks. When I briefly caught a glimpse of him, the smirk was back. I huffed and firmly placed my empty flute on a table to continue my work.

"I realised today I hardly know anything about you," he said.

It took me a few moments to understand him as he switched to Italian. The words brought with them memories of the previous evening. I shook my head and replied with the foreign words. "You don't need to know anything about me except for the fact that I am your girlfriend's assistant, and since she is my employer, you are also my employer, and I would prefer to keep our relationship professional."

"Oh, my darling Emilia," he purred, "we're the furthest from professional that two people could be."

"I'd like it to go back," I said.

"I'm afraid that'll be impossible."

I met his gaze. "Why?"

"Because I know what it's like to kiss you," he replied. "And I know how much I want you."

I rolled my eyes at his comments. Fortunately, Georgina didn't understand a word of Italian. But he knew that, and that was why he switched to the language. "You have a very strange way of showing it."

"I don't know how I could make myself clearer."

"It doesn't matter, anyway. I work for your girlfriend. If she were to find out about anything, my career would be over."

His eyes lit up. "So you want me as well?"

I gave him a sideways glance. One I hoped conveyed my complete exasperation. That wasn't the point I was trying to make.

"What if she didn't find out about it?"

"That's beside the point!" I exhaled. "I would know and I would feel guilty."

"Even when it involves a woman who treats you like she does?"

I was completely stunned by his words. Actually, what stunned me was the fact that he was even suggesting this... whatever it was he wanted from me. I had always considered him to be so nice. So personable. So... not this. Not a playboy or a philanderer or anything requiring this type of arrangement.

"You're not supposed to be like this," I said. "You're supposed to be Prince Charming. You're supposed to be kind, and funny, and gallant and... and... perfect. Not someone who preys on weak women and openly cheats on his girlfriend."

The left corner of his mouth quirked up in amusement. "Someone has been looking at too many of my interviews."

"It's all you've ever been around me! Well, at least, before now!" I turned away from him and grabbed a handful of chiffon. "How was I supposed to know that underneath you were just a typical man?"

"It's merely one mask I wear."

"You have more than one?"

He shrugged. "My public and private selves aren't really all that different from each other. I'm not perfect, though, and you shouldn't confuse Public Alexander with Private Alexander. I'm still that man you barely know, I just don't show the truly private side to everyone."

"Oh, lucky me." My voice dripped with sarcasm.

"I thought you would understand. You make a habit of hiding from the world as well," he said.

I folded a pair of linen trousers and laid them in a pile with others. "I have no idea what you're talking about."

He sighed. "I watched you last night. You walked around, skulking in the shadows like that's where you think you belong."

"It *is* where I belong," I said. "I'm not on display here. That's Georgina's job."

"It's *not* where you belong. There is a passion in you, dying to be set free. Something's stopping you from realising it, though."

I balked at him. *Yeah, reality.* "You don't know what you're talking about."

"But I do."

I stopped what I was doing and looked at him squarely, hands on my hips and true frustration flaring inside me. We covered this conversation—no, argument—already. Yet I couldn't pull myself away from it or him. Some twisted part of me wanted to hear him out. But

I knew I had to stop it.

"Look, I don't care what you think," I growled. "I don't want whatever you're offering. I want you to be the old Alexander. I don't want you to touch me or kiss me or do anything else to me but smile and move on your way so I can do my job."

He stood from his seat, righting his long body on equally long legs and stepping over to me. We weren't touching, but the heat of his body near me warmed my bare skin as we stood toe-to-toe, chest-to-chest. I had height going for me in my shoes, but I felt diminutive in front of him. His presence was massive, but not oppressive. The heat between us was not body heat. It was an acute consciousness of his passionate vitality stealing my breath away.

I was nothing more than a fish hooked on a line and he, ever so slowly, began to reel me in to shore. And just like a fish, I struggled fruitlessly against the unrelenting pull of the line.

"Are you absolutely certain you want that?" he asked, his voice so low I scarcely heard it above the pulse pounding in my ears.

I hesitated. The truth was that I didn't know if I *was* sure. I wanted this man. So much. He called to me like some male version of a siren—it could only end poorly.

A slow grin spread his lips to reveal a row of perfect white teeth when I didn't immediately answer. He brushed my hair back behind my shoulder, fingers tracing along my jaw behind an ear, down toward my chin as he leaned into me. He held me hook, line, and sinker in the palm of his hands. He knew it. I knew it. And I began to brace for the contact of his lips, but a heaping dose of reality shot through my brain at the last possible moment.

I shifted away, just enough so he couldn't reach my lips. His soft mouth brushed my cheek. "Yes, I'm certain I don't want whatever it is you're offering me."

Everything changed when he dropped his arm and took a step back. He sighed in aggravation, balling his hand into a fist. He met my gaze. I didn't see anger there, thankfully, only a reluctant acknowledgment of my wish for the replacement of his mask of happy indifference.

He breathed again and looked behind my shoulder at something. "I should go check on Georgina. We're late."

It was back to business as usual when he disappeared down the hall into the bedroom. I stood bewildered, aroused, and miserable in the centre of the room, staring dumbly at the rest of the clothing I had yet to fold before I went out.

If I went out.

Alex had sapped all the energy from my body; I had no will to do anything now. I only had enough to finish my work, go back to my room, and crawl into bed.

I looked up when I heard both people coming back down the hallway. Georgina was beautiful, as always, this time in a pale pink mini-dress she picked up from Donatella in Milan. It played up her fair, delicate features brilliantly. I would never measure up to that, and I found it rather impossible to imagine what Alex saw in me when he already had someone like Georgina. Not that it mattered now.

Alex helped Georgina into her coat before putting on his own. Georgina looked pointedly at me. She produced a piece of paper with a list of items and thrust it under my nose.

"I need you to find these things tomorrow before you leave for London," she explained. "Use the credit card."

"I will." I nodded, glancing at the list and ascertaining that it consisted of wines and chocolates and other things difficult to get through customs. My unlucky job to do.

Georgina smiled her fake smile. "Splendid. Feel free to have some champagne… and have a wonderful night, Emilia."

I nodded my head as she turned and walked out the door. Alex held it open, but paused and looked back at me.

"Thank you, Emilia," he said in Italian.

"For what?"

"For… everything," he said and left the room, the door shutting heavily in the jamb.

I waited for them to reappear, but when they did not, I grabbed the champagne flute and went for the bottle in the dining room. Thinking better of it, I grabbed the whole Moët bottle out of the ice and carried it with me over to the sofa where I sat down to drink what was left.

For the first time in my life, I longed for London. Cold, dreary, grey London was preferable to the colourful, confusing upheaval taking over my life.

CHAPTER 5

WHEN THE AEROPLANE'S WHEELS bumped onto the tarmac at Heathrow the following afternoon, I let out a careworn sigh. We came out beneath heavy, wet clouds, and from what I could glean from the ground crew in thick winter coats waiting to service the jet, the bitter cold had not abated since I left the country.

Part of me had wanted to stay in the milder Venetian climate for a little longer, but one thought about what transpired there not only got me on the plane, but it also made me, once again, incredibly anxious to get back to my London doldrums. At least I would be safe from Alex's influence while he was on the other side of Europe, likely enjoying the warm weather and lapis beaches of the Grecian archipelago.

I waited until most of the passengers disembarked and gathered my computer bag and handbag before stepping out into the aisle. An attendant smiled politely at me when I passed him on my way out to the bridge and terminal. I pulled my coat tighter around me as I breezed through passport control and customs and made my way to baggage reclaim. As much as I wanted to return to England and to be rid of certain distressing Venetian events, there was just something about the damp cold that permeated my skin down to the bones. Heat inside the building only did so much to give me any warmth.

The group of people in front of me pushed through the exit into the waiting area, allowing me to see the modest crowd waiting to collect travellers. My eyes scanned those waiting, but I didn't expect to find anyone for me; I planned to hail a taxi to lug all of the bags returning to London with me. Yet, I couldn't ignore the sudden flood of relief when I spied the two most important people in my life standing at the end of the blocked railing, holding a vibrantly coloured sign and a bouquet of white daisies. My sagging shoulders and deep exhalation were telling of how I truly felt.

I had never been so excited—and relieved—to find Sam and Lindsay waiting, their faces smiling brightly at me, though Sam was just a little more excited than strictly necessary. They were my beacons of home and normality more than anything else in the world. Two months away with no proper amount of time at home with them was too much for me, and the toll it took hit me like a brick wall. I could barely move as the exhaustion overcame me.

Sam broke free of the barrier and ran toward me in complete glee, opening his arms wide. I allowed him to pull me into a giant hug, though he forgot his strength for a moment before I made a small sound of discomfort. "Oh, sorry, Em."

"I'm fine, love." I brushed a bit of his dark hair out of his wide-set, slightly crossed eyes. He blinked back at me through his thick eyeglasses. As I always did after these long trips, I took a moment to verify he'd been taking care of himself while I was away.

"Em! I missed you!" he exclaimed, trying to get my attention away from him. "You were gone too long!"

"I know I was," I said with a sigh, feeling the tears I had kept away in Venice welling dangerously close to spilling level. I hugged him again and breathed in his familiar scent. No matter how many times I tried washing the mothball odour out of his clothes, I had yet to achieve success. I refused to have anything having to do with mothballs in the flat—it reminded me too much of our childhood spent with our grandmother—but he still managed to smell old and musty. Even after I bought him new clothes. His smell mixed with the aroma of rasher grease and coffee, though; Lindsay had probably cooked him a fry-up for breakfast before leaving for the airport. "I missed you so much, Sammy."

He giggled happily and stepped back in the process of grabbing my hand. "Come see Lindsay! He said this morning that we could come get you. And we did. Did you see my sign I made?"

"I did!" I glanced at the big man standing silently and stalwartly behind the railing with the sign. He looked as polished as ever in his starched and simple black suit.

Lindsay finally grinned and enveloped me in his strong arms for a long hug. As wonderful as Sam's hug had been, Lindsay's was even better. He smelled of soap and aftershave, and it was instantly warm, inviting, and blocked out the bone-deep chill following me through the airport. As massive as a bear in body size, but without the claws and bite, he always made me feel loved, welcome, and safe when we hugged. When I finally had enough, for the moment at least, I looked up to find concern in his brown eyes.

"What's wrong?" he asked, his chest rumbling in his lovely Scottish brogue.

"I'm tired, that's all."

He squinted, eyes crinkling at the corner. He didn't believe me, but he didn't press the subject. Which was a surprise, considering he loved to debate and argue for information. It was why he chose politics over a more sedate life in academia.

"Well, let's get you home," he said decisively. "I have a meeting in an hour. Come along, Sammy."

"How did you manage any time away from the office?" I asked Lindsay, linking my arm with Sam's. Sam grinned at me and leaned his shoulder against mine.

Lindsay shrugged. "Benefits of a senior staffer. I can make the others do my work for me."

"I'm sure they appreciate that," I mused.

He smirked in response. "It's nothing I didn't have to do as an underling."

We walked together toward baggage where I again looked up at the big man beside me. "We'll need a trolley."

"You left with two bags," he said, confused.

"I came home with five."

"What?"

I held my hands up in feigned innocence and gave him a small smile. "Georgina asked me to bring things back."

"Where do you expect to fit all of it and us in my car?"

"I could put all the bags in the car and Sam and I could use the Tube," I offered.

"No!" Lindsay exclaimed. "The dragon lady and all her things can sod off if they don't fit in the car. You and Sam are riding with me."

I glared at him. "Come on, Lindsay, don't be like that."

"Yeah, come on, Lindsay!" Sam chimed in.

"It should fit. The other three bags aren't large," I said. "They would have all fit in a cab, so your car shouldn't be difficult."

Lindsay rolled his eyes and continued on to the carousels in the baggage reclaim without us. I looked at Sam, who stared back at me with wide eyes. "He's not happy with you."

"No," I concurred. "But he's unhappier about my job than he is with me."

Which makes two of us, I added in my head.

We turned a corner to find Lindsay hovering diligently at the carousel. He grumbled at me. "What do the other ones look like?"

"Louis Vuitton brown." I turned to Sam. "So how was footy yesterday?"

"Great!" he said, excited. "I scored a goal. We played Hammersmith. Roger was goalkeeper and he went out like this…"

Sam illustrated his point, reaching his arms out over his head and then bending to the side.

"And he fell down," he concluded. "An ambulance came. But he was fine. And then…"

I watched and listened to my brother recount the match from the previous night, laughing at some of his tall tales, but trying to rein in the storytelling to a manageable level until we were not in a public space. Only too late did I realise I hadn't managed it as well as I hoped when Sam took a diving leap as if to protect his imaginary net. He stumbled into a bank of chairs along a wall. He caught his balance, but not without the curiosity of the other people standing around waiting for their baggage.

I chuckled, helping him up and brushing the dust off his shirt. "Are you all right?"

"I'm fine, Em." He pushed my hands away. "Stop."

"Let's go back to Lindsay." I motioned to our big friend and Sam complied. As I stepped over, I took the opportunity to look around at the other people standing around the carousel while their attention faded from us. I froze on a chiselled, masculine face I did not expect to see. A mop of straight black hair fell into his ocean water eyes as he glanced up from typing something into his mobile. He grinned and waved; I returned the gesture.

When I stopped beside Lindsay, my friend looked down at me.

"What?" I asked.

"Do you know who that is?"

I shrugged. "Yeah, it's just Tobias."

I had worked with the man on multiple occasions in the past. He was beautiful. But most of the men I worked with were beautiful, even if this one was particularly so, as though carved out of the purest marble and imbued with some magical property. He emitted a radiance like some old Hollywood movie star.

"*Just* Tobias?" Lindsay repeated, speaking out of the corner of his mouth in a low Scottish grumble. "How can you—"

I shook my head. "Yes, and my boss' boyfriend is Alexander Thorne, and I work with many famous faces. I thought you'd be comfortable with that by now."

"You know the obsession I have with *Evergreen Hills*," he replied.

"I know. And it's unhealthy," I added. "Especially since the final series was last year."

"But… but…" Lindsay started. "Oh, God, he's coming over here."

Lindsay was never more flustered than at that moment. He faced down multiple utterly terrifying MPs and other government officials—many from across the globe—on a daily basis. But when presented with the possibility of meeting one of his favourite actors, I couldn't believe how he folded under the pressure. I laughed lightly and quickly tried to talk myself into not behaving like a total nutter either; at least one of us needed to form sentences around the man. As many celebrities as I met, a few still made me feel star-struck. Tobias Sinclair was one of them.

A uniformed man carrying a rolling piece of luggage followed behind Tobias, but stayed a respectful distance away when Tobias stopped in front of me. It must have been his driver. I smiled. "I thought you weren't supposed to arrive until Wednesday."

Tobias shrugged. "Originally, yes, but my engagements in Asia were moved to a later date… so I have a few days to relax."

His cat-like eyes crinkled at the corner when he smiled. Even though he said he would use the few days to relax, he and I both knew he wouldn't actually use them for that purpose. When his gaze tracked up behind my shoulder, I realised he had spotted my companions and expected an introduction.

"Oh! Right!" I turned to them. "Tobias, this is my brother, Sam, and my best mate, Lindsay."

"Pleasure." Tobias shook their hands and returned his attention to me. I shifted uncomfortably underneath his inspection. What was it with these men looking at me like this? Never before had I received such positive regard. "Would you mind if we meet up tomorrow for my fitting since I'm home early?"

I spluttered. "Of course, that would be fine. Our rep at Burberry should be able to get it to me tomorrow morning."

"Perfect," he said with a toothy grin. "Ten o'clock? At Georgina's studio?"

"Yes." I nodded. "I'll see you then."

"Good," Tobias replied with another smile. "Have a wonderful evening."

He turned and left us standing there; I turned back to a speechless Scot and my confused brother. Lindsay finally unfroze and shook his head. "I don't believe that just happened."

"You're such a fangirl," I chastised. "Would it be a huge inconvenience to collect my baggage and go home?"

"But…"

"No buts," I said. "Baggage. Car. Home. Sleep."

Lindsay scowled at me, but followed my directions. In no time, we were travelling the motorway toward Westminster while Sam chattered about things he saw on the drive. I had missed the happy, ambient noise my brother seemed to create despite not fully getting my mind off of Venice or the encounter with Tobias at the baggage reclaim. If I were being honest, meeting Tobias there felt rather odd, far beyond the discomfort and awkwardness of seeing a professional acquaintance outside the context of the work environment. Perhaps I was chalking it up to mean more simply because of the interconnectedness of the people within my life at the moment: Alexander had introduced his friend to Georgina after which Georgina became Tobias' stylist.

I couldn't escape, not even for a day.

When we finally arrived at our flat, with all five pieces of luggage sitting in the middle of our reception area, I escaped to my bedroom for a moment of peace. I found immediate comfort in knowing it was just the way I left it, with the walls covered in artwork and the shelves and flat surfaces littered with bric-à-brac from my life. My wardrobe door remained open with half of its contents missing and in the luggage down the hall. I dropped onto my bed and buried my face into a pillow, enjoying the smoothness of the pillowcase on my cheeks and the fruity scent left from the lotion that had transferred to it before I left. Finally rolling over and staring up at the ceiling, I let out a long, deflating sigh.

Home. Safety. No Alex. After two months, this was exactly what I needed.

Someone rapped lightly on the closed door.

"What?" I asked.

Lindsay's rumbling voice seeped through the wooden barricade. "May I come in?"

"I guess." I didn't bother to get up from my sprawled position on the bed. If I had a choice, I wouldn't leave this spot again for the rest of my life.

The lumbering man entered the room and shut the door. He stood at the side of the bed, tilting his head to the side like an interested bird. "Are you ill?"

"Huh?" I frowned. "No. I'm fine."

"You are not 'fine' and if you don't talk me, then I'm going to have to get it out of you another way," he threatened.

Sometimes he was such a mother hen.

"Don't doubt me. I have an army of trained interrogators at my beck and call. They could get it out of you," he said.

"Lindsay, you get tea and take calls," I said. "You could no sooner have me interrogated than you could become Prime Minister tomorrow."

"Wow." Lindsay scoffed. "Well, excuse me, Your Royal Highness, but when did you do anything but walk dogs and arrange your boss' life?"

I glowered at him.

"At least I'm doing something useful in government," he said. "You're off attending soirees and premieres making sure some celebrity doesn't end up on a worst dressed list. Hardly curing cancer or ending world hunger, I should think."

I threw a pillow at the man and groaned angrily. Of course I knew it wasn't ideal, and in fact was a waste of my time, but I had no other options. And our conversation only made that knowledge worse.

"Look," Lindsay said sotto voce, "I know something is bothering you. I'm here right now and I want to make it better. Just tell me what's going on."

I pulled myself up and hugged my knees to my chest. Lindsay sat down on the bed, jostling it with his weight. "I really don't want to talk about it. I want to forget about it. I'm tired from my trip. I'm tired of two months of non-stop Georgina herding. I want to sleep in my own bed, eat my own food, and watch some telly with Sam."

Lindsay shook his head. "You really think that after all these years together, I'm going to let you get away with that answer?"

"You will, because you won't be happy when I tell you to sod off," I stated drily. "Please go to your meeting. Perhaps I'll be in a better state to talk to you later."

He huffed and stood from the bed. "Fine. I'll be back at seven. Don't forget Sam has to be at the club at five for his practice."

"Thanks," I replied glumly as my friend swept from the room. I heard him yell his farewell to Sam, who yelled back his reply, followed by a slamming front door. Knowing Lindsay's temper, he wouldn't speak to me at least until tomorrow, and then it would likely only be about my fitting with Tobias. I was just fine with that.

I tried to close my eyes and relax into the bed, but I was acutely aware of the fact that I had to get Sam across town for his footy practice in an hour. So I groaned, gathering what little energy I had left, and trudged back down the hall for my luggage to begin emptying them out and washing the dirty clothing.

Only once did I stop to think about what it might be like to be on the deck of a sleek white yacht while sipping champagne in the warm Mediterranean sun. When the thought skipped across my mind, I turned on some music—loudly—and waited for it to take me in another direction.

CHAPTER 6

THE RUNNER FROM BURBERRY arrived with the delivery at
Georgina's Kensington studio at half past nine, leaving me only a
short time to set out the three suits while taking messages off my
mobile and checking emails from various people—though the majority of them were from Georgina herself. I never understood why
she couldn't switch off.

If I were on that illusive yacht touring Greece with my gorgeous
boyfriend, work would have been the absolute last thing on my
mind. Guaranteed. Rather, my thoughts would revolve around loads
of sex with said boyfriend followed by getting as much time as possible to see the historically significant sights around the archipelago.
Then I might think about taking a dip in the ocean and sunbathing. I
wouldn't worry about a bill requiring payment within the next thirty
days for the stationery I purchased with my new logo.

As it was, I was elbow deep in a box of post the maid had left on
my desk, looking for the specific account statement Georgina wanted, when someone knocked at the front door. The black Pomeranian
and the fawn pug I freed from the pet hotel earlier in the morning
erupted in fits of barking and wheezing. Their little paws clicked on
the wood flooring as they danced at the door.

I rushed to the door, opening it a crack and bending down to stuff
both animals under my arms in one smooth movement before they

could escape. Using a foot, I kicked the door the rest of the way open. Of course it wasn't the most professional way to greet clients, and Georgina probably would explode if she saw me do it, but I figured it was either a delivery or Tobias. The first wouldn't care, the second would likely smile and offer to hold one of the tiny wiggling beasts.

Tobias stood in the doorway, hands shoved into the pockets of his jeans, bundled up in a dark coat and scarf, topped off with a newsboy cap and reflective sunglasses. On a cloudy day. Which meant he wanted to hide from paparazzi.

"Hi, sorry, come in."

I smiled shyly and moved away to allow him entrance into the foyer and out of the cold. He shut the door behind him and reached out for me; I almost moved until I realised he intended to scratch the pug's head.

"Hey there, Gucci-boy," he cooed and moved to the excited Pomeranian, "and Coco." With his other hand, he pulled off his sunglasses and smiled at me. "Good morning, Emilia."

"Come on back."

I didn't wait for him to follow me toward the open-air work area which comprised our clean and sterile studio. The dogs went into the tiny kitchenette I blocked off with a low gate so we could work unimpeded. I turned back around, rubbing my hands on my jeans as though they would sufficiently clean them. They wouldn't, of course, and it would be yet another thing Georgina might harp over, but she wasn't around and I wasn't too worried. Deflecting Tobias' attention—well, at least attempting to deflect—I pointed to the three suits hanging from pegs along the wall. "So these are the suits."

"I only needed one," Tobias said with a laugh.

"You know Georgina likes options," I replied. "You know the deal… try each one on. I'll snap a photo and send them to Georgina for her approval."

"Are you sure you'll be able to reach her?" he asked. "I thought she was in Greece with Alex."

I laughed at him. "If Georgina wasn't micromanaging someone, she'd be dead."

"And then she'd probably still find something to micromanage?" he joked, the corner of his mouth quirking up in a smile.

"You have no idea." I sighed. "Which one first?"

"Which one do you like best?"

"I don't know, I haven't seen them on you."

"Fair enough," he acknowledged in his low voice. "I suppose we can begin with the grey one."

I grabbed it from the peg and handed it over. "Please be careful since we haven't officially purchased them yet."

Tobias disappeared around the corner into the single changing room. I listened to the rustling of clothing and zippers and metal accents clinking, but tried to focus on what I was doing, looking for the stationery bill in the box of post. Why did she even need stationery with everything and everyone going paperless? All of our files were digital.

I found the envelope and extracted the paper inside by the time Tobias toddled out of the changing room. The suit fit him like a glove—I was almost certain all of the suits would because they had been pulled to his measurements—but this one wasn't right for him.

"So?" he asked, turning around smoothly, adjusting the jacket on his shoulders.

"I like darker colours on you. This grey is too light."

"I agree." He slicked his hair back when he stopped to look in a full length mirror.

I grinned. "But how does it feel?"

"Like it was made for me," he replied, playing with the slim-cut coat sleeves. "You know, I remember when I would go down to Harrods, grab a suit from the rack and take it home before trying it on for size. Now I have to pay someone to do my thinking for me because I can't go to the shop without being bombarded with fans and paparazzi."

I nodded. "I don't envy you…" I grabbed my mobile. "Let me take a photo, though."

He posed while I snapped the image. "I'll try the navy next."

I handed it over and watched him disappear into the changing room. We repeated this process until he came out in the last suit. It was a dark charcoal, nearly black. The seaming followed the shape of his body perfectly, and knowing Georgina's thinking, it would be her choice. The trousers seemed slightly loose in the hips, but we could fix it with a belt for one night—or he'd just have to eat a heavy meal and pray it went to his hips like it did everyone else. When he stood in the long mirror to look at himself, I stopped beside him, trying to locate the source of bagginess from a visual inspection alone.

He glanced at me. "Hmm?"

"May I, uh…" I hesitated, pointing to his hips. "I have to check the fit on the trousers."

He lifted his arms. "Please, be my guest."

I lifted the bottom of the coat and slipped my fingers along the waistline of the trousers, brushing warm skin and the elastic waist of his pants. Try as I might, I couldn't prevent a blush from filling my cheeks, but I hoped he didn't notice it.

It wasn't often I did any of this work. Georgina typically ran fittings because our clients were rather prickly about who touched them. And honestly, I didn't know if there would ever come a time where it became second nature as part of my job: the part that required touching handsome men in intimate locations.

"You know, we've been doing this for near on five months now," he remarked, "and I've never asked you how you got into this business. Were you a seamstress or designer or something?"

I looked up to find him watching me with interest. "No. Actually, I was a model."

"A *model*?"

I cringed at the astonishment in his voice. People had described me as swarthy in the past—thick, darkly coloured, and solid—but it was the somewhat exotic appearance which interested the talent hunter in the first place. I wasn't the fair skinned nymph in the ilk of Kate Moss or the delicate Georgina Cavendish, but I didn't consider myself a complete loss no matter how many failed to see it when compared to my waify counterparts. "You don't have to sound so incredulous."

"Oh, no, it's not that," Tobias quickly amended. "You're a beautiful woman, Emilia… it's just that I never expected someone like you to be a model."

I released my hold on the trouser leg and stepped back from him. "Someone like *me*?"

He huffed. "Oh, goodness, I'm making a mess out of this. You're not like them… I mean… you're far too grounded and intelligent."

"I know a lot of grounded, intelligent models," I defended.

"It's just… your personality is different," he said. "I think it's the fact that you have a personality. And a nice one at that."

I chuckled.

"How did you even get into modelling anyway?"

"They 'discovered' me at uni."

"And…" he continued.

"And it's in the past."

Tobias didn't press the matter. A momentary kindness, perhaps, but a text message alert jingled and saved me from saying anything else about it. Georgina had passed down her verdict.

"Georgina says to go with the one you're wearing," I said. "Do you feel comfortable in it?"

"All of them have been comfortable," he replied and looked in the mirror again. "As comfortable as a straight jacket."

I ignored him. There hadn't been a fitting with him where he hadn't complained about having to wear a coat and tie. He despised dressing "the part" for the public.

"Is it loose on the hips?"

"The belt is fine to keep it in place." Tobias sighed and turned to me again. "Which one is your favourite?"

"I actually prefer the navy one." I glanced at my mobile as another message came through dictating the shoes Tobias should pair with the ensemble. "It makes your eyes look bluer."

He grinned mischievously. "You like blue eyes?"

I snapped my gaze to his, fully aware of what he said. My brain, however, took awhile to fully puzzle out the situation and what the playful tone in his voice might mean. Especially when a flash of the bluest pair of eyes I knew, framed in a gilded Carenvale mask, danced across my memory.

"Huh?"

"Nothing." He laughed and removed his coat. "I'll take the navy suit."

"Oh, God, please don't do that," I pleaded. "Georgina will see the pictures and she'll—"

Tobias held up a hand to stop me. "I'll tell her that *I* decided on the navy."

"You're sure? You could end up on the worst dressed…"

"And of course I would be positively gutted if that happened." His deep baritone dripped with sarcasm. "My goodness! The end of my career as I know it if I show up in a navy rather than a black suit that look virtually interchangeable to me."

"But they're not the same," I protested weakly.

He stepped over to me and rested his hands on my shoulders. "Stop. If it makes you feel better, bill me for both suits and I'll use both on this press tour."

I sighed in defeat.

"But I'm going to wear the navy to the premiere Wednesday."

I rolled my eyes and pulled away from him. "Please go change out of the suit."

He followed my directions and disappeared around the corner. I went to my desk and flopped down into my seat, staring blankly at the wall until he once again passed in front of me. He carried both suits draped over one arm.

"The, uh, garment bags are over here." I jumped up from the chair and grabbed them from the rack; Tobias helped me with both. We finally stood back, admiring the zipped, white garment bags with the Burberry knight logo emblazoned across the front. "Are these good? Do you need anything else?"

He turned to look at me. "Yes, I do."

I frowned. "What do you need? You didn't tell me you needed more. I didn't call for anything."

"Calm down." He chuckled. But then his laughing expression turned serious. "What I need has nothing to do with these costumes."

"Oh, well, then I can't help you with that."

His eyes turned soft when he smiled. "You might be able to help me anyway."

I looked back at him sceptically.

"You see, I need a date."

"A date?"

He grinned at me. "I'm not speaking Greek, am I?"

"No," I said softly, squinting my eyes as though it would help me determine his sincerity.

He had to be joking. Actually, the gods had to be joking. They had to have set this up just to compound what happened in Venice. They were testing me. For what, exactly, I was unsure, but they must have all been having quite a laugh at my expense.

"These things can be so dull without a friend," he added to convince me of his honest interest.

I laughed manically. "I'm sorry. I just… I just don't know why you would want me there when you'll be busy with all the press stuff. No, I guess I just don't understand… Why me?"

He shrugged. "Why not? From what I hear, you could do with a little fun now that you have a few weeks off."

The tiny hairs at the nape of my neck stood on end. "Who told you I had time off? Did Alex tell you?"

Tobias frowned. "I don't know what you mean."

"Did he orchestrate this whole thing?" The only people who knew of my time off were Georgina, Alex, Lindsay, and Sam. I knew Georgina hadn't communicated anything to Tobias about it because she wouldn't think to mention it. It wasn't important to her.

Did Alex think he could pass me off onto one of his single friends after I had refused him? Fury flared inside me.

"Okay, he may have mentioned it last we talked," Tobias said. "I thought I'd give you more time off by coming by the studio earlier for the suit."

I shook my head. "I'm going to kill him."

Tobias laughed lowly and stepped closer, setting his hands once more on my arms. "Believe me when I say you're not the only one who would like to."

"You want to kill him too?" I said, interested. "For what?"

"It's between us," he replied curtly.

"We should start a club."

"With shirts and everything."

"I know people," I said in a laugh.

Tobias pulled away from me and grabbed the garment bags from the rack. "So what do you say? Tomorrow evening?"

"What time?"

"Carpet is at seven," he replied. "Film at eight. Party afterwards."

I shook my head. "I would love to, Tobias, but I've already made plans that go until eight-ish."

"Oh?"

"I'm going to watch my brother's footy match," I said. "It's a very big to-do. The opposing club is one of the best in the Special Olympics system."

Tobias' smile was warm and understanding. "I wouldn't want you to miss that, but if you could make it to the after party, that would be lovely."

How could I refuse him? Really, what woman could refuse a lovely man like him? Compared to Alex, Tobias was a saint and it was nice to be valued in a way that wasn't purely physical. While my blood didn't thrum with want around Tobias in the same way it did when Alex walked into the room, it was just as nice to have his attention. It seemed more proper. More acceptable than anything Alex offered me, even if my relationship with Tobias never went anywhere beyond friendship. Frankly, at this point, I was willing to do anything with another heterosexual male to get my mind off Alex.

What would going out with Tobias harm, anyway?

"I'll try," I said.

"Perfect!" he exclaimed. "Let me have your address and I'll messenger over a ticket for tomorrow."

I walked to the desk and scribbled the address on the back of the envelope which once held the stationery bill. When I handed it to him, he shoved it into his jeans pocket and smiled again. We walked to the door, where he quickly replaced his cap over his hair and put on his sunglasses. He stepped onto the front stoop and turned to look at me.

"Hopefully I'll see you tomorrow evening."

"I hope so, too." I really did.

"Have a lovely afternoon!" And with that, I watched him bounce down the stairs and out onto the footpath. He paused again. "Oh, tell Sam good luck!"

"I will, thank you!" I called.

Sam wouldn't know who Tobias was, but he would appreciate the wish for luck. More than anything, it made my icy heart melt that he remembered Sam's name and that he cared enough to mention anything before he left.

With a giddy sigh, I shut the door behind me and locked it. I took a few minutes there, letting the past hour replay itself in my head. Finally, only because my mobile began playing the foreboding Toccata and Fugue, did I forcibly remove myself from the door.

Reality called.

CHAPTER 7

BY THE TIME THE MESSENGER arrived the following morning, I talked myself out of going to the party with Tobias. Even though I'd technically be his date, I had attended my fair share of these events in the past and they all amounted to nothing more than glorified and incredibly expensive back-slapping and brown nosing opportunities for all involved. It wasn't my scene, especially immediately following two months of it in Georgina's employ. Besides that, I didn't aim to be *that girl* who mysteriously showed up on the arm of one of Britain's greatest treasures.

However, my resolve did not last long. Or, perhaps, it did last well into the night, even after I was already dressed up and preparing to step out of the car onto the red carpet, but Lindsay's insistence that I attend was impossible to overcome. When he returned home from the office and saw the envelope on the table, he nearly flipped out. No, not *nearly*. He *had* flipped out and told me to go, and there would be no argument about it. Of course he used a long list of rather sound evidence as to why I needed to go out for myself, but none of it seemed compelling enough without his insistence.

Tobias including extra tickets for both Lindsay and Sam, should they wish to join me, didn't help matters either. Whether he intended kindness or not, this wasn't going to be a real "date," which made the appeal of braving the masses even less, well, appealing. I would have rather stayed at home and caught the film with both Sam and Lindsay when it released in cinemas in a week. Anything was better than shimmying into a flouncy dress and stilettos when it wasn't strictly required of me. Still, it was wonderful to include both Sam and Lindsay in something rather than leaving them behind.

Sam, still on a high from his club's hard-fought win over his football opponents, imagined himself the star of the show and hammed it up for anyone interested in talking to him along the endless line of photographers and reporters lining the red carpet. Lindsay stayed with me, as though he were my bodyguard, even though he was shaking in his boots with the possibility of meeting the object of his fantasies again. I simply walked, trying to work both men back into the cinema as quickly as possible. As it was, Sam's match finished early enough that we could attend the premiere, but it didn't leave us as much time as my brother wished on the carpet. The film was due to start, and I refused to be seated late or cause a scene.

As we neared the doors into the theatre, I heard the familiar baritone voice of my quasi-date. Lindsay, whose arm I held, froze in his spot, alerting me to the fact that the large man found the source of the voice over the heads of all the shorter people. A group cleared out of the way, revealing Tobias. He stood on the other side of the wide red carpet in front of a microphone and at least three cameras giving an interview. Tobias caught sight of us, pausing his interview for a minute with a smile and a wave.

I grinned and herded Lindsay and Sam further along until I felt another body beside me and a large, warm hand slide from my low back around to a hip.

"You look lovely," said the baritone voice in my ear. A shiver skittered up my spine.

"As do you." I smiled. "That suit looks impeccable."

Tobias laughed. "My stylist's assistant knows a smart suit when she sees one."

I finally looked up at him and playfully nudged his shoulder. "Yes, well, you don't have to deal with the shit storm I'm going to face when she sees the press images."

"I'll give her a ring tomorrow," Tobias said.

"Thank you."

I felt an elbow in my other side and realised I neglected Lindsay and Sam.

"Oh, Tobias, you remember Lindsay and Sam."

Sam jumped in front of us; since that morning at breakfast, I had tried to explain to him who Tobias was and why he was important. It took several attempts, but after showing him pictures of Tobias as some of the characters he had portrayed, it slowly started to connect. His glee meeting the actor nearly eclipsed that which he felt for winning his footy match.

Tobias was gracious with him, asking him questions and—I noted, much to my own delight—didn't talk down to him. Lindsay didn't utter a word until we were seated together and Tobias joined his cast mates for an introduction before the film.

"I don't believe this is happening," Lindsay whispered. "I don't believe I'm sitting in a room with all these celebrities."

"Would you calm down?" I pleaded. "And you wonder why I don't include you in more of my work events."

Lindsay scowled at me, but couldn't retort before the lights dimmed and the director of the film appeared on the stage to introduce the actors and talk about the story for a little bit. When it concluded, Tobias came back to us and slid into the empty seat beside me. It was comfortable and companionable, but I still couldn't shake the feeling that he didn't intend it to be a real date.

But, then again, that was only me jumping to conclusions. Tobias was such a lovely man, I knew I had to give him the benefit of the doubt. It would have been stupid of me to ignore his interest, however reserved, especially when he was such a practical choice for a potential suitor. Not that I had a huge pool of suitors. With my life consumed in work, I had been unable to seriously look. If I *had* been looking, Tobias was all the things which made a suitable love interest—he was respectful, kind, gainfully employed, and he wasn't completely hard on the eyes.

Most importantly, he didn't have a girlfriend and use me to cheat on her.

Still, something seemed off about the whole situation and I couldn't put a finger on it.

A few hours later, the lights came up to well-mannered applause. Tobias excused himself to chat with others before going to the party venue, and I grabbed Lindsay and Sam to go on our own.

Tobias didn't arrive for another hour, but that didn't stop us from partaking in the open bar and free food until the man of the hour arrived. The instant Tobias appeared beside me, I sensed the intensity of interested onlookers watching us. I tried to ignore it, but Tobias made me forget them.

"So how'd you like the film?" he asked between sips of his drink.

"It was wonderful," I replied. "But there haven't been many roles I haven't liked you in. You have good taste in selecting your roles."

He smiled. "It's been pure luck, trust me."

I laughed lightly and shook my head. "Well, whatever it is, you were wonderful. Lindsay and Sam loved it, as well. Speaking of whom… thank you for thinking of them."

Tobias shrugged. "I knew I couldn't be with you all night, so I thought you might like company."

"It was appreciated," I replied. "I almost talked myself out of coming before Lindsay saw the envelope and extra tickets."

I flinched when I realised what I said—I never intended to be so blunt about it. But Tobias grinned like a wise old owl. What did he know anyway?

"I also had a feeling you would try to talk yourself out of it."

"I'm so sorry," I apologised and tried to mask my blunder. "I didn't mean it to sound like that. I'm grateful for the gesture and everything, and you're lovely, I just… I didn't think I should waste my time."

"Who says you're wasting your time?"

I sighed and pressed my hand on his back until he turned in the direction I faced. "You have your pick. There are gobs of beautiful women in this room watching you, undressing you with their eyes, and wondering how they can get you away from me."

"What a way to make a chap feel awkward," he said with a genial laugh. He shifted his shoulders about and stood taller.

"But they are," I insisted. "And while they're all trying to undress you, I'm really only concerned about keeping this fabulous suit on your body. Because I have to. Because it's my job."

Tobias' thick black eyebrows furrowed in confusion. "You haven't thought about taking it off at least once?"

I laughed at him. "That's not the point."

"But that *is* the point," he remarked.

I removed my hand from his back. "You're trying to distract me from my point."

"Hardly." Tobias faced me and stepped in closer. "You're trying to convince me that all those other women deserve my interest more than you do. You're deflecting attention when you really should be concerned about who's looking at you."

To illustrate his point, his hand circled around my waist and turned me around in a full revolution, making note of a few curious male glances as we moved.

I looked at him and shook my head, unconvinced. "They're looking at you, Tobias."

"I promise you, they aren't."

"How can you—"

I stopped when a large shadow fell over us.

"Em?"

I looked up at Lindsay. "Yeah?"

"I've got to head home… early meetings and all that tomorrow," he said. "Are you coming with?"

Tobias answered before I could. "I'm not going to be here much longer, I'd be happy to share my car with you, Emilia."

"Oh," I said, "I, uh, that would be great. Will you take Sammy home, though, Lindsay?"

Lindsay bowed his head in solemn acknowledgement, but the expression on his face filled with a mixture of mirth and giddiness. "Let me know if you're going to be out… late."

He winked and used air quotes. No one could accuse him of subtlety. My face burned with embarrassment. He thanked Tobias profusely for the invite, and when he was out of words to say and had stopped squealing internally, Lindsay turned back to me.

Lindsay grinned. "Don't do anything I wouldn't do."

"That leaves it pretty wide open," I replied.

"Indeed it does."

I rolled my eyes. "Please leave us alone. If you embarrass me anymore, I don't know what I'll do."

"Oh, please, you love me," Lindsay said cheekily, stepping in to peck my forehead. "Just be good."

"Go forth and end world hunger," I ordered. Lindsay turned and mock saluted once before going to find Sam. When we were finally alone, I looked back at Tobias. "I'm sorry about that."

"What does he do?" Tobias asked.

"He's an aide to an MP," I said. "So basically he keeps calendars and serves tea and writes documents with bravado and legal mumbo-jumbo. But we like to think he's finding the key to ending world hunger."

Tobias laughed at my answer. "I'm sure he does more than at least half of the Parliament combined."

I shrugged my shoulders and glanced around the room again, content that the curious onlookers had mostly moved on from us. A server with a tray of filled champagne flutes passed by us; I grabbed one and took a long sip.

"Let me take you around and introduce you," he offered.

I followed him like an obedient puppy. We spent about an hour more posing for pictures, moving through introductions and short conversation with others, but mostly with the other actors and crew members Tobias worked with on the production. I was content staying on his arm and allowing him to work the room; he never neglected me, making sure I enjoyed myself as we moved around the room and included me in conversation as much as possible.

However, I was ecstatic when he asked if I wanted to leave. I agreed immediately. We slowly made our way outside to the valet where a sleek black Audi pulled to a stop in front of us. I gave the driver my address, and once we were in the quiet vehicle moving through the streets of London, I let out a sigh. Even though the night mostly involved dealing with the parts of the industry I disliked, I had to admit to having a good time with Lindsay and Sam, and then with Tobias. He, at least, behaved like a gentleman and didn't push me into dark alcoves only to leave me completely befuddled. Not at all like someone else I knew.

"Thank you for coming tonight," Tobias said. "I hope it wasn't too terrible."

I chuckled and looked at him. "It was actually pretty lovely. Better than many fashion events I've been to recently."

"Oh?"

"I've never met a community of people who are more exclusionist than models and fashion designers. If you aren't like them, then you're out of the club," I said. "I seriously go to these events with Georgina and watch them float everywhere, filling up on booze and hovering over the food like some sort of ravenous zombies. But there's a force field around the food so they just sort of come over, admire the way it looks all spread out, smell it, and walk away looking forlorn. It makes everyone so cranky that they don't talk to each other."

By this time, Tobias had broken into a full, long laugh. "The sad thing is that I know what you mean."

"My God!" I was on a roll and knew I wouldn't be able to stop myself. Not with him egging me on with the interested laughter in his voice. "People always question me about what it's like to be a plus size woman in the fashion world. I tell them that someone has to eat the food that everyone else won't. I'm as good as any other to meet that challenge."

"That's perfect." He wiped a tear out of his eye from the laughter and shook his head. "Completely terrible, but a perfect reply."

I shrugged and folded my arms over my chest. "They all just sort of sniff at me like I have five heads when I say it. Personally, I like food. And I like good tasting food. If they want to keep subsisting on air, alcohol, and the fad diets and cleanses of the day—then they can go right ahead and stay miserable."

Tobias chuckled. "I take it you didn't last long as a model."

"Fuck no," I replied with a sigh. The truth was, I didn't mind modelling much. In fact, I actually loved working the catwalk and the living it provided for me. I only wished the industry had been more welcome and open minded to me. "After my first agent moved on to editorial work, they signed me to a new contract and told me I wasn't thin enough for plus size samples on the runway and asked me to lose weight. I refused, so they refused to book me for anything other than print advertisement because they could Photoshop my imperfections."

Tobias looked at me closely—almost too closely. His eyes slid from my face and down my body for a brief moment, but it was enough to make me shift in my seat from discomfort. He smiled. "I just can't imagine what imperfections they would have to Photoshop away."

I laughed and playfully dug my elbow in his side. "Stop."

"It's true."

With a blush, I met his eyes.

"I guess you know that flattery will get you everywhere," I teased.

He sat back in his seat and folded his hands in his lap. I pursed my lips, wondering why he moved. Of course he was so proper—so

English in his reserve around me—but I was surprised at the sudden change. Had I said something wrong? It had only been in response to his comments.

"But are you *really* happy?" he asked quietly, glancing at me.

The question stunned me because it came from out of nowhere. What shocked me even more was a negative knee-jerk answer practically falling from my lips.

"Happy about what?" I said instead, hoping to buy some time.

Tobias shrugged. "It's just that you basically said that everyone in the fashion world is cranky and unhappy. You aren't like them, so I want to know if you're happy with who you are and your life."

I stared at him for a long time. Probably, for much too long a time. No one had ever actually asked me that question point blank and it upset me. I fidgeted in my seat. "I'm happy."

He looked at me askance.

"I *am* happy."

I wished I believed it as much as I wanted to make him believe it.

"All right, if you say so," Tobias said.

I shrugged, but was thankful when he ceased the questioning.

"I am happy," I repeated again. This time, I said it softly. "It was a good night and I got to spend time with people I like."

Tobias' smile was slow as he turned his head toward me. He opened his mouth to reply, but closed it when the muffled jingle of a far off mobile sounded in the vehicle. We both reached for our own; Tobias hummed at his screen as he looked at a message. He turned his body slightly away so I could not read the screen. Not that I could have if I wanted. I had multiple messages of my own.

One from Lindsay saying he and Sam made it home with little incident.

Ten from Georgina. She, apparently, had haunted the Internet in wait for pictures from the premiere and found photos of Tobias in the navy suit. Her words were scolding, but she hadn't fired me, so I marked it down as a victory for me. The last message, however, completely incensed me.

> *Georgina: I truly hope you didn't guilt Tobias into taking you.*

So, there were photos of me with Tobias. For the briefest of moments, I was gobsmacked at how quickly the images became available online. But then I remembered what Georgina said, and it just made me grumble all over again. I clicked off the screen and heatedly tossed the device into my clutch, snapping it shut.

"What's wrong?" Tobias asked.

I sniffed. "Georgina."

"What'd she say?"

"I'd rather not talk about it."

"Are you sure?"

"Yes, I'm certain."

The rest of the ride continued in silence as we neared my flat. His driver parked the car and jumped out, coming around to my side. I thanked Tobias again for inviting all of us.

He merely smiled. "Maybe we'll do it again sometime?"

"For another premiere?"

My tease was not lost on him. His grin widened. He shook his head. "Maybe something a little more intimate? I have a bit of a break when I fly back from America next week."

I sighed and pursed my lips. He was like a sphinx. I couldn't read him and it bothered me. Did he ask because he was truly attracted to me and wanted to get to know me better, or was there something else? I still didn't feel as though our night were a real date, but there was a chance that in a more intimate setting, circumstances would be different.

I decided to answer him truthfully. "Oh, Tobias, I had a lovely time tonight, but I'm not sure…"

"Think about it. I'll ring you next week and we can discuss it a little more."

I nodded. "Please."

He leaned over and gave me a chaste, brotherly peck on the cheek. I felt absolutely no flutter in my chest, nor did my belly do any acrobatics; he didn't linger or try to do it again in an attempt to get a response. It was just plain odd.

"Have a good night, Emilia."

I slid out of the car and smoothed my dress down, gathering my wits about me before moving toward the front entrance. Even as I entered the building, I had absolutely no idea what to think about the night, about Tobias... about anything really. So, in my confused state, I went straight to bed and hoped by morning my dreams would work it all out for me.

ALEXANDER
UNMASKED

As LUCK HAD IT, I didn't see the object of my infatuation for any decent length of time over the following weeks. She and Georgina had many events out of the country while I continued preparations for my new theatre engagement in *The Taming of the Shrew*. The few times Emilia was around ended up being swift and perfunctory in their mannerly greetings and farewells and did not give me the opportunity to get to know her better.

However, Emilia's and Georgina's absence made me unduly excited for Georgina's annual Halloween soirée, despite the rather distracting theme requiring women to dress in their most revealing lingerie. Emilia's attendance was compulsory as a condition of her employment and I hoped it gave me ample time to stare at her like some infatuated school boy.

That was, of course, how I found myself going through the motions, trying to feign enjoyment. I hated it. Only the liberal application of whiskey eased the pain, but it was only a partial numbness. It forced me to listen to Georgina and act like I cared. The addition of a close friend's presence made it almost bearable, though that friend seemed even less thrilled than I was.

"So where is this woman you wanted me to meet?"

I glanced at the stone-faced man as he fell into place beside me in front of the blazing fire. "She hasn't arrived yet."

"I'm beginning to think she doesn't exist," Tobias replied, sipping the dark liquor in his heavy-bottomed tumbler.

Sighing into my glass, I sipped the stringent liquor. I held it in my mouth for a moment and then swallowed slowly, enjoying the slow burn it created down in the pit of my belly. It was the best option to buy some time before answering the inquisitive man. For as little as I actually saw of the woman in question, I was also beginning to wonder if she existed or if she was merely a figment of my imagination—a welcome oasis in the desert—brought on by the unhappiness in my love life.

The source of that particular unhappiness came into our visual path wearing some kind of pastel frock. I supposed it was some ridiculously expensive negligee made by some big name designer she insisted she show off to the rest of her money-grubbing, fame-hungry friends. I sighed and closed my eyes, shaking my head.

"She's just eating the attention up," Tobias remarked.

I sighed. "It keeps her quiet and away from me."

Tobias rolled his eyes and took another sip of his drink. After he swallowed, he looked at me seriously. "Why did you ever agree to go on a date with her if you loathe her so much?"

"Because," I said, "she was attractive and she was interested."

"You mean she hounded you until you couldn't take it."

"It wasn't like that," I defended. "And she's not all bad. When she's not with these people, she can actually be pretty decent to spend time with. She's also okay in bed."

Tobias leaned on the decorated mantelpiece, pushing his arms against the autumn garland strung across the ornate mouldings. He picked absently at the plastic gourds attached in a cluster to a silk vine. "Wow, it certainly sounds like true love."

"It isn't," I said with a clear of my throat. "It's the furthest thing from love, and you know it."

"You're the one that got yourself into this mess."

Tobias made a good point, just like everyone else in my life had after I met Georgina. Unfortunately, I barked so far up the wrong tree that I didn't know how to turn around and come back down. My only option was to fantasise elsewhere and frantically look for some way out of my relationship with the woman, even if I knew there might never be an easy one.

I glanced across the room and noticed her watching me with the sick predatory look I had quickly learned was her scheming face. It was the one that portended plans made without asking and the expectation that I follow blindly along behind her without any care for my own needs and wants. The one that continually emasculated me for no other purpose than to prove she was a heinous shrew.

"Alexander!"

Her voice, high-pitched and grating, made the hair on the back of my neck stand on end in icy frustration. I adjusted the high clerical collar around my neck. Why had I even agreed to put the damn thing on? I detested the premise of Vicars and Tarts parties, no matter how lavish and high class they were, or whether they were dressed up and packaged as something else. Georgina had attempted sexy and provocative, but it just came out as terribly gauche, much like the rest of her over-styled self.

"Yes, Georgina?" I asked as pleasantly as possible when the small woman stopped in front of me.

She tossed back the rest of her champagne. "Why aren't you smiling? This is a party!"

I pulled the last shreds of festiveness from the depths of my soul and managed a small smile.

She set a hand on Tobias' arm. "And Tobias! Come on! I have so many lovely ladies for you to meet."

Tobias merely patted Georgina's hand as though she were a small child. "I'll find you in a bit. Alex and I are catching up."

And then he gave her the award winning goofy smile.

Georgina grinned a row of fluorescent white teeth. "Well, all right, if you say so. Just don't be a wallflower. We're supposed to have fun tonight!"

She shimmied off to her other guests and we both watched her go. When I turned to look at Tobias, I noticed the abject horror riddling his face. He drew a breath through barely parted lips. "Well, at least she likes playing hostess. There's always a plus to that, you know. You'll never have to plan another thing in your life."

I groaned and drank what was left of my whiskey. That was exactly the problem: I had absolutely no control over anything in my life. More than that, I willingly went along with it. "I need more liquor. How are you?"

"I could use a top up."

Tobias followed me through rooms filled with people I didn't know and didn't care to know, toward the bartender set up along one wall in the reception room. The man making the drinks looked thoroughly bored, but filled our order with expediency. As he pushed the drinks across the makeshift bar, he glanced up and past us, a smile on his face.

I felt her presence before I actually turned to look at what or who the beatifically smiling bartender noticed. I couldn't ignore the low zing of pulsing magnetic energy running through me. Seeing her there in all her splendour was a cross between a shock of electricity and bathing in fizzy seltzer water.

"Hello, Paul!" Emilia called as she rounded the bar. "How's everything going? Do you need anything?"

I wanted to reach out and touch her; I felt like a child in a sweetshop and my impulse control barely matched that of a five-year-old. She wore the most fetching fancy dress I could have imagined in this setting. Her costume consisted of more coverage and fabric than the rest of the female attendees combined, but what she did show made my mouth water.

I felt an elbow digging in my side and tore my eyes away from the residence they took up on her tanned legs. Tobias looked at me expectantly and I blinked at him to clear my mind. He expected an introduction, but I didn't know if it was one I could give.

"So that's her?" Tobias asked with a lazy, slightly slurred cadence. He wasn't drunk on alcohol, that much I knew. The woman, then?

I nodded. "Yes."

Tobias sipped his drink. "You certainly weren't overstating."

When I finally took a moment to really look at my friend, I noticed the telltale sign of a man in lust. But I knew my friend, and I knew he wouldn't overstep himself. My eyes fell back on Emilia as she shifted her weight on her stiletto-adorned feet. She played with a long curl of dark hair as she talked. My hands itched. I wanted to sink my fingers into the thick waves and tug at them as I kissed her senseless. Why had she left it to cascade down her back like that? Didn't she know what she was doing to poor bastards like me?

The curl sprang back into shape and came to a rest in the dip of ample cleavage visible in the open neck of the filmy white blouse.

Something must have caught Emilia's eye because she stopped mid-conversation with the bartender and glanced over at us. Maybe it was the drool down my chin or Tobias' subtle preening—he adjusted his coat and stood taller—but it was enough to be noticed in the middle of the room. She replaced a headset on her head and connected it to a receiver on her hip. I supposed she used it to keep track of the service operations throughout the party. After a few more words with Paul, she pushed herself from the bar and slinked her way over to us with a slight, provocative sway of her hips.

Where had she learned to walk like that?

"Gentlemen," she said with a small smile, a visible heat rising on her cheeks. "I hope you're enjoying yourselves."

"We are," Tobias affirmed.

Both looked to me for an introduction, but I found none.

Tobias rolled his eyes and offered his hand to Emilia. "I'm Tobias Sinclair."

Emilia grinned. "I know."

She was completely star-struck. I knew the signs well. Glassy eyes.

Insane thousand-wattage smile. And a slight hitch in the smooth richness of her voice. "My name's Emilia. I'm—"

"Georgina's assistant," Tobias finished for her and laughed, reaching out to touch her arm. It was a chaste, friendly touch, but the familiarity of it bothered me. I thought I made it clear to Tobias that he was invited for reconnaissance and nothing more.

She giggled, playing with the flashy bejewelled necklace resting on her clavicles. She let go of the jewellery with a sigh when her eyes flicked over to me. "Hello, Alex."

"Good evening," I replied. "How are you getting on tonight?"

She shrugged. "It's just like any other of Georgina's parties. I'm running around wild and directing everyone."

A momentary silence fell between all of us; I was content to just stare at her, and she seemed to be waiting for me or Tobias to lead the conversation or, at least, change the subject. Tobias, ever the observer, didn't intrude. Georgina's obnoxious laugh and grating voice took care of that.

"Oh, Emilia! *There* you are!" she called, appearing at Emilia's side. "Excuse us, Alex and Tobias. I need to talk to her about a few things."

We watched Georgina practically drag an unwilling Emilia into a corner to chat. When they were far enough away, Tobias turned to look at me again. "You know the best part about this situation?"

I frowned and looked at him. "What is that?"

He swallowed what remained in his glass—it was a lot to drink so quickly, but he merely hissed at the burning—and set the tumbler on the table beside us with a *clunk*. "The best part about this cock up with Georgina is that for once you get to be my wingman."

"Tobias…" I warned.

He held up a hand to stop me. "I suspect you invited me here not only to meet her, but also to infiltrate enemy lines for you."

I sighed.

"Well, that comes with a price," he said. "And that's entertaining Georgina while I do the dirty work of chatting up Emilia."

My knuckles turned white around the tumbler in my hand. He was right, naturally. I wanted information. I had to be completely sure I wasn't making the wrong decision should I end my relationship with Georgina.

My very livelihood and career depended upon it.

"You're right," I conceded.

Tobias nodded. "If you want this done, you better go sidetrack Georgina."

I blew out a long breath and took another pull of whiskey from my glass. Wingman for the night. My only hope was that it didn't become a permanent position, especially with Emilia involved.

CHAPTER 8

AT PRECISELY SIX O'CLOCK on my first Friday morning at home, an impromptu Toccata and Fugue symphony catapulted me out of a sound sleep and out of my bed into a dark room. My senses took awhile to return to a somewhat functional state after the sudden jolt, but as they did, the fogginess of sleep gave way to a clearer head. The electronic organ music pounded through the room while I stared and blinked dumbly at the device, wishing the song would cease, so I could crawl back under the covers and salvage what was left of a restful night's slumber.

It didn't stop. As soon as it ended, it started anew. I cursed Georgina for redialling my number and not leaving a message. Were my grandmother still around, the words leaving my mouth would have earned me quite the punishment. However, I was thankful she wasn't alive. The only phrases acceptable at such an ungodly hour were the ones I uttered between clenched teeth.

I fumbled with the mobile in my hands, connected the call, then dropped it on the floor before finally managing to place it against my ear.

"Hello?" My voice sounded scratchy from sleep. I swallowed and reached for the glass of water beside my bed.

The screech coming through the line practically pierced my fragile eardrum. "I have been trying to reach you for the past hour! Where have you *been*?"

I grabbed the fleece blanket previously thrown from my body in surprise and pulled it around my shoulders. "I'm sorry, Georgina. Did you text me? I didn't hear the mobile. I was asleep."

"Whatever," she dismissed. "I need you to book me a flight from Athens."

Her words weren't making any sense to me yet. "Huh?"

"I need a flight from Athens!" Her voice rose several octaves.

I frowned. "I hope nothing's the matter—"

"Everything's the matter!" she shrieked. "Alex has ignored me this whole time with his—well, whatever he's doing on the islands. I give him the perfect opportunity to propose sometime on this cruise and he's more anxious to go look at some crumbling stone building or a statue of a naked woman."

Six in the morning was entirely too early to listen to Georgina's complaining; she clearly hadn't thought Alexander would want to actually absorb the Greek culture and history on his trip. He read History at university and commented more than once in my presence how much he wanted to take an extended sail around the archipelago; I suggested the destination to Georgina when she began searching for an appropriate location for a holiday. But I wasn't surprised she expected a holiday meant to focus on him to revolve around her. She would blame me for even suggesting Greece when she returned, but until then, I planned to take what little amount of pleasure I could in the fact that she didn't get what she wanted all along.

"And then his mother has to go and trip over a cat or something a few days ago mucking everything up—"

"Oh my, is she all right?" I exclaimed in worry, but she ignored me and continued.

"… He flew back last night to be with her for some reason. It's only a couple broken bones or something. Doesn't he have siblings or somebody else to look after her? And aren't there doctors and nurses and caregivers? He's worth so much money, couldn't he—"

"But is his mother all right?" I asked again with a stronger voice, stopping her rant dead in its tracks.

"What?" The impatient confusion in Georgina's voice made me wince.

"Is his mum all right?" I repeated again.

A forced sound of disgust met my ear. "It's not my concern at the moment. I need you to do your job and find me a flight as soon as possible."

I chewed on my lower lip, trying to ignore the anger simmering inside of me at her quick dismissal of Alex's mother. Of course my new feelings for Alex weren't particularly kind, but Georgina hit a new low with her flippant disregard for his mother's well-being. If she was so keen on Alex marrying her, then she might do well to get to know the woman.

"Emilia?" she called. "Honestly, Emilia! You can't skive off right now."

Her disdain irked me. Didn't she see how much I did for her on a daily basis?

"Yes, Georgina. I will get you a flight out from Athens as soon as possible," I said evenly, hoping it hid my irritation. "City or Heathrow?"

"Neither," she replied. "Send me to Paris for the next week. I called Martinique and Jenny. We're to meet there for a bit of a girls' holiday. I need to work Jenny over for dresses for the Oscars."

And she didn't plan to come home to help the man while he cared for his injured mother.

"Yes, Georgina." I grabbed the magazine and pen beside my bed to scribble notes down on Heidi Klum's airbrushed face. "Shall I make reservations at the Four Seasons as usual?"

"Yes," she said. "Make sure you get me one of the penthouses. I don't want to be stuck with people above me again."

I nodded for my benefit alone. "When would you like to return?"

"Sunday next. And I'll fly into City. Plan to meet me at the airport with the driver. I'll be bringing back loads of new things from Paris."

Great. I would have to sort and catalogue it. Not my choice of a fun day at the office, not that there were many of those. "I've got it. Travel from Athens to Paris, Four Seasons until Sunday. And you'll be returning via City. Is there anything else?"

"No," she said. "Martinique's driver will meet me at de Gaulle."

Lovely.

"I expect to hear from you in a half hour."

"Of course, Georgina."

"Good." Her voice was short and snippy, even though her hysterics had subsided a little. "I will need you to get flowers or something for Alex's mother. Not some half dead bouquet from a street vendor, either. You know what I like."

I sighed and rolled my eyes toward the ceiling. Of course I knew what she liked, but seeing as this was a gift for someone else, it would take some thinking. Georgina wouldn't ever see them. They'd be dead by the time she returned from Paris, anyway.

"I'll let you take care of that while I manage the yacht," she said. "Half an hour, Emilia."

"Yes, good bye."

I dropped the silent mobile on the bed and laid out across the rumpled covers. Pulling the blanket more snugly around me, I let out a loud yawn along with some of my frustration. The first bits of periwinkle streaked the morning sky outside my windows and I heard movement from within the flat—likely Lindsay bumping around like a zombie in preparation for work. Ceramic dishes clinked together, followed by running water and rummaging in the cupboards. A harsh Scottish curse followed and then more bumping around.

I yawned into my hand again and somehow summoned enough energy to complete my tasks. After a few more minutes, I pulled myself from the bed and reached for my laptop to do the work needing to be done. At least I could try for a little more sleep after I finished.

I STOOD OUTSIDE the front door of a charming brown brick cottage in Wandsworth many hours later, reconsidering what exactly I expected to get out of my visit. Delivering the wrapped bouquet in my hand was one task I was required to complete, but I couldn't help but feel like a masochist going through this trouble for a boss I only tolerated… and for an infuriating man who had an ego the size of Russia.

Even though I made sure to leave our relationship professional in Venice, it was our first meeting since the hotel ultimatum; I wasn't at all prepared for the occasion. Georgina wasn't a hallway away tempering his actions or words, and I was fairly certain hand delivering the flowers along with a care package did not border on the truly professional. I feared he would see it as me disregarding all of my previous wishes and act accordingly. More galling to me was that I couldn't blame him if he did. I was not keeping up my end of the agreement and staying on my side of the proverbial line in the sand.

The situation became completely personal to me after I realized what little regard Georgina had for her potential mother-in-law. Not so much in the fact that I thought I could be a better candidate for such a position, but more because I believed Alex's mother, Mary, deserved to be the centre of attention in her time of need. She deserved the best because she did just as much for everyone else.

Mary and I had only conversed for five minutes a few months earlier, but it was enough time to learn that she was a goddess amongst women. Not only had she maintained a successful career as a museum curator, but singlehandedly raised four productive, intelligent, and beautiful children; she loved her family fiercely, and they adored her in return. She wouldn't back down from a fight, but she was also the kindest woman imaginable. Rather than ignore me, she personally sought me out and thanked me for the hard work I put into the party at which we met. That gesture alone made my toil over the whole thing worth it.

Honestly, I fell in love with her before I developed my own starry-eyed interest in Alex. I wondered idly, as I stood on the front stoop of Mary's cute cottage, if my appreciation for her hadn't coloured my image of her son in such a positive light. Now that I knew the truth, not even her involvement could save him. He only put on the "good boy" show in public; hundreds of interviews and positive fan encounters proved as much. The truth was far from the image I had constructed in my head.

And yet...

And yet, he ended one of his dream holidays early just to fly home for his mother. No one told him he had to come home to care for her. He did, actually, have siblings nearby who could help. Had he no regard for his mother or was as much of a Don Juan as he appeared to me in Venice, he wouldn't have found the first flight out of Athens. I hoped there was more to him than he let on, but I found it incredibly difficult to reconcile what I knew of him now with what I learned about him a week previous.

Still, I knew I should have asked the florist to deliver the flowers; doing so cut down on the inevitable awkwardness of arriving at her home unannounced or facing him before I thoroughly prepared. I was, however, beginning to wonder if anyone was even at home—or if I had the correct address. Or worse: if he packed his mother off to his place while she recuperated. When I received no answer from my first knock, I knocked once more.

"Alexander! If you don't answer the door, I will get up."

I smiled at the sound of the plucky woman yelling from somewhere inside her home.

"All right, all right!" a second voice said, close to the door. "No, you stay in that chair and don't move. You heard the doctor's orders!"

Exasperated more than angry, I wouldn't have disobeyed the authoritarian tone in his voice. An irritated, disembodied grunt of frustration followed.

I saw the dark outline of him in the cut glass panes in the door. Two eyes peeked out the clear glass, blinked a few times, and then pulled away. For a second, I thought he wouldn't open the door; I heard a small intake of breath on the other side before he flipped the deadbolt and pulled it back.

He didn't welcome me immediately. Fortuitous, seeing as my tongue felt like a lead weight in my mouth and would have kept me from replying if he spoke to me. Instead, he surveyed my face, then the bouquet of flowers in my right hand, and the basket hanging on my left elbow before meeting my gaze again. I did the same; he looked sun-kissed and well groomed, but consternation filled his face. I sincerely hoped my visit wasn't the reason for it.

"Yes?" he asked coolly.

I swallowed around the lump forming in my throat. "I, um... Georgina asked me to deliver these flowers."

"Did she?" A well shaped brow rose in mock surprise. "How kind of her."

The vitriol in his voice stunned me, but it clearly wasn't for me.

"I wasn't aware she even cared," he added.

"Alexander!" called the woman from the other room. "Either invite the girl in or shut the door. It's rather chilly."

Alex's eyes lifted to the ceiling as though praying for some sort of serenity. After a breath, his eyes were back on me. "Would you care to come in?"

"Oh, I don't know," I said. "I just wanted to drop these off..."

"We're about to have tea," he replied. "You should stay."

I blew air out of my lungs and shook my head, knowing even before stepping foot into the house that it was a bad decision. "Fine."

Alex stepped aside and waved an arm to allow me inside the cottage. It was bright and airy with colourful artwork on the basic ecru walls. Vibrant jewel tones from garnet to deep sapphire seeped into the other modern furnishings. I felt a hand on my shoulder and tensed at the touch.

I practically heard his smile. "Let me take your coat."

"Thanks."

I sheepishly switched the basket and bouquet to one hand as he helped me out of my coat on the off side. I moved them to the other as he completely removed it and turned to hang it up in a small cupboard near the door.

He wordlessly led the way into the living room where his mother sat propped up in an overstuffed chair. The lower part of her right leg was covered in a white plaster cast and elevated on an ottoman. Her right wrist bore a matching cast, the other simply wrapped in an elastic brace. An ugly, scabbed cut followed the curve of her chin.

"My darling Emilia!" The thin woman, elegant even in her current state, tried to stand but remembered she couldn't. She grumbled unhappily and fell back into her seat, tucking some of her curly silver hair behind an ear.

I moved over quickly to take her hand in welcome, for which she seemed grateful.

"Oh," she said, discouraged. "These damned things… I'm sorry I couldn't get up."

"Don't think anything about it, Mary."

Her face brightened instantly when she spotted the gifts in my hand. "What beautiful flowers!"

"Oh, right!" I held the bouquet out to her. "I've come to deliver these. They are from Georgina. She sends her best wishes for a speedy recovery."

Mary made no attempt to keep distaste from surfacing on her face. I sighed. So the feeling was mutual between both women.

"Georgina picked these?" she asked with an eyebrow cocked.

I fidgeted under her scrutiny. When I didn't reply, she barely nodded her head and lifted the fragrant bouquet to her nose.

"These are delightful. I do so love sunflowers… and the irises compliment them so well."

I laughed. "I'm glad you like them. They're one of my favourites. They just seem so cheerful."

"They'll certainly brighten up a gloomy day." She set them aside with care and turned back to me. "And with all this grey weather, it's especially welcome."

"Indeed." I nodded my head and held out the basket I brought with me. "This is from me, however."

She smiled kindly, looking through the teas, reading materials, and the plate of chocolate chip cookies from the batch I baked for Sam after my return to London.

"I remember at the Christmas party we bonded over chocolate," I recalled, "and chocolate makes everything better, so I thought you might like those."

"We'll have them with tea!" she called. "Alexander! Weren't you going to make tea?"

I followed her gaze behind me, remembering Alex had stalled somewhere back there. Apparently he had been quietly observing the situation. He shook his head to clear his thoughts, clapping and rubbing his hands together. "Right. Tea."

"Thank you," she replied.

I looked back at her and she motioned to the sofa beside her. Carefully sitting down and letting out my own sigh, I tried to ignore the banging of cupboard doors coming from the room where Alex had disappeared. "He's been in such a mood recently. I apologise for his behaviour."

I choked a bit on my saliva and coughed into my hand. "I haven't noticed."

Her face softened and she shook her head. "Of course you're too kind to draw attention to it, but something's bothering him."

I kept my mouth shut. I could no sooner divine the reason behind Alex's unhappiness than I could the weather the next day. But I could say with some measure of an educated guess, based on experience, that it would rain tomorrow and Alex and Georgina were obviously experiencing troubles in their relationship.

"I'm sure he'll be fine," I finally offered.

Her astute blue eyes—the same as Alex's, I noted—watched me for a few moments before she finally nodded. I wasn't going to say anything, and she had the better judgment not to push any further.

I was thankful when Alex reappeared with two cups and their matching saucers, handing one to each of us. He, presumably, disappeared into the kitchen to retrieve his own, so I took a small sip of the tea and looked at his mother again. "So how'd you do it? How'd you hurt yourself?"

"Oh." Mary laughed and pointed across the room to a window sill where a black cat had curled up on a pillow. "I tripped over poor Womble. It was the middle of the night coming down the stairs and I didn't see him."

Alex came back into the room with his tea and lowered himself onto the sofa beside me, displacing the cushion and jostling me slightly. I cleared my throat and sipped the delicious brew again before placing the cup and saucer on the table in front of me.

"How's the tea?" he asked.

"Great," I said absently, standing to retrieve the plate of cookies from the basket. "Just enough cream and sugar for me…"

Then it dawned on me that I never told him how I liked my tea. I caught the smug expression on his face and the infernal raised eyebrow of challenge. He lifted his teacup in a soft salute at me. What was he trying to prove anyway? That he'd been watching me? That he was so amazing he remembered how I took my tea? So what? He was perceptive and had a decent memory. Nothing more.

"These are quite tasty," his mother said of the cookies after they had been passed around and placed on the table between all of us. "Thank you, again, Emilia."

"No problem." I sipped my tea only to occupy my mouth.

"It's nice to have a bit of a nosh on something that isn't half burnt," she continued. "Alex was gifted with many talents, but cooking isn't one of them."

"Don't look at me." He held his hands up defensively. "You have other children who could come cook for you as well."

"Oh no!" I laughed. "It can't be that bad."

She shook her head. "It is. It's either this or beans on toast for every meal."

Alex kept silent at his mother's good-natured ribbing, but I couldn't tell if he was truly upset or if he chose not to fuel her fire.

"You shouldn't be subjected to that while you're on the mend," I said. "We can set up a meal service or have a chef come in… I have a full list of contacts in my mobile I could give to you. I could even cook you a meal or two."

What the fucking hell was I doing? Why had I offered? It would only mean—

"That would be lovely!" Mary said in exaggerated happiness before I could amend my initial statement. "How about this evening?"

I realized then that not only was Alex incredibly perceptive and cunning when it came to convincing people to do what he wanted, but his mother did it better. I walked right into it. She deftly ascertained my ability to cook from the taste of the cookies. Then she sprang her trap.

"I, uh, I'm sorry," I stuttered. "I can't. I have plans—"

I didn't, of course. My night would consist of sitting in front of the telly watching a recorded episode of *Luther*, followed by a few hours of *Doctor Who*. Sam and Lindsay would join me for those. After I sent them to bed, I planned to finish the *Downton Abbey* Christmas special I still hadn't finished from December. That was my life. When I wasn't chasing after Georgina, my life was utterly boring.

But I fashioned it that way on purpose.

"Oh, that's okay, then." Her face fell in disappointment. I couldn't take the guilt. My grandmother would have been ashamed with the lies I told an elder.

"But I could do it tomorrow if you like," I offered.

Stop. Just stop. I repeated it in my head, but my mouth kept running. I had such a tendency to do that. Sometimes I thought about implanting the metaphorical foot in my mouth permanently.

"You should bring Sam," Alex suggested.

It was clear to me he still didn't know who Sam was; I found it surprising that Tobias hadn't mentioned our night out to Alex. What if I had read that excursion all wrong? What if Tobias hadn't invited me out on Alex's insistence? What if…

What if Tobias had actually wanted to go out with me?

I fidgeted in my seat and picked at imaginary lint. "I don't know if that'll be possible…"

"Come on," Alex urged.

"Who's Sam?" asked his mother.

"No one," I said too quickly. It wasn't that I was ashamed of Sam—I was as proud of my brother as any big sister had the right to be— but I sure as hell did not intend to introduce him to a man I hoped would not be in my life for much longer. It wasn't good for Sam to get attached, especially when I would then have to explain to him why they couldn't see each other again.

"Either Emilia's boyfriend or girlfriend," Alex explained. He didn't take his eyes off of me. He was searching for some kind of confirmation in my reaction. Or, at the very least, trying to see how I felt about him.

Mary seemed excited. "Well, whoever Sam is, please bring him or her along. I would love to meet Sam."

I gritted my teeth. "We'll see… but I should be going. I have to make it all the way back to Westminster in an hour or so."

Alex set his teacup on the table and stood up, offering his hand to me. I looked at it for a length of time I imagined would seem suspicious, but no one said anything. The last time I had allowed him to help me, we were boarding a gondola. I knew what his touch did to me then.

It would be impolite not to take it, though, especially in front of his mother. So I did and regretted it immediately. The familiar warming shiver reacquainted itself with my body. He pulled slightly as I stood.

I turned to Mary. "How about seven for dinner tomorrow?"

She nodded. "If you need to come earlier to cook anything, please do."

I smiled, nodded, and followed Alex to the front where he helped me back into my coat. At the door, I paused and looked up at him. "The flowers… they should be put in water. And you need to cut them on the diagonal about two to three centimetres up. And there's flower food attached to the package—"

"I've got it, Emilia," he said softly. "Thank you for delivering them for Georgina. I'm sure she'll appreciate all the trouble you went to."

I snorted. "It wasn't any trouble. Not for your mum."

He smiled genuinely, I thought, for the first time since he answered the door. "Thank you."

I shrugged my shoulders and turned on my heels, feeling as though I should have kissed him as I left. As though kissing him was the natural thing for me to do and I subverted nature by walking away. What was it about that man? He had to have his own gravitational field or something equally as attractive.

When I was a suitable distance away from the cottage, I fished my mobile out of my coat pocket and dialled Lindsay's number. It went directly to message. "Hi. It's me. I have a huge favour to ask you and you're probably not going to be happy about it, but… yeah, I'll see you at home."

I clicked off and slipped it back into my pocket, speeding up my steps against the bracing chill. Lindsay would hate me when I told him my plan.

CHAPTER 9

"YOU WANT ME TO DO *WHAT*?"

The next afternoon, I sat in the bleachers of a football stadium, looking at my closest friend—the person who knew me better than I knew myself—and simply blinked at him. He had heard exactly what I said, and I wouldn't repeat it. I couldn't find the nerve to repeat it.

"You've gone bloody barmy!"

Lindsay's exclamation drew attention from a pair of older ladies sitting in front of us. Even though his words were becoming more incomprehensible in his irritation, and I was sure the old ladies with hearing aids did not understand him, they definitely heard him raising his voice.

I placed a hand on his coat-covered arm to quell his outburst. Glancing at the women, I gave them an apologetic nod.

"Lindsay! Please!"

The ladies turned back around to watch the last minutes of the football match playing out in front of us. The other club kicked the ball into the goal box, but the goalie came out from his net to retrieve and punt it to the other end of the pitch. Sam stopped the forward motion of the ball with his chest, letting it roll off for his teammate to herd it in the opposite direction.

"Would you just hear me out?" I pleaded.

Lindsay folded his hands in front of him and kept his eyes trained on the match. "When you left the message on my mobile, I thought maybe Cruella had called you to France and you were leaving again and I would be taking care of Sam. I didn't think…"

I sighed and looked at my hands, picking at the fresh coat of sparkly red lacquer the manicurist applied earlier in the morning. "Linds, I'm sorry… but I have no one else to ask."

"Haven't you got a boyfriend?" he asked. "What about Tobias?"

"Forget about Tobias." Honestly, I was trying everything I could to forget about him, too. "He's not here. I need you tonight."

"I've spent most of the years of my life hiding what I am for my family," he replied. "And that's an awfully long time. Now you want me, just after I've become completely comfortable with myself, to pretend to be straight again? Do you realize what you're asking of me? Even for one night?"

I groaned and raked my fingers through my curly hair. "Lindsay, I know. I just need you to pretend to be my boyfriend for one night. Just be like you are now… just don't… don't…"

He set his jaw and finally turned to look at me. "Nancy about?"

"Ugh!" I shook my head angrily and tried to focus on the game play. "You make it sound so bad. It's not that bad."

Lindsay pressed his lips together in heated silence for several minutes until he blew out a loud, aggravated breath. "I just don't understand why you need me to pretend to be your boyfriend. You have been acting so odd since you returned from Venice. What's going on?"

"Don't make me explain it all."

He merely rolled his eyes and looked back at the players running around the pitch. I didn't have a chance to say anything else as he jumped up, all six-foot-five of him, and cheered and screamed for the team. Sam had taken the ball and scored a goal a few seconds before the end of the game to win it for his team. I joined him and the rest of the crowd in cheering, but when the fervour quieted and Lindsay looked at me again, I knew there would be no escape.

I threw my hands up. "Fine! What do you want to know?"

"Everything."

I pursed my lips. We sat back down while Sam finished his af-
ter-game routine. Then I told Lindsay everything about Venice. As
Lindsay usually did in times of intense listening, his face remained
stone solid and betrayed absolutely nothing about his thoughts. It
was a beneficial trait in his line of work to have the best of poker
faces, but it aggravated me to no end waiting until I talked myself
out to discover them.

When I finally stopped, he sat in silence and looked out on the
pitch. I grew worried when, after a few more minutes, he still hadn't
said anything.

But then he laughed at me. "Oh my God."

"Don't laugh at me!" I said.

"You are still the fucking calamity queen, aren't you?" he asked.
"Absolutely nothing has changed since uni."

I slugged his shoulder and crossed my arms over my chest.
"Lindsay! Come on! Be serious."

"I *am* being serious," he responded. "I don't know how you do it,
but trouble always finds you. No matter if you keep your head low
or not."

"I hate you."

He shook his head. "You love me. Now… do you want my advice?"

"Why not? It certainly can't hurt to consider it."

"Quit your job with Georgina and fuck that man six ways from
Sunday."

My huff was indignant. "And how will I take care of myself? How
will I take care of Sam? His care isn't going to get any less costly as
time goes on. I sure as bloody hell can't just slip right back into modelling after being gone for so long. And doing that would just cause a
whole cascade of problems for me that I don't want to consider. You
know what happens every time I actually do what I want to do!"

He shook his head. "Well, then, it sounds like you've already made up your mind. Why are we even arguing? Continue living a boring life taking care of Sam and doing what your grandmother told you to do before she died."

He paused for a beat and looked at me. "Or you could possibly find complete happiness and sexual fulfilment with a man who is sex on legs."

"What about Sam?" I said. "I could never…"

"That's not what I'm saying," Lindsay said with an almighty sigh. "What I am saying is that you can't keep putting your life on hold for him. Yes, you've made some rash decisions and mistakes and have had to pay for them, but that's what life is about. You learn from them and move on."

"This will ruin my career."

Lindsay laughed. "Love, *what* career are we talking about, exactly? The one where you're living someone else's glamorous life because you're too afraid to live your own? Being a personal assistant is not a career. There is no upward mobility. You will never be yourself as long as you stay with her."

"Wow." My voice sounded flat—hollow—as I considered what he said. Lindsay had never had any tact in his personal life; he always let me have the truth even when it was painful. This was no different.

Lindsay took my hands in his. The large warm paws thawed my frozen fingertips. I met his eyes and he gave me a soft smile. "Sam's a big boy. Constant molly-coddling isn't going to do him any favours. He can mostly take care of himself, and when he can't, I'm also around to help out."

I chewed on my lower lip while I thought about it.

"You've got nothing to lose," Lindsay said. "Be crazy. Have an affair. Have fun. The worst thing that'll happen is that Georgina hates you and fires you, but I'm not entirely certain she doesn't already hate you. Frankly, it would be a huge relief if she *did* fire you."

"You just make it sound so easy," I groaned. "But it's not that easy. It's not!"

By my estimation, I had quite a lot to lose, but I refused to fess up to that. Still, something told me he already knew what I was talking about. We lapsed into silence once more and looked out at the now empty pitch. Sam sat with his teammates drinking energy drinks and listening to the coaches talk.

"That still doesn't solve my problem for tonight," I said. "I can't introduce Sam to them. You know how he gets."

Lindsay sighed. "Then don't take him. Go on your own."

"Lindsay!" I whined. "Please go with me and pretend to be my boyfriend. I just need a buffer there while I try to figure this out."

"Emilia!" He imitated my whine, almost too well.

I pouted. "I would have to borrow your car anyway…"

"You're not driving my car," he growled.

"Well, then…"

Lindsay shook his head and scratched his neck. "*Fine*. Whatever. I'm not kissing you."

"That's fine," I said. With a big laugh, I threw my arms around him and kissed his bristly cheek. He caught me and pulled me close. "Thank you, Lindsay."

"You owe me big time."

"Of course."

"I mean… like… *huge*."

"Yes."

He looked directly at me. "Find the hottest and gayest of Alex's friends and set me up with them."

"You cut straight to the point," I replied, rolling my eyes.

"I'd settle for one of Tobias' friends as well," he added, and then gave me a curious look. "How the hell did you end up with the attention of two of the finest men England has to offer? Some people might accuse you of witchcraft."

I shrugged. "Trust me, if I knew the answer, I'd tell—"

Lindsay interrupted me and motioned to the group of people in the grass. "Oh, they want us down there."

I grabbed my handbag and followed my friend out of the stands. Sam ran up to us, sliding on the wet grass just before he bowled us to the ground. "They want to know who's gonna be in the family match. Are you gonna do it?"

I looked at Lindsay, who had been Sam's choice in years past. "I suppose I could, but don't you want Lindsay? He's better."

Sam shook his head. "No, I want you."

"When is it?"

Lindsay cleared his throat. "Next month."

"All right, Sam, I'll do it," I said and allowed him to pull me across the pitch to his coaches, grateful that the topic had changed for a little while.

WHEN WE ARRIVED AT OUR DESTINATION that night, we sat in the car staring at the front door. I looked down at the still-warm apple pie resting in my lap; I wasn't ready to go in, and Lindsay, apparently, was attempting to step into his role as my boyfriend for the evening. Even before I reached over to open the car door, I knew going through with it was wrong and would amount to a terrible idea by the end of the night. But we were already at the house. There was no turning back.

Lindsay turned to look at me. "Don't tell me you expect me to open the door for you, as well."

"I can open the sodding door myself," I snipped.

He sighed and reached over to pat my leg. "My beautiful, darling friend… we don't have to do this. I can just drop you here and pick you up later."

"No," I replied. "We're doing this."

Lindsay nodded. "Then we ought to go in before they get suspicious."

Of course he was right. I pushed open the door in the chilly, foggy night and manoeuvred my way out of the car while balancing the pie in my hands. After successful extrication, I nodded to the backseat. "Will you grab the pot and bread from the back?"

He simply got out of the car and smoothed his crisp button down over his barrel chest. "You only brought me for the heavy lifting. I see how it is."

"Of course." I laughed. "I might as well put those big Scottish muscles to work."

"Oh, stop." He waved his hand at me and bent down into the car to retrieve the large stock pot I used to concoct our meal.

Our wait for someone to answer the door wasn't nearly as long as the previous afternoon. Alex opened the door almost instantly and took a step back, flicking his eyes along my body before shifting his gaze to my date. He made a lengthy perusal as I watched the silent interaction. The energy changed when I realised it wasn't just a simple perusal; the men were weighing and measuring, completely critical of each other. And even though Lindsay was not a romantic partner by any stretch of the imagination, it certainly didn't stop him from puffing out his chest and straightening his spine to tower menacingly over Alex.

I half expected antlers to extend from their heads in preparation for a battle of strength, followed by a florid dance filled with colourful tail feathers fanned out in display. Alex's tail feathers, I was certain, would have been magnificent. I was tremendously disappointed when it didn't happen. But that wasn't to say that Alex cowed to Lindsay, or Lindsay to Alex. Judging from the wary sideways glares at each other, it was easy to see they would continue the same intricate dance throughout the evening.

"Emilia?"

I startled from my thoughts and blinked hard, looking at my friend. God, I had to stop letting my mind wander. "What?"

"We're going inside now." Lindsay jerked his head toward the door where Alex stood waiting for us to pass him.

"Oh," I said dumbly and stepped into the house before Lindsay.

Alex directed us back to the kitchen. "Do you need the cooker or anything?"

"Just need to heat the stew up for a bit," I replied as I set the pie down. "I only took the pie out just before we left, so it'll be warm enough."

"Have at it, then." Alex motioned to the appliance and stepped back as I let Lindsay through to set it on a burner. "I'm Alex, by the way."

I glanced to the two men shaking hands. Well, at least someone still had some manners. "Lindsay Morrison."

"Not Sam?" Alex asked. One of those damned eyebrows rose in curiosity when he glanced quickly at me.

"No," Lindsay said. "I'm her *other* boyfriend."

I could have died. No, check that. I did die—it was a small, agonising death. Lindsay and I went over our story a million times. He swore to me he had it. He'd spun so many yarns through his political career—and had kept all of them straight—I was sure he would be able to handle a simple story. And yet he couldn't remember this one?

Alex coughed into his hand and began to say something, but his mother interrupted us when she called from the other room. "Excuse me."

As soon as he stepped out of the room, I punched Lindsay's arm. "What do you think you're doing?"

"It was a joke!" he said with a laugh.

"This is no laughing matter."

Lindsay shook his head. "Yes, it is, but you fail to see it."

"Just stick with the story," I hissed at him when we heard footfalls coming through the hall.

Alex swept back into the kitchen. "Sorry about that. Would either of you care for any wine?"

"Please." Lindsay and I both answered at the same time. We glanced at each other, and Alex smirked. He disappeared again, I suspected to procure our wine, giving me time to lean into Lindsay.

"What?" Lindsay asked.

"Please."

"Don't pout at me," Lindsay said. "You know it does nothing."

"How do you think I got you here?"

Lindsay moved away from me just as Alex reappeared with a bottle of red wine and three goblets dangling through his fingers. They clinked together as he righted each one on the counter top.

"Do you need bowls or plates for the food?" he asked.

I frowned. He nodded toward the pot. I scrunched my face. "Uh, bowls would be better."

"Wonderful," he replied. "Please take the wine and see my mum while I finish laying the table in the dining room. That is, if you're done there."

"Yeah, it just needs to heat through for about ten minutes," I said. I took the wine he offered me and sniffed the bouquet of the ruby coloured beverage though I didn't taste it instantly. When I realised Alex was watching me, I gave my attention to Lindsay. "Let's go."

Lindsay followed obediently behind me into the sitting room. Mary sat in the same spot she occupied the previous day, but she seemed more at ease on her makeshift throne. The scab on her chin wasn't nearly as gruesome and the brace on her left hand was missing.

"Hello, love." She grinned and moved her head to look at the man trailing behind me. "I hear you didn't bring Sam?"

I shook my head. "No. This is Lindsay."

Lindsay introduced himself with a smile and an incline of his head before he sat down on the sofa beside me.

"What part of Scotland are you from?" she asked.

"Born in Aberdeen, raised in Edinburgh," Lindsay told her. "But I've been in England nearly… twelve years, is it?"

He looked at me for clarification. I nodded.

"Yeah, it's been ten years since I started at Oxford—that's where we met," I said to her and then turned back to Lindsay, "and you were at uni before me."

Mary smiled. "My father was from Paisley, originally. That's why I asked." Then she focused on me, those sharp blue eyes curious for more information. "You went to Oxford? What did you do there?"

I sipped my wine for fortification. "Modern languages."

"Alexander did say your Italian was perfect. But then he says that a lot with you in context."

I accidentally inhaled the pungent drink, spluttered, and coughed. Lindsay patted my back in an even rhythm as though I were a baby and it would actually help the burning in my lungs. Mary grinned gleefully. When I finally had my breathing under control, I looked at her. She knew much more about our trip to Italy than she let on; I saw that much by the humour covering her face.

Alex popped his head into the living room. "Is everything all right in here?"

"Just fine, darling." His mum smiled. "We're just chatting about speaking Italian and that Emilia read modern language at Oxford."

Only then did I see that they were a tag team. Had Alex enlisted his mother in his quest? Why would his mother help him? Did she hate Georgina that much?

I sighed and looked at the wall clock, finding my escape. "I need to check on the food."

With precise movements, I stood and fled with a speed I wished was swifter. I made it into the quiet kitchen and leaned against the countertop, still trying to clear my sinuses—and my lungs—of the acidic wine. I was then aware of the additional presence behind me and turned to find Alex.

"What happened?" he asked.

"I choked on wine." I wiped at my watering eyes and sucked in a deep breath. "You told your mother about Venice?"

Alex's resulting triumphant smile was enough. "I didn't tell her everything. She was curious about what I did during my trip, so I explained the highlights."

"*I* was a highlight?" I blurted, incredulous.

He merely stared at me for a few beats in that very hungry way. He finally responded. "How could you think you weren't?"

"Pfft." I brushed off his attempt at flattery, though I blushed nonetheless.

"You do speak Italian rather well," he said. "Better than I do."

"I thought you did fine."

He shrugged. "Perhaps. But I don't think I conveyed my intentions as clearly to you as I could have had I said it in English."

"You made yourself pretty damn clear." I pushed away from the countertop toward the pot simmering on the burner. "I need a large spoon."

Alex reached into a drawer beside the cooker and handed one to me. "Not as clear as you made yourself."

"Good," I said.

He sighed and pointed to the bag with the bread in it. "Do you need butter for that? Or something else?"

"Butter. The bread needs to be sliced."

He extracted a small dish of butter from a cupboard and then reached to a butcher block of knives.

"Did you make everything?" he asked, pulling the dense loaf of brown bread out of the bag.

"I did."

"Where did you learn to cook?"

"My grandmother."

"Not your mum?"

I huffed. "My mother left us right after my brother was born."

"Oh, she passed away?"

"Worse," I said. "She dropped us on my grandmother's doorstep and took off with her latest *petit ami de la journée*."

"Ah."

I shrugged. I really didn't want to talk about my childhood with him. Doing so would mean a deeper level of acquaintance—friendship?—whatever the bloody hell he wanted us to be. And yet, I felt somehow powerless to resist discussing it with him. Frankly, I found it immensely flattering someone was finally interested in me and not everyone else around me. Even if it was *his* interest.

"How thick do you want these?"

"Huh?"

A low rumble of laughter. "The bread. How thick do you want the slices of bread?"

"Meh." I shrugged, holding my thumb and index finger a few centimetres apart. "Like this."

I watched him arrange the dense loaf on a cutting board and begin the process of drawing the sharp serrated knife through it with perfect technique.

"So you have a brother?" he asked with false nonchalance.

I closed my eyes and shook my head. Of course. "Yes."

Alex paused and looked up from his task, his eyes knowing. But I prevented him from continuing.

"The food's ready," I chirped. "You should help your mum into the dining room."

He bowed his head in acknowledgement and disappeared, leaving me a moment to catch my breath and to prepare myself for the meal ahead.

OVER PUDDING, the conversation turned from formal pleasantries to more probing questions. Mostly, Alex's mum led the charge. She was relentless digging for the information she wanted out of me. Lindsay and Alex merely sat back in their seats to watch the volley, both with silent smiles of amusement stretched across their mouths.

"So if you read modern languages at Oxford, what are you doing wasting your time as Georgina's assistant?"

She was blunt, I'd give her that.

Lindsay coughed behind his serviette. Alex sipped his wine for too long and looked over the clear glass rim of the goblet. Somehow

I was in the inquisitor's chair and my jury of peers hung on every word.

"I, um... well... I didn't finish. I left school after the Christmas holiday of my second year."

"Why would you do that?" she asked.

I played with the silver fork sitting on the edge of my plate. My half-eaten slice of apple pie stared back at me, trying to tempt me to eat it, but I couldn't under the circumstances. "I didn't like school."

Lindsay shifted in his seat uncomfortably. He knew the whole story and he wanted to tell it with his own flavour of sarcasm. Mary turned her gaze to Lindsay. "Why would you let her do that?"

My friend barked with laughter. "I had no say in the matter. Emilia is a force to be reckoned with when she's got her mind set on something."

"I admit it was a stupid and rash decision," I elaborated, "but why waste my time there when I wasn't attending lectures or going to my meetings with my tutors? I learned just as much—even more—about the modern languages travelling around after I left uni."

Lindsay smiled and placed a hand on my shoulder.

"Going to university and becoming some great lecturer or high ranking official or businesswoman was my grandmother's dream for me," I explained. "It was never mine."

There was silence, but Alex was the first to ask. "Then what was *your* dream?"

"It's not important now," I said curtly. "I made my choice to do the modelling thing which eventually led to Georgina."

I glanced at Lindsay, who clamped his mouth shut into a thin line. I omitted a lot from my tale, but none of it needed to be brought up in the current company. They didn't need to know any more about my rash decision making and how much trouble and heartache it caused me along the way.

Alex, most of all, didn't need to know why I refused to give into my urges. Doing so would only give him ammunition to use against me. His aim already proved deadly when it came to turning things around in his favour.

"You sound a tad like Alex," Mary said. "I made him go through university because we didn't believe in the acting thing."

"That was Da more than it was you, Mum," Alex mumbled, fidgeting in his seat like an uncomfortable schoolboy in the headmaster's office. I learned quickly over dinner that as much as he liked figuring people out, he absolutely hated others doing the same to him.

I took pity on him, though he didn't deserve it. "But it worked out for him anyway. Modelling never really worked for me because I didn't have the drive—or time, for that matter—to fight the waify fashion industry. I wanted to make money without trying."

"You must have drive and talent in something. Everyone does," Mary said.

Lindsay could no longer keep his mouth shut. "Emilia's an amazing artist."

I hung my head. Leave it to Lindsay.

"But she hasn't done much since she started with Georgina," Lindsay added. "She's getting calls at all hours of the day and night to do things. She has no time."

"Lindsay…" I hoped my tone warned him to stay away from the subject.

"What? It's the truth," he protested. "She treats you like an indentured servant. You have no life but to live hers for her."

"She does have some good qualities," I defended—or at least, tried to.

Lindsay shook his head. "And now she suffers from Stockholm Syndrome."

"Alex is in love with her," I finally said. "I'm sure that has to be a point in her favour."

I was unsure if it was a point for or against her. The nice, obliging, fun Alex I always thought he was might have given her a point. The man I had come to know over the last few weeks, not as much. Still, my pronouncement made Alex choke on his coffee, his mother to smile knowingly, and Lindsay to shake his head.

"Love is such a... *strong* word, don't you think?" Mary asked the universe, although none of us missed her meaning. Alex stood from his seat and cleared his throat before he began picking up dishes from the table and taking them to the kitchen. Lindsay jumped up from his chair to help him. Soon, both men were chatting in the kitchen as they did the washing up, leaving me alone with her.

"I'm sorry, Mary," I apologised. "I didn't mean to..."

Her lips stretched into a soft smile. "Don't apologise for anything, love. I knew who Georgina was the moment she walked into my son's life."

The whole situation was so confusing. How could a man who otherwise cared so much about his mother not listen to how she felt about Georgina?

"But we shouldn't speak like that about my boss... or about Alex's girlfriend at his mum's home," I said. "It's not polite."

She sighed. "Perhaps. But I certainly don't fault you for it."

"Alex—" I began but she raised a hand to stop me.

"He's a big lad and can handle criticism."

I pursed my lips and looked down at the linen tablecloth. What was she trying to do anyway?

With a sigh, I pushed back from the table. Mary stopped me, though, with a hand on my arm as I passed. I turned to look down at her. "Will you be working this week?"

"There are some things I need to do at the studio," I replied. "Probably Monday and Tuesday."

"Wonderful," she said. "How would you like to take an old woman out for an afternoon?"

"I—"

She interrupted and pointed to her wheelchair. "I'll take care of everything as long as you push."

What was I going to say? No? This woman was as close to a

mother as I would ever get, and she seemed to be perfectly content playing that role for whatever nefariousness she had planned. And Alex wouldn't be around; I wouldn't have to worry about him every waking moment.

"All right," I agreed. "What day?"

"Let's say Wednesday," she said. "You collect me around noon and we'll make a day of it."

I nodded and Lindsay appeared in the doorway that led to the kitchen. He smiled. "Are you ready to head out? It's getting late and I have to meet my parents for breakfast in the morning."

"Oh, right!" I said.

Alex escorted us to the door. He did not say much and seemed rather sullen, but he remained civil as we put on our coats and exited the house. When Lindsay and I were finally in the car and driving down the street, he turned to look at me.

"So you want the good news or the bad news?"

"News about what?"

"What do you think?"

I frowned. "Why don't you just give me both? I'm sure they'll both be equally horrible."

"He was asking why you and I aren't married," Lindsay began, turning his eyes to the road. "You know, after being together for ten years and all that…"

"Great. And you said?"

"We have an open relationship."

And before I could lift a hand to pinch him or slug him, he held up a hand.

"Before you do that, please consider the fact that I am driving and hold both of our lives in my hands."

"I can't believe you!" I yelled. "We had a story!"

Lindsay shrugged. "What do you want me to say? He obviously fancies you. I didn't want to cut him off at the knees…"

"That was the reason you came with me tonight! To cut him off at the knees!"

"It was? I thought I was a bodyguard so he didn't manhandle you."

"I just… I just can't talk to you right now." I crossed my arms over my chest and fumed at the cars passing us on the motorway.

Lindsay let a few kilometres of darkened road pass before he opened his mouth again. "There's more."

"God," I groaned. "What?"

"He was prattling on about his appointment with a jeweller this week."

The words were like a sucker punch to my gut. All at once I couldn't breathe and I couldn't think. The blood rushed through my head, audible in my ears, much in the same way it had that night at the masked ball when he first kissed me. The news should have been a relief. Georgina would get off my case because her scheming had worked. Alex clearly planned to move on from his infatuation with me. And I would be left to do my job, free of complication.

Never mind that I suddenly felt so cold and hollow.

"Well, good," I said. "That's for the best."

Lindsay looked at me doubtfully. "Is it?"

I nodded in the affirmative. "Yes. He'll stop bothering me."

"If you think an overpriced lump of coal can stop a man's eyes from wandering, you've got another thing coming," he muttered.

"I'm not so naive that I believe that," I said. "But there is a level of permanence that comes with it. It means he's got the point that I don't want to do anything to jeopardise my life and working for Georgina."

Lindsay grumbled something about me being completely dim, but I couldn't make it out. "We'll see."

"I don't want to talk about it anymore," I replied. "My head hurts and I just want to go home."

He nodded and focused on the road ahead of him.

CHAPTER 10

GEORGINA'S ABSENCE DID NOT COME without some real perks—perks not particularly limited to freedom from her propensity to micromanage me until I wanted to scream. For one, I could go into the studio at my leisure and find the time to do the housekeeping work I normally dropped in deference to the more urgent tasks she created throughout the day. The true urgency was always debatable, but the days that I planned to do this sort of work, without fail, ended up full of side projects Georgina considered life or death.

A part of me wanted to luxuriate in all the time off, especially considering how rare it was, but after a week at home finishing my personal housekeeping, I felt as though I might go completely stir-crazy if I didn't do something useful. I quickly rationalised my need to work, repeating to myself about how doing the inventory would only make things run more smoothly for me when Georgina returned. Our extended fashion week tour had resulted in an incredibly out-of-date inventory. With a huge influx of fashions coming back with Georgina from Paris, having our existing stock accounted for would keep me sane.

Having the studio all to myself provided the other benefit of blasting my choice of music from the hidden speakers placed throughout the open space. Filled with reflective surfaces, the studio created a platform for a soul-filling sound I could lose myself in while I worked. It made everything worrying me—every thought, emotion, whatever—slip far, far away from my mind. For the first time in two weeks, I thought I found peace.

But it didn't last long.

It happened after I took up residence in the middle of a pile of footwear, checking off serial numbers and ordering the shoes by colour and style. Some obnoxious Cher Lloyd song kept replaying on my playlist, but I couldn't get it out of my head and the dock was all the way on the other side of the room; I didn't fancy getting up from my position just to skip the song again. So I gave in and bopped my head along to the catchy beat as I continued work on our selection of black boots.

In my movements, a strand of curly hair fell across my sweaty forehead and into my eye. I reached up to brush it back, but a flash of light and movement in the mirror made me do a double take. From my vantage point, I saw into the entrance hall; the front door opened onto the sunny day and cast a beam of light through to reflect on the mirror.

However, I had locked the door when I arrived earlier in the morning. Barring any natural force like a gust of wind, there were only two other people with a key—Georgina and Alex. I definitely didn't want to see either of them, though I preferred one more than the other.

The tall man appeared in the arched entrance to the main studio floor. He wore his Georgina-free wardrobe, a backpack resting on one leather coat-covered shoulder, and carried with him a large brown paper bag. He set the bag on my desk and the backpack carefully on the floor, but took his time to remove the sunglasses from his eyes. Then he stood in full view of mirror with his hands on his hips.

"Aren't you supposed to be on holiday?" he shouted over the music.

I shrugged noncommittally and went back to my work, but he walked over to the dock and turned the sound down as though he owned the place.

"Hey! I was listening to that!"

He merely shook his head and pushed his sunglasses into the v-neck of his simple tee. "I can't keep yelling. I'm on voice rest."

I shot him a pointed glare and checked off one of my favourite pairs of Ferragamo riding boots from the inventory list. "Then don't talk at all."

"What are you doing?"

"Inventory."

He crouched into a squat beside me, picking up a cobalt blue stiletto. "How do you girls even wear these things?"

I huffed. "*I* try not to."

"Only when you have obliging gentlemen to help you back into them?" he teased.

The heat on my face was instantaneous; I didn't even have time to hide it. Pleased with the reaction, Alex set the shoe down and grinned.

"Here I thought you were just being gallant," I said.

He chuckled lowly.

"Not that you wanted something more from me."

Alex bowed his head and shook it slightly. Then he met my eyes and licked his lips. "I thought *you* wanted something more."

His comment enraged me. But why? I *had* wanted more. So, so much more. Long before he first kissed me, I hung on his every word. Afterward, when reality set in… well, that was another story.

"Why are you here, Alex?"

He let out a small sigh and placed his hands on his thighs as he stood to his full height. He looked down at me. "I brought you lunch."

"How did you even know I was here?"

"Lucky guess," he replied.

"Your mum told you I was working this week, didn't she?"

I stared at him. He raised his shoulders in a small shrug.

"How do you know I haven't had anything yet?"

Alex rolled his eyes in exasperation and looked at me. "Because in the past seven months I've not once seen you stop for food during a work day."

"You haven't been around much until recently," I countered.

Georgina hated any foodstuff in the studio. There were practical reasons behind this unspoken rule—if food wasn't in the studio, it couldn't damage the clothing and accessories which were often only on loan to us from their respective design houses—but she didn't even allow it in the kitchenette in the back. I swore she could smell a bag of crisps from a kilometre away if I tried to sneak one during the day. She'd appear before my desk, look at me accusingly and then move on her way leaving me to dispose of whatever I had.

It wasn't surprising, considering she was a woman who subsisted on air, protein smoothies, and extra-large caffeine shots from local coffee shops. Eating didn't matter to her. Sometimes I saw her nibble on a biscuit with her tea or a handful of chocolate, but then she wouldn't consume anything but liquids for weeks on end. That was when her sense of smell was at its most acute. Since I didn't want to put up with her silently accusing stares, I abstained from substantial food in deference to her hypersensitivity.

Still, I was fairly certain he could guess the reasons why I tried not to stuff my face whenever I was in Georgina's employ. I didn't dignify his curiosity further with an explanation.

"Touché," he replied. "But you can eat now. It's getting cold."

"You're not going to leave me alone until I agree to stop what I'm doing and give in to your orders?"

He grinned. "Something like that."

I puffed out my cheeks with air and shook my head. The sooner I ate lunch, the sooner I could insist he leave the studio. I slipped my pen onto the page I stalled on and closed the cover in the binder book before setting it aside.

Alex helped me up from the floor with little effort after I reluctantly slipped my hand into his. The man was surprisingly strong for having such a lean build. He left me standing there and sauntered over to my desk.

I caught a glimpse of myself in the mirror and realized how atrocious I looked in my stretchy paint-splattered yoga trousers and a threadbare tee I had cut the neck out of because it bothered me. When I dressed that morning, I planned on hard labour completed with no interruption, and chose my wardrobe to fit that goal. At least, I figured, I would know he was really into me if he saw past the frizzy hair piled on my head and the thick rimmed glasses sliding down my oily nose.

Shoving an errant curl into the elastic of my headband, I turned around and walked to the desk. "What did you bring?"

"Indian."

"Georgina would die if she knew that was in here," I said.

He turned his steady, meaningful gaze to me. "But she's not here, is she?"

My mouth went dry at his tone. Was that the point? She wasn't around so I was a replacement for her only when he needed it?

"Let me go get some plates."

I left him standing there and nearly ran to the kitchenette. But he wasn't far behind me, claiming the pretence of rummaging through the fridge for the bottled beverages we kept on hand for clients.

"What do you want?" he asked.

"Water."

He took two bottles out and placed them on the countertop. I returned to my task and opened the cupboard door next to my shoulder. The glassware was placed on the lower shelf—we used the glasses most often to serve beverages—and the dishware set on the shelf above given that we never used it. Those pieces were only there for decoration, just like the food at industry events which went uneaten; it was there for show to hide a world rife with eating disorders.

I reached for the plates, but my fingertips barely brushed the edges of the cool ceramic. I grumbled and reached again, this time on my toes, refusing to be defeated.

"Let me help," Alex offered.

"I've got it." I reached for them once more, but only succeeded in pushing them farther out of my reach.

"Emilia... stop."

His voice spoke of amused frustration mixed with pure adoration. It was at once sweet, yet commanding. My noisy heart thudded in my chest when he stepped closer to me; I was convinced he heard it as well as I heard the rush of the erratic pulse in my ears. I stood completely still, not wanting to move for fear of further inflaming the situation.

His warm body pressed from behind, pushing me against the counter in the small space. The action flooded every single sense I possessed. He smelled heavenly—the same scent of clean cologne and man I found so intoxicating—and the weight of his body against mine, though overwhelming, made me sigh in comfort. A long-fingered hand rested on my left hip, burning through the thin material covering it. I struggled to breathe and swallowed down a parched throat that made it feel as though I had marched through the Sahara with no water for miles.

He reached past my arm's length and grabbed two plates with his free hand. I attempted to turn around and extricate myself from the situation, but doing so only gave me pause when I accidentally met his eyes. Were I not so tall, I would have stared at his lower neck or his chest, but at my height, it was difficult not to flick my line of sight just a few centimetres up, however unintentionally, and recognize the hunger dripping from his gaze.

It was my undoing.

Standing this close to him, my bum pressed against the countertop with the weight of his taught, lean muscled body, it was next to impossible to resist him or the temptation. What woman in their right mind would pass him up?

"A-Alex..." I stuttered lowly, trying to maintain some level of detachment from the heat coursing in my veins and begging me to give in this one time. A tingling ache settled into my lower abdomen and cried out for fulfilment. I wilfully ignored it. "I…"

"Don't," he murmured. "Don't say it."

I shook my head and pressed my hands to his chest in an effort to push him away. He stepped back, allowing me enough space to wiggle out from the tiny kitchen into the main studio. The chill of the studio air hit my inflamed body like the ocean cooling molten lava. I leaned one hand on my desk to catch my breath, bowing my head and swallowing again around the knot in my throat.

"Em," he called, his voice low as his fingers encircled my arm. The electricity of his touch made me tremble. "I'm sorry."

I hadn't expected him to say something like that. As a matter of fact, he had seemed fairly unapologetic since Venice, as though all of it was my fault. As though my refusal of his advances had made the situation awkward—not his multiple attempts to cheat on his girlfriend.

"What are you doing, Alex?" My voice sounded weak and breathless.

"I only grabbed the dishes for you because you couldn't reach them."

I shook my head and set my fisted hands on my hips. "So… what? Touching me like that was just collateral damage?"

"I would hardly call it 'damage.'"

I rolled my eyes. "Don't for one minute fool yourself into thinking I'm an idiot. What I meant was what are you doing here? Why did you come? Did you intend to proposition me again?"

He held his hands up in defence. It was the first time he acted that way; he always seemed so confidently cool. So quietly powerful and above ever showing remorse to anyone. "I came because my mum said you'd be here. I wanted to do something nice for you, after what you did this weekend for my mum and me. I get the feeling that you take care of everyone else and don't take care of yourself enough."

I flinched at his words. It was as though he had peered into my mind and read it as easily as he did an open book. What he said was the truth, but I refused to acknowledge it.

"And?" I challenged.

"And what?"

"Nothing else?"

He shrugged. "I do not pre-emptively limit the possibilities of the situations I put myself in. I see where they take me."

"Alex, I'm going to say this plainly so neither of us get it confused," I said in warning.

"Say what?"

I drew in a deep breath and then exhaled, meeting his eyes. "I can't keep doing… whatever this is."

"But you want to. You like it."

"You don't get it!"

He sighed and left me; he prowled around the desk and then slid into my office chair. "Why won't you just give in? You want it. I want it."

"I want millions of pounds in my bank account as well, but I sure as bloody hell am not going to rob a bank any time soon."

Alex chuckled and shook his head. "You're quite stubborn."

"Oh, I'm only getting started," I sassed.

His grin only widened at my pronouncement.

My arguments fell on deaf ears. Or, at the very least, were being defiantly ignored. "Aren't you getting ready to propose to Georgina, anyway?"

"Am I?"

I frowned.

"It's news to me if I am."

"But Lindsay said…"

Alex shook his head and clicked his tongue against his teeth. "Speaking of Lindsay, he isn't your boyfriend, is he?"

I crossed my arms over my chest. "Why do you say that?"

"You didn't kiss or touch each other the entire time you were at my mum's."

"We don't have to show it that way after ten years."

One brow rose. "I'm an excellent judge of character, darling. I can also tell when someone's lying to me. He's not your boyfriend."

It was a matter-of-fact statement; nothing more, nothing less. Had he known all along? I wanted to throw something at his smug little head. So, yes, he figured out the puzzle on his own. He didn't have to be so infuriatingly sanctimonious about it. Did he want a gold star pinned to his chest?

"You want the truth?" I snapped in indignation. "Fine! I'll give you the truth. No, we aren't in a relationship. Yes, I brought him as a buffer to your mother's because I didn't want to encourage your attentions. Yes, I've wanted you ever since I first met you. But now that I know the *real* you, I'm questioning what I ever saw in you. Do you make a habit of sleeping around while in committed relationships?"

He shook his head and held my gaze. "If I did this often just for the sex, don't you think I would've learned to choose a woman who would willingly fall at my feet when I commanded it? Not one that I would have to convince—repeatedly—of my intentions only to come up empty-handed?"

"What *are* your intentions?" I demanded. "In plain English, if you will, so there aren't any misunderstandings."

He leaned forward in his seat. "I want you. In every way imaginable."

"While you're still in a relationship with Georgina?"

Alex stood and stalked back around the desk, stopping in front of me. I felt his body heat, but he hadn't trapped me. I could run if I wanted. The intensity of his stare, however, rooted me to my spot. I hung on to every last syllable he spoke in his slightly lilting voice.

"Yes."

"What about the sort of situation that puts me in?"

His lips pressed into a firm line as he considered my question. How selfish could one man be? When he didn't reply to me, I threw my hands up in disgust.

"It's not going to happen."

He pushed a curl behind my ear and drew a finger along the line of my jaw. My stomach fluttered and my breathing hitched. "Are you sure?"

I nodded forcefully, but hated the guilt of knowing that I had to keep convincing myself I was sure of my choice.

"Even if I tell you that there are things you don't know and don't understand about my relationship with Georgina? Things that might change your mind?"

"I know the important thing," I stated. "That you're still together and I'm not jeopardising my future for one amazing night of sex."

His voice turned into a seductive rumble low in his chest. "Oh, and I assure you, it would be amazing."

I wasn't prepared for the moan involuntarily slipping from my mouth. Judging from Alex's reaction, he hadn't expected it either, but his pleasure surfaced almost immediately in the slow smile tugging at the corners of his mouth.

"And it wouldn't be just *one* night," he added.

I was absolutely floored by this. As though trying to convince me to sleep with him one time wasn't bad enough, he wanted an ongoing relationship of creeping around in the shadows while he lived a public relationship with Georgina? Was he ashamed of his obvious attraction to me? Was that why he couldn't just break it off with Georgina and begin dating me like a normal person?

I quickly reminded myself, even if he did break it off with her, I still wouldn't give in to him. Alex was a huge star and our relationship would be public before I knew it; Georgina would see the press and relieve me of my duties. I would be back at square one. I told him as much back in Italy. No job. No money. No way to take care of responsibilities as Sam's caregiver. Perhaps I hadn't said it in so many words, but he hadn't earned the right to know everything about me or my life. If there was any honour left in him he would take my word for it.

And what if he truly loved Georgina and he simply wanted to use me? Why would I get into this relationship when I had other viable options? Real options that could lead to a lifetime of happiness?

Georgina always believed in having as many options as possible during styling appointments; couldn't the same be said about relationships? An arrangement with Alex might not fit me, but a relationship with Tobias—who wasn't ashamed to be seen in public with me—could become something more than flirtatious friendship and end up fitting like a glove.

Tobias was, after all, the proper choice. He was husband and father material. Alex was everything else. He was fun and wild and exciting. Everything that Old Me would have wanted. But I really couldn't bring myself to give in now…

Or could I? I wouldn't know if the Alex thing "fit" without trying it on for size.

Alex's hand slipped beneath my chin, pushing up until he forced me to meet his piercing gaze. I swallowed hard.

"Give in to me," his silky voice implored while he searched for some acceptance of what he offered me. My knees were weak with want. With need. With… everything.

I reluctantly pulled away from him. Leaving was my only option.

On unsteady legs, I walked around the desk and collected my things, slinging my tote bag over a shoulder. I grabbed my mobile and slipped it into the bag. I looked at him again. "Please lock up when you leave."

And with that, I left him standing in the middle of the studio. I stepped outside into the cold early spring air, only realising I forgot my coat halfway to the Underground station. The rest of my walk to the Tube and then from the station to my flat would be brutal without it.

I stopped in the middle of the pavement a few streets down and looked in the direction of Georgina's, weighing my options. Did I go back? Did I face him again? Did I tempt myself again? I wasn't completely sure of my ability to withstand his advances another time.

Neither did I know if some small part of me—the same small part of me that had no business ruling my brain—was using my missing coat as a convenient excuse to return.

My conversation with Lindsay at Sam's football match came unbidden to my head while I grappled with my warring thoughts: *"Quit putting your life on hold… You've got nothing to lose. Be crazy. Have an affair. Have fun. The worst thing that will happen is that Georgina hates you and fires you, but I'm not entirely certain she doesn't already hate you."*

The possibilities with Tobias might have been proper and long lasting, but nothing said I couldn't play the field and have an affair until the time that something became more serious. I wasn't the one in a committed relationship, after all. Alex was the one who would have to suffer from the guilt, if he was even capable of the emotion. And as long as we kept the appropriate secrets, no one would know otherwise.

A strangled, rueful chuckle rose in my throat.

Who was I kidding? I made my decision back in that damned Venetian ballroom. The moment I allowed myself a dance with him, I was lost, set adrift in the churning sea of Alex's intoxicating energy. He knew it even before I had a chance to work through it myself.

I was exhausted doing everything that was expected of me as an employee, sister, and friend. Couldn't I have a little fun, too?

I turned so suddenly I nearly ran over an old man walking his dog behind me. Apologising profusely, I stepped around him and started for the studio. The cold air burned my lungs and stung my skin. Adrenaline pumped through my body. I felt as though I was coming out of my skin.

I felt alive. Vital. Just like the night of the ball when anything was possible.

When I reached the studio, I walked up to the door and tried the knob, but it was already locked. I didn't dig out my keys from my tote; the Powers That Be had ultimately intervened on my behalf and made it clear that I shouldn't go through with what I wanted. It was probably for the better. All the other rash decisions in my life blew up in my face. Why did I think this time would be any different?

I stepped down the five stone stairs at the entrance and prepared to step out onto pavement again when I realised I still needed my coat.

"Damn," I exhaled and went right back up the stairs, digging my keys out of the bottom of my bag. Jitters had overtaken my body with the excess adrenaline, making it difficult to stick the key in the lock with such shaky hands. The door fortunately squeaked open on a second try. I stepped inside and let out another calming breath. He was gone. The lights were off and I was alone.

I thought.

A floorboard groaned beneath a heavy weight further down the hall and I looked up in the direction of the sound. Alex appeared around the corner leading to Georgina's living area. I froze.

I opened my mouth to speak, but I didn't have the wherewithal to form words in my breathlessness before he pressed me back against the hallway wall. My bag dropped on the floor with the suddenness of the movement and hit my foot. The contents flung everywhere around me, but I hardly cared when I registered the intensity in his eyes.

Strong, urgent lips latched on to mine, sending my mind spinning and spirals of heat down into my belly, reigniting the hot ache I had sensed there earlier. There was no going back as I succumbed completely to the demanding strength of his mouth against mine.

"Alex."

It came from me in a sigh, a soft entreaty for more. For my part, all I could do was hold on for dear life and try to remain upright. Even with his weight leveraging me against the wall, my knees had turned to mush. I wanted to fall to the ground in a heap of overexcited, overheated, formerly repressed sexual tension.

The cork in the metaphysical bottle where I stuffed all my

frustration had popped; it burst open with a rush I could barely handle. It was difficult to control myself, to slow down and really enjoy what he was doing to my earlobe, then grazing his teeth against the line of my jaw, sucking a pulse point just enough to drive me wild but not leave a lasting mark.

Large hands frantically grazed my arms, hips, thighs, before slipping beneath my shirt. Wet lips pressed against my shoulder as finger pads ghosted over the skin of my back, fumbling with the hook-and-eyes of my bra before giving up. I clawed wildly at his shirt in an effort to get it off of him, but abandoned the task when he lifted one of my legs, hand roughly clenching my thigh, to wrap it just so around his waist.

I was the perfect height for him; I felt the growing bulge in his low slung jeans against my centre, grinding, teasing in the almost imperceptible movements of his hips. I struggled to reach between us to undo the buttoned closure on his jeans, but failed in my attempt as he thrust up, the sudden pressure shooting a thrilling streak of delight through my body.

My body arched into the sensation and he took the opportunity to devour the exposed column of my neck, hands squeezing my bum and creeping up into the small arc of my back. I clenched his shoulders and lean biceps before digging my fingers into the sinew that corded around his shoulders and back.

"My God, Emilia," he breathed finally, near my ear. "You are amazing."

His scratchy and wiry beard tickled my sensitive flesh when he drew my earlobe once more between his teeth. My knees buckled. If I didn't get to a horizontal surface soon, it wouldn't be pretty, but I couldn't leave his embrace. I just couldn't...

He seemed to sense my conundrum, like he did in every other situation, and pulled away from me with a great deal more self-discipline than I could claim. Just as in Venice, when he led me into the waltz in time with the music, he manoeuvred us away from the wall and around the corner into the main studio. We nearly fell in our haste, but he course-corrected neatly. We both seemed to be rushing toward our destination without taking our time and thoroughly enjoying the journey, but I couldn't have cared less. I needed him.

Fumbling and grasping for bits of each other kept most of what was left of my logical brain busy. He tugged my shirt off and threw it somewhere in the room when the back of my legs finally hit a solid surface. We had made it as far as the chaise set up in the corner of the room with two other chairs—our de facto waiting area. Tickling fingers skittered up my sides and slipped beneath the elastic lace and underwire of my bra, teasing across the tightened, pebbled peaks of my breasts. I inhaled at the sensation but moaned in displeasure when he quickly moved on to the hook-and-eyes again.

"How many bloody things are there?" he complained in a moment of frustration, his lips barely a millimetre from mine.

I giggled and looked up at him from under thick eyelashes. He was biting his lip in consternation. It amused me that this man—this man who was so sure of himself, so powerful, so dominant—couldn't figure out the workings of my bra closures. The knowledge made him more human somehow; more real to me than he ever seemed around the other people in his life. It was a glimpse, I hoped, of what was truly underneath his supposed affectations.

Contorting my arms, I reached behind me and easily snapped the two ends apart. His pupils dilated infinitesimally more as I drew my lower lip through my teeth and pulled off the loosened material, holding it out to my side and dropping it. "I've got a lot to hold in there, you see. I need more than just a few."

"I see," he rumbled.

I had never been particularly squeamish about showing off my body—as a model, one usually dressed and undressed in front of hundreds of people on any given work day. Romantic situations were far different though, and even my own confidence could be shaken with the wrong look or comment. Alex, however, didn't let that happen. I felt needed. I felt wanted.

I felt beautiful.

I thought he might bury his face in his bounty for a moment, but he surprised me again when his lips returned to mine until my legs gave out. I sat onto the chaise, thankful it wasn't the hard floor beneath it. He eased me back onto the wide surface of smooth white leather, once more in complete command of the situation. Our urgency seemed to have evaporated. In its place was a heady, almost unbearably slow, cadence.

I leaned my weight on my palms. His mouth skimmed over my chin and down my chest to the valley between my breasts. There he paused for a split second, grinning up at me mischievously, nipping lightly and playfully at the underside of one heavy mound. The ever increasing heat between my thighs reached epic proportions when he levelled that heated gaze at me. That one that told me I wouldn't get what I wanted right away.

He clearly preferred torture through teasing. Perhaps he wasn't hardcore enough to have his own collection of the Marquis de Sade's works, but I had little doubt of the pleasure he received when I completely relinquished control to him. He wanted it all along. The control, at least. I wanted to give it to him, even though I knew I shouldn't. My belly fluttered with anxiety at the thought, but I banished it from my mind before it grew into a monster.

Alex knew exactly how to play me as he climbed the peak of a breast with a deft, wet tongue, circling around the puckered flesh. He closed his lips and drew his teeth lightly across the taut nub. Kneeling down onto the floor, his hands gripped the tops of my thighs and massaged as they slipped to the sides and further down my legs. Alex sat back on his heels and looked up at me, making a show of grabbing each leg in turn and quickly whisking away the boots covering them—much easier than trying to stuff my fat calves into them had ever been.

But then, I was lucky my clothes didn't just spontaneously vaporise whenever he looked at me from across the room. There were a few times I was surprised they hadn't.

He pressed a kiss on my trouser-clad shin and moved up again, walking his fingers gradually up with his body. His pace slowed and I found it completely maddening. I needed him. Now. I needed the comfort of his lean weight pressing my back onto the chaise and the feel of his skin rubbing against mine as we each worked toward our release. I needed all of him.

Growing anxious at his continued, almost plodding, discovery of my body, I leaned forward and ran a hand through his hair. His eyes fluttered closed for a brief moment with a sigh of contentment. I gripped the wire-silk strands more vigorously in an effort to coax him along but avoided pulling them completely and harshly. He opened his eyes, a new glimmer of hunger taking over the serene blue. A wicked smile played at his lips.

"Yes?" he asked.

"Didn't your mum ever tell you not to play with your food?"

He laughed and pushed up on his knees, rising slightly to crawl up the length of my torso. Lips smothered mine again with demanding mastery and coaxed me to follow along until I forgot my train of thought. His fisted hands sank into the lounge on either side of me, supporting his weight as he laid me back onto the furniture.

Pushing a jean-covered thigh between mine, he knelt above me and finally broke the kiss. "I'm not playing. I'm savouring."

I raked my nails down his back and gathered his shirt's thin material in my hands. I easily pulled it from his body. "Savour later. I've been waiting for this since you left me high and dry at the ball…"

"My apologies," he replied.

I arched an eyebrow at him. He wasn't truly apologetic. "You should've followed through."

He grinned and leaned down, resting his weight against me and fitting his pelvis into the seat of mine. The instant hot streak at the friction made me gasp. "Should I have?"

"I was putty in your hands," I remarked, breathing out.

"And you aren't now?" A hand cupped my breast. His fingers tweaked the hard peak as his hips rocked against me again and again.

Robbed of the ability to speak, I merely twined my fingers togeth-er behind his neck and pulled him down to me. His wandering hand slithered into the curve of my waist and over the wideness of my hip, slipping it back under my thigh to guide my leg around him.

I squeaked at the contact. "Please don't make me beg."

"Of course not, *bellissima*," he purred against a nipple, the vibra-tions sending white-hot pleasure through my body to add to the coiled ache in the pit of my belly. God, I needed him. "At least not this time."

The cool studio air engulfed the inflamed skin beneath my trou-sers as hands hooked onto them and my knickers in an effort to pull both from my legs. He shifted back on his haunches once again, which I found as highly annoying as the leisurely pace he had adopt-ed. So I took matters into my own hands.

Sitting up, I reached for his hips and fumbled with the button and zip on the front of his jeans. His fingers pushed under my chin, raising it so that he could draw me away from any form of coher-ent thought. But I was intent on my task and quickly pushed boxer briefs and jeans down his straight hips to free him from the tortur-ous denim confines. He sucked in a breath and groaned low in his throat as I circled my fingers around him.

I was impressed at my tactile perusal, to say the least. My mouth watered at the thought of tasting him, however I did not have the chance as he tossed me back on the lounge and out of arm's—or mouth's—reach of his proud and prominent anatomy. No wonder the suits we dressed him never fit him exactly right in the area.

"Do you have—"

Before I could even finish, he reached and fumbled with the low-ered-but-not-removed jeans. From the back pocket he extracted a foil wrapper. I watched in interest as he quickly opened and rolled the condom along his length.

"I don't know whether to be excited—"

He rested against me, drawing both of my legs around him this time and then pinning my hands with one of his over my head. I twined my legs with his in an attempt to pull him closer. I needed his heat. I needed to feel the fullness I had so long been without.

"—or mortified—"

I saw stars when he touched me again. The streak of pleasure shot from my centre to my head and back again. I wanted to reach out and touch him, to run my hands along the expanse of hard, masculine torso, but his grip on my hands refused any movement.

"—or furious that you thought I was a—"

He shifted a fraction, slipping a hand between us, thumb circling the bundle of nerves at my centre. My eyes must have rolled back into my head because I couldn't see a thing after he did that.

"A what?" he breathed, close to my ear.

"A—"

He massaged with more and more persistence. "You're glorious, bellissima."

I whimpered and bit my lip as he pressed the tip of himself against me.

"A what?" he queried again.

"Hmm?" I blinked rapidly, trying to focus on the hovering man over me. "Oh, right, that you thought I was a—"

He pushed in an inch. My toes curled.

"I won't go any further until you finish your thought," he said calmly, though I felt his restraint quickly waning. His determination to hold steady knit his brow.

I swallowed. "Then stop making it so that I can't concentrate!"

Alex gave me an impish grin and stilled. "Go ahead."

"That you thought I was a foregone conclusion," I finally uttered.

"There you go, bellissima." He growled and filled me completely.

I yipped while my body struggled to accommodate him. The

fullness—the stretch somewhere between pure ecstasy and pain—was exactly what I needed. I cried his name as though it were a dirty oath when he began an exasperatingly unhurried rhythm with his hips.

"I never thought," he said, his breath wavering, "you were a foregone conclusion."

He lay against me for a moment, pushing at my thighs until my untrained muscles could no longer accept the pull. They burned and tingled and it was oh so wonderful that I didn't even care I would ache afterward.

"I'm an eternal optimist," he added.

He released his hold on my hands and dropped them to my hips. Sitting back, he lifted me with the movement and rested my bum on his thighs. I lifted into a sitting position and as I righted and wrapped my arms around his neck for leverage, I saw blinding light. He drove deliciously deeper at this angle as I clutched at his shoulders in search of an anchor. His masterful lips seared a trail down my exposed neck, nipping, biting, and sucking as we searched for release from the coiled pressure low in our bodies.

Mine came suddenly in a rush of scorching warmth and light. Every part of me was on fire for him; it was almost painful to feel his hands glide up my back and over slightly slick, perspiring skin. Everywhere he touched burned me a little deeper, a little closer to the part of me I wanted to keep out of this arrangement.

He laid me back on the chaise, the cold leather kissing my fevered skin. I breathed out a sigh and he inhaled it, driving faster with more force until at last his movements became erratic. He sought my lips one more, just in time for a growly groan to fill our mouths. He finally stilled.

"Oh, Emilia," he said in a breathless, sated chuckle.

He sagged against me, off to the side a bit, but unwilling to leave. I stared up at the ceiling, spent and struggling for my own air as the world began to shift back onto its axis and continue on in its day.

Alex buried his face in the crook of my neck, peppering his lips here and there, dropping a kiss behind my ear. "Bellissima."

My body hummed at the soubriquet.

"I'm glad you came back," he whispered, lips moving against my neck with his words.

I purred and drew my right hand over his shoulder and across the leanly muscled arm holding me against him. "I only came back for my coat."

Alex's body shook me with his low rumble of laughter. "Was it worth it?"

I replied honestly. "I'm still trying to figure that bit out."

His head popped up, his eyes ablaze with challenge. He knew what I meant—about everything—but he teased about the sex instead. "Then I didn't do it right if you're still unsure."

I buried a hand in his hair and kissed him. I didn't dare reply. Honestly, I was more confused than anything. Well, not about what we had just shared. I was more confused about myself and how I could have possibly talked myself into believing it was a good idea.

I couldn't ignore him after this. Every time I saw him, I would remember how he worshipped me and wonder about the next time—if there were a next time. I would remember how he treated me. How he cared for me in small ways. How, despite my better judgment, other ideas and emotions were already sneaking into the mix. That knowledge, most of all, was what worried and frightened me.

My heart had absolutely no place in this affair.

CHAPTER 11

THE FOLLOWING MORNING, I woke to a knock on my bedroom door and an anxious brother poking his head inside.

"Emilia? Are you awake, Emilia?"

I groaned and curled deeper into the cocoon of warmth created by the voluminous bedding. Praying he would get the hint to leave me alone, I kept my eyes closed and turned away from him. In the periphery, I listened to his shuffling feet as he came around the other side of the bed. He reached out and placed a thumb on my eye, lifting the lid.

"Are you awake?" he asked again.

I batted his hand away and turned back to the other side with a gravelly grumble. "What do you want, Sam?"

"Are you sick?" He lumbered around to the other side and stood beside my head. His ice cold hand sought my forehead this time. He pressed it there for a few seconds. "Oh, you are burning up!"

I cracked one eye open and stared at the concern on his face, trying to convince myself that murder wasn't the answer for someone waking me so early in the morning. Sam never bothered me before he left for work in the mornings unless it was an emergency. The fact that I wasn't awake at my normal time probably didn't help, either.

"You should go to the doctor," he said with all the certainty of a loved one convinced I was dying of cancer.

Rolling onto my back, I stared up at the ceiling and scrubbed my hands over my tired face. "I'm fine, Sam."

"But you have a fever."

"Your hands are too cold," I replied. "I don't have a fever."

I wasn't sick; I was exhausted. I didn't arrive home until late the night before, having stayed at Georgina's to finish the footwear inventory, which had to be done after finally convincing Alex to leave the studio. It took no small effort since he saw it as his responsibility to shift my attention back to him. Even after the first time, and the subsequent seconds and thirds and an hour long nap afterward, he remained as incorrigible as he was insatiable. The only thing to ruin his little bubble of pleasure was a call from his mother asking when he would return home.

He left, and with him he took my favourable outlook on our temporary arrangement. Left alone in the quiet studio with nothing but the clothing and the shoes, I noticed the familiar emptiness settling in again, only this time accompanied by something which made my stomach churn unpleasantly. It didn't take me long to figure out what it was; after all, my grandmother took great pains to instil this particular dreadfulness in me from the first moment I came into her care.

Guilt was a powerful tool in controlling an innocent child. More so as an adult.

How could I have given into him? Why did I sleep with another woman's significant other—no matter what their relationship status was? Why didn't I have better morals or ethics? Why couldn't I be more like my stonewalled grandmother and not my wishy-washy mother? Everything that happened made me positively ill with regret when I convinced myself to go back to work.

Lindsay saw the shame written all over my face the instant I walked into the flat. He offered me a slight harrumph and remarked on the short time it took me to change my mind, as though he wasn't surprised it had taken so little. Of course he said it in a jest, but it had still added to the weight sitting squarely on my shoulders.

"I'll be fine," I said when I realised Sam wasn't leaving my bedside.

"You sure? I can stay home and take care of you, you know. Gran always told me I have to take care of you," he offered.

I smiled. "Did she?"

He nodded. Sam was deathly serious about two things in life: football and me. Sometimes, in my weaker moments, I assigned that devotion to mean he knew he liked to be taken care of more than he enjoyed taking care of himself. Anything which might potentially hinder my ability to care for him—an illness, my leaving, my possible death at any moment—would put a crimp in his cushy life, much in the same way a cat only deigns to show his owner any love because it's worried about who will open the next tin of food. Not because it genuinely cares.

Of course, I knew none of that was actually true. Sam's devotion to me came from a deep brotherly love—and I loved him just as much; sometimes performing for him while barely able to care for myself made me angry. Lindsay helped me divide and conquer in taking care of Sam more than I would ever be able to repay him, but I was still the final say. It didn't matter if I had my own issues; his worries were mine as well.

"I'm fine, really," I insisted. "Did you need something?"

Sam looked at me sceptically, but moved on to my question. "Lindsay said he had an emergency meeting this morning and that he couldn't take me to work."

And then there were times I just wished he could go to work on the Tube like everyone else. But he couldn't, because of the Great Transportation Debacle of 2013. I certainly didn't fancy a trip all way to Wembley again to retrieve Sam from the police because he took the initiative to board the train in Paddington one afternoon after being let off work earlier than expected. Who knew where he would end up if he started in Westminster.

I picked my head up and looked at the clock. Six thirty; he didn't have to be at work until eight. "Let me get ready. I'll be out in a bit."

"Good." He promptly disappeared out the door and closed it behind him, leaving me in the chilly room.

My body groaned as I threw my legs over the side of the bed, more so than it usually did when I woke in the mornings. Muscles pulled and ached and burned in areas where I didn't realise I had muscles. Memories from the day before filled my head and made me sigh in recollection. Even with the guilt eating away at me, I couldn't deny that Alex was an excellent lover and that, for a time, I felt powerful and marvellous.

Before my shower, I popped a pill to relieve the pain. The steamy, pelting water from the showerhead massaged my neck and upper back well enough, but as soon as I stepped out and dried off, the aching returned. I cursed the fact that I would have a constant reminder of him the whole day.

After dressing and gathering my things, we left the flat at half past seven. At eight exactly, I watched Sam stroll into the football club's office like he owned the place. He didn't say goodbye. He was too concerned with a cute girl who had run up to greet him. I was not unaware of my brother's popularity among the ladies in the office; he had, after all, given me a complete rundown of his many new girlfriends the second night after I returned to London.

Knowing that I had been discarded so easily made me grunt in irritation, but I shook my head anyway and turned back down the street. I took my time making my way toward Kensington. There weren't many days where I had the luxury of moseying about London without any demands on my time this early in the morning and I enjoyed watching the hustle and bustle of the city going to work. My travels took me to Hyde Park where I spent a good hour strolling through the western bound trails to loosen many of my stiff muscles, but it ultimately made me tired and hungry.

My rescue came in the form of a Starbucks I rarely visited though it was less than a five minute walk from the studio. Georgina considered their coffee to be inferior to an expensive little Italian café seven minutes away, but it would suit me just fine. Their caffeine would do exactly the same thing.

I was oblivious to the interest of a pair of ocean blue eyes watching me as I walked down the street, and only noticed their owner at the last minute. Sitting along one edge of the outdoor seating was the man I had all but forgotten in the events of the previous afternoon. His infectious, goofy smile and the crinkles at the corners of his eyes made me grin. I waved as I stopped beside the railing.

"Fancy seeing you here! I was just thinking about popping over to the studio," Tobias said.

Tobias stood and leaned over the railing. He kissed my cheek in greeting. I tried to ignore the slight flutter in my belly as well as the curious onlookers around us. Even though I knew the fluttering to be a reaction—in some part—of my womanly interest in him, I liked the public attention more than it had anything to do with whether or not I saw him in a romantic light.

It wasn't at all like Alex who treated me like a dirty secret.

I couldn't help my grin or the warmth of a blush that filled my cheeks. I refused to think about Alex at the moment. "When did you get in?"

"Yesterday afternoon," he replied. "Then I went home and passed out for fourteen hours."

He looked good, if a little tired since the last I saw of him. His flannel button down was a bit rumpled over a white tee, and his straight dark hair had been combed then windblown and finally tousled with fingers. The haphazardness of his dress made him all the more delectable despite wanting to appear unappealing, and at the very least, normal. He failed every single time.

"You deserve it," I said. "I didn't know you lived around Kensington."
"I don't."

On cue, I sensed another presence beside us. An overwhelming presence like a dark cloud covering the sun. Damn actors and their dramatic entrances. I breathed out and glanced to my side, blinking rapidly at the man holding a large caffeinated beverage. He seemed invigorated, but he did not smile at me. Didn't I, at least, deserve a smile from him?

"But Alex told me to meet him up here after his run," Tobias explained. My eyes dropped to Alex's body and noted the jogging clothes and trainers.

"Hi," I said in a rush of air.

Alex's lips quirked up into a smirk as he set his drink on the table and sat down in an empty seat. "Good morning, Emilia."

Tobias nudged Alex's shoulder. "You could at least make yourself useful and go get her a drink."

"Oh, no, that's quite all right," I assured him. I felt the intense urge to run away; I didn't want to—and certainly couldn't—face them together. How could any woman, really? What was more, I had an even better excuse than most. "I'm just going to grab something and head over to the studio."

"You shouldn't be working on your holiday, Em," Tobias said. "I insist you come sit and enjoy the morning with us."

I shook my head. "I don't want to intrude. Alex obviously had something to—"

"Don't be silly," Tobias cut in. "You're never an intrusion."

Alex once again adopted the aloof indifference I had come to expect from him. When Tobias looked to him for support, Alex merely inclined his head as though giving me permission.

Sighing heavily, I glanced at Tobias. "All right. Let me go get something."

Tobias triumphantly sat back into his seat as I walked into the shop and placed my order. I waited around at the counter for them to make my latte, glancing out the large windows to watch the two men waiting for me.

I wished I were a better lip reader, but all I saw was a heated discussion and two men completely unconcerned about where I was. Tobias sat up with his arms resting on the table while Alex lounged back in his seat, basking in the cold sunlight poking through the morning haze. He seemed much more at ease than he should have been given the awkward circumstances.

The barista set my drink on the counter with a smile, after which I grabbed it, took a tentative sip, and turned to go outside. I slipped into the outdoor seating area and reached the small table with little fanfare, but both men stood in unison to reach for the empty chair. Then they paused, looked at each other, and laughed at the situation. The laugh, however, bothered me. I didn't know Tobias well enough to understand what his hesitant laugh meant, but I knew Alex's. It wasn't Alex's mirthful laugh. It was the polite chuckle he reserved for annoying paparazzi and autograph hounds—the one that meant everything but joy.

Still, he ceded the responsibility to Tobias by lifting his hands in defeat and sitting back into his seat. After everything had been ironed out and I was comfortably set up around the round table, I looked at the two men. "Thank you both."

I sipped my drink and held the warm cup in my cold hands, hoping that they would start talking to fill the void between us, but it didn't happen. So I relied on the standard fallback. "I'll be so glad when it warms up."

"Everyone will be," Tobias said.

"At least you'll get to enjoy some warmer weather out in L.A. when we leave next week," Alex added.

I nodded.

Tobias smiled. "Will you be going out for the Oscars?"

"Will Georgina be there?" I asked.

Alex's lips pressed into a firm line, but it wasn't exactly a grimace. He nodded slightly.

"Then that's where I'll be." I picked at the cardboard sleeve on my drink and I looked between both men. "We actually have a lot of jobs and consults planned the week leading up to the show and since Georgina will be attending with Alex, I'm manning the ship for her the night of with the two actresses we're dressing."

"So you wouldn't be available to be my date for the show?" Tobias asked me, but gave Alex a smug grin.

Alex fidgeted in his seat. I didn't know what to say. "I, uh, no, I'm sorry. There's no way I'd be able to get everyone ready at the hotel and then get ready myself."

"I guess it is a distance back to Malibu," Tobias agreed thoughtfully.

"Oh, I'm not staying with Georgina at Alex's house," I explained. "I'll have a hotel room."

Alex's interest increased with my admission.

Tobias frowned at Alex. "You're letting her stay at a hotel when you have like twenty bedrooms at your new place?"

"Five bedrooms," Alex corrected Tobias and then looked at me, but Alex continued, "And I didn't know you weren't staying at the house. Won't Georgina need you there?"

I nearly choked on my latte, but recovered easily. Didn't he mean if he needed me? "Oh, sorry. It was hot…"

"Emilia," Alex continued, "wasn't it the plan when we were out there for the Globes that you were going to stay at my house? I insisted on it."

"You can insist all you want, but it still doesn't make it feasible," I said. "It's easier for me to be in the middle of everything since I'll be running all the errands."

"Still…" he tried to argue.

I rolled my eyes at him. "Sometimes, Alex, in the real world, you can't always get what you want."

Tobias snorted in laughter at his friend's expense, which only put Alex in a foul mood. Alex crossed his arms over his chest and leaned back in his seat somewhat like a petulant child. Maybe that was the problem; maybe he had become too comfortable with always taking and getting what he wanted. It wasn't out of the realm of the possibility that his stardom spoiled him, despite how gracious and humble he appeared to the public.

And I, unfortunately, only reinforced the notion that he could have whatever he wanted whenever he wanted it by giving in to him.

"It's no use arguing," Tobias interjected.

I looked at Tobias and sighed. "Sorry. I didn't mean to sound ungrateful... but we all have to remember here that I am Georgina's employee first and foremost. And as long as I am her employee, and she's footing the bill for me to accompany her out there for the purpose of helping her, I'm bound to her whims and choices. If she wants me at a hotel so I can coordinate everything, then I'll be at a hotel."

Even as I explained it, I saw the wheels working in Alex's head. Taking no for an answer was not a forte of his, but he did not continue to press the subject. Though it was nice to think he did it for my benefit—who wouldn't want to stay at a beautiful beach house for a week?— if he did succeed in getting me to stay, it would be more for his benefit and peace of mind. I'd be around when he wanted me and he wouldn't feel guilty about me languishing away in a hotel room somewhere due to Georgina's ungraciousness.

"Well, there's a lot going on during the week," Tobias said. "I'm sure there will be one day we can do something."

"I'd like that." And I really would, whether it was romantic or not. "But what about while we're still here? Don't you owe me dinner or something?"

Tobias's face lit up. Alex made a small sound of indignation in his throat. We ignored it.

"I believe I do." Tobias grinned. "What do you feel like?"

"I'm pretty open. You decide."

Tobias nodded and pulled his mobile from a coat pocket. "Are you free tomorrow?"

"Georgina planned to stay a few days after the Oscars. Maybe you could at least have a few beach days then," Alex suggested out of nowhere.

"I can't," I replied to Tobias as I looked at my own calendar. "I have plans all day tomorrow."

Although I mucked things up with Alex, I still intended to take his mother out for the day. I couldn't penalise her for what happened with him.

"Then Thursday?" Tobias asked after a moment's counsel with his mobile.

"That should be good," I affirmed.

Alex sat forward in his seat, somewhat blocking my view of Tobias. The jealousy was palpable in his hard azure stare. "Would you care to move over to my place after your Oscar duties are done?"

I groaned. "Georgina didn't say anything to me about staying beyond the Monday after the Oscars. That Wednesday I have practice for a football match."

I said it mostly for my benefit and forgot my company. They both looked at me like I had gone mad. "For my brother's team. It's family athletics day."

Tobias smiled. "Sam roped you into playing footy?"

"I'm actually quite good," I asserted. "I played all through school until uni. I'm out of shape, though, so Sam said I have to practice."

"Wait." Alex frowned, furrowing his eyebrows. "Sam is your *brother*?"

"Who did you think he was, Alex?" Tobias asked, clearly enjoying the rapid fire volleys between us. He was getting a little too much delight out of the friction we had created.

Alex shrugged, relaxing back in his chair. "I don't know. I thought a lover or boyfriend or something. She wouldn't say."

"I can't believe you didn't connect it after you found out I had a brother," I said. Really, I was surprised.

"Is he young?" Alex asked. "You talk about him like—"

"Twenty-one," I shot back to Alex and then looked at Tobias. "Thursday is perfect."

Tobias nodded and typed it into his calendar. "I'll pick you up at seven?"

"Sounds lovely." I clicked off of my calendar and slipped my mobile where it belonged in my pocket. This was where I saw my exit from the uncomfortable situation. "I really do need to get to the studio, though. So I'll see you two later."

Tobias followed me as I stood and leaned over to give me another peck on the cheek. I inadvertently caught the murderous glare Alex shot in Tobias' direction. As much pleasure as I took in the two men vying for my attention, I really didn't relish the thought that I might be responsible for really and truly driving a wedge between their friendship. I wasn't that sort of girl. But then, I once thought I wasn't the sort of girl who slept with her boss' boyfriend, so my argument was tenuous at best. Even so, Alex had no room to complain about anything. He was dating someone. And he cheated on her. He had absolutely no standing in this.

"You'll be over to collect my mum tomorrow, right?" Alex asked pointedly as I stepped back from Tobias. It was a parting shot for which he seemed quite chuffed; Tobias didn't seem to care one way or another about it—which was weird. But I pushed the thought away.

"I've already set it up with her, thank you." I hoped the curt response was enough to cut him off at the knees.

Alex began to stand and lean over in the same way Tobias had, but I took a step back, putting my chair between us.

He took the hint. "Thanks for the chat."

I gave him a tight smile and lifted my Starbucks cup in silent salute. After saying goodbye, I escaped the seating area, praying no one would follow me or think me impolite.

Only when I reached the inside of the studio and threw the deadbolt on the door did I fully breathe. Relief flooded my senses. I felt more conflicted and confused than in all my twenty-eight years of life. Considering how dodgy my past was, that was saying a lot.

CHAPTER 12

WELL INTO MY PRODUCTIVE AFTERNOON, my mobile rang and cancelled out the music coming from the dock. I contemplated letting it go to message so I didn't have to drop the heavy pile of beaded evening gowns thrown over one arm, but thought better of it. I thought it might be something important. Maybe I won the lottery.

Though the mobile did not recognise the number, I could ascertain the American prefix. I answered it anyway. Georgina wouldn't be calling from the States and with the Oscars less than a fortnight away, some reservation or scheduling conflict could need my attention.

I shoved the phone between my raised shoulder and ear. "Hello?"

"Girl! Please tell me you're comin' out here for the Oscars!"

The excited Southern twang in the other voice made me smile. I missed the sound of this particular sultry drawl more than I cared to admit. It had been much too long since Jordan and I last had the opportunity to talk.

"I planned on it. Are you going to be in town?"

"Not only am I gonna be in town, but I'm doin' a shoot with Alex Thorne. Henriette just called me with the booking."

Oh, great. I sighed heavily.

Her perkiness lowered considerably in her concern. "You don't sound happy."

"I am happy." I just wished I felt like it. "I've missed you so much.

There's just… there's a lot that's been going on. I've got a lot on my mind."

"Well, then it's perfect that you're comin' out!" Jordan exclaimed. "We're gonna go out, we're gonna go dancing, and we're gonna drink too much. Heaven knows you need a break from Cruella and I need to fill you in on the last seven months."

The mobile slipped slightly from my shoulder. I grabbed it in annoyance and flipped on the speaker to continue working hands free. "I don't know if I'll have the time for that, but I do want to see you. We'll see each other at the shoot for Alex, at least."

"That's not good enough for me," she complained. "I got y'all for exactly one day before my wedding last summer. I need girl time and I need it with you."

"I'm telling you, the schedule is pretty busy."

I dropped the stack of evening gowns on an empty rack and walked back to the desk, reaching for the tablet sitting in the middle of it. As I was already well aware, the six day trip was jam-packed with activities; most of them were Georgina attending some party or gala either with or without Alex, but I never knew when she might require me to be at her side. Even though she employed a publicist, he did not travel around with her like Alex's did with him. My responsibility involved shepherding her around wherever she went on business and keeping her on schedule.

Jordan grumbled on the other end of the line. "You know, you keep doin' this and I'll start to feel like you're avoidin' me."

"I'm not avoiding you." It sounded false, even to me.

"We both had a day in Paris we could have met up," she said. "I didn't have a job. Cruella was off with Martinique at a trunk show. But you said you couldn't grab lunch with me because Georgina asked you to pick up a birthday present for Alex."

I blew air from my lips, remembering the day in question. I had literally been knocking on death's door and only had the energy for one errand. "It wasn't like that, Jordan."

"Yes, it was," she said. "I was ignored for a shoppin' trip for your boss' boyfriend."

"Look," I said in exasperation, "I just wanted to find the perfect thing for him. That takes time."

I could almost hear Jordan rolling her wide brown eyes at me. "When will you realize that woman's never gonna pat you on the back and say job well done? It's just not gonna happen, honey."

I had heard that particular chorus far too much as of late.

"Have you been talking to Lindsay at all?" I asked.

"We've sent a few e-mails back and forth," she replied. "But he's even harder to pin down than you are. Why do you ask?"

"Because Lindsay has been on this rant recently."

Jordan chuckled lowly. "Honey, we just keep sayin' it because it's true. She won't give you the approval you want."

Even though she was right, it was best just to ignore her. A moment of silence passed in conversation as I fiddled with the tablet.

"Unless…" her voice broke through the silent studio.

I waited for her to continue. "Unless what?"

"Oh my God!" The sudden shock and accusation in her exclamation made me jump. "Oh. My. God! Why in the world didn't I see it before?"

"See what before?"

Jordan chuckled. "You're not doin' it for her approval. You're doin' it for his approval."

I refused to dignify her comments with an answer, but I honestly didn't know how to respond to her accusation. Was I looking for his approval? Of course I was, on some level. Before Venice, the sun rose and set on Alex Thorne. His absolute compassion, effortless charm, and friendliness won me over before I ever had a chance to resist. I thought he deserved the same. He deserved someone just as thoughtful and caring as he was to me, holding doors, thanking me, and exchanging small jokes when Georgina was out of earshot. His concern for other people beside himself had mystified and entranced me. I just wanted him to realise that someone else cared about him as much; not everyone used him like Georgina.

Then Venice happened. And dinner at his mum's happened. And then the afternoon on the chaise lounge happened. Did he find me an easy target? Had he thought, because I was so willing to please and to be praised, I would fall easily into a trap I wasn't entirely sure he hadn't planned from the moment we met? I still didn't quite grasp how he could be all of those wonderful things I first came to know about him, but so demanding and domineering as well. No one person could maintain such a level of diametric opposition in their personality without going mad.

"You see? This is what happens when I don't see you or talk to you for months at a time," Jordan continued. I blinked as her words shot through the thoughts in my head. She'd been babbling as my mind drifted.

"Jor," I said with a sigh. "You can't even begin to comprehend what the fuck has happened in the past month alone."

"Then you have no excuse. We're gonna go out and have a good time," she said. "Tell me what night you have free in L.A."

"Probably Wednesday night," I responded. "But I don't know for sure."

"Well, you have my number."

I nodded for my benefit. "What number did you call from?"

"Oh, that's the ranch's landline," she replied. "You should probably save it in case of emergency."

I opened my mouth to confirm I would but stopped when I heard the sound of a key turning the front door lock followed by the pitter-patter of small canine feet running at top speed from the kitchen. Coco and Gucci erupted into a barking and crying fit when the door opened, doing their job to alert me in case of intruders. I had purposely liberated them from the pet hotel for the day to be my guard dogs. Alex wouldn't then have the opportunity to mysteriously appear with lunch or more wicked intentions.

"What's going on?" Jordan asked in confusion.

"I have to go."

Alex greeted the animals vying for his attention, but paused and then yelled, "Emilia? You here?"

"Is that who I think it is?" Jordan demanded. "Am I on speaker?"

I reached for the mobile. "Yes… now…"

"Well, hello Mr. Thorne!"

"Jordan!" I cringed and looked toward the entry as his lean body filled it. "I'll let you know about L.A. later. All right?"

"No! Don't hang—" The room went silent when I hit the appropriate button to end the call. She wouldn't let me forget it, but at the moment, it was all I could think to do.

I set the mobile on the desk and ignored Alex. I marched back to my work and the beaded evening gowns. He stayed at the entrance. "Is Georgina back?"

"No," I said. "Why?"

"The dogs…" he muttered.

I frowned at him, but then realisation dawned on me as to why he would be concerned about them.

"Oh, I hate that they spend more time at a pet hotel than they do at home," I explained. "And I like the company."

"If you wanted company," he said lowly, "all you had to do was ask."

"Not your kind of company."

He sucked in a breath and lazily walked around the desk. "Who were you talking to?"

"A friend."

"Ah."

Ignoring him was just as difficult as I imagined it would be, and I found myself, as I continued separating evening wear from day wear, stealing glances in his direction. He hadn't attempted to say anything and instead played with the dogs, then leaned back in the chair to relax. The mechanisms creaked with his weight as he crossed a leg over the other and rested his head against it. I sensed his eyes on me before I confirmed it with another glance. His attention did not waver.

I felt like prey in the African bush, stalked by some beast preparing to pounce. Only my bush consisted of multiple clothing racks and my beast was an incredibly handsome actor. An actor who, for his numerous faults, still had the power to make me feel amazing. Wanted. Needed. Even though what we did might have been considered morally and ethically wrong, nothing had ever felt as right as his hands, his mouth—his body—worshiping all of me. Not even his overbearing, mostly infuriating, personality could take those facts away.

He wove a pen between his fingers and dextrously flipped it around each digit without using the other hand. "So who's your friend?"

I shrugged. "Her name's Jordan."

"American?"

"Yes," I replied. "She's a model. I met her at one of my first modelling jobs. She taught me how to strut down a catwalk."

A slow grin spread his lips. "Remind me to thank her for that."

I rolled my eyes at him and began arranging blouses.

"Are you close friends?"

"Relatively."

Why was he so interested? It felt like he was deflecting or trying to prolong the conversation before getting to what he intended to do or say to me.

"She based in L.A.?"

Placing the last blouse on another rack, I stood back and surveyed my work. It was as good as it was going to get. The articles of clothing that needed to be weeded out and sent back to their respective designers were pushed off to the side for the messengers, and everything else was in order. I only wished I had more work. I didn't want to give Alex all of my attention.

"Emilia?" he asked again when I didn't answer him immediately.

I pushed a rack back to the wall. "No. She and her husband live on a ranch outside of Nashville. He's a musician. Why do you care, anyway?"

"I want to know everything about you," was his answer.

The bark of laughter that escaped my throat surprised me. I looked at him. "You don't get it, do you? You don't get to know everything about me. This thing between us… it can only be sex. And it can only be you and me. You can't go around trying to stake a claim on me in the middle of the Starbucks outdoor seating area."

"Why not?"

"Because people aren't idiots," I said. "If it gets out in the press…"

He grunted in anger. "If I have to listen to one more bloody thing about the press getting into my business—"

"It's the life you chose, Alex."

He directed a terrible scowl at me.

"Don't give me that look."

He stood from his seat and changed the subject. "You aren't seriously considering going on a date with Tobias, are you?"

"It's none of your concern."

"It's not?"

I shook my head and turned around, coming chest-to-chest with the man. A waist-high shelf holding a glass vase full of opalescent pebbles and a single silk orchid impeded my step of freedom backward. The vase wavered before Alex's right hand darted out to steady its movement.

"No, it's not," I said.

"So you're saying that it's none of my concern that the woman I wake up thinking about and fall asleep only to dream about is out with some other guy?"

His question, spoken with such a deep earnestness, absolutely floored me. If I wasn't completely incensed at his possessiveness when he had so little standing, I might have swooned at the comment. Instead, I merely shook my head at him. "Maybe you should've thought about that before you seduced me into having an affair with you."

"But it's not just an 'affair' to me," he said.

I pursed my lips. "Then what the hell is it? There's no room for your pretty platitudes or romance or anything like that. It's not rainbows and butterflies. You're the one who created this monster. Perhaps you should have—"

"Of course, it'll always be my fault," he remarked, though I felt the comment wasn't entirely directed at me. For the briefest of moments I saw sadness flash in his eyes. I wanted to comfort him.

He promptly replaced the mask of impassivity he had worn since Venice. He was undaunted by my arguments.

"What if I wanted more? What would happen then?"

"You've already taken so much, Alex," I said, shaking my head. "I don't know if I have any more of me to give. Or that I want to give to you."

However, I was confident he already held everything important, including my heart, no matter how twisted the situation happened to be. When I glanced back at him, I noticed the muscles in his jaw clenching and unclenching.

"Clearly, you and I had different visions about how this arrangement would go. Let me enlighten you," I offered, letting my words hang in the air for maximum effect. "If I want to go on a date with Tobias, I'm going on a date with Tobias. If I want to fuck him, then I'm going to fuck him. If I want to have a relationship and marry and have children with Tobias or anyone else I find, guess what? I'm going to do it and you're not going to stop it. Because you have no right to do so."

"How do you know he's not just using you?"

I balked at his remark. "You mean just like you are? Pot, have you met the kettle yet? My God, this isn't the bloody Dark Ages where men get to have all their fun and expect women to waste away tending home and hearth only to drop everything they're doing at their husband's or father's or brother's beck and call. You don't get to go around lording it over me and strong arming things just because you want it to happen. You haven't earned the right."

"I'm asking you," he said evenly, "no, pleading with you… don't start anything serious with him."

"Why? Give me one good reason why I shouldn't, and please don't say it's because I should just trust you."

Alex's fists balled at his sides. He opened his mouth to reply, but no words came to him. He shut his mouth with a nearly audible snap, his thin lips pressing together in rage.

I tugged at my shirt and squared my shoulders. "Didn't think you'd have one."

"I do have a reason," he claimed.

"What is it, then?"

He opened his mouth and froze, making a slight gurgling sound in his throat. "I—I… I'm sorry. I can't say."

I threw my hands up in disgust. "Look, I'll make this easier. If you want this," I said and motioned to my body, "then you'll have to square with the fact that you don't own it. You can't command it. I get a say, and you most definitely can't always try to dominate me into submission."

I wished I could live up to my own words. The fact of the matter was that I found it incredibly difficult to resist anything to do with him. Still, I had to try, and he wouldn't know just how pliable I would remain to his commands. Over time I hoped it might become easier to resist his unrelenting pull, the one set deep in my bones. He had been spoiled for too long, taking whatever he wanted from me without a care in the world; I needed to change that.

"We can be friendly and continue to work together but no one… and I mean no one… can know about it. You can't go off trying to piss all over me like a dog marking his territory. Got it?" I held his gaze as the words seeped into his brain.

He didn't show any recognition of them for quite some time. The eventual nod of his head was begrudging and curt as he stepped away from me. I tried to ignore the hurt in his eyes; acknowledging those emotions existed in him would be my end. Seeing his emotion would only make me wish we could have more than what I had allowed him. I had to be strong in the face of this new turn in my life.

Because being in "love" with the insufferable man was already killing me.

"Alex," I said as I reached out to him and set my hand on his shoulder.

He turned in his spot.

"I'm sorry, but I have to do this for my own sanity." The momentary power I gained from asserting myself quickly vanished. In its place was remorse. I didn't want him to leave. And yet I didn't want him to stay, either. God, why was everything so difficult?

The crack in his imperious wall shone through his eyes. He seemed contrite. As though I clipped his wings. He reminded me of the Alex I had secretly fallen in love with when I first met him.

"Emilia…"

"What?" I whispered.

He sighed and shook his head. "Nothing."

There was more he wished to say, and it absolutely killed me that I would never know what it was. But then I remembered who stood in front of me. He used his vulnerability as a trap and nothing more. Any gifted dramatic actor could.

"All right." I sucked in a breath, replenishing the supply I lost with him so dangerously close to me. "I'm leaving for the day and taking the dogs back to the pet hotel."

"You won't come back like yesterday?"

"No. This time I'll remember my coat." To prove my point, I grabbed it from the coat rack and slipped my arms through it.

He merely shook his head and walked around the desk. "I'll see you tomorrow then?"

"If you're at your mum's," I said. "Gucci! Coco!"

The dogs skittered from the other room and immediately sat at my feet. I pulled their leads out of the coat pocket and clipped them to their collars. "You guys ready to go back to the hotel? I know you don't want to go, but it'll only be for a little while longer. Your mummy will be back in a few days."

Gucci yipped and jumped, placing his tiny paws on my knee for leverage. I scratched behind his ears before standing up and glancing at Alex.

"Were I that dog," he mused.

I laughed at his remark, feeling a sudden lightness about the situation. The weight and guilt which made it next to impossible to get out of bed were officially things of the past. I felt better with boundaries and limitations imposed. At least with them, we knew how this was going to go.

Of course, we actually had to follow the rules for them to work. There was a very real possibility that he wouldn't obey them. I pushed the frightening thought away, instead deciding to hope that Alex had a shred of integrity left. And that I had the willpower to see them through.

I gathered the rest of my things and headed toward the door. Alex followed close behind me. I pulled the door back a centimetre before he thrust his arm out and shut it again. I spun around to complain, but he was there, his lips hungrily devouring mine. However, he did not allow it to last. He lingered just long enough that I would remember it as I left the studio and then regret my decision to leave without giving him more.

He misunderstood my resolve, however, to remain strong in the face of his calculated strategy to get me and keep me in his bed.

"Goodbye, Alex."

"Have a lovely evening, bellissima."

At this, he reached for the handle on the door and opened it for me, allowing me out of the studio without any more impediment.

CHAPTER 13

MARY FLEW OUT THE DOOR when I arrived for our outing. She had car keys in hand along with her handbag, neglecting to wait for Alex's help out of the house. I would have laughed at the rushed scene and Alex's look of utter vexation as he followed behind her if I hadn't felt the overwhelming dread mixing with the strange craving he created every time I saw him.

For once, however, the feeling was remarkably fleeting as I quickly turned my attention to helping his spitfire mother into her car. She had a bit more mobility than the previous Friday; the doctors had replaced her plaster leg cast with a plastic walking cast, though she remained confined in a wheelchair for the time being.

"Come on, love! We should be on our way or we'll lose our table."

I laughed at her and made the mistake of peeking at the man standing beside me, his hands thrust deep into his pockets. He turned to me, one brow arching in question. "You think you can handle her?"

"Please," I said, waving him off. "Compared to everyone else I have to handle in my life, your mother is a walk in the proverbial park."

At my meaningful look up at him, he grunted. I decided to ignore it and he didn't press the subject. It was a relief when he let it go, but also a worry that he ignored it so easily. Did he not see what an arse he was? Because he had turned into the biggest arse I had to contend with on an almost daily basis. Perhaps even more so than Georgina.

"Emilia?" His voice broke through my thoughts.

I blinked and looked up again, realising he said something else to me. "What?"

"I was just saying that I have an event to attend tonight," he repeated. "So I won't be here when you return. Do you think you could stick around for a bit and—"

"For your mum? Of course," I said. "How late do you think you'll be?"

He shrugged. "I can never tell with these things. It'll be later this evening, though. Just make sure she has dinner."

"Goodness, Alexander!" His mother's voice floated from the open car door. "You make it sound as if I'm a complete muddlehead. I'm not entirely useless in my dotage."

"I know you're not, Mary," I called to her. "We'll be fine. I planned on offering to cook dinner anyway."

"Oh?" He rubbed his hand on his trim abdomen. "What do you have planned?"

"Don't know." I shrugged. "Have fun at your event."

Leaving him standing there without a definitive answer would likely irritate him, but I didn't care. When I got to the car, I grabbed the vacated wheelchair and folded it down before slipping it into the boot. Mary handed me the keys after I climbed into the driver's seat.

"Right. Where are we off to?" I asked, adjusting the seat and mirrors.

"Hyde," she answered. "Lunch at the restaurant by the Serpentine."

With a final nod of my head, I moved the car into gear and slowly backed out onto the road. Before I switched gears again, my eyes caught a glimpse of Alex standing on the front stoop of the house, his hands back in his pockets. I might have considered it an innocent, boyish look if weren't for the smug smile on his face. He seemed more than a little pleased with the situation. I could only try to ignore it, lest all my attention remain on him when I needed to concentrate on Mary and driving through London.

The traffic wasn't nearly as congested as I imagined it would be, but it did take us some time to reach a car park and to dawdle our way over to the restaurant with Mary in a wheelchair. Luckily, the restaurant hadn't given away our table. A host seated us quickly out on the patio overlooking the Serpentine's sparkling water on the crisp, clear day.

Glancing around at all the professionals dressed in smart business attire, I thanked my better judgment for telling me to wear something nicer than jeans. Even so, I adjusted the sleeves of my ankle-length dress and sat up a little straighter. These places always made me uncomfortable; Mary relaxed as if she were back in her living room at home.

"You look lovely, Emilia," Mary assured me with a knowing grin. "I'm sure you could wear your worst and you'd still be beautiful."

Caught red handed in my anxious fidgeting, I reached for my sunglasses and pushed them to the top of my head. I peered at the woman beside me, folding my hands in my lap. "Thank you."

Mary waved her hand in dismissal when the server appeared to take our drink orders: water for both of us. We sat in friendly silence, enjoying our surroundings and commenting sporadically on the scene in front of us. Everything seemed very civil—never strained—but I found myself lulled into a false sense of peace by the time we were enjoying our field greens with raspberry vinaigrette and walnuts.

"You handle a wheelchair very well," she mentioned in an off-handed way. She always began her information mining like this. She started with something rather innocuous so the subject didn't know what happened to the conversation before it was too late.

I smiled and sipped my water. "I've had a bit of practice. My grandmother was wheelchair bound from the time I was fourteen until she died a little over three years ago."

"Oh, that's too bad," she remarked, nibbling a walnut. She swallowed and dabbed at her mouth before continuing. "You lived with her?"

"Didn't Alex tell you?" I asked.

She smiled. "He tells me a lot of things, but I think it's your story to tell."

I sighed softly and looked out on the water as a rowboat with two men in it glided by the patio. "My mother left me and my brother on my grandmother's doorstep when I was six. He was only a few months old then. Our grandmother raised us."

"Ah," Mary replied. She pursed her lips in thought and prodded some more. "You haven't seen her since?"

"Once. When I was in Paris—that's where she went when she left—during my second fashion week there," I admitted.

I could hardly believe I divulged the information to her. I had never breathed a word of it to anyone. Not even Lindsay. But once the leak of information started, it was only a matter of time before the dam burst from the pressure. Mary had no problem capitalising on my weakness.

Mary nodded solemnly. "It wasn't happy, I take it."

"No."

The memory was seared into my brain. One look at my mother's pockmarked and jaundiced face confirmed she had started using again, and had been for quite a long time. Her beauty stayed with us when she left England.

In France, she was nothing more than an emaciated wraith.

I shuddered as I remembered the cold clamminess of a bony hand clenching my wrist, bruising my skin with an intimidating drug-induced strength. One good breeze and she would have fallen over, but the way the fingers dug into my flesh hurt me. When she finally had my attention, rather than hug me or cry over seeing me, she asked me for money.

My reaction to the situation wasn't one of my proudest moments. I hated myself for it. I was with a group of other models at the time—a group I desperately wanted to infiltrate for the sake of my modelling career—and I shrugged her off like I didn't know her. My only consoling thought was that I didn't know her, not really, when it came down to it. She was just another blip in my past. A woman who gave me life, but had never been a true mother to me. A woman who abandoned me to a cold, resentful, and oftentimes cruel grandmother.

Mary interrupted my thoughts. "It wasn't my intention to bring up sad memories."

It was your every intention, I mused.

I smiled despite the unpleasant ghost of a memory haunting me. "It's okay. It's who I am. Where I come from. There were some good times, too."

Mary leaned an elbow on the table and rested her head on her hand. "Tell me about one of the good times."

"When I was about four or five, my mum would take me to Notting Hill on Saturdays. We'd get cheap art supplies and some food for lunch, and we'd come to the park together to paint and draw and have a picnic," I said with a small laugh as I met Mary's assessing blue eyes. Despite all the bad memories, this happy one was the easiest to recall of them all. "Which is funny since you decided to come here for our lunch, because you're the closest thing I have to a mum right now."

Mary's smile was warm. "That's a lovely memory."

"It is," I agreed and shifted uneasily in my seat.

"Is it why you didn't pursue art in school?" she asked, point-blank.

I took a moment to collect my thoughts and sipped my water again. Once I started talking, I wouldn't be able to stop. "I guess, somewhat. Everything always goes back to her, unfortunately."

Mary watched me attentively. I wasn't going to get out of explaining myself. This was most important to her—figuring out why I didn't do what I wanted and what made me who I was. Maybe she hoped to discover the reason as to why I refused to—or couldn't—leave my position with Georgina.

"My grandmother thought I was too much like my mother. To stop me from going down the same wild, drugged-out, irresponsible path my mother chose, she made it imperative that I become a productive, hardworking citizen. So she guilted me to do that. Pressured me into excelling in my education and choosing a field that would benefit me later in life. Nothing I ever did was good enough for her. She couldn't see how being an artist could put food on the table and take care of Sam."

Mary balked at the reasoning. "You could have done so much with it… just because your mother couldn't do it, doesn't mean you would fall to the same fate."

"But I nearly did—fall, I mean," I explained. "That's the worst part of it. I was so bloody selfish, just like her. I went off the rails and left uni and became a model. I was so sick and tired of always worrying about everything and everyone. I did the cooking and cleaning and errands and everything else in addition to school and working a job when my grandmother could no longer do it. And I just left Sam and her to take care of it themselves as I…"

I couldn't finish the sentence and paused to gulp down more water.

Mary, meanwhile, grabbed my hand, squeezing it comfortingly. "Love, I think it would be fair to say that you never had a childhood, and what you did at uni—that was making up for lost time."

"But I was older then. I should have known better."

"Everyone needs a time to rebel," Mary said kindly. "I lived through four children. I know all about it."

I started to reply that Alex would never rebel, but stopped myself when I remembered who I would defend in the process: the perfectly imperfect man who cheated on his girlfriend with me, and who had a much darker side than his public image. Thinking about Alex rebelling as a teenager made me sigh.

Chewing on my bottom lip, I finally met the woman's eyes. "But if I rebelled, it didn't just affect me. Most kids have the luxury of stretching their legs and growing under the supervision of their parents. They don't have adult worries like buying groceries or caring for a sibling."

Mary nodded. "You are right. I'll give you that much, but I still think you're being overly hard on yourself."

"I'm not." I shook my head, refusing to let her convince me otherwise. "I wasn't there… when my grandmother died, I didn't hear about it until a month afterward because I hadn't given Lindsay my new mobile number. By the time I made it back to London, Sam was in government care. I broke into a thousand tiny pieces when I saw him—saw the sadness on his face. He's the one who found her, you know? When she died…"

Mary said nothing, but she nodded and let me continue.

"I was so selfish," I said. "So completely selfish. I abandoned them… I abandoned Sam just like *she* did."

Mary squeezed my hand until I looked at her. She gave me a warm smile and patted my forearm. "Love, you needn't go on if it's bothering you."

This time, I heard the sincerity in her voice.

I sighed. "It's why I stay with Georgina, you know. You were trying to figure it out Saturday evening… why I would stay with her when she is so dreadful."

"Because you're worried you'll become your mother," she said. "You think that leaving your position with her would be like when you left university. Maybe it's why you're so scared about getting back into modelling again and having something that's your own?"

Hot tears stung my eyes as she spoke. She reached over and gingerly pushed a few strands of my hair behind my ear. The gesture was gentle and loving, as I imagined a mother would act, and it made the tears spill down my cheeks. It was just so nice. So lovely.

I sniffled and wiped my face with the backs of my hands. "I'm sorry."

"It's my fault," Mary admitted. "I pressed you for information."

"But you understand now, don't you?"

She nodded.

"I can't just leave my job," I replied. "If I leave my job, then there's no income to provide for us, and Sam goes back into government care. Especially if I go back into modelling and it's too late to make anything of it. They may not want me. I mean, I'm getting older. I can't take the chance. I can't do it… I just *can't*."

"Emilia, you're a strong, intelligent girl," Mary said. "I think you're capable of doing anything you put your mind to. But Georgina is toxic and you need to get away from her."

"If I pay my dues with her, it opens up so many doors."

Mary gave me a censuring, maternal look. "She is a vile person and you need to quit. Start looking for a new position now, so you don't have any gap."

"I don't have any other experience except in fashion, and those jobs aren't really traditionally advertised." I shook my head. "You just fall into them."

"You speak several languages. You are a fantastic assistant, judging from what I saw at the Christmas party and from what I hear from Alex," she said. "Lots of people need assistants. I think you're scared to actually do something you love. To actually take the leap of faith and do it."

I sat silently, letting her words seep into my brain. Instinctively, the woman knew I needed comfort and yet a good knock on the chin to put on my big girl knickers and get on with my life. They were exactly what I needed to hear. But that didn't make it any easier to digest. Especially when I considered the possibility that Alex may have put her up to it.

The sinking feeling in my stomach made me ill. What made it even worse was that I couldn't question her further about it without giving away my tawdry affair with her son. God, what would she think if she knew what Alexander and I were doing?

Unless, of course, she already knew.

I chose to err on the side of caution and not broach the subject.

Thankfully, our server appeared at the table with our main cours-es, effectively interrupting the conversation and allowing us to lapse back into pleasant companionship as we ate our meal.

Even though I was thankful the grilling had ended, I was also glad it happened. It was nice to talk to someone like Mary—someone who didn't have years of history with me. I was a hopeless case and I knew it, but Mary's resolute confidence in me was a nice feeling to have.

Me leaving Georgina was a slim likelihood at this point. I never had any time between work and personal commitments to actually search for new opportunities, much less the ability to find the time for interviews without Georgina knowing. She would relieve me of my duties before I even had a chance to defend myself.

With another sigh, I decided to concentrate on the scrumptious meal. I needed to repair the depleted stores of energy our conversa-tion had used. There was no telling what else the woman had in store for me before I left that night.

CHAPTER 14

MARY DIDN'T NEED MY HELP preparing supper or around the house. Of course I didn't mind helping her because I quite enjoyed her company, but I did wonder why Alex thought she was incapable of caring for herself in her injured state. His endearing, if misplaced, worry contradicted the image of the domineering and spoiled actor I had formed in my head of late, and leant more credibility to the fact that public Alex—the happy, intelligent, unequivocally nice man—was really him.

I wanted to watch him with others. With his friends and the rest of his family. Somehow, I thought, I'd discover the truth about him if I had the time to observe his interactions with the others close to him, not entirely unlike an anthropologist studying some reclusive tribe in a remote part of the rainforest. However, socialising with them was out of the question. I set our boundaries and vowed to keep them. That included getting overly chummy with the people in his life. Well, people other than Mary.

I shot myself in the foot with that one, I supposed, but I refused to give Alex the pleasure of knowing I was the one to amend the rules for my purposes. I pictured the raise of an eyebrow as he tried, fruitlessly, not to smirk at me. He would never explicitly say "I told you so," but it would definitely be implied. Moreover, by second-guessing myself and changing the rules to suit my needs, it would cause a fundamental breakdown of the tenuous authority I actually held in our affair.

The thought made me sigh in irritation, but it turned into a yawn as I focused on the glow of the telly in front of me. Womble the cat curled himself in my lap, his little body vibrating with a rumbling, motorboat-like purr. He nudged my hand for a scratch; he had grown rather fond of me after I opened a tin of wet food for his dinner. The feline seemed cuddly despite his participation in injuring his owner.

"He likes you," observed Mary in my periphery.

I blinked and looked at her. "Huh?"

"Womble. He likes you."

The pause that followed and the twinkle in her eye made me wonder if we weren't talking about someone other than the cat.

"Well, you know men," I replied with a giggle. "You feed them and give them a little scratch behind the ear, and they're yours for life."

Mary let out a long laugh. "If only it really were that simple."

I nodded and looked back at the television, trying to get into the programme, but my thoughts were elsewhere with little chance of diversion.

"So, *are* there any men in your life?" Mary asked. "Since Lindsay isn't actually your boyfriend?"

Her question didn't exactly stun me, but it did surprise me that she waited so long to bring it up.

"N-no," I replied. "There's not."

She nodded. "Alex said you were going out on a second date with Tobias."

Did the man tell her everything? Lord, I hoped not.

"Well, it's really a first date. Tobias only took me to a premiere the last time. That's not much of a date."

Scepticism filled her kind face. "With them, that's a date."

I hissed at the cat when his claws extended mid-knead and buried into my thigh. He didn't seem to care about my human pain, but I carefully moved his paws away from my leg. In return, he fully animated, stood up, gave me an indignant sniff, and strutted down to the other end of the sofa. He circled and laid down to sleep.

When I glanced back at Mary, she was still watching me. "If you date Tobias, that's what life will be all time."

"Not all the time," I countered. "There are nights when there's nothing going on and it can just be the two of us."

Her scepticism did not waver. "Maybe four or five years ago there were nights like that. But it seems like Alex, at least, is off to some event or in a different country working all the time. Tobias is likely the same way."

"Alex's been back here for a little while to do the play," I offered to her, even though it was useless to argue. If one person operated on a busier schedule than mine, it was Alexander Thorne. Alex's publicist and I dealt with each other on numerous occasions trying to schedule time for both Georgina and Alex to spend together because there was so little of it. "And now that the run is over… he has time."

"For a bit. Then he's back off to do another press tour."

What point did she want to make anyway? Was she trying to convince me not to see Tobias, or not to look to men like him for a stable future? I felt as though she meant it as a warning about the dangers of relationships with actors, completely contradicting my belief that she had occupied a spot in Alex's corner all along. It sounded to me like she was advocating for any other man but her son or his friend.

My friend.

I shrugged. "Honestly, I don't even know what's going on with Tobias. We're only friends."

Mary didn't reply after that. I couldn't tell if she was happy, relieved, or ambivalent about my admission. Honestly, I thought she might want to say a lot more, but she chose not to, which of course only added a little more uncertainty to my present situation. Maybe she intended to pull for Alex, after all.

With all the concentration I could muster, I focused on the telly for the next hour or so until Mary looked at me and announced her intent to go to bed. "Go home, love. No need to stay around while I'm asleep. I take pain medication and I'm usually down for the count."

"I don't mind," I said. "And what happens if you need something before Alex returns? I don't want to be responsible for you tripping over Womble again."

Mary laughed and waved her hand at me in dismissal. "I promise I won't leave my bed."

"I told Alex I'd stay until he returned."

She gave me an impish grin. It was suspiciously familiar, as though I had seen it somewhere before. "Unless, of course, you just want to see Alex. Which is more than fine with me."

And... there it was. I blew out a small puff of air and shook my head wildly. "No, Mary, I—"

The woman patted the top of my hand. "Love, as I said before we left for lunch this afternoon, I'm not a complete muddlehead. I could see it the moment you walked in here with those flowers last week."

"But I..."

She sighed.

"He's in a relationship," I spluttered, trying to think of some believable defence while tap dancing around the issue.

"So it would seem," the woman conceded bitterly and with an unsettling shake of her head. A yawn overtook her when she focused back on me. "But that's a conversation for another night. You are, of course, welcome to stay if you wish. Just to be certain that *I'm* all right."

The mirth in her voice and smiling wink made my skin hot with a blush. She wheeled herself toward the downstairs bedroom Alex or someone else had set up for her while she could not climb the staircase. Her door eventually clicked shut and left me in the deafening silence of the living room, punctuated here and there with dialogue from the television. She was right, I didn't need to stay. She could take care of herself.

That I actually wanted to stay was only because Alex would be home soon after. Despite my misgivings about our little situation, I could not go back to the way things were. I figured I might as well enjoy it while I could, whether it ruined me or not. It was a matter of principle, and no self-respecting woman would turn it down. Not in good conscience. The thought made me laugh in spite of myself. Of course I would claim anything to make my decisions seem like they were good ones. Only *I* could convince myself of something so preposterous. All I could do was hold on and hope I came out of the maelstrom with minor injuries.

Tired of rationalising, I finally turned off the television and poked around for something to occupy my time until Alex returned. There was still some washing up to be done from dinner; Mary told me to leave it and someone would do it in the morning, that someone being Alex. But I couldn't inflict that torture on the man, no matter how troublesome he was. I was a messy cook and the crusty pots and pans more than illustrated the story of my war with the mushroom risotto.

I grabbed my mobile from the table in front of me and went to the kitchen, shutting the door so as not to bother Mary. Choosing my music and setting it on low, I tied my hair up with the elastic on my wrist. But I wasn't a few minutes into my task when I heard the front door open and shut followed by keys dropping on a hard surface to herald his arrival. Hard-soled shoes tapped on the wood floors as the owner moved his way back to the kitchen.

He pushed open the door and I turned to glance at him.

"Hi, sorry," I said. "I had to finish this stuff from dinner."

Alex did not reply, but a slow smile spread across his lips as he moved further into the room. The long, lean length of his body pressed into my back. Strong arms encircled and pulled me away from the sink. I dropped the pot in my hands.

His lips, oh those lips, ghosted across the shell of my ear and grazed my earlobe as he bent to place a more solid kiss low on my neck where it met my shoulder. I shouldn't have been surprised by my own eager response to his attentions, but something in his lips—in the possessive clench of his fingers on my waist and hips—completely weakened my resolve. And he knew it.

He swayed with me to the soft strains of music coming from my mobile, unwilling to release me from his arms as he shifted the weight on his feet. "Where's my mum?"

Sharp teeth grazed my neck. One of his hands travelled around my torso and splayed across my abdomen, dipping lower to the apex between my thighs. He pressed firmly until I shifted, my bum fitting perfectly against his pelvis and the hard length beneath his trousers. I purred gently and shut my eyes. "She's gone to bed."

"Good," he quietly—dangerously—breathed against my ear.

I shivered, though I was burning for him. Gooseflesh rose on my skin and tightened my nipples uncomfortably against my clothing.

Alex reached out to shut off the running water. I didn't need confirmation, in that moment, to know exactly what he wanted and why he asked me to stay until he returned from his work engagement. Though I had no doubt of his concern for his mother's comfort and wellbeing, his true intention was to get me alone. As ashamed as I was to admit it, I was completely fine with that.

I turned to face him. He wasted no time claiming my lips for his own. My body hummed to life and I succumbed to the insistent, intoxicating strength. His hips pressed against mine, pushing me back until I connected with the countertop and sink behind me.

"I thought about you all night long," he murmured against my mouth, his tongue slipping between my parted lips when I opened them to reply.

I lifted my arms and wrapped them around his neck in an effort to bring him closer to me. I needed some solid tether to the physical world, but realised too late my hands were still covered in soapy water. Soapy water and his particularly hot McQueen suit did not go together.

I pushed back on him with my hips. He tried in vain to ignore it. before reluctantly stopping his seduction with an angry growl.

I didn't try to hide my ire. "Oh, stop. Would you please just hold on a minute?"

My eyes darted around for the tea towel I set out before I began the washing up, but located it across the room. Why had I left it so far out of reach? I didn't want to leave my spot. Not in the least. But it had to be done. If Alex stained the coat in any way, I would be responsible for finding a replacement. I didn't delight at the thought of the extra work.

I wiggled out of his grasp and walked over to the towel, glancing back at Alex, who finally seemed to understand. His body relaxed and he silently looked toward the ceiling as though it warranted a prayer. As he did this, he carefully slipped out of the coat and tossed it across the clean counter top. "I would have taken it off for you if you asked me."

My laugh wheezed from my lungs. I shot him an incredulous look. "You really don't understand that I can barely breathe with you around, much less talk."

His only response was to give me a hungry, wolfish grin before he advanced on me once more. He wasn't going to waste a moment more on pleasantries, and honestly, I didn't care. The way he approached me set my blood on fire. I already ached for blessed release from the agony building within my body.

"I'm glad it's the same for both of us, then," he finally whispered.

"Is it?"

His dark, throaty chuckle made me tremble as I found myself once more pinned to the cupboards. He kissed me with the sole purpose to disorient; I was sure of it when his fingers tugged at the cloth covering my hips. The soft fabric inched slowly up my legs, tickling, sliding, bunching in his hands until it was at my waist. I couldn't stop him had I wanted to, as his hands finally reached beneath my skirt and massaged the underside of my thighs. He grabbed two handfuls of flesh and lifted me a centimetre, his hips pressing until I had no option but to sit back on the hard counter.

The stone surface chilled my blazing flesh, but it was a welcome sensation as overheated as I was with my need for him. I clawed at his chest, searching for buttons on his shirt and finding none. They had to be around somewhere, but my patience, already worn thin, refused to slow down. I fisted the back of his shirt in my hands and drew the tails from where he had tucked them into his belted trousers. He hooked his fingers into my knickers and they were down my legs and tossed aside so quickly I barely registered what happened.

"You're so lovely, bellissima," he hummed against my mouth, a thumb circling my centre. I hissed at the searing heat rocketing through my body and arched back, but bumped my head on the cupboards behind me. A strangled cry of fleeting pain flew out of my mouth and mixed with a laugh, but he devoured the sounds with a soul-deep kiss. He shushed me when a moan replaced my laugh. "She will come out if we're too loud."

I couldn't have cared less and rotated my hips as much as my position would allow in time with his marvellous fingers. The coil within me tightened to an unbearable degree. I needed him to release it, but he refused to give me any satisfaction. His hands disappeared from my centre and skated the tops of my thighs to my bum, sliding me a bit until I teetered on the edge of the cupboard.

"Will you be quiet?" he asked, a simple entreaty spoken lightly as though it were something he asked every day. I was confused by the question until he pinned me with a serious stare.

"I could use that towel to gag you, though…" he offered playfully. "Or my tie."

"Don't," I panted and paused to catch my breath, "Don't use the tie."

Questions filled his face, his fingers stilling near my centre again, but not touching. His teasing frustrated me and I let him know it with a disgruntled whine. I attempted to move my hips to achieve the contact I desperately needed, but his hands grabbed and held me firmly in place. His strength was rather surprising. I loved it and hated it at the same time.

"But the *towel* is acceptable?" he asked in amazement.

I lifted my shoulders in what I supposed was a coquettish gesture. "I'll try anything once."

He cocked his head to the side and looked at me as though I was the biggest, most perplexing curiosity he ever met, but the pleasure of finding out that information outweighed everything else. With a ravenous grin, and a challenging lift of an eyebrow, he kissed first my mouth and then the point of my dress where the neck formed a v between my breasts. The blue gaze flicked up to my eyes for a moment and I saw nothing but mischief before he slipped lower and rested on a knee between my legs.

It was difficult to maintain my silence, however, when he pressed his lips to the burning flesh on the inside of my thigh. I sucked in a breath and reached for him, twining my fingers in his curls as he drew his tongue along my skin. He paused and blew cool air down the moistened path, lighting a new fire in its wake. Teeth nipped nearer to my core, pushing a low keen from my lips.

"Don't tempt me to actually use it," he warned against my skin, draping one of my legs over his body, knee bent over shoulder.

I bit my lip the instant his mouth settled onto my heat, nearly coming out of my skin. The back of my head thudded softly against the cupboard door when I rested against it, in the hopes it would hold me upright during the onslaught of sensation and pleasure.

"Alex, come here," I pleaded with him. I needed him. I needed all of him. He wasn't listening to me; or was he listening and wilfully ignoring me?

"Please," I tried again.

I wanted to make him listen, but it was useless. My voice was unconvincing in the wake of his ministrations. His tongue worked like a ratchet, tightening and seeking and building the pressure within me. The blood in my ears pounded as his glorious fingers joined his mouth, fucking me until at last I reached my breaking point. My body tensed and I clamped my teeth down hard on my lip. His hands steadied my hips until I settled, heat and euphoria pumping through every cell in my body.

With a final kiss on the opposite thigh, he rose on his feet. Through heavy-lidded eyes I watched his hands undoing the belt I had neglected before he sidetracked me. I reached for him, but he deflected my hand.

"Don't," he said sternly, drawing the zipper down.

"But I…"

A muscle in his jaw clenched. He caught me around my waist and shifted me further away from the counter until I had to put my shaky legs on the ground. I hardly had any time to steady myself on the gelatinous muscle and bone before he turned me to face the cupboard.

"If you touch me, I'll lose it," he intoned in my ear, just above a whisper. I shivered at the sensation of his warm breath there. "And I want to do that here." His hand cupped my sex. "I was completely honest when I said I'd been thinking about you and about this all night. I'm sure the photos from the event will cause quite a stir."

Sure fingertips pressed on the hollow of my back, bending me until I set both hands on the cupboard in front of us. I moaned at the feeling of him pressing into me, stretching me. He paused and sucked in a breath as his hands clutched my hips and thrust the rest of his length, groaning with the movement. My fingers curled into the cold, hard stone beneath them. I hated that I couldn't watch him, but loved the fullness I felt in our position.

Then, he withdrew and thrust again. I saw stars. Beautiful, brilliant supernovas in a black velvet sky. He wasted no time setting a punishing but steady rhythm with his hips. I lifted and pressed my back against the scratchiness of his still-clothed chest, reaching behind his head and turning to kiss him. He released a long, somewhat strangled, hum of pleasure and emptied himself a moment later. I bent to accommodate his deep, dying thrusts; he followed me down, his hands partially covering mine and gripping the stone counter for support.

We stood like this for a few moments, waiting for the world to right itself on its axis. My heartbeat slowly evened out and the blood rushing in my ears gave way to our ragged breathing and the sounds of soft music still coming from my mobile across the room.

Lips brushed at the nape of my neck. "Will you stay awhile longer?"

"I should leave soon," I said quietly. "If I'm taking the Tube."

He chuckled and righted us, turning me around to face him. My dress worked its way over my hips and fell back around my ankles. I felt the proof of our activities between my legs and shifted uncomfortably. He arranged himself in his trousers and I stepped forward, kissing his lips gently, dragging my fingers through his messed hair.

He shuddered. "I'll take you home later."

"But your mum will be left alone," I argued.

"Then stay the night with me," he said.

I stared at him in the oddly quiet room with the soft music playing in the background. "I have to leave early. I don't want your mum to think—"

"I'm sure she's already figured it out."

I closed my eyes. She hadn't said anything to me about it, but even I had to admit she probably knew about us. Still, it didn't feel good to admit to having an affair. Not even when his mother didn't like Georgina.

"Stay the night with me," he asked again. "I've not finished with you."

With a sigh, I shook my head. "Fine."

"Switch your mobile off." He looked toward the device across the room. "And let's go upstairs."

I followed his commands, hoping I didn't seem too eager to comply. As much as I didn't want to face his mum in the morning and explain what happened, I couldn't very well resist him. Not after that.

How could I ever actually refuse him? God help me, I wanted *more*. I wanted it all.

When I turned back around, he stood there with his hand outstretched and waiting for me. I took it without reluctance.

CHAPTER 15

I COULDN'T REMEMBER A MORNING where I woke in such a state of relaxation that all I wanted to do was stretch my sore limbs and snuggle in the soft sheets covering me. I wanted to bask in the glow of the feeling. I felt no urgency. No need to get up and perform. The sedate laziness filled me with a sense of peace.

That was, of course, until I remembered, in my groggy waking mind, where I was and what we did. I looked at the clock and sat bolt upright, clutching the sheet to my bare chest to prevent it from falling away.

Where was Alex? Why had he let me sleep so late? Lindsay and Sam were probably wondering what happened to me. Lindsay probably deduced where I ended up when I didn't come home, but there was still a chance that he called out the Met to search for me.

I was furious that Alex hadn't listened to me. He promised, before we both fell asleep, to sneak me out of the house before his mother woke; it was the price for staying with him longer than I should have.

The last thing in the world I wanted to do was face Mary as I scurried out of the house in the morning, tail tucked between my legs in shame. I had yearned for a "mother" like her my entire life. Having found something like it in her, I was convinced helping Alex cheat on his girlfriend might ruin it all. Though she kept no secrets about her position on Georgina and Alex's relationship, what would it say for me sleeping with her son while he was still in the relationship? I didn't want her to think poorly of me. I couldn't stand even more guilt.

I jumped out of bed and rummaged through the room for my clothing, finally finding my dress crumbled in a heap beneath the heavy blanket Alex discarded at some point in the night. My knickers, on the other hand, were either missing or stuffed somewhere impossible to find in my haste to dress.

In the edge of my memory, I recalled Alex tossing the garment aside in the kitchen. I couldn't remember picking them up after we decided to continue upstairs to his room. A moment of mortification surged through me, and I prayed either Alex picked them up or Mary hadn't gone into the kitchen. That would only make matters worse, especially since I didn't intend to inquire about them. Fortunately, my ankle-length dress wouldn't make it too conspicuous that I wore nothing beneath it going home on the train.

Stopping off in the connecting bathroom, I did what I could with a comb to tame my hair, but the fine-toothed thing barely made a dent in the curly-headed helmet. I silently wished my elastic hair tie hadn't snapped when Alex buried his hands in the mess at some point in the night. There was another tie and a proper brush in my handbag, but it would be a task getting to it without anyone seeing me in such disarray.

In resignation of my plight, I stood tall, rolled my shoulders back and lifted my chin. This would be one of the most epic walks of shame ever endured, but by God, I was going to own it. After I went downstairs, there was no going back.

I slowly descended the old staircase and paused when I heard voices talking quietly somewhere on the ground level. The hushed nature in which they spoke told me I wasn't meant to hear their discussion, but I couldn't help but pick out my name in the mixture of words.

"I hope you know what you're doing with Emilia, Alexander," Mary was saying.

Alex sighed dramatically. I pressed back against the wall even though the staircase let out into a long corridor; none of the rooms had a good view of it. It made me feel better.

"She's a lovely girl," she continued. "And I don't want to see her hurt by my son. I raised you better than this."

"I know, Mum," he replied.

"If it comes down to it, I'm keeping her and getting rid of you."

It was an ultimatum if ever I heard one.

"Geez, thanks!" He sounded incensed, but I almost whimpered aloud knowing I made such a positive impression on Mary. I was loath to see the disappointment in her eyes when I appeared downstairs. Clearly, she knew I spent the night.

"I'm serious," Mary said.

Alex mumbled something under his breath. "I just... I just have to—"

When he stopped, I leaned forward, stretching and craning my body in an attempt to get closer... to hear in the otherwise silent house. Perhaps he was having trouble finding the right words. But then I remembered this was Alexander Thorne and the man had an uncanny ability to always fill the void with words even when no one wanted them.

He took another breath. "I just have to—"

A floorboard on the stair beneath my feet groaned loudly with the change in pressure.

No!

"Emilia?" he called.

I righted myself, patted my frizzy hair down and smoothed out my rumpled dress. With a fortifying intake of air into my body, I stepped down the last few stairs and continued into the living room. Alex's mum sat propped up in her chair, and Alex looked at me over the rim of a porcelain teacup. He set the tea on the table and stood up as he brushed off his hands.

"Good morning," he bade, back to polite business as usual. He looked freshly showered and well-groomed compared to me, who looked appallingly bedraggled. It infuriated me even further, if that was at all possible.

"Alex said you fell asleep on the settee and he offered you the second guest room so you didn't have to go back in the middle of the night," Mary explained with a pleasant smile. "How did you sleep?"

My mouth dropped open in confusion at her words, and I stared at her for longer than was strictly necessary in my dumbfounded state. Did she really believe that? The sparkle in her eyes and the words I overheard confirmed that she knew exactly what we were up to all night, and that I hadn't even seen the inside of "the second guest bedroom" nor knew there was another. But then I relaxed. Even though nothing could diffuse the awkwardness of the confrontation, she did make it possible to leave with some amount of dignity intact.

Bless you, Mary.

"Uh, um," I began, searching for words and wishing my mind hadn't gone completely blank in my shock. "I, er, slept well, thank you."

Flicking my gaze up to Alex, his smug grin made my stomach flutter with excitement, but also made me want to slap it off his face. He didn't even care we were discussing our sex life in front of his mother without really discussing it. I wished the ground would swallow me whole and end my torment. Anything was preferable to this situation.

"I, um, I need to go home." I paused a second to swallow away the stiltedness in my voice. "I'm sure Lindsay and Sam are worried about me."

"I'm sure." Alex bent down to grab the key ring from the table where he dropped it when he came home. "I'll drive you—"

"I'm fine," I said in a rush. "No need to do that."

I grabbed my shoes from the floor beside the table and slipped them on before spinning around and trying to remember what I did with my—

"Handbag?" The laughter in his voice was not lost on me. He held it out in one hand.

I grabbed it from him but did not put it on my arm. "Thanks."

Alex inclined his head and took the moment to touch my back, his hands burning through the thin layer of clothing covering my body. The fingers shifted over the curve of my hip and bum possessively, ascertaining I had not found my knickers. Right in front of his mother, no less! I almost punched him, but ultimately restrained myself.

"Coat," I commanded and pulled away, not able to meet Mary's eyes as I escaped into the foyer. He followed me lazily as I took my coat from the cupboard and slipped it over my shoulders.

"I'll take you home," he reiterated.

"What if someone sees you?" I whispered. "Us?"

Alex shrugged. "We'll be fine."

"Famous last words," I shot back, heading toward the door. I made it outside into the warm sun and took a deep breath.

Alex yelled back to Mary that he would return soon and warned her not to do anything crazy while he was away. She agreed, but I had learned enough about Mary to know she wouldn't sit still with him gone.

He strode over to his Land Rover and turned to look at me. "Well?" he inquired with an expectant tone, waving his arm toward the open passenger seat.

I looked down the street both directions and then back at him. As much as I didn't want to give him the satisfaction of winning, going home in a private car was preferable to facing the half knowing, half laughing strangers on the Tube. They would take one look at me and correctly work out just what my night had been like.

With a huff, I marched my way around the vehicle. He held the door until I relaxed back into the leather seat, then made his way around to the driver's side. I dug the small plastic hair brush and emergency elastic holder from inside my handbag and pulled down the visor mirror to attempt a miracle. Alex climbed into his seat and looked over at me with no little amount of amusement at my current state. He released a contented laugh and shook his head before sticking the key in the ignition.

"It's no use, you know," he remarked, sliding his aviators on his face and checking mirrors before backing the vehicle out of the drive.

The momentum of the vehicle forced me to pause the hasty brushing, something which would just make my curls bushier, but the worst of the snarls would be worked through enough to pull them back.

At his words, however, I turned to him. "And why not?"

"Because you look thoroughly fucked, whether you fix your hair or not," he answered.

I grumbled something incomprehensible at him.

"You're prickly in the morning," he said.

"I can be prickly any time you ignore my express wishes. You just let me hang out there and your mum knew all along."

Alex sighed. "I told her you slept in the other bedroom. I gave you an out."

"I've known your mother for like five minutes and even I know that your mother didn't believe it."

"Where am I going?" he said, confusing me for a moment before I realised he was asking for directions.

"Westminster." I hit a nasty tangle and cringed at the pain in my scalp. "Why did you let me sleep in anyway? Do you just do these things to upset me?"

The smile remained on his face, but he did not answer me.

"Well, you bloody well did. I hope you're happy."

When he still did not reply, I stopped what I was doing and looked at him. He huffed. "No, I didn't do it to upset you. I did it because I thought you needed the rest."

"I don't care if I haven't slept in twenty fucking days," I said hotly. "When I ask you to do something, just listen to me and do it."

He was unmoved by my complaint and actually seemed to become more aloof in his comportment. "I don't regret my decision to let you sleep. As a matter of fact, I'm glad I did it. Why can't you just let go for a bit and let things happen the way they do?"

"Because then bad things happen."

"You don't always have to be on a schedule or plan things."

"Yes, I do."

"No, you don't," he said. "Constantly trying to control when things will happen and when they won't happen is going to get you nowhere in life. All that pressure? All that worry? It's not healthy. It's going to get you a major breakdown by the time you're thirty-five. You'll go off the rails and you'll be nowhere but back where you started."

I scoffed. He clearly didn't know that I already had a nervous breakdown. Nor did he know that it happened at the ripe old age of nineteen and I had been clawing out of the hole ever since. "Someone has to be in control. Otherwise it would be utter chaos."

"Of course someone has to be in control," he acknowledged. "But you could at least share the load with someone else."

"Oh, so you think you're the one I should share it with?"

He glanced at me. "Tell me you wouldn't be happier letting someone else dote on you."

"I want nothing more than to not have to care all the time. To not have to worry about running someone else's life. Or taking care of my brother. Sometimes I just want to do things that involve me, and my art, and my passions, but I don't have that luxury. That's the luxury of the rich," I explained. "It's the luxury of someone else who doesn't have so much to worry about."

"What if I could give it to you?" he asked. His voice was soft but firm, with no amount of jest or untruth within the words.

"And you think you can give that to me?" The incredulity in my voice made him flinch. "You think you can do that while you're in a relationship with *another woman*?"

"Well…" He drew out the word as though he were contemplating it. But he didn't add anything.

I shut the visor and slumped back into the seat with my arms crossed over my chest. Tense silence followed as we continued toward Westminster. I just didn't have anything left to say to him and I didn't want to think about what he said. Eventually, I threw my hands up in disgust, unable to take the uneasy silence much longer. "Look, I'm just angry because it was your mother this happened in front of."

"It was only my mum," he said. "She doesn't care."

"No, but I care!" I exclaimed. "You don't get it, do you? I've never had an actual mother figure in my life and she's just… she's been nothing but amazing to me. I don't want to jeopardise that."

Alex sighed and turned to look at me when we stopped at a signal light. "I'm fairly certain my mother loves you more than she does me at the moment."

I pursed my lips.

"And unless you were to… I don't know… murder someone, I don't foresee that changing," Alex continued. "Not even if we were to have loud sex everywhere in her house, which I considered last night, by the way."

His comment absolutely floored me. The shamelessness of his sexual appetite was both completely aggravating and intoxicating. Once again I wondered how one man could be so bloody confusing.

"Where am I going exactly?" he finally asked.

"In life?" I replied with an ill-tempered, challenging arch of my right eyebrow.

He cast me an exasperated glare. "No, what is your address?"

"I'll direct you when we get there," I said. "Turn right after three more signals, though."

In the lull in conversation, I fished my mobile out of my handbag and finally turned it on to hundreds of emails, calls, and text messages. I started at the top of the list with the most recent. And then I nearly had another nervous breakdown.

"Fucking fuck!" I swore at my mobile. "Did you know?"

"Know what?"

I held my mobile up though he couldn't read it as he drove. "That Georgina is on her way back *early*?"

Alex looked at me. Of course he did.

"She's due to land in forty minutes," I read aloud, trying not to hyperventilate. "It'll take that fucking long to get to the airport."

"Emilia, calm down," he told me.

"Oh, God. I have no time to call the car company. I can't get cleaned up... I can't..."

Alex slammed on his brakes and pulled into a parking spot on the side of the road. He turned to look at me.

"I will collect her from the airport. Don't worry about the car company. Take a deep breath."

I wanted to hurt him.

"Emilia... breathe," he commanded.

Squinting my eyes at him, I finally let out a long breath and then took another gulp of air. After a few minutes of watching me, he seemed to relax.

"Now... I'll drop you at your flat and I'll go after her," he informed.

"There's no time," I repeated, still anxious. "Just leave me here. It's not that far."

He didn't seem at all pleased with my insistence to be let out of the car, but ultimately he was defeated. He knew I was right. "All right. Fine."

I slung my bag on my shoulder and reached for the door handle. He grabbed my arm and pulled me back against him. When I turned to him, his fingers buried deep into my hair and his lips covered mine in a punishing exchange in front of the whole world passing us by on the pavement. Anyone could see us. Anyone could figure out who was in the driver's seat.

I struggled against his chest until he released me, and then tried to ignore my stomach flipping and the hot tingling centring low in my abdomen. God, my anger was so absolute I could barely think, but all I wanted to do was feel him against me, near me... in me. How could I have let it reach such a point? Why had I done it?

We stared at each other in our breathlessness for a long moment before I carefully and silently backed out of the vehicle. I shut the door and glanced at him as he adjusted his sunglasses and smoothed down his hair. I hadn't realized I messed it up during our kiss.

But I refused to worry about that. My priorities involved getting home and making it over to the studio before Georgina arrived. And I had to do all of it without thinking about him, or how I felt falling asleep in his arms, or the amount of pleasure he gave me those few times I totally lost myself in him. The only emotions I could work with were urgency and anger. They were the only two that wouldn't give my true feelings away to the world.

ALEXANDER
UNMASKED

(THREE MONTHS BEFORE THE MASQUERADE)

CONTRARY TO WHAT EVERYONE BELIEVED, there were good days with Georgina. They were the days we spent little time together; perhaps dinner or some red carpet event would bring us together. After, we'd proceed back to her home where I always spent the night. Those nights inevitably evolved into uncomfortable mornings and bad days before I finally slipped far enough out of her grasp that she couldn't pull me back into her web. After the night of the Halloween party, however, I realized I had to make a serious change in my life. No one deserved living like I did, least of all a man like me with needs not fulfilled by a woman like her.

I resolved to do something about it immediately following the party; even if Emilia didn't want anything to do with me, without Georgina's cumbersome baggage weighing me down I could, at least, find some sort of happiness. But business called Georgina away immediately after Halloween, and she did not return until the beginning of December.

I wasn't about to let another opportunity to end it pass by, so I made my way to Georgina's without delay after calling her to say we needed to talk. Warning her with the standard, if cliché, message seemed gentlemanly enough. I wanted her prepared for what we were about to discuss. It saved me from seeing her immediate anger and, hopefully, leave me with a calmer, more rational person to confront. However, almost instinctually, I knew as soon as I stepped into Georgina's home that fateful December day, I wasn't leaving a single man as I intended.

When I first came into the main room, I found Emilia balancing precariously on a ladder, covered in glitter and attempting to affix an angel to the top of a red and gold themed Christmas tree. The rest of the room looked as though the season vomited all over the place. There wasn't a surface without some sort of Christmas paraphernalia decorating it.

Emilia caught sight of me and puffed her cheeks. "Oh, hey, Alex. Georgina just called. She said she'd be back in a few minutes."

"Lovely," I said, clapping my hands and rubbing them together. "Do you need help with that?"

"Huh?" she asked.

I pointed to the angel in her hands.

She shook her head. "Oh, no, I've got it."

She lifted onto the balls of her feet, teetering on the edge of the topmost ladder rung. The tip of her pink tongue stuck out of her lips and between her teeth until the angel at last slipped into place. The triumph in her eyes was infectious.

Covered in the debris of Christmas' trimmings, Emilia was gorgeous. She gracefully inched her way off the ladder and looked up at her work before seeking my approval. "What do you think?"

"She's splendid."

Emilia hummed. "She?"

I blinked. "Oh, the angel."

The woman didn't believe me, but she shrugged it off and returned to work.

"Why are you doing the decorating anyway?" I asked, hoping to change the subject.

Emilia folded the ladder and set it against a wall. "She doesn't like strange decorating companies in the house."

"No, I guess what I mean is, why doesn't she do it herself?"

She shot me a glance. It spoke volumes. Of course Georgina wouldn't dare to dirty her hands with such a menial task. I couldn't imagine not doing something like this myself. Holiday decorations were a deeply personal thing for me; Christmas was my favourite holiday of the year. I literally waited on tenterhooks for the day my mother called to set up a time to decorate her house. She said she only needed me because I was tall and could reach high locations, like the tops of trees, but I didn't mind. I loved it. The season always turned me into a little kid.

It was the one day or so in the year where I didn't feel all the weight of my thirty-four years on my shoulders. I had no cares. No job. No sycophantic people using me for their own gain. In the place of all those things were family, good food, and lots of laughter.

"Do you like doing the decorations?" I asked. It was important to me to know she liked them.

Emilia shrugged. "It's okay. I rather not be covered in glitter for a week afterward, but I like the sparkle and the lights just fine."

I nodded and walked over to a chair, relaxing as much as I could into the stiff leather. "Do you have any traditions?"

"Not really," she replied, placing a small box on a side table. She gingerly unpacked the protective cushion innards.

Realising she wasn't going to give me her whole life story—even if I asked her bluntly—I sighed. Clearly, I needed a different tactic. "Do you want anything special for Christmas?"

"Not particularly."

She was completely exasperating.

"Well, I do want to go see *The Nutcracker*," she added as an afterthought. "I've always wanted to see it, but I never have."

"You've never seen *The Nutcracker*?" My words came out more incredulously than I intended. I just couldn't imagine someone never seeing the iconic ballet. Even I watched it on occasion—and I did not claim any particular fondness for the theatre format of a ballet. It was mind numbingly dull.

Emilia's annoyance came through her glare at me. "I've seen recorded versions. But I want to see it live. With the Royal Ballet."

"Ah," I replied. "Well, maybe Father Christmas will bring tickets for you."

She chuckled. "Maybe."

"Baby?"

Georgina's nasally voice shot through me like ice, forcing a simultaneous cringe and shudder from me. I covered my sigh and looked around for her. She dawdled in through the studio door, a large handbag on her arm and black sunglasses over her eyes despite the gloomy weather outside. After divesting herself of her coat and carelessly tossing everything on a couch, she stopped to look at the decorations.

"Thank you, Emilia," she said. "You may finish tomorrow."

"But I'm almost—"

Georgina cut her off with nothing more than a pointed stare. "Have the afternoon off. I won't need you until the morning."

Emilia nodded. "Yes, of course, Georgina. Good night, Alex."

She scurried through the door into the studio, closing it behind her. Georgina made one revolution around the tree, carefully assessing the decorations with a critical eye. I listened to Emilia exit and lock up. Georgina moved a few ribbons around, switching ornaments here and there. Shifted a garland on a branch. Nothing too strenuous, of course.

After all of the nitpicking, she made her way over to me and crawled straight into my lap. "How was your day?"

"Exhausting," I told her, shifting uncomfortably under her negligible weight. "I don't have much time before call, though."

"I didn't expect you until after the show."

I swallowed. "Well, I didn't want to wait. I wanted to talk to you... get something off my mind."

Georgina's shrewd aquamarine eyes shot me a pointed, glaring look. She pushed away from me and stood up, hands on hips. "You seriously aren't going to do this to me right now!"

"Georgina, let's be serious," I said. "We were never a real 'thing.' We drive each other up a wall. We had our fun. You got what you wanted out of me."

"What was that, pray tell?" she asked shrilly.

I didn't bother to contain the derisive guffaw I emitted. "You got a leg up. You got the paparazzi attention you wanted."

Georgina rolled her eyes. She walked over to her purse and opened it, rummaging for something, though it was likely her compact. Whenever she didn't want to look at me, she checked or reapplied her makeup. It drove me mad.

"It's just not working out," I announced.

She stood back from her purse with a paper clutched between her bony fingers. With little more fanfare, she shoved the paper beneath my nose, demanding that I read it. At first, the black type on bright white paper didn't make any sense. I could have been reading gibberish for all I knew, but slowly, the letters began to grow clear.

As did the meaning.

It sucked all the air from my body. "What?"

"You read it."

"Are you sure? You've been to the—"

She huffed. "I've just been. Where do you think I got this pamphlet?"

"You can't be," I protested. "We used—"

"Did we?" She arched one of her perfectly groomed brows at me.

"How far along?"

She sighed. "Five weeks. It was Halloween—"

"How did it happen?"

She puckered and smacked her lips like she had sucked on a sour lemon.

"Well, I know how it happened… but it just *can't* happen," I said. "Not now."

Georgina tore the paper out from under my nose. She stomped

back to her purse. "Well, it happened. What are you going to do about it?"

"Just because it happened…" I let the words die on my lips. "We can't stay together, Georgina. I can't stay with you."

"You will stay with me. At least until—"

"No, I won't," I said. "Of course I'll help you out and everything, and we can discuss—"

Georgina spun around and advanced on me with fire flaring in her eyes. "You *will* stay with me."

I couldn't believe it. Of course she would insist; I supposed it was her right to do so. But I couldn't. Even for the sake of an unborn child, how could I, in good conscience, stay with her? I did not love her and I was convinced I never would. Particularly not while I pined for another.

"Georgina, please, be reasonable," I tried to placate her, even though I was asking the impossible.

She huffed again. "If you leave, I will tell everyone—*everyone*—how you left your pregnant girlfriend to deal with it on her own. I don't think Jack wants that kind of public relations nightmare, do you? Do you want it? With a predominantly female fan base?"

"But I wouldn't abandon—"

"Perhaps not." She shrugged. "But that doesn't matter to them. What matters is how it *appears*, right? Isn't that what Jack's always saying? Image is built from appearance, not actual fact? I could spin anything in my favour and make it stick. Because *I'm* the innocent one in all of this. Well, your child and I are."

I jumped from my seat, driving her back a few steps. I hated the momentary fear passing over her face, as though she expected me to physically hurt her. As furious as I was at the situation—at her—that she thought I could ever do something like that killed me.

"Look," she breathed. "We can make it work. It'll help both of us. You can be the doting father-to-be, and it'll soften my image a little bit."

"I'm not doing this. I'm not." I shook my head and pushed past her to go to the front door.

Georgina followed quickly after me. "We won't tell anyone about it until after the first trimester or when I start showing."

"This isn't—" I stopped dead.

What was I going to say? It was her fucking choice, after all, and people would quickly and easily guess who the father was. When they found out I wanted nothing to do with Georgina, and by extension my child, my image would take a hit. A huge hit. She wouldn't have to say anything to anyone. The court of public opinion was unforgiving at the best times and downright ruthless in their crusade for moral correctness at the worst. They'd all jump to the same conclusion.

Not for the first time I wished the veracity of my career were based on my skill as an actor, not on the person I appeared to be in an interview.

I fisted my hair in my hands and closed my eyes, praying for guidance. None came. So I looked at her and shook my head. "If I do this, we are absolutely not going to say anything to anyone, especially the press. I do not want them in the middle of this. I'm at my wits end being followed and hounded because of you."

"Alex," she said matter-of-factly. "They'll find out eventually."

"Yes, but for right now, while I sort this monumental cock up out…"

Georgina rolled her eyes at me. I put my hand on the door knob and opened the door.

"Where do you think you're going?"

"I'm leaving," I said. "I need to go. Right now."

"We have to discuss this."

I spun on her. "I couldn't give a fuck what we've got to discuss. I need time to process this."

"Alex—"

"No!" I yelled. "We have nine months. We'll figure it out. But certainly not right now. I'm too fucking angry right now."

Her fingers curled around my arm in a death grip. "Alex…"

I peeled her fingers back and stepped out onto the stoop. Georgina snarled at me, stomped her foot and, seeing her imminent defeat, slammed the door in my face. I stood staring at the carved wood for a decent length of time, letting the situation fully sink into my brain, but the freezing rain dripping on my head from the roof overhang didn't allow me to do so for long. I turned and ran down the steps toward my vehicle.

Slipping inside, I sat there, staring ahead through the rain-glazed windscreen. I just couldn't work out how it happened. I had been careful. I was always careful with women, for this purpose alone. And she certainly never fostered my trust in that respect. But stranger things had happened.

How was I ever going to be a father? I wasn't prepared to be a father. Not at this point in my life… in my career. Of course I would do my best, because I never backed down from a challenge. I would do what needed to be done. But it couldn't have possibly come at a worse time.

A throbbing began in my head, first at the base of my neck and slowly spread further up the back of my head. I needed to go. I needed to stop thinking about it. My only recourse was to escape to the theatre, where I would have to be in an hour anyway, hoping I could lose myself in the character. But even poor old Petruchio could barely handle his secrets or his Shrew.

What hope had I of doing the same with mine?

CHAPTER 16

ALEX HAD PARKED his Land Rover in front of the studio door by the time I arrived and they were nowhere to be found. Half running, half speed walking from the Tube, I slowed my steps in an attempt to catch my breath before bursting into the studio. My lungs burned with the chilly air and my head refused to stop spinning with the whirlwind the morning brought. Georgina wouldn't suffer my tardiness, least of all after she attempted to contact me more than ten times before leaving France, but I prayed that moving quickly was enough to mitigate any terrible punishment.

Of course, if she did punish me somehow, I probably deserved it. The responsibility for mucking it up rested on my shoulders. I switched off my mobile and spent the night with Alex without being more vocal about what I needed him to do in the morning. I let him have control of the situation, giving him the power to wake me when and if he saw fit, or to warn me if she was coming home early or not.

It was exactly as I had feared. I lost track of myself and my obligations for one night of bone-melting pleasure. Perhaps last night was but a small dose of it, but what would happen on a larger scale? What if I truly went all the way down the rabbit hole with him and ended up having to face a fate worse than Georgina's reprimand for not answering her calls? As much as I wanted to follow him, this only proved to me that I couldn't trust him or myself. I had to stop before it was too late.

After I finally caught my breath, I climbed the front steps like they were Mount Everest and entered the studio. Alex and Georgina's raised voices—neither of them happy—seeped through the walls from the living portion of the building. Someone shut the door dividing the two sections, for which I was equally glad and disappointed. What could they be arguing about? Despite Georgina's nature, Alex never argued with Georgina. Well, at least they didn't do it as loudly and never around me. He always seemed so above it all by choosing not to engage her in any of the fights she picked. Something had changed.

I stepped into the once-organised studio to find a disaster zone. Ten pieces of luggage were all stacked and lined up in the centre of the room. Five black garment bags from various fashion houses were thrown over one of the clothing racks. An eleventh piece of luggage lay opened to the right of the stacked luggage with the contents spilling out as though someone had started the process of emptying it but became sidetracked in the process—

Or thought better of the manual labour and left it for me to do.

I set my bag down on the desk. The arguing ceased abruptly and the door opened on creaky hinges.

"And where have you been?" The bitterness in Georgina's voice made me sigh.

I breathed in deeply and turned to greet her. "My apologies, Georgina… I was—"

She cut me off with a hard look, her posture ramrod straight and frosty. Alex popped up behind Georgina, following her into the studio. "I gave you an informal holiday. I expected you to be near your mobile at all times."

"I'm sorry, really," I apologised again. I dared a look at Alex. I saw fury in his eyes barely restrained in a mask of indifference, his hands sullenly shoved into his pockets and his back rigid with discomfort. I almost felt bad for him.

Almost.

He deserved whatever Georgina gave him, as far as I was concerned. After the way he treated me—not telling me she intended to come home earlier, just to name one infraction—I couldn't care less how much she upset him.

Georgina breezed over to the open piece of luggage and bent down to pick up a blouse. "I'm very disappointed, Emilia."

I sighed again. There wasn't anything else I could say or wanted to say.

"It really made me question my need in employing an assistant," she continued. "If I could do all of the rescheduling myself, why do I need you?"

"I apologise, Georgina." I absolutely refused to grovel, but I had a feeling that was exactly what she wanted.

"You're really very lucky Alex was able to get away from his *injured* mother to retrieve me from the airport."

Injured fucking mother, my arse. If she only knew what he had actually been doing. I snorted in my complete annoyance, but realised too late I did it loud enough for her to hear and it would only make a bad situation much, *much* worse.

Georgina froze and narrowed her eyes at me. "You think that's amusing, do you?"

"No, of course I don't—"

I stopped when she held up a hand.

"Apologise to Alex."

I would be damned before I ever said anything remotely apologetic to the man after the way he had behaved, even if my words had the power to smooth over the situation.

"Georgina…" Alex spoke through gritted teeth.

She fixed him with a glare. "What? You don't think it was completely rude of her to make that noise?"

Alex's lips pressed into a firm line and I looked at Georgina.

Georgina scoffed. "She's being completely insolent and you're going to let her do it?" She turned to me again. "Apologise to him."

"I refuse to apologise," I said. The words were lifeless within me as I stared at the man over Georgina's head. Alex made no movement, his face expressionless. We both knew his mother was just a comfortable scapegoat. He understood why I refused to ask for forgiveness for the sound. I only wished I could shout my own frustration at him.

Georgina was furious. "Do it or I'll be forced to… to… fire you!"

Her threat truly made me laugh. Right in her face. She turned red with rage and a volley of hateful words clogged in her throat, the sound resembling a choking animalistic snarl before it died on her lips.

I exhaled. "You can fire me, but you wouldn't have anyone to handle your scheduling or your appointments in L.A. You and I both know you're not going to fire me because word would get back to Clémence and you'll stop getting styling jobs from her. I also know that you really, really want to go to the Oscars with Alex, and if you don't have an assistant to make sure your two clients are dressed, you can't go with him. So, no, I won't be apologising to him."

I wished I had an accessible camera to snap a photo of her unadulterated hatred and disbelief for later, but my mobile was in my handbag on the desk. No one would believe I actually stood up to the cruel beast without visual proof. But Alex saw it. I hoped that meant something to him. I didn't know what, exactly, just something.

Georgina made a small sound and closed her mouth, clenching her jaw for a moment before she spat, "We leave for Los Angeles tomorrow. You need to call and reschedule the jet and our transport when we arrive."

"But Georgina—"

She raised her hand again and advanced on me. "I don't want to *hear* another word out of you."

"Yes, Georgina," I replied contritely.

"We need to leave in the morning. I took two more editorial shoots. One for Saturday and one for Monday," she explained. "Saturday is a

Vanity Fair shoot for Morgan King. Monday is one for me at *Modiste* where I will be giving an interview."

I nodded and returned to the desk to search for my tablet. I clicked through to my calendar; she already added all the pertinent details into the files. My intention was to ask her what her interview with *Modiste* was meant to include. Clémence Dubois, the creative director, was a good personal friend to us both. She launched each of our careers, first as models, and then when Georgina transitioned into styling. But it was unlike Clémence to schedule something without requiring my presence as well, usually in a bid to convince me to come back to modelling. However, I never got to those questions. Not when I saw the other appointment we scheduled for the same day.

"You're double booked on Monday, though. Alex has a shoot—"

"I'm aware of that," she snipped. "You'll go with Alexander and style the shoot."

I eyed him from my spot, searching for some indication of his complete rapture knowing I would be captive to him during the shoot. Had that been the cause of their argument?

"*Vanity Fair* will provide the wardrobe for Morgan," she said, unconcerned with my discomfort. "I will sort my own and pack it. I do, however, need you to empty all of this luggage. I need to refill it."

"Yes, ma'am," I replied. "I'll call and change my reservations for the hotel as well."

Georgina sniffed. "You'll be staying with us for the extra days. There's no sense in paying the ridiculous Oscar week prices at the hotel when you don't need to be there until the middle of the week. Though, now I'm not sure Alex wants you at his house with the way you treated him."

He wouldn't want me there? Ha-fucking-ha. *I* was the one who didn't want to set foot in the place. I glanced up at Alex again and noticed the smug smile on his face. He won. Somehow he worked it out to his advantage. I would have to stay at his home in L.A. It only added more anger to the already roaring fire in my belly. How dare he?

It was wrong and he knew it, but I used up what little leverage I had when I refused to apologise at Georgina's insistence. As it was, she would make me suffer for that insolence. I didn't want to tempt fate.

"Emilia is welcome at the beach house," he said to Georgina.

Georgina nodded. "Get to work. You're already behind on the day."

With her final pronouncement, she whisked herself from the studio and into her living quarters. The door shut with a slam. Alex stood still and then stepped closer to me, pushing me against the wall, out of sight of the door.

"You should have just apologised," he murmured, his voice low. He leaned over to kiss me, but I was quicker than him for once, shoving my hand between our lips before he made contact.

I pushed back on his face until he took a step away from me. "Don't touch me."

"Come on, Emilia…"

Had I not known him, I would have considered it begging. But it was nothing more than a whiny little boy not getting what he wanted.

"Fuck off," I bit out tersely. When he didn't move, I looked at him again. I had never seen the man so upset. "Get out of here! I have work to do, no thanks to you!"

I went to my desk and sat in my chair, desperately trying to work through everything spinning around in my head. There needed to be a definite plan of attack for the work I had to finish before the next morning. Forgetting something might spell my ruin.

When Alex didn't say anything else to me, I finally dared a glance to see if the fury still filled his eyes. He was gone, however. My shoulders sagged in relief and I reached for my mobile.

The calls couldn't wait.

AT SEVEN O'CLOCK THAT EVENING, I finally escaped Georgina's clutches. She stayed fairly silent throughout the day, though it was not due to her forgiveness. When she did deign to speak, the words were snippy and snide in a way that not even her false charm hid them. This was Georgina's brand of the silent treatment, and it appeared I was to be the lucky recipient of it for some time to come. Not that I found it particularly terrible that she spoke to me as little as possible. Without her constant interruptions as per her usual, I finished more work and did it more efficiently.

Even so, the work load did not ease in the mad rush to sort everything before we left in the morning. I staggered home from the Tube that night at nearly eight, half dead from exhaustion, with at least another four hours of work ahead of me at home. There was laundry to do in addition to my own packing, all the while trying to come up with some way to deal with the stress of managing Georgina and my affair with Alex. The situation seemed to be unravelling at an alarming rate right before my eyes, and all without enough time to truly enjoy the guilty pleasures of it. Perhaps it was better this way, but I was still upset.

I let out a soothing sigh and let myself into the flat, only to be bombarded by enthusiastic yelling. Surprised by the sudden sound, I jumped, but then realised Lindsay and Sam were only watching the Man U-Chelsea match they had geared up for all week. No, not watching. Viscerally feeling the match as they complained about the yellow card one of the referees gave a Chelsea forward. They were not, adding insult to my battered ego, excited to see me.

Lindsay was in the middle of some indiscernibly Scottish rant when I stepped into the living room and saw that the uproar also included one other. He looked up at me with a wide, laughing smile and his sparkling ocean water eyes. My stomach dropped.

"Oh my God. Tobias! I feel like a prize idiot."

He looked wonderful in a black suit and dress shirt, the top buttons undone with no tie. Also, I noted, feeling completely at home as he rested in one of the overstuffed armchairs across the room. "I completely forgot we were going out… things happened at the studio… and, oh… I'm just really sorry."

His kind smile didn't leave his face. He gracefully stood from his seat and crossed the room to me. "Don't worry about it, Em."

"Well, it wasn't right," I mumbled.

Tobias's grin widened and he pressed a warm hand on the small of my back. "You can make it up to me by going out for a bite to eat now."

"But I've got so much work I still have to do tonight…" I looked at Lindsay and Sam. "Georgina took on more work and I leave in the morning for the week."

Sam frowned. "Will you still be back in time for practice?"

"Yes, Sam," I assured him quickly. "I'll be back in plenty of time. Don't worry about it."

Come hell or high water, I wasn't staying one minute longer in California than what was currently planned. Georgina could shove it.

"But you've still got to have dinner, right?" Tobias asked.

I nodded. "Well, yeah, but I need to be here to do laundry and stuff. I can't go out."

"No problem," he replied smoothly. "I'll go pick something up and bring it back."

"Where are you going?" Sam asked.

I closed my eyes and shook my head. The subtleties always went over him like a lead balloon. "Sammy…"

Tobias ignored me. "What do you want, Sam?"

"Pizza!"

Tobias laughed at him and clapped his hands together. "Then pizza it is. Where from?"

All three men launched into a debate about which takeaway pizza was better, thus the restaurant they would order from, and then about what toppings, allowing me a moment to slip away from them.

Frankly, I didn't care what they ordered. My stomach had suffered through tight knots all day. There was a slim chance I would actually consume anything. Except a liquid. Like alcohol. I could do alcohol. A *lot* of alcohol.

I stopped in the kitchen and found a bottle of wine, setting it on the countertop. "All right, I'll leave you three to opening and pouring. I'm going to get comfortable."

By the time I switched into my favourite fuzzy jumper and a pair of stretchy trousers, there was more yelling at the telly and Tobias ordering pizza from the closest restaurant. Someone popped the cork from the wine. I paused, with my hand on the handle of my door, listening to the three men bellyache about the play that incited their yelling.

They talked until they laughed at each other. It was so nice to hear that it made a little bit of my stress evaporate. This thing with Tobias, though still rather odd, was nice. And rather than being someone who intentionally tried to interrupt my life, he seemed to slide into my life so naturally I hardly believed it. Nothing like this would ever happen with Alex. Had I even wanted him around my family, I wasn't certain he would fit in with them.

With another sigh, I stepped out into the hall and made my way back to the kitchen to check on the wine. A large goblet of Merlot sat on the counter. I took a long sip, letting the scent of the liquid and the taste on my tongue fill my senses.

"Tobias?"

From his seat in front of the television, he turned to look at me over the breakfast bar. "Hmm?"

"Do you want to come back while I pack?" I asked. "I mean, you're more than welcome to stay out here and yell at the telly, even though it doesn't matter because *they can't hear you.*"

"It makes us feel better!" Lindsay yelled.

Tobias grabbed his wine from the table beside him and joined my side. "It does have a calming effect. I heard that you once threw a shoe at the telly when they killed Lord Putney off of *Evergreen Hills*."

"I did no such thing," I said, aghast and glaring at Lindsay. I was inconsolable when Tobias' character died a spectacular—and aggravating—death in the last series of the show. "Lindsay may have mistaken my shoe for his girly heels."

Lindsay merely lifted his hand and flashed me a reverse V-sign. "Keep your door open, Emilia. We don't want anything untoward happening."

I rolled my eyes and grabbed Tobias' hand, leading him down the hallway to my bedroom. Once we were inside, I closed the door partially to block out the yelling from the other two and glanced around the room. Tobias moved over to the far wall where I kept one of my large landscape paintings on display. He appraised the canvas from top to bottom, side to side, like a seasoned art critic inspecting every visible brush stroke for imperfection. I wondered if he ever looked at me like that.

"Is this yours?" he enquired. "Alex said he found out you were an artist when you were in Paris for Fashion Week."

I cringed at the mention of Alex's name and the fact they talked about me. "It's mine, yes."

Tobias shook his head and whistled lowly. "Why aren't you doing this professionally?"

"It's a sordid tale that I can't really go into tonight," I said. Really, I didn't want to think about it. I set my goblet of wine down on my chest of drawers and opened the cupboard where I stored my luggage. Tobias finally settled on the foot of my bed.

"You know," he began, setting his wine down on the floor beside him, "I think this is the quickest I've ever made it into a girl's room."

I laughed at him and unzipped the luggage in the middle of the floor before returning to my wardrobe to select clothes. "Yes, well, I'm easy, apparently."

Little did he actually know. Some terrible part of me wanted to exclaim that I was fucking one of his closest friends, too, but my filter stopped the words from forming. Even though I really was and it was proof positive of my easiness, I couldn't hurt him like that. Especially if he truly fancied me. Well, unless he already knew...

He chuckled lowly. "No, you're not. If you were, I would have been invited back to your flat the night of the Halloween party at Georgina's."

I paused and looked at him. Memories of the night floated through my head. He and Alex were both exceptionally attractive that night, all prim and proper in their clerical collars and suits. I felt like a bloated, uncomfortable beast in a too-tight corset and a suspender belt pulling obnoxiously on my silk stockings. In a fit of bravery, I wore my hair down. By the end of the evening, I was so sweaty from running this way and that, that I felt even more disgusting. But I remembered Tobias' interest above everything else. He kept me entertained for the better part of the evening between my ordering the help around the party and listening to Georgina complain. Funnily enough, though, I still couldn't recall his interest feeling anything more than platonic.

To divert the path my thoughts were going, I grabbed a handful of hanging garments and tossed them unceremoniously into one of the pieces of luggage. It made Tobias laugh. "That's quite the packing technique."

"I so badly want to leave it in there like that," I remarked. "I'm so sick and tired of emptying and refolding and washing clothes and sorting shit like this. It's all I did today from ten o'clock on."

"I'm sorry," he said sincerely. "I take it that it was a tough day."

I plopped on the floor to begin folding the shirts. "It's been an utterly miserable day."

He slipped down onto the floor with me, stretching his long legs out in front of him with his back against my bed.

"You're going to ruin your lovely suit," I chided.

Tobias laughed. "I know where to go if I need another."

"Do you, now?"

He nodded his head and sipped his wine.

I looked down at what I was doing. "I'm really sorry about tonight. I know this isn't what you had in mind."

"Actually," he murmured, looking at the dark garnet liquid in his glass. "This is pretty close to perfect."

I smiled. "You're being too kind."

He grew silent and watched me as I worked. It wasn't nearly as unnerving as when Alex did the same thing, but it still made me wish we could fill the space between us with words. As much as I liked him, I wasn't comfortable sitting in silence with the man.

After a while, he sighed and leaned forward. "Emilia?"

"Yeah?" I looked up at him, some hair falling in my eyes. I blinked and tossed my head to the side to move it, but it lodged on my eyelashes. Instead, I pushed it back behind my ear.

"Can I be honest with you?"

"Oh, goodness, that doesn't sound good," I said with a little chuckle, refraining from looking at him. I wanted to shield my reactions if what he was going to say hurt me.

"It's just really bothering me and I need to tell you… You know the Halloween party?" he asked.

I nodded.

"I monopolised your time that night in the service of a friend."

The blood drained from my face and my chest constricted. Of course Alex had his hand in it.

"I don't really know why I did it," Tobias continued. "He's a grown man who should be able to do it himself, but he asked me to get to know you because he didn't want Georgina to be suspicious. To be honest, I thought it was a little dubious."

I couldn't physically make myself continue my work. Instead, I sat back and looked at him.

"So you were helping him," I managed to say. "Are you helping him now?"

Tobias met my eyes and held my gaze. "No, and I have no intention to do so in the future. He's been behaving very poorly of late… I mean, there's a lot going on in his life… but I just can't keep doing it. Mostly because I've developed my own feelings for you."

I all but whimpered. Why was this happening to me? Did the universe have it out for me? It was different when I lived in the nebulous, unsure world of "did he or didn't he" to say I could sleep with Alex and unofficially date Tobias. But this announcement changed everything. "You have?"

"I have."

"Why?"

He openly laughed at me. "Why? Because you're the most interesting, intelligent woman I've met in quite a long time."

My face warmed in a deep blush. "When did you know?"

"When I saw you across the airport," he answered.

"Oh," I said dumbly.

"Oh, is right."

I chewed on my lower lip. "Well, it does make sense, I suppose. You were hot and cold all night at your premiere. I couldn't get a sense of what you were getting at. If it was just a friendly kindness to invite me, or if there was something else."

He laughed in spite of himself, picking at imaginary lint on his trousers, an innate, shy boyishness in his actions. "You were sensing my own confusion. I've tried so hard to be a good mate to Alex, being there to help you when he couldn't because he was stuck with Georgina… but I can't deny that I am attracted to you as well."

"You are?" I blurted out.

Of course he is, you ninny. The man already said so.

"I am." He said it with such a finality that a shiver shook my body.

I leaned against the door of my wardrobe. Puffing my cheeks, I shook my head. "Alex has an uncanny ability of convincing people to do stupid things."

"He's very persuasive when he wants to be." Tobias chuckled. "Though I suspect his tactics with you are different than the ones he's employed with me. At least I *hope* they have been."

I refused to discuss Alex any further with Tobias, especially since I couldn't trust him. What if all of this was just an attempt to get more information out of me for his friend? Or worse, if he was just mining for information to determine if I was a bit of a slag? He wanted to know how far Alex and I took our relationship. If Alex hadn't told him, then I sure as hell wasn't going to do so, though I was fairly certain the wildly intelligent man sitting in front of me could deduce enough without a genius level IQ. The painful hitch in his voice, however, gave me pause, as though he suspected I would automatically choose the other man due to those "tactics."

"I guess what I'm trying to say is I would like to get to know more about you without Alex always looking over my shoulder," he said.

"He'll always be looking over our shoulders," I said flatly. "He'll always be there. Pushing and sidling and being rude and possessive and forgetting that the woman he should be concerned about is off being her tactless, ingratiating self."

Tobias let out a low breath and chuckled again, shaking his head. "So you've really gotten to know Alex."

"Unfortunately."

"Has he been so terrible?" Tobias asked.

I sighed and played with my hair, my folding forgotten for the moment. "I'd prefer not to talk about it."

Really, I didn't want to talk about him. As a matter of fact, I wanted to forget about Alex for at least the next twelve hours until the car arrived to ferry me to the private jet. I wanted to forget about the way my heart raced the second I sensed his presence in the same room, and how the touch of his hands and lips on my heated body weakened my knees, and how he felt inside me as we made love in the wee hours of the morning.

I wanted this man sitting in front of me, all boyish shyness and charm, to touch me, and kiss me, and make me weak in the knees though my heart didn't race in the same way. Still, I rose up on my knees and carefully scooted over to him. Tobias watched me, his gaze boring into mine in silent curiosity and expectation.

When I reached him, I took the goblet from his hands and set it aside, throwing one leg over his lap. It was forward, I would admit, even for me, but I had to follow through. I had to push everything negative out of my head and his soothing manner into it. Dropping a large hand to my waist, he drew me closer. Tobias felt like a balm to my wearied nerves, especially when his hands dove into my hair to pull me down to him.

Our lips met in a slow, thoughtful connection, his tenderness kindling glowing embers of warmth within me. My heart thumped inside my chest, a deep beating that quickened as I settled my weight back onto his legs. He moved with me, unwilling to stop, a hand slipping to support the small of my back while the other held my neck, fingers curling and pulling at the long strands of my hair.

Despite his mild-mannered reactions to my temptation, I couldn't mistake a gentle fervour thrumming just below the surface of his cool and collected exterior. He hid a wealth of untapped passion underneath, all waiting to be let loose. I felt it in the way he held me and in the way his strong fingers massaged my scalp. Nothing about him was rushed, or needy, or calculating, or punishing, or angry.

It made me sigh softly. It was amazing, yet too perfect.

I loved having a man pining—yearning—for me. I wanted to feel that all-consuming heat. I wanted to be pushed against a wall and fucked. Or bent over a kitchen counter and taken from behind. I needed clawing and ripping clothes and missing knickers in the morning. Would—*could*—Tobias ever reach such a point? I didn't know. Acknowledging that truly pained me. Otherwise, he was perfect.

Before I really realised it, I had compared this interaction with those shared with Alex. And it was a major disservice to Tobias. Because Tobias was the type of man—the silently strong, cool type of man—you married and started a family with. He was the man who created a stable life with you. He was a partner.

Alex was the man who stole your breath away and used the force of his power to dominate you. He was the searing heat that eventually burned you and left you bereft and hurting at the end, but still shaking your head in fond remembrance.

I couldn't ignore the fact that as much as I wanted to feel the same pull for Tobias that I did for Alex, I just didn't. And it was a terrible shame. I wondered, if maybe, just maybe, my life would be different if I gave us a chance. Perhaps, just like Tobias, it was a fire that needed to be stoked. Maybe we needed to get to know each other outside of anything having to do with another man.

"Emilia! Pizza's here!"

The shout wrenched us apart. In the process, we bumped foreheads and laughed at each other.

"Oh, geez," I said, clutching my forehead. "Sorry."

He chuckled. "You've got to let me up. I have to pay the delivery person."

"Right." I shifted to the side and sat back onto the floor. He stood up and smoothed out his clothing before turning to me, offering a hand. I took it and stood on perfectly working legs, silently following him from the room and to our awaiting dinner.

There wasn't a wobble in my step or a fear that my bones were mush like they were every time Alex finished with me.

ALEXANDER UNMASKED

IT WAS PRETTY AMAZING TO ME how little I saw of Georgina after her baby announcement, but I suppose it worked out for me in the end. Our time together included a few parties and work events without the need for spending "quality" time together. We came together, took our fill of each other, and went our separate ways—just long enough to forget that we loathed each other—and then came back together to do it all over again for the cameras. It worked for me, it worked for her, and I saw no reason to change it.

I did what I did best in the face of adversity: talk, make people laugh. Listen. It was my disguise, this happy, friendly, and kind Alexander Thorne. It hadn't always been that way, but I felt more and more compelled to put it on just to shield the utterly bone-deep revulsion building inside of me.

My fans didn't deserve to watch their favourite actor crumble from such a lofty pedestal; they deserved to think I was a being worthy of their adoration. I owed it to them—for what their undying support had done for my career. I wanted to prove to them, and by extension myself, that the public mask I had created wasn't a total sham. I couldn't stand the thought of anyone thinking poorly of me, be they fan or friend or family—even if it meant I died a slow death under the weight of my obligations.

The Christmas cheer didn't touch the misery growing in my heart.

I had hoped throwing myself headlong into what remained of the season would change my attitude, or that I might, at least, come to a place of acceptance. Each time I saw Georgina, however, I hated her a little more. Hated everything she was. Resented the tiny child growing in her belly. I had always expected having children would be the happiest time of my life. But it wasn't. It was the absolute worst.

Worse yet, I lost more and more of myself in the process.

Nevertheless, with civility firmly in place, I forged ahead by myself, too ashamed to draw anyone else into the mess. Not even my closest friends or my family knew. I couldn't bring myself to actually voice the words to them. Least of all did I want to see the disgust on my mother's face. She had always been critical of Georgina and warned me against the relationship from the outset, but I hadn't listened to her, thinking I had handled little flings like Georgina before and could easily do it again.

I had not prepared for a fling who didn't get the hint and leave.

My mother knew something was wrong, though she did not ask me about it. It was our English way not to talk to each other except for the basics—and we certainly never talked about our feelings. Those were our own to deal with, not to spread around; my siblings and I learned that lesson early in life. She did not smother me with questions. She believed I would come to her when and if I truly needed help. As a man of thirty-four, I never thought I would actually *need* her help, much less that I had to overcome my own pride to ask her for it. But even then, I refused to tell her. Not yet. How could I tell my mother someone as horrible as Georgina was the mother of her first grandchild?

It didn't help matters when my mother took an instant liking to Emilia at Georgina's party. My mother's preference for the company of the hostess' assistant rather than the hostess herself was a slight Georgina would never overlook it considering our current and future connection. While it didn't surprise me that my mother had zeroed in on the only person in attendance not drawn into the glimmering light of the glitterati, my heart ached for what I couldn't have.

What I would never have, if Georgina had her say.

At one point in the evening, lost in the sea of sycophants and my own neurosis, I found myself wandering over to where my mother and Emilia stood. I picked at a table of sweets set up for grazers like me, trying to overhear their conversation without appearing too interested. I figured my mother would draw me into conversation if I hovered long enough.

Fortunately, I was right.

"Are you going to come over for a chat or do you plan to finger the rest of the macaroons, Alexander?" my mother called with a jovial laugh.

I snatched my hand away from the treats and looked at my mother. Hopefully it appeared more contrite than it did jubilant. Emilia peered into the empty champagne flute in her hand, a slight pink hue tingeing her cheeks. She seemed more beautiful with the blush.

A wayward waiter happened by and I stole two flutes of champagne from the silver tray. Emilia accepted one and set her empty one aside, sipping at the golden liquid to occupy herself. When she finally met my eyes again, they very briefly slid past me onto the scene over my shoulder. Her face fell.

"I'm sorry, excuse me," she muttered and pushed away from us. I followed her retreat until she stopped in front of Georgina. When I turned back, my mother stared at me with a twinkle in her kind eyes. She could barely contain a smile.

"What?"

"She's lovely, Alexander," she said.

"Georgina is," I replied automatically.

She shook her head. "You can play coy all you want, but I wasn't born yesterday."

I looked again for Emilia. She was gone and Georgina had returned to a conversation with her friend.

"I'm in a relationship with Georgina," I confirmed. My voice was monotone, on autopilot. Maybe repeating it would make me believe it. Maybe.

"Regardless," my mother countered. "Emilia is special."

I sipped my drink. I didn't want to answer her. Georgina caught my eye and ended her conversation to start a path in our direction. The woman stopped in front of us with the same plastic smile that made my skin crawl.

"I hope you've enjoyed everything," Georgina said in greeting. "It's been such a chore putting this party on. All the work! You wouldn't believe it."

My mother and I shared a short sideways peek at each other. She hid her smirk behind the flute of champagne. I felt no mirth—not even the sardonic kind—so I stared blankly at the woman I loathed.

"But it's been lovely," my mother said and looked up at me for reinforcement.

That was enough to engage Georgina and my mother in conversation. By extension, I could not leave, as I was the only tangible link and topic between them. That Georgina blocked my exit and had an arm holding me firmly in place didn't help either. Thus I stood and listened to her dullness, hoping my mother didn't think too poorly of me, for what seemed like ages.

Eventually the revellers began dispersing for their homes. Nearing midnight and anxious to get some sleep, I started making my way for bed. The morning would bring with it loads of time spent with the rest of my family—and Georgina. I couldn't even begin to comprehend what sort of torture Georgina would bring into my life in the morning. I needed all the sleep I could get.

I moved through Georgina's house after seeing my mother to a cab, dodging vendors as they packed in their wares. Crates that white-coated chefs and line cooks stacked on the back staircase throughout their service blocked my preferred escape. I didn't want to go out through the front—that would require me facing Georgina again as she bade farewell to the guests who overstayed their welcome. My graciousness wore thin and I couldn't guarantee any pleasantries for them.

I ducked out the back door into the garden. Twinkling white fairy lights strung through shrubbery and twisted around tree trunks welcomed me into a magical escape from my obligations. I wished I had utilised this fairy land at some point throughout the evening. Despite the biting cold and tiny patch of land we city dwellers called a garden, the sudden serenity which overcame me matched no other. I breathed out, the hot air from my lungs curling into steam. The air felt heavy and cold, and silent, too, but for the faint sounds travelling from the interior of the house.

I stood in the stillness looking up at the moonless sky for a long time until I heard the doors near the living room open and close.

"Thank God that's over," said a familiar whiskey-tinged voice in a sigh of relief.

I poked my head around the corner; Emilia startled at the intrusion and giggled at herself.

"Sorry. I didn't know you were there," she apologised. "I didn't mean for you to hear—"

She stopped talking when I raised my hand and stepped closer to her. "You don't have to worry about it. I know Georgina can be quite a pill."

A slight nod of her head followed. "Did you enjoy yourself tonight?"

I shrugged. Sure, all the parts without Georgina were fine. "I would have preferred to have a quiet Christmas Eve in front of the fire."

She looked at me doubtfully. "There's never a quiet night like that with Georgina, you know."

"I'm aware," I admitted.

The conversation stalled there, for which I was eternally grateful. I didn't want to answer more questions or talk about Georgina. I wanted, just for a few moments, to stand in Emilia's company and not worry about my life.

I wanted to enjoy myself, no matter how fleeting our time together might be.

A visible shiver spread through her body. She crossed her arms over her front. I thought to take my jacket off and give it to her, but didn't. If I made the mistake of purposefully or accidentally touching her, I would be lost forever and hate my situation more than I already did.

"Do you do anything special on Christmas?" I queried instead, to take my mind off the cold nipping at my nose.

She shrugged. "I sleep in as late as possible, I don't take my pyjamas off all day or comb my hair or brush my teeth, and then I sit in front of the telly."

"No gifts? No family time?"

Emilia cringed in what I could only understand as pain for a brief moment. "There is. When we first get up. There's only three of us, so at the first of the month, we draw names to see who we'll buy a gift for. It's small and uncomplicated. But nice."

Her fond smile made me smile despite the thoughts in my head. We lapsed into silence again, but it was pleasant company.

"It feels like it's going to snow," Emilia remarked.

"You think?" I looked up at the starless night. Fluffy grey clouds had blanketed the city all day, threatening some sort of precipitation. They lingered in the darkness.

She nodded. "One can hope. White Christmases are the best."

The wistfulness in her voice made something tug the corner of my lips into a smile. It was infectious. Her spirit was infectious. "Are they?"

Emilia laughed. "I like the fantasy, you know? Even if things aren't going great in your life, the stillness of snow and the magic of the season can transport you to some other place."

"Maybe you're right," I agreed. It was difficult to believe a little snow could make me feel anything more than a frostiness to match the ice growing within me.

"I *am* right," Emilia asserted. I adored her authority on the subject. "Don't laugh at me."

"I'm not laughing at you."

"There's amusement in your voice and on your face," she said. "I can see it plain as day in your eyes."

I shrugged. "I guess I'm only surprised by your whimsy. You always seem so to-the-point. No nonsense."

Emilia chuckled softly and pushed a few pieces of hair behind her ear. Then she opened her mouth and hesitated. I gave her my full attention to encourage her to continue. She blushed and giggled again.

"What?" I asked.

"It's nothing."

"Tell me."

She hesitated for a moment.

"When I was a very little girl, we couldn't afford anything—not even a Christmas cracker—we were so poor. But when I woke up one Christmas morning, there was a small package on the kitchen table wrapped in newspaper. It had my name on it. I tore into it and inside was the most beautiful snow globe. The snow inside was white and sparkly and fell on the limbs of a large evergreen and on the heads of a group of laughing, smiling people. They were all drinking and having a wonderful time while watching a little girl dance with a nutcracker in her hands. It played the Dance of the Sugar Plum Fairy." She paused for a moment. A lone tear fell down her cheek. She turned to casually wipe it away.

With a clear of her throat, she continued. "For a little while I completely forgot about being cold and hungry and not having a Christmas tree or one of those ridiculous paper crowns. Whenever I had a bad day or I went to bed hungry after that, I would wind the snow globe and shake it up and watch the snow fall. It transported me to another place. A place where I could be happy. So snow is important to happiness."

I stood enthralled with her story, though my chest constricted with new emotion. I had so much to be thankful for this holiday, but I completely ignored it in favour of wallowing in my own self-pity.

I put myself into this situation, after all. I had to live with it and make the best of it. In eight or so months, I would be a father. And that wasn't something to hate, as much as I loathed Georgina. I had my health, as did my family. I had banked more money than I would ever use in this life thanks to the new movie franchise deal, which made my future comfortable. I had a home with food, and heat, and Christmas crackers galore. There were so many things to be thankful for that I thought perhaps Georgina wasn't as bad as I made her out to be.

Despite the hate in my heart, I decided to give the spirit of the season a chance to do its work.

She gave me a content little sigh of a woman remembering fond memories. "Someplace a nutcracker turned into a prince and made me his princess."

There was nothing I could possibly say to her. My mouth went dry and I wished I could be that man for her, but it was impossible. There were others more qualified for the task, even if Georgina and the baby weren't in the picture. But it didn't stop me from wanting to taste her sweetness or to feel her bare skin under my fingers.

She laughed lightly. "Sorry. I get carried away with the fantasies sometimes."

"Don't be sorry," I replied. "This has been a difficult holiday for me, and it was nice to hear your story."

Emilia shrugged. "Count on me to bring the angst."

I smiled and reached into my jacket, fishing for the envelope I put in the pocket before coming to the party. "I intended to leave this on your desk for when you returned after Boxing Day, but now seems like a good time."

She gave me a look laced with bewilderment. "You got me a gift?"

"Of course I did."

"But I didn't get you anything."

I chuckled. "I don't want anything."

Anything she would be willing to give me, at least.

She took a step back and waved her hands in objection. "Alex, I can't."

"Please. Just open it. You don't even know what it is."

Emilia eyed the red envelope with trepidation. I saw the war going on in her beautiful hazel eyes until she convinced herself to take it from me. When she finally snatched it from my fingers, I exhaled a puff of steam into the night air. She pushed back the flap with agile fingers and withdrew the contents. I waited on bated breath for her to read it. Her brows furrowed in confusion and her face softened. She bit her lower lip, wide eyes darting to mine.

"Alex—" Her lip quivered. More tears threatened to spill down her cheek. "You can't be serious."

I nodded. "I am serious."

"They were all sold out as soon as they went on sale," she continued. "Where could you have possibly found them?"

"I know people."

She gave me a watery laugh. "I really can't take these. They're too much."

"You will take them. And you will enjoy yourself. I command it," I said. "Hopefully you have someone special to go with."

Emilia slipped the tickets back in the envelope and looked up at me. "I don't know about special like that, but I have someone. Yes."

I smiled, though her words broke my heart. "Well, that's good."

She held the envelope close to her heart. She didn't have to verbalise how dear a gift it was to her. My heart felt light knowing I was responsible for such a reaction. "Alex, I don't know how I could ever thank you enough."

"I've seen how happy it's made you," I said quietly. "That's all I need."

She frowned upon hearing the unhappiness in my voice. What she did next, however, completely surprised me.

My arms were suddenly full of the warm, soft woman and it was everything I could do not to react inappropriately amorous. Instead, I chuckled uncomfortably and wrapped my arms around her, burying my nose in her hair and inhaling the perfume of cinnamon and vanilla. I would remember the spicy scent forever.

"Thank you, Alex. Really."

She hugged me closer, with a strength that made me somehow content, despite the shambles of my life. This was a hug. An embrace. It was real, pure, and everything a hug should be. What was more, she meant it. I closed my eyes and forced myself to enjoy the moment without thinking of anything else.

However, an icy wet plop on my cheek made me blink my eyes open. Another dot of iciness landed on my hand. And then I realised what was happening.

"Emilia?"

"Huh?" she said, pushing back from me.

I felt bereft without her in my arms. I pointed above us. "It's, uh, snowing."

She turned her face up to the sky as fluffy white flakes dropped onto her cheeks and into her eyes. Releasing a giddy laugh, she stepped further away from me, arms outstretched. She spun around. "You see? I knew it!"

I couldn't help but laugh with her.

The magic of the moment, however, came crashing down on us when the doors behind blew open to reveal a foot-stomping Georgina.

"What are you doing, Emilia?" she demanded. "You're supposed to be directing everything… oh, God, it's snowing? I hate snow."

The woman shivered for good measure. I wondered how she could hate it; if anyone was *the* Ice Queen, it was her.

"I'm sorry, Georgina," Emilia replied, slipping the red envelope into the pocket of her trousers.

Georgina disappeared, but not before levelling a warning glare at me. Emilia and I were left looking at each other.

Emilia smiled softly, almost pityingly. Did she know?

"Happy Christmas, Alex."

"Happy Christmas, Emilia," I whispered back.

The words swirled into the increasing snowfall as Emilia returned to her duties inside the house. I wasn't sure she heard them.

A deep shiver travelled the length of my spine. Perhaps there was some magic left in this little snow globe of ours, after all. Finding it in the dark was a task, but I wondered if Emilia might be a light to show me the way.

CHAPTER 17

AS I SNUGGLED INTO A SOFT LEATHER SEAT in the richly appointed private jet the following morning, I thanked the gods for allowing me a relatively easy time rounding up Georgina and the luggage needed for our trip to Los Angeles.

My night with Tobias had drawn on much longer than I originally planned. It resulted in a massive headache created from too little sleep, almost a full bottle of wine, and no food in my stomach. I only picked at the pizza Tobias ordered, and ultimately didn't consume much as my anxious stomach refused to release the knots into which it had tied itself after our kiss.

A part of me hoped above all hopes the kiss would help me determine where my heart lay—or could lie, as it were—but it only made my decision more difficult and perplexing because there hadn't been an "ah-ha!" moment. The Earth never quaked beneath us. Neither did my body quiver in the same way it did for the other man in the equation. My heart only fluttered in a few of its beats.

There was little magic despite the pleasantness of the kiss. I wanted more. I *needed* more. However, I wasn't certain a whole lorry load of the most powerful magic would help me out of this ridiculous pickle of hopelessly divided loyalties.

The choice should have been clear cut to me. I *should* have fallen head over heels for Tobias, the man who did and said everything I ever wanted out of a possible mate. I *should* have easily pushed aside any thought of Alex, the man who refused to release me from his spell and did as he pleased.

I couldn't make myself do it. I just couldn't disregard Alex as though he didn't mean anything to me. Because he meant quite a lot to me for a time, which was only changed by his behaviour since Venice. It was this shared, albeit brief, history making the situation all the more difficult. Alex used it to his advantage while I remained utterly lost in love with a man who I feared would ultimately be incapable of the same love.

Some sick and twisted part of me hoped Alex would move past whatever shackled him to Georgina. I wanted him to look at me and see what Tobias saw—or at least treat me as something more than a piece of meat. I loved that Alex found me so completely irresistible that he couldn't keep his hands off of me, but I needed more than that to be able to give up on Tobias. I needed commitment of some sort. The type Tobias was willing to give me. Legitimacy. No dirty secrets and slinking around in the shadows.

While one man had me intellectually, the other ripped the heart right out of my chest and kept it locked away for his use when he needed it. It made my life a living hell.

I tried to push the wretched thoughts from my pounding head; they were the absolute last things I needed to worry about as we flew into a wild work week. I needed some decent, uninterrupted sleep if I had any hope of making it through the madness ahead of me, not only balancing my obligations as Georgina's assistant, but also engaging in a skilled tap dance between Alexander and Tobias while I tried to grasp where I stood in all of it.

Georgina flounced around the jet for a bit before she chose the perfect seat to commandeer, as though she would actually pick one other than her customary seat near the front of the cabin—a lone seat away from the rest of us. Sweeping her eyes over the cabin one last time, she grimaced with a small, annoyed sniff and plopped down into the aforementioned seat. I hummed in contentment, knowing that despite all the upheaval in my life, Georgina remained the same person and would stay the same person. I could always count on her to be herself. I knew how to handle her. She never gave me any surprises.

It was a remarkably comforting thought.

Georgina shifted around in her seat, somewhat like a dog digging and clawing at a bed before it settled, and then fished a pill bottle out of her handbag. After popping a few of her favourite sedatives, Georgina would numb herself to the world and fall asleep for the duration of the twelve hour flight from London to Los Angeles. It would be a blissful flight.

Well, it would, I supposed, if Alex wasn't scheduled to share it with us. The movie studio hired the jet for both Alex and Georgina, as she had been contracted to dress three of their biggest names for the Oscars, Alex being one of them, and she needed the cargo space to transport all her bits and bobs many thousands of miles. Georgina had absolutely no problem with the arrangement.

I had every problem with it.

It meant spending twelve hours in a pressurized metal tube at cruising altitude with a man I couldn't decide whether I hated or loved—not to mention with his girlfriend who also happened to be my neurotic boss. There would be no means of escape, save pulling the emergency exit and chancing it with a parachute. And yet, I couldn't help but feel this was exactly where he wanted me: held captive.

I was, however, thankful he planned to find his own ride to the airport and I hadn't faced him at Georgina's. After my somewhat surreal evening with the perfection of Tobias Sinclair, I wasn't ready to face the imperfection of Alexander Thorne, nor how I readily responded to him.

Jack, Alex's grey-haired publicist, popped his head inside the cabin first. His instant warm smile prodded a smile from me despite the pounding in my head. I had liked the man from the moment I met him. His job was not one I envied; wrangling someone like Alex, who had ideas and plans of his own on red carpets and in interviews, never made it easy for a guy trying to maintain his client's image. Alex did listen to him—mostly—but there were times when Jack seemed so completely exasperated he nearly dropped his most successful client. Now I understood why. Once Alex set his mind on something, nothing could change it, whether it involved sleeping with me or talking with one fan too many when he ran late to a premiere. But Jack seemed to manage it with startling aplomb.

"Still at it then, Emilia?" he greeted with a cheery laugh as he searched the cabin for Georgina.

I nodded my head. "Still at it."

"Good," Jack replied. "I like working with you."

He heaved the bag hanging from his shoulder onto the mahogany table flanked by two sets of double seats. Without wasting a moment, he pulled out his laptop and paperwork, setting up in preparation for the work he apparently needed to do. I had no doubt it could pile up if it were left unattended for too long, judging from the work Alex and Georgina's relationship generated.

Alex's long shadow darkened the entrance and momentarily distracted me. He wore a rumpled button down and low-slung jeans, both of which would drive Georgina mad with anger once she saw them. No doubt Alex went for comfort, but that didn't matter to the woman. He removed the sunglasses from his face and folded them into the unbuttoned neckline of his shirt, his gaze holding mine briefly before sweeping through the cabin. I watched with interest as his eyes flicked quickly over Georgina, who was none the wiser to Alex's entrance. There wasn't even an attempt on his part to say hello; in fact, his face fell, a grimness overcoming his features. It ignited a firestorm of questions he would never openly answer for me.

He dropped his bag on the seat across the aisle and sat in the seat facing me. "Good morning."

I muttered something in acknowledgement and looked out the small porthole window at the ground crew loading Alex's and Jack's luggage. No one spoke, but that didn't stop Alex from studying me closely as the pilot announced a quick departure. I leaned my head back and closed my eyes, hoping to forget the staring man—the man who alternately infuriated me or drove me to the highest level of physical pleasure possible.

When we were finally in the air, I reclined in my seat and curled up beneath a blanket to further protect myself, like a turtle in its shell. I prayed for sleep to come and for the constant flow of disturbing thoughts in my mind to abate for a little while.

OBNOXIOUS DINGING WOKE ME from my slumber. I opened my sleep-filled eyes and blinked to clear the blurriness from them. The plastic ecru-coloured ceiling came into sharp relief in the shadows and light filling the small space. Propellers and machinery hummed and buzzed, creating the peculiar droning white noise only possible at cruising altitude in an aircraft.

I yawned into my hand and pressed the automatic reclining button on my seat with the other, righting and orienting myself once more with my surroundings. Georgina hadn't moved from her spot fast asleep at the front of the cabin, but Alex was gone from the seat in front of me. He and Jack sat at the table, talking just under the aircraft drone so their words were lost in the sound. Alex wasn't happy with the conversation—that much I saw in his body language.

The clock on my mobile said I was out for six hours or so—which helped my headache, though I felt fuzzy and groggy. And I needed the loo desperately. Standing and stretching drew both Alex and Jack's attention, but I ignored them when I passed the table for the facilities. While there, I made my hair presentable and splashed cold water on my face, though nothing would help my appearance. The mental exhaustion was as evident on my face as it felt in my body.

I stopped for a bottled water in the galley and came out into the main cabin. Jack smiled up at me and motioned to the seat beside him. "Come sit with us, Emilia. We need to have a chat."

"About?" I asked softly, praying the shakiness in my words went unheard. How could anyone possibly take that as something good? It couldn't be.

"Alex said he'd like to have a get together with some friends at his place while we're in California," Jack said. "And I need to see what the schedule is for Saturday or Sunday with Georgina."

"Oh, just the shoot with Morgan Saturday morning, but you knew that since you work with her, too. The evening is free," I replied. "And Sunday she has nothing planned."

Jack nodded and typed the information into his calendar, looking over the top of his laptop at Alex. "Saturday then?"

"Sure," Alex agreed.

"Do you need any help pulling it together?" I offered. "I have a few catering numbers and such… I know Alex can't cook."

The muscles in Jack's jaw clenched. A smile tugged at the corners of his mouth, but he refrained from letting it grow, glancing first at Alex and then at me. It was the smile of a man who knew the bigger secret, was deeply amused by it, but out of respect didn't draw any attention to it. "No, I think I have it. It'll just be a few of us if Amy and Gabriel are available. And their kids."

I frowned. As much as I liked Amy and Gabriel Costa, their brood now numbered four little ones between three months and six years. "Are you sure that's a good idea?"

"Why?" Alex said, a note of cynical amusement in his voice.

I glanced at him for the first time since I sat down and motioned with a thumb behind me to Sleeping Beauty across the cabin. "Not, uh, everyone will be particularly, er… thrilled… to have the children there. Maybe you should schedule it when she's busy?"

Alex scowled and I thought he directed it at me. He shifted uncomfortably and excused himself with a few clipped words. He retreated into the galley before I turned to Jack, who also watched his friend disappear.

"I didn't mean..." I tried to explain. I sighed in exhaustion. "I'm sorry. It's just that I want everyone to have a good time, and I don't know what Georgina will do."

Jack held up a hand to stop me. "You don't have to apologise, Emilia. Both Alex and I understand what you were getting at."

"I mean, one time Evelyn Warner was visiting Georgina and brought her son with her. Phineas was colouring with a marker and jumped on Georgina. He hit her with it. It was a big blue mark all across her face. Georgina flipped out," I said.

The actress and I had laughed. Georgina yelled at the child. And that was the reason why Evelyn Warner no longer required our services.

Jack doubled over in laughter and shook his head. "I know I shouldn't be laughing, but I would have loved to see that."

It was contagious, and I found myself laughing with him. "Stop laughing!"

"Oh, come on, it had to be wonderful," Jack managed to say between giggles.

I sighed and nodded my head. "It was the best bloody day of my life."

Jack grinned, turning back to type an email.

I cleared my throat. "It's just that I've never seen her more ill at ease than she is with children. I don't want everyone else to suffer because Georgina is such a tit."

"Aren't we all already suffering because of her?" Jack said at such a low volume that only I could have heard him.

"True enough," I replied. "I just don't want the kids to get hurt."

Jack thoughtfully tapped his finger against his lips and then lifted his shoulders in a shrug. "I'm sure Alex knows what he's doing by inviting all of them. We have to trust him."

"Well, if you trust him," I said with a noncommittal shrug. To be honest, I didn't know if I should trust his judgment. Alex didn't have the best track record in exercising sound judgment with me, no matter how much I enjoyed it.

Jack nodded but did not look away from the computer. I found his silence suspicious. I wanted to ask him about it, but Alex returned with a teacup and lowered into his seat.

Jack looked at his friend. "You all right, mate?"

"I'm fine," Alex muttered. "Perfect. Living the dream."

The biting acidity of Alex's comment surprised me, but not as much as the way he disregarded his friend's concern in such a nasty way. Jack didn't seem terribly upset by the comment. He merely sighed and clicked through a few things on his computer. He finally shut it down and closed the lid.

"All right, I'm going to try to get some sleep," Jack announced to both of us as he ran a hand through his short hair. He cast Alex a cautious look.

I didn't want him to leave us alone, but he gave me an expectant look to let him out of his seat. Of course he would choose now, when I had no conceivable excuse to escape Alex's attention, to have a nap. Unless that was his plan…

With a reluctant exhalation, I stood up and let Jack out of his seat. He wandered away to an empty space and sat down. I felt warm fingers circle around my wrist and I turned to find Alex watching me.

"Sit," he commanded.

I moved to sit in the seat across from him, but his hands squeezed around my wrist and tugged.

"No. Here." His eyes swept momentarily to the seat beside him. I fidgeted nervously and peered across the cabin.

"No."

"Yes."

"She's right over there, Alex," I said softly. "We can't…"

His lips flattened into a thin line. "She's dead to the world. You know that."

"Alex—" I started, but before my mouth closed with the end of the syllable, he stood from his seat and pulled me into the galley.

There, he shut the door with a snap, but did not lock it. He couldn't lock it. A lock would have made me feel invincible, but at least we were out of sight.

"What do you want, anyway?" I asked him in a feeble attempt to avert my thoughts.

His eyes met mine. "You, of course."

I swallowed around a sudden hard lump in my throat and squirmed under his serious stare. The unabashed arrogance was back and I wanted to throttle him. I would have, if it wasn't for the fact that his damned gaze pinned me—yet again—in my spot. My skin prickled with excitement as he inched closer but did not touch me.

"But I'm not sure you want me," he continued. "Not after what happened yesterday."

"Is this you apologising to me?" I shot back at him. "Because you're rubbish at it."

He shook his head. "I won't apologise for what I did."

"Why are you so infuriating?"

"Am I?"

I rolled my eyes. "You know you are."

Out of nowhere, the jet threw us to and fro. I stumbled against the cupboards, clenching my fingers on the lip of a closed drawer to stay upright; Alex stepped toward me to balance himself. He did not return to his spot. His fingers, instead, dug into my denim-clad hips, steadying both of us against the wall of labelled and latched cubbies. The warmth of his breath fanned away the strands of hair that fell in my face.

"You okay?" he murmured, lips and teeth taking the opportunity to nip experimentally at my mouth. I moaned at the feel of his scratchy beard and wrapped my arms around him, playing with the longer auburn curls at the nape of his neck.

"I'm fine."

"Just fine?"

"I don't really like turbulence," I divulged. "I'm fine flying, but turbulence—"

The intercom dinged overhead and the pilot's American accent flooded the space. "Looks like we're going to be running into some mild turbulence for a while, folks. Please return to your seats and fasten your seat belts."

"We should go," I said, motioning to the door.

He refused to loosen his grip. "It'll be fine."

"Alex—"

The jet rattled again, but he wedged us so snugly into a corner, we hardly moved.

"We really shouldn't," I tried again. "They're right outside that door. And I don't want to die being thrown around a plane."

"You're never going to find a safer place than right here." His lips teased my neck just behind my right ear. I had no option but to lift my head and give him better access. The curve of a smile against my skin was unmistakable. A warm tongue darted against the angle of my jaw and slid up, sucking an earlobe into his mouth.

I moaned. "This is the least safe place to be."

"I'll protect you." His sure fingers slipped below the hem of my blouse, teasing at the naked flesh. I marvelled at their strength and yet he touched me so delicately. "Jack doesn't care, and Georgina won't know. No one will hurt you."

"No one?" I breathed. "Can you protect me from yourself?"

To his credit, the words didn't go over his head. He stopped and craned his neck until he held my gaze. A heartrending sincerity filled his stormy blue depths and mixed with such a dark anger it staggered me. Perhaps phrasing it as I did hurt him, but it was the most truthful thing I ever uttered to the man.

Strange, though, that the pain reflected in his eyes happened to be mine as well. It made me uncomfortable. I wanted him so desperately to be everything I needed, but he seemed to confirm for me he could not be what I needed. The line in the sand was back between us. I either had to accept that or move on.

I couldn't stand it and pulled him down to me, kissing his lips long and slow. The tension in his body eased and I finally sighed into his mouth.

The aircraft wobbled again, this time forcing him to take a marked step back and woefully disengaging his mouth from my body.

"Let's go sit down, please?"

"We'll be fine," he insisted in an odd sort of chorus that was doing nothing for my anxiety. To illustrate his point, he stepped forward and held me firmly against the wall, a strong thigh wedged between mine.

"Yeah, we'll be fine until the jet shakes and you or I go tumbling about and someone ends up with a concussion," I said in a last ditch attempt to draw his attention away from me. "Let's try to explain that to everyone."

His hands on my hips drifted lower over my thighs, trying to change my mind. However, in this, I was resolute. I pushed him away and inched out of his steadying embrace.

"I will sit with you, but I am doing it strapped into a seat."

I opened the door and stepped out into the main cabin. Alex did not follow right behind me, but I realised we wouldn't be able to sit together anyway, because the dragon stirred from her slumber at the front of the cabin.

With an unsettled sigh, I found my original seat and buckled the belt across my hips, new unpleasant feelings invading my thoughts.

CHAPTER 18

WHEN WE ARRIVED AT ALEX'S BEACH HOUSE, he and Jack stayed only long enough to drop their bags off and disappeared under the pretence of grocery shopping. It left me with a bitching Georgina because she had to sit in traffic for ninety minutes on the 405 from LAX. I hadn't spent a lot of time in Los Angeles, even in the height of my modelling days, but the city was notorious for its poor traffic. This fact didn't register in Georgina's life. She expected cars to part ways for her like the Red Sea did for Moses. So, true to fashion, she took it out on those close to her when things didn't go her way. I was the unlucky recipient.

I wanted nothing more than to decamp to my room to relax after such a harrowing flight, especially knowing the luxury waiting for me. Alex had, after all, assigned me to the one bedroom guest house situated by the garden pool. It boasted two huge glass-paned doors which opened onto a wrap-around deck overlooking an expanse of golden sand and the Pacific Ocean; he gave me a quick tour of the property when we were out for the January award shows and I had marvelled at the view then.

My only wish was to escape to that deck, sit in one of the lounging chairs in the warm afternoon sun, listen to the rolling waves, and smell the ocean breeze, preferably until I felt sleepy enough to retire for the night.

I should have known none of that was going to happen. Before I could grab my bag from the pile in the middle of the tile foyer, Georgina ordered me to unpack her things in the master bedroom. She showed me the way and carried a small bag on her arm while I lugged two heavy Louis Vuitton bags up the flight of stairs and down a long hallway. I wasn't sure why she felt the need to show me again, having done the exact same thing back in January, but it wasn't unlike her to forget or take some measure of delight watching me struggle with her bags.

Though I considered the task just another aspect of my job and it definitely was not one of my favourites, it never made me uncomfortable. This time, however, I couldn't help but liken it to a cruel form of torture I wished upon no one—except, perhaps, Georgina herself.

The room felt different. Heavier. The bright white cleanliness made my stomach ache in the worst way. Alex's king-sized bed with the driftwood headboard looked luxuriously soft. It begged for someone to curl into the fluffy down comforter and mess up the neatly aligned pillows. I wanted to smell the scent of his clean, masculine cologne left over on the pillow after a good night's sleep. I wanted to wake up beside him. I wanted to be more than what I was.

But that wasn't possible. It was for Georgina. Georgina and Alex.

"Emilia?" said Georgina, her voice grating on my last nerve.

I sighed and blinked hard.

"Emilia!"

I turned to the demanding woman. My fingers itched to strangle or punch her—anything to stop the vile nails-on-chalkboard voice from screeching my name for a little while. Georgina stood with her arms crossed over her chest, tapping her foot impatiently on the light-coloured hardwoods beneath us.

"Yes, Georgina?"

Georgina held the small bag out for me to take. "This is my jewellery. There is a safe in the closet. Please make sure you put it in there.

Alex will lock it when he comes back."

I frowned. "You won't be here?"

"No," Georgina said. "I will be out until late."

"May I ask—"

Her cutting glare silenced me.

"So I can tell anyone who asks," I finally voiced.

"Tell them I'm working."

She said nothing more and left me standing in the middle of the bright room with the wall of floor-to-ceiling windows and the panoramic view of the glorious Pacific. Once more I wished I was on the beach squishing gritty sand between my toes rather than hanging clothes and loathing every minute of my current situation.

Eventually, I took a breath, blinked my eyes again and looked around me. I opened Georgina's bags and hung her garments, placing others into a chest of drawers, and organised her personal items into the en suite marble-encrusted bathroom that would have made the Queen jealous. I made two more trips down to the foyer for her remaining luggage, leaving Jack's and mine to the side, and hauled Alex's hanging and wheeled bags to the room. He hadn't brought much with him because he kept a basic wardrobe at the house, so I didn't mind. After all, the suits needed hanging or they would wrinkle. I despised semi-wrinkled suits on handsome men and I wasn't about to let Alex fall to that fate no matter how much he bothered me.

I slipped a Tom Ford jacket back onto its hanger when I heard male voices coming up the hallway toward the bedroom. Back in the large closet, I couldn't make out their muffled words, but instead heard the deepness in octave enough to know it wasn't a woman or women doing the chatting.

"Georgina?" Alex called.

I cleared my throat. "No."

He grunted, but I couldn't really say he sounded upset. Did he want to find Georgina? I desperately pushed the thought away lest it incense me more.

"Where are you?"

"Closet," I said.

He stepped into the doorway, hands in pockets. Nothing about him seemed relaxed. His shoulders were rigid in his shirt and the muscle in his jaw developed a slight twitch as he gnashed his teeth. I froze under the hard look in his eyes, clutching another of his suit coats to my chest for protection.

"You didn't have to do that.

"Didn't have to do what?"

"Unpack for me." He motioned to the garment in my arms. "That's not your job."

"Well I…"

He sighed. "It would never be your job to do any of this, if I had my say."

His gaze flicked momentarily to the other side of the walk-in, where I lined up a row of beautiful floor length evening gowns, most of which Georgina would wear at some point over the next week. The meaning of it was not lost on me.

I shrugged my shoulders anyway. "I don't mind."

Even though I did.

Alex shook his head. "Have you had *any* time to relax since we arrived?"

I turned around and put the coat in my arms with the others. It was then that I realised it was the McQueen he wore the night I stayed over at his mother's house. Warmth flooded my cheeks. The memories surged through my body to my fingers as they skimmed along the buttery velvet.

"Are you going to answer me?" he added after I had ignored him for too long.

I grabbed two more coats and three pairs of trousers to line up next to the others. "Answer what?"

"Have you been over to the guest house and decompressed?" he asked again.

"You already know the answer to that," I returned, "so why ask it?"

Alex straightened his shoulders. "Then stop. Come with me. I'll show you the way."

"I'm fine, Alex," I insisted.

My answer was unacceptable. His hands covered mine and tugged the next garment from my grasp. He tossed it over the cushioned ottoman in the centre of the room and turned back to me. "No."

"No, what?" My throat felt like sandpaper. I swallowed. If he didn't take no for an answer, why must I?

His fingers slid beneath my chin and nudged it up until I had no option but to meet his steely gaze. "I don't want you to do this for me. You aren't my employee or my servant or whatever it is you are to Georgina."

My heart ached at his words. If I wasn't any of those things, then what was I?

"What am I, then?"

He shook his head.

"Answer me, please," I asked him. "What am I to you?"

He didn't have an answer; for the first time since I met the man, he didn't have some pretty words to fill the space between us. I didn't know what to expect from my question, and honestly, I wasn't sure I truly wanted an answer. Having a label in which I did not feel comfortable would only make it worse.

Fortunately for us both, he didn't have to answer with a lie or some small platitude. Jack popped into the closet to interrupt us. "Alex! Haven't you heard me calling you?"

Alex didn't jump away though caught red handed, but I did. His shoulders slumped and he turned to Jack. I hid my face from Alex's friend. There was no mistaking the intimate nature of our interrupted conversation. I felt ashamed. Even though other people knew what had been going on, I wasn't prepared for someone walking in on us kissing or arguing or doing anything else, for that matter.

"No," Alex answered. "What is it?"

"Your, uh, car is here," Jack informed him. "For the thing tonight at the Marmont."

Jack's inquisitive assessment of the situation unnerved me as I stiffly finished the work Alex expressly forbid me from doing. My awkwardness got the better of me, however, and after hanging one more article of clothing, I quickly left the room. I pushed past Jack on my way out and nearly ran to my bag downstairs, leaving through the back door for my sanctuary. Something told me, though, it still wasn't far enough away from Alex.

When I got to the guest house, I threw myself on the bed and started running through my schedule for the next few days to forget what happened. I tried to rest, then I tried to sleep. Despite my mental exhaustion, my body was not tired, and I found myself staring dumbly at the ceiling fan. The shadows reflected above slowly moved with the setting sun, until periwinkle and orange light bathed the room. I thought about getting up and turning the bedside lamp on, but couldn't muster the strength.

Eventually, I heard a light tapping on the glass panes of the door leading to the expansive pool area. I contemplated ignoring it. Perhaps I could say I fell asleep if someone asked what happened.

I couldn't, however, ignore the deep voice on the other side.

"Emilia? You there?"

Jack.

"Yeah," I replied. "Hold on."

I struggled out of bed and opened the door. Jack held a six pack of beer in one hand and a bag of crisps and a tub of something in the other. He smiled and held up the bag. "Tortilla chips and salsa. And really horrible American beer."

I laughed at him. "When in Rome, eh?"

"Exactly." He grinned. "Though I could do with a margarita. A little tequila would not go amiss right now."

"You, too, huh?"

Jack chuckled and shrugged his shoulders. "Would you care to join me?"

"You read my mind," I said. "How about we sit out on the deck?"

Jack agreed. In no time, we claimed two large cushioned lounges out on the deck and began sipping watery beer and digging into our repast of salsa and guacamole with salty tortilla crisps. After a suitable amount of silent companionship, I looked at Jack.

"How is it you're off tonight? I thought herding Alex was a full time job?"

"I'm not on the clock until next week," Jack explained. "But he's only going out for a dinner meeting with the director and producer for a new movie. I would be superfluous. Besides, I think you needed a friend and beer more."

"When don't I?" I held a sip of the thin liquid in my mouth for a second. I swallowed it and cringed at the label. "This is really terrible."

Jack chuckled. "But it does the trick."

"Touché." I held my bottle out to him. He clinked his with it and we both gulped some more.

The sun hung low on the horizon, mostly snuffed out by the curve of the ocean, but the dying beams ignited the fluffy clouds in a vivid display of purples, pinks, and oranges. It was beautiful sitting and listening to the calming ebb and flow of the ocean, watching late day joggers and little old couples strolling hand-in-hand through the surf.

It wasn't easy for curious onlookers snooping for celebrities to see in, but our vantage provided enough of a view of them. The guest house, and all of Alex's property for that matter, sat far enough away from the beach and was elevated on a picturesque bluff. A locked gate hidden in tall pink bougainvillea bushes on the other side of the pool gave way to a sandy path and stairs down the side of the hill for beach access. Further down the row, when individual houses turned into flats and smaller cottages that opened directly onto the beach, it would have been a different story. I personally loved the quiet serenity of the spot. It was difficult to stay angry for long.

"I love it here," I said with a contented sigh. I set my beer on the low table between us.

"It's nice," Jack agreed. "But I would miss London."

I nodded. "So would I. I'd never leave permanently. I just like the change. The laziness of beach life."

"And the sun." Jack smiled and stuck a chip in his mouth.

"Definitely the sun," I echoed.

We lapsed into silence again, though I sensed Jack wanted to talk about something, and my intuition told me that something revolved around his star client and what we were doing in the closet. For Jack's part, he remained respectful, a sort of silent support system like Lindsay. I was convinced Lindsay would probably really like Jack despite the fifteen year age difference. So I used that to change the subject before the one about Alex began.

"Are you single, Jack?"

Jack choked and spluttered on his beer. He quelled his fit of coughing and looked at me, red faced. "Sorry. That was the last thing I expected you to ask me."

I shrugged. "No, I'm sorry. I'm just thinking out loud."

He laughed. "But as an answer... Yes, at the moment, I am."

"Looking?"

"Are you trying to set me up with someone?"

"Possibly."

Jack shook his head. "You and everyone else. I swear I'll find someone in my own good time. But my life is a little too busy right now. I just took over as director of our London office in addition to all the clients I still manage."

"Sounds like you need more help," I said.

"I do." After a beat, he glanced at me with a playful smile on his lips. "You want a job?"

I laughed, but when I realised he wasn't following, I turned back to him. "Wait. You're serious?"

"We are expanding and hiring," he confirmed with a slight nod of his head.

It sounded like the answer to all my prayers. A different job. A boss infinitely better than Georgina. Freedom. But then I remembered it entailed work with Alex, and I still wasn't certain how our liaison would work out. Least of all did I think I could do the work. I had absolutely no education or training in the area. I told Jack as much.

"Public relations isn't so much about the education you have," he pointed out. "It's instinctive and it's how you handle people. How you talk to them, communicate to them. And it's also in who you know. You have all of those qualities… and Alex said you're multilingual? Do you really speak six languages?"

I nodded in confirmation. "If you count my conversational knowledge of Japanese and German, which really could use some work."

"You're perfect for a junior publicist," he said. "We train the right people."

"I…" I hesitated and stopped myself. "Did Alex ask you to do this?"

Jack sighed. "He may have mentioned it, but I was already thinking about it. It's no secret that you're unhappy where you're at."

"Who could ever be?"

"I can't guarantee I'm an amazing boss," he replied with a faint smile, "but I do hope I'm better than her."

I couldn't believe I was about to say it, but I didn't stop myself. "It's flattering, Jack, that you would think highly enough of me that you want me to work for you. But I can't. I don't want the job because Alex made it so. I may be at my rope's end with Georgina, but I'm even more tired of the game he seems to be playing."

Jack inclined his head and pursed his lips together. Momentary anxiety crossed his face. It was the indecision of a man who had something else to say, but wasn't entirely sure it should be said. Then he sighed again. "It's not a game, Emilia."

I snorted. "It's pretty damn close to one."

"He genuinely cares for you."

"He has a funny way of showing it."

Jack groaned in frustration and leaned back in his seat. He looked up at the sky. "You're perfect for each other. Abso-bloody-lutely perfect for each other. And the worst part is neither of you will admit what you truly want to yourselves. You both talk without *listening* to one another. And you… you see without actually *seeing*."

The man had never raised his voice in annoyance before, but this subject clearly bothered him. On the plane, he had been a sphinx. That certainly wasn't the case out on that balcony. Or maybe he felt he could openly say what he wanted with neither Georgina nor Alex around.

"What am I supposed to hear and see, exactly?" I asked.

"That Alex is miserable with Georgina."

"That doesn't excuse what he's doing by going behind her back and cheating on her."

He gave me a long, hard look. "*You're* the one he's cheating with. What does that say about you?"

And there it was. Jack's words hit me like a sack of bricks. I clamped my mouth shut and ground my teeth. I refused to yell or burst into tears; I was unsure which emotion would show itself first. I looked toward the horizon as the words rang in my ears and tried to calm myself. I didn't want to fight. I liked Jack. But that didn't take the sting out of what he said. It hurt. It was the truth.

"Why won't he leave her?" I asked finally. "Why can't he do that if he's so miserable? It's not like they have a contract or anything."

Jack shook his head. "No, they don't."

"Then why?"

Jack didn't want to answer me, but our conversation backed him into a corner. He let too much slip already. I saw him trying to negotiate a way out of the situation, but he failed with all the alcohol clouding his judgment.

His shoulders sagged. "Because he felt sorry for her."

"What?"

Who in their right mind would ever feel sorry for Georgina Cavendish?

He exhaled. "When she lost the baby right before his birthday—"

"Baby."

Jack clamped his lips shut.

"Baby?" I repeated. "What *baby*?"

He sighed and continued, ignoring my bewilderment. "Despite all the shit she put him through, he still felt sorry enough to stick around and play it up for the cameras for a little while. He was finally going to break it off with her, but then that happened and blew it all to shit."

"Baby," I repeated again, not really making sense of what Jack was telling me. I didn't care who felt sorry for who. Or why. "Pregnant?"

"You didn't know she was pregnant?"

I shook my head.

Jack's expression was grim. "She hid it well, I guess, considering how she loves to act in front of the media."

"No," I said. "No, she wasn't pregnant."

"Yes, she was three months along," Jack elaborated. "Whether you want to accept it or not."

I stood up quickly. My knee hit the chair and nudged the table with our food and beers. "No! She wasn't pregnant. She couldn't have been pregnant."

Jack looked at me like I was an adult who refused to accept the fact that Santa Claus wasn't real.

"Listen to my words," I enunciated slowly. "She's not able to get pregnant."

"How do you…"

"Because I live her life for her!" I raised my arms in exasperation and began pacing the boards of the deck with small, measured steps. "I know everything about her! I mean, I don't know all the details, but she got pregnant with her last boyfriend, it was ectopic and there was some complication, she severely haemorrhaged. They ended up having to give her a hysterectomy during her surgery to remove the rupture. She was laid up for a few months because of it. She almost missed the February shows—it was back when Alex was doing *Macbeth*, long before we ever met. I remember because my friend, Jordan, was in London and had gotten us tickets. I missed the show because I was taking care of everything for Georgina while she was in recovery."

Jack sat in stunned silence, his face slackening bit by bit while the words slowly seeped into his brain. He opened and closed his mouth a few times, and then he looked at me. "You're… sure."

"Yes, of course I am," I told him firmly.

"But Alex said she showed him a print-out from the doctor's office."

I shrugged my shoulders. "Unless it's the Immaculate Fucking Conception, and God radically healed her, then she wasn't pregnant."

"Oh my God." Jack shook his head in disbelief. "I can't believe she would actually… Oh. My. God." He ran his hands through his short hair, scratching at his neck. "Are you sure it couldn't be aliens implanting something?"

I rolled my eyes.

Jack blew out a long breath and scrubbed his hands over his face. "You can't tell Alex."

"Why the bloody hell not? If he knows, all of this is done. He can break it off with her. All the weirdness and everything going on with him—done! We won't be sneaking around… we won't…" My voice trailed off before I concluded. "It's the answer to everything."

Maybe for me, it was the answer. Jack quickly disabused me of any notion that this information coming to light would actually solve anything, at least for his friend.

"Not exactly," Jack contradicted. "There are other issues here. Big ones."

"What could possibly be bigger than that?"

He sighed. "We're going to need hard liquor."

Without waiting for me to reply, he jumped up from his seat and disappeared around the side of the guest house, I hoped to procure liquor rather than to run away from me and my questions. I needed more information.

As I stood there in befuddled silence, realisation slowly dawned on me. Maybe some of my problems would be solved, but the fact of the matter remained that Alex still decided to start our arrangement with no end to his relationship with Georgina in sight. And that actually did more to cure me of my obsession with him than it did to strengthen it.

Jack returned with shot glasses and a bottle of tequila. He poured two shots and held one out to me. After we swallowed them, he took a deep breath and started from the beginning.

ALEXANDER UNMASKED

(ONE MONTH BEFORE THE MASQUERADE)

O N THE NIGHT OF THE SCREEN ACTORS GUILD AWARDS, I remember stepping backstage and feeling as though the weight of the statuette in my hands was an immovable anchor, holding me in place and allowing me no chance of escape from a stifling world. The two weeks leading up to it were nothing but a whirl of award show after award show, dinner after dinner, all of which I attended and most of which I won. But it felt empty to me. Meaningless. What should have been one of the most triumphant times in my life—finally earning the respect of the film world for my work and contribution to the medium—made me empty.

The people around me were jubilant enough, but they conveniently forgot to share any of their enthusiasm with the person who needed it most. I felt dead. Like I had given too much of myself to too many people and they had done nothing for me in return to replenish my stores of energy. Georgina wanted me to kiss her. Jack wanted me to smile—not only for the blinding camera flashes on the red carpet, but also for the television cameras recording us at our tables during the opulent award show.

I wanted to scream.

I couldn't force a smile. If my peers only knew what a fraud I was sitting amongst all these Hollywood greats, unable even to act happy or plaster a fake smile on my face while they clapped politely for me.

I managed nothing more than a tight, mechanical smirk which had received criticism from some sources for being unnecessarily surly, ungrateful, and arrogant.

An Internet gossip columnist first brought the unhappiness hiding beneath my mask to the world's attention after the Golden Globes aired the week prior. They pointed out how I hadn't been as pleasant or as gracious. I didn't do what was *expected* of me. As though I owed it to the world to perform at the drop of a hat like some caged animal in the zoo, all while I fell apart from the inside out. I barely functioned in that oppressive world without screaming at the top of my lungs for freedom. How did they expect me to put on a convincing show when backed into a corner like that?

I suppose I let it happen to myself. I was the one who played and pandered to the whims of my fans and the press to please them. To gain status in their eyes. To make my name—my mark—in an industry in which I so desperately wanted to be a power player. As I pandered more, the more they came, *expecting* me to do this and *expecting* me to do that, because it was my image. The image I wanted.

For my fans, I would literally do anything. But then there were those factions with dishonourable intentions. I allowed them access to my world without scrupulous inspection, personified in one, Georgina Cavendish. She brought with her headaches and paparazzi hiding in bushes and sitting in dark-windowed SUVs waiting for a salacious story. She was the ringleader of this circus and I was the lion, agitated and roaring in the corner for the amusement of others when all I wanted to do was maul and claw the way out of my cage.

I swore to myself when I got into this business, I wouldn't let it happen to me. I had heard too many horror stories of disillusionment to ever want to travel down that path. Now, it wasn't to say that I didn't understand some give and take of it in this industry, but I never imagined it would reach the point where I would stand backstage at the SAG Awards, at the peak of my career, wishing I wasn't there. Wishing I was only young Alex Thorne, stage actor, doing local theatre. Not Alexander Thorne, international super star and sex symbol, who sold out cinemas and had studios begging him to star in movies. Not thirty-five-year-old Alexander Thorne, on the verge of a breakdown, backed into a corner by duty and honour despite a seething disregard for his girlfriend and wanting the one thing he couldn't have.

I lived with my choices because I didn't want the people in the stands to turn on me when I didn't do what they expected of Alexander Thorne, the gentleman British actor who loved life and lived every day to its fullest. To reveal the cracks in my façade would ruin me even more completely than it would to continue the masquerade.

So it was, with heaviness in my chest, why I stood backstage at the SAG Awards trying—mostly unsuccessfully—to prepare myself for the madness awaiting me when I realised I didn't want the award in my hands. Everything I had ever wanted in my life seemed like nothing, like biting into an apple and expecting it to be sweet and juicy, but finding nothing more than a wax decoration. If this thing was tangible proof of the hell my life had become, I didn't want it. I didn't want any of it.

Hot, stinging tears filled my eyes. I couldn't go into the green room in such an emotional state. Sure, it might fool them into thinking I was only overwhelmed after receiving such an accolade from my peers, but I couldn't risk it. I couldn't. The handler stood at my elbow, trying to edge me toward the green room. I stopped him and shook my head.

"I just need a few minutes," I said. "Is there a quiet room where I could—"

The handler looked at me as though I had twenty heads, but then found a door, knocked and pushed it open. "Five minutes, Mr Thorne."

I gave the guy a curt nod and stepped into the room, letting out a heavy sigh in the silence, away from the discord of the backstage area. I wondered what would happen if I snuck out the back door. What would they do if I didn't show up to the green room to answer their questions in my typical song and dance? Would it end my career? Would people think poorly of me?

A knock at the door made me groan, thinking it was the gruff handler again. Jack stepped into the room and sighed when he saw me there with red-rimmed eyes. He shut the door and stared.

"Why aren't you in the green room?"

My voice cracked. "I can't do it."

"You have stage fright? Right this instant?"

I looked at him askance and shrugged my shoulders. "I just can't face them… I can't… my life…"

And that was where it happened.

At the age of thirty-five, at the top of my career, in a tiny prop room backstage at the 22nd Screen Actors Guild Awards show, I melted down. I wanted to simultaneously punch something and scream at the top of my lungs, but even then I was cognisant of who would hear it outside the room. Instead, I gripped the foul statue in my hands until my knuckles turned white, twisting my fingers around it in place of someone's neck.

Jack's demeanour softened, though he did not reduce his stance of power. He came over to me, resting a friendly hand on my arm until I looked up at him. "Alex, I know your life isn't exactly perfect at the moment, but you have to go out there and do it."

"I don't think I can."

"I know you can," he replied firmly.

"I can't keep doing this, Jack. I have to get out of this hell."

When I met my friend's eyes again, I saw the concern in the frown lines on his forehead. He had been right there by side, watching me slide into this role for the last half year. He had warned me all along and I ignored him for most of it. He told me to change course while I still had the chance. But I said I was fine—that I knew what I was doing and that I could handle it.

"What do you want to do?" Jack asked. "I need to know what you want. Do you need a long break? Do you need me to find you a therapist? Do you need me to call out a hit on Georgina?"

I blinked at him.

"I would do it if my best friend would come back for a little bit," he said with no humour in his voice. "If I could just see him smile again."

I didn't doubt him.

"I don't know what to do," I confessed. "I know it starts with leaving Georgina, but if I do leave her, she'll ruin me… my image."

Jack stepped away. He stubbed his toe onto the concrete floor, shaking his head. "Yes, well, this unhappy, half dead Alex isn't exactly helping your image, either."

"I can still perform my job with that image—but with half my fans turning on me because I left my pregnant girlfriend, where does that leave me? We both know I only got the new franchise deal because of their insistence. It would ruin me and it would ruin them and my name wouldn't be worth a bloody thing."

"Alex, is the fame and the money really worth it?" he asked. "You're killing yourself trying to put on a happy face for everyone. You have to start thinking about yourself, not what everyone else wants you to do."

"But I owe so much… how could I ever…"

Jack cleared his throat. "You do owe some things to them, Alex, but it's not because of them that you're here. You're here because you made sacrifices and had the talent in acting that scored you these iconic roles. *You* put yourself here. They have supported you this far, why do you think they wouldn't eventually get over anything Georgina could invent in a publicity blitz?"

I chewed on my lower lip anxiously.

"Do you want to know what I think?" Jack asked.

Licking my lips, I held my hands out in a gesture for him to go on. Why wouldn't I want to know what he thought? Everyone else thought it was appropriate to tell me their opinion.

"I think your own ego is the one to blame for all of this," he said. "You don't want to be seen as anything less than what you think is appropriate, and now you're faced with the fact that you can't be everything you intended. You're failing under the pressure and you're freaking out about it."

His words sank deep into my brain, but it was difficult to hear them over my internal screaming.

"You want to control your life, but you've reached a point where complete control is out of your hands," he said. "And you can't handle that."

"I want it back," I said. "I want to be able to control my life. I want to make my own choices. I want something that's my own. Some piece of my life that I don't have to share with everyone else."

Jack nodded his head. "That's what I thought."

I slumped into a nearby folding chair and let my shoulders sag. I felt defeated and deflated.

"You're scared someone might see you as imperfect, and that terrifies you," Jack concluded.

Was it the truth? Had I really become so arrogant to think I was perfect—whatever "perfect" meant? That I couldn't show my vulnerabilities outside of acting a part? That because I thought I had to be Mr. Perfect, I had gotten myself into some terrible situations of late? Jack was right, though. I couldn't tender the thought of seeing my weaknesses splashed all over the tabloids. The possibility of it happening caused enough fear in itself to make me neurotic.

"So I ask you again," Jack said. "What do *you* want?"

"I want control."

Jack inclined his head. "Okay."

"And I want Georgina gone."

"We'll work out a PR plan and discuss it over the next few weeks," Jack said. "I need to think about this and strategise, but I won't do anything without your approval, of course."

I nodded.

"As much as I hate asking it of you, you need to continue playing along with Georgina. You need to be seen going to doctors' visits and such with her," Jack advised.

"She doesn't have another until we get back from Italy."

Jack pursed his lips. "All the same. Really try doting on her. Make it seem like you love her. Then we can spin a break up as something that you really tried working on, but it ultimately failed."

I hated this. It was just another lie—another mask I had to wear to protect myself. But there was a change. There was some hope there, deep down, that this nightmare would eventually end. At what cost, I couldn't know, but I prayed for its swift conclusion.

"We can't do anything before the Oscars," Jack went on explaining. "It would be bad publicity and the studio wouldn't appreciate it after all the time and money they've spent on promoting your nomination."

The ache started anew in my heart.

"Six weeks," Jack said reassuringly. "That's all you need to hold out. But if you feel like you're going to lose it, you come to me. Please."

I sighed. "And in the meantime…"

Jack levelled a long stare at me. "Yes?"

"What am I supposed to do to cope in the meantime?"

Jack stared at me, unable to find anything worth saying. Many celebrities before me had turned to drugs and alcohol to help them cope with the pressures of their public lives, but neither of those ever exactly appealed to me. They might give me the release I desperately craved, but it wasn't something I wanted to start while I was reclaiming control of my life. There was, of course, one other option that poked through the haze, but I couldn't do that to her.

Could I?

Jack didn't have a chance to answer me before the door to the room opened up again and the handler appeared in the doorway.

"Excuse me, Mr. Thorne," he said, "but we have to get you to the green room now."

I looked at Jack. My friend closed his eyes and swallowed. Gingerly I stood, arranging my tuxedo coat on my shoulders. With another sigh, I glanced at the bronze statuette in my hands. The Actor held masks of Tragedy and Comedy, as though deciding which one he wanted to wear. I couldn't help but feel some level of solidarity with him while I convinced myself to stretch my lips in a passable smile and walk toward the door to meet the press.

I felt ancient under the weight I carried, but they insisted on Mr. Perfect. And Mr. Perfect was what they were going to get.

CHAPTER 19

SLEEP ELUDED ME THAT NIGHT, even with the amount of tequila I had consumed while Jack and I talked. His words echoed and swam around in my alcohol-soaked brain for a few hours before I finally started to sober, and then they stayed there like bright neon lights on the ceiling above me.

Around five the next morning, I conceded defeat and dressed myself, waiting for the first streaks of dawn to light the sky. Eventually, I slowly made my way down to the beach to take what I hoped would be a cleansing walk. Or, at least, I hoped it gave me time to further process all the information Jack had poured into me so my heart stopped aching for a man I still wasn't convinced deserved such loyalty.

Georgina had played one of the most heinous mind games on Alex, but he didn't need to remain complicit in his own destruction. He did too much to appease Georgina to save his career. Of course, I was no idiot. I understood the power of image in our industry. One bad article might derail a movie's publicity. One box office bomb destroyed many a commercially promising career. Some errant comment on social media could spark—and had sparked—media firestorms. It could snowball to epic proportions, no matter the evidence to the contrary, and become a black mark on the record of a publicly recognisable name. Jack's profession had been created to minimise the black mark on public figures, but he said even he couldn't spin Georgina's story in Alex's favour.

Jack didn't know what this would do to Alex; that was the reason why he asked me to stay mum on the topic until after the Oscars. Learning something like this would drive me over a cliff into a pit of unending fury and despair. Alex's fragile psyche could fully shatter in front of the world at the worst possible time. With the week ahead of us, Jack needed Alex's head in the game as much as possible. Since Jack could not plan how the final shattering would manifest, he didn't want to risk it. When they were both back in London, he would tell him and work doubly hard to extricate Alex from Georgina's clutches.

I agreed with Jack. Against my better judgment, I would keep my mouth shut. I did not fancy being the one responsible for Alex spiralling further into his abyss. Lindsay would tell me to stop being a martyr, but I couldn't stop myself from feeling the way I did, not even with the full story at my disposal.

At some point during the night, I started to empathise with Alex. His reaction to a life careening out of control meant grasping for some form of power in the only place he could find it. I was the weakest target, half in love with him due to our friendly acquaintance, and he seized the first opportunity I gave him the night of the masquerade. His mask in Venice had not been the gilded bauta, after all, but the one of indifferent arrogance he built up to hide his excruciating grief and rage. He literally took matters into his own hands and reclaimed a part of the life he lost.

On my way back to the house after my hardly productive walk, I came upon the man in question sitting in the sand watching the gently rolling waves. He had folded his long legs up in lotus pose far enough away so as not to get wet in the foaming surf. From the appearance of his casual attire, he had been running and stopped to enjoy the morning. His trainers were off and sitting beside him. The look of complete serenity on his face, however, made me pause.

The new day's sun poked through the morning beach haze, catching and igniting his messy auburn curls on fire. He had closed his eyes from the glare of the sun, his lips stretched into the faint ghost of a smile. It was no mischievous smirk or pained sneer. For the first time in a long time, I realised, it was a genuine emotion of complete comfort and happiness. Witnessing such peace made me smile, too.

I couldn't bring myself to interrupt him and diverted my path to make a wide berth, but I didn't get far when I heard his voice. I sighed and closed my eyes.

"Emilia," he murmured again, my name rolling off his tongue and surfing over the sound of the breaking waves.

I turned to him. A smile pulled at his lips again and he patted the sand beside him. I desperately wanted to leave him there, but I couldn't help myself. I had absolutely no self-control with this man. He was an addiction; I knew what taking another hit would do to me, and yet I craved him.

As I made my way over, he unfolded his legs and stretched them out, burying his feet ankle deep in the loose golden sand. He pulled the earbuds out of his ears and stuck them into the front pocket of his jumper.

"I didn't mean to bother you, Alex."

He sighed in apparent exasperation. "You don't bother me."

I smiled at him and settled into my spot. Our shoulders brushed, but I made sure a safe distance remained between us.

"I saw you earlier when I got up for my jog."

He motioned his thumb behind him. I didn't have to turn around to know he had motioned toward the house. However, that also meant we were in clear sight of it. I inched a little further away. A strong hand gripped my thigh, pressing down until I couldn't move.

"Stay. You're fine. I saw you walking across the pool deck, not down here."

"She could still see us."

"If she woke up this early, then I would say yes." His lips flattened into a thin line for a minute. "It's like you can't get away from me fast enough."

I glanced at him. "I can't."

He frowned.

"I don't trust myself. I make stupid choices when I'm around you."

Alex's hand slipped a bit and insinuated itself on the inside of my thigh. Still respectable, but there was no question as to the intent or meaning behind it. The move was possessive and intimate. "Don't run away from me."

It was my only option, as far as I was concerned, and yet I stayed right there with his hand possessively securing me in the space beside him.

A pair of svelte female joggers bounced across the surf in front of us. I couldn't take my eyes off of their scant clothing or their toned bodies. They were either models or actresses, but I didn't know them. And they didn't pause to notice us. When I looked back to Alex, his eyes had trained on my face.

"What?"

"Did you get any sleep last night?" he asked.

I shook my head. "I look that bad?"

Alex shrugged. "So you didn't?"

"Not very much. A lot on my mind."

"Jack?"

"Yes," I confirmed.

"Did he…"

My mouth felt dry and I swallowed, looking at him. "He did."

Alex showed no outward reaction but for the fact that his fingers dug, ever so slightly, into the cloth and sinew on my thigh. "So you know…"

"I know," I said. God, I wanted to tell him *what* I knew. He needed to know. He did.

But I promised Jack.

"Does it make it easier for you to quit working for her? Now that you know?"

I was utterly gobsmacked at his question. Of all the things he could have said—what he needed to say to me—I couldn't understand for the life of me why he chose that. "Alex, I've always loathed her, that hasn't changed."

"And yet you stay with her," he observed.

"I don't particularly like you half the time," I said. "And I'm still sitting right here with you."

Chastened, his eyes blinked and he looked out at the ocean. After a few minutes of nothing but listening to waves and watching his impassive profile, he glanced back at me.

"Why do you stay with her? What hold does she have on you?" he asked.

"Other than the fact that I have to?" I said. "I have to support myself and my brother. It's not just me in the equation."

"Is your brother unable to care for himself?"

"You wouldn't understand."

He rolled his eyes. "Try me."

"He has Down Syndrome. He can do a lot himself—though he likes to make it seem to strangers that he needs a lot of help—but he won't ever live alone or hold a full time job to support himself."

Alex's face didn't show as much surprise as I thought it would. I wondered if he knew all along, but I couldn't let myself think that. If he knew it and still thought I ought to abandon my only source of income in a whim of fancy, consequences be damned, then I didn't want anything to do with him. I couldn't see him as that selfish without completely hating him. But then, I supposed, maybe I needed to wake up and realise that he *was* that selfish.

"Hasn't Jack mentioned that he's looking to take new people on?"

"He did last night and I declined."

Alex looked at me as though I were insane. "Why the fuck would you do that? Don't you want to be free of her, too?"

"I also don't want to be given a job as a favour," I told him. "I want to be asked on my own merits. I want to feel useful in the sense that *I* achieved something. I'm tired of you going around and sorting things for me because you think it needs to be done."

"I'm only trying to help you," he said.

I laughed at him and shook my head. "Did it ever occur to you that not everyone wants nor needs your help?"

His lips clamped shut, and he said nothing more to me. I looked out on the glittering waves and rested my palms over the large hand clinging to my leg. He twitched beneath me, but relaxed as I curled my fingers around his.

"You're trying to control my life because you can't control yours," I stated. "You're being incredibly selfish."

He didn't like the laundry list of character defects I was making. I saw it and felt it in his tensing body. A sheet of thin ice had formed beneath me, and I had started a tap dance on the weakest part.

"But I get it. I do. I'm selfish, too," I added. "By giving into you, I gave into my own selfishness without really paying attention to my obligations. It was a mistake."

"Please," he breathed, his voice breaking. His Adam's apple bobbed with his emotion. "Please don't say it was a mistake. Don't end it all now."

I chewed on my bottom lip. I hated that he wouldn't look at me, so I reached over and pressed my fingers against his cheek until he turned to me. "I-I'm not ending anything. I'm only saying what I've been saying all along. It's not as simple as you've made it out to be in your head and I need you to understand that. I can't just say fuck it all and ride off into the sunset with you when you finally break up with Georgina, no matter how much I may want to do it."

"You want to do that?" He sounded like a little boy, hopeful he was about to be awarded some big prize due to a technicality in the rules which would have otherwise disqualified him.

"I don't know what I want, truthfully."

My reply was honest, at least. My indecisiveness sat at the crux of all the problems in my life. I had no idea what I wanted out of anything; a healthy guilt gifted to me from my grandmother, my complete resistance to ending up like my mother, my love for my brother and Lindsay, and my indecision between two incredibly different men were warring within me. But I couldn't heap all that on Alex. Not with all I had learned in the past twenty-four hours.

I had to pull myself up by the bootstraps and figure that out for myself, without relying on someone else to do it for me or allowing them to sway my decision one way or another. When I learned how to do that, I would fix everything wrong with my own life. Even the character deficit which led me to being such a perfect target for people like him.

I leaned toward him and brushed my lips against his; he wasted no time burying his fingers in my hair and pulling me against him. Like the first time he kissed me in Venice—and every time after—I lost track of who and where I was. It didn't matter that there were people moving up and down the beach in their morning exercises or surfers catching little waves out in the distance. Or the fact that Georgina could wake up at any moment and peer through her second story floor-to-ceiling windows.

Our embrace ended too quickly; he was conscious of our surroundings, after all. I shifted away from him and turned to gaze out on the horizon again, waiting for my heart to return to a normal pace and my breathing to regulate. He slipped the possessive hand back on my thigh.

"Emilia," he said finally, "I know I haven't been the best example of good behaviour, but I hope you know that I considered my relationship with Georgina over the day she told me she was pregnant."

I pursed my lips. "I hope you know how terrible that sounds."

He sniffed and chuckled ruefully. "The irony is not lost on me. But it was all for show. We didn't... we haven't slept together since then."

"What about the night after the masquerade in Venice?" I asked. "I remember picking up that mess in the morning."

"I tried," he admitted. "I had to get you out of my system some-how. I didn't want to—God, I didn't want to drag you into this mess. Believe me. But there you were, ripe for the taking. I couldn't help myself."

I dug my fingers into the sand beside me, sifting the granules through them a few times.

"But I couldn't make myself, er, feel anything with her... if you know what I mean," he continued. "And then the trip to Greece was unbearable. I was so thankful that damn cat tripped my mum and gave me an excuse to get away."

"Don't say that," I chided.

He shrugged his shoulders. "I love my mum and would never wish her harm, but it's true. You belonged on that yacht with me, Em. Not Georgina. I know you came up with the idea and planned it all with me in mind, because I told you how much I loved Greece in passing a few weeks prior."

I gave him a small smile, though the confirmation that he realised such a thing made my heart melt. It was all I ever wanted: recognition for my toils. But I also knew what he was doing; either consciously or unconsciously, he seemed to be controlling me through my reaction to these words. He knew what I wanted to hear.

"It was brilliant, by the way," he said. "The gift was. But I should have shared the experience with you." He let the words drift off into the breeze, but his silence didn't last long. "Now that I really think about it, you've always been more of a girlfriend to me than she ever was."

"She got all the benefits, though," I replied. "Well, at least in the beginning she did. But it's always been like that. I live her life for her, and she is merely the mask I wear."

Alex made a small indecipherable sound in his throat. He sighed and squeezed my thigh. "Look at us. Both being who we're not to fool everyone into believing we have it all together."

I nodded. "I think the correct terminology is 'two peas in a pod.'"

He laughed.

We sat together for some time before going back to the house, neither of us daring to speak again. I didn't want to face the hard truths of our arrangement any more than I had to, and it seemed like Alex was content with that. We neither moved forward nor moved backward. We remained in the same place with each other.

I tried to ignore the other things he told me. If I didn't ignore them, then I might consider his feelings for me to be deeper. I couldn't allow myself that comfort. Any knowledge of such feelings only made the difficult decisions facing me—sooner rather than later—next to impossible.

CHAPTER 20

I CONSIDERED ESCAPING to my little guest house as soon as we returned to Alex's after a lengthy morning and afternoon at Morgan King's photoshoot. However, the futility of the thought became clear the instant I set one foot in the front door.

Georgina walked ahead of me and tossed her bag and coat over an obliging chair in the entrance rather than hanging them on the coat rack one foot to the left. She turned to say something to me, but I ignored her in favour of concentrating on balancing two bulky garment bags and an accessory tote in my hands. When I finally set the things down and gave my aching arms a rest, I queried Georgina again. However, she never got the opportunity to repeat herself, startled as we were by a thundering herd of wildebeests running through the house. A growling and exasperated Spaniard yelling a string of indecipherable foreign curses followed the noise. Then there was laughter and high-pitched squealing.

A little boy cried. "Papa! Stop!"

"Mama! Help!"

"Uncle Alex! Uncle Alex!" called a demanding little girl.

"What is it sweetheart?"

I froze when I heard Alex's velvety purr. There was no mistaking how highly Alex thought of the girl who called to him; the sound of adoration made me sigh in contentment. He was excited to be doing whatever he was with his friends and their children. Such carefree moments must have been in short supply of late, and I was relieved to hear he found some happiness among it all.

"Will you colour with me, Uncle Alex?" asked the girl.

"Of course, my darling." He laughed amid a shriek of jubilation from the child.

I thought about monopolising Georgina to protect that sacred time for him. As soon as she walked through the house and found them, she would turn into a wet blanket, smothering all the joy out of the evening. But I didn't mobilise swiftly enough.

She cast me an ugly eye-rolling grimace and continued through the foyer into the living portions of the house. Even though I didn't witness the others' reactions, the energy in the whole house changed as soon as Georgina made an appearance. What was once filled with bright happiness now seemed to be a stormy cloud. And yet, in the interest of civility, Gabriel and Amy both received her warmly—though formally—into the fold. The children were not discussed.

"Where's Emilia?" Gabriel asked, his accent thick and sultry. I could listen to him read the dictionary.

"Oh, she's just bringing in some things from the shoot today."

The dismissal in Georgina's voice made me sigh. Even though I had long known I was a pebble in her shoe, I still wanted to hear a bit more concern for my person, struggling as I was to carry in bloody heavy garment bags full of beaded and embellishment-encrusted red carpet gowns. I hung the bags up in the coat closet and stuffed the tote inside until later.

"And Jack?" Alex asked.

"Still with Morgan."

I stopped in front of the large mirror in the hall, adjusting the diaphanous white button down and black skinny jeans I was wearing. Despite the hectic photoshoot, I remained unfrazzled; my makeup looked fresh and my hair mostly stayed in the knot at the back of my head except for a few wayward coils. At least I looked presentable.

Sucking in a breath, I stepped around the entrance into the huge family room-kitchen combo. I noticed Amy first. She stood behind the large granite island, stirring something in a saucepan over the flame of the gourmet cooker. Groceries and pots and pans were spread out over the expansive counter space, but she looked right at home moving amongst the controlled chaos of the kitchen. But I supposed it was to be expected of a professional chef.

"Ah, there she is!"

I turned to Gabriel, who took three long strides to reach me. He was the only man, other than Lindsay, capable of making me feel small in stature, especially since Gabriel started an intense physical regimen in preparation for a new movie he refused to tell anyone about. Instead of shaking my hand in greeting, he pulled me into his giant arms and hugged me close. Any other time, I might have died a happy death while being squeezed by such a gorgeous man. This time, it only made me more uncomfortable.

A crooked smile stretched across his stubble-dusted face. A dark, long lashed eye winked at me. "Everything all right with you, Emilia?"

I chuckled at his apparent enthusiasm and shrugged my shoulders noncommittally. If I actually said how I felt and aired my grievances accordingly, none of them would like me very much. Thankfully, he accepted the shrug as an answer and muttered, "I understand."

Georgina didn't hear it, thankfully. She was too busy filling a goblet with some kind of fruity concoction which looked suspiciously like sangria. Amy came out from behind the kitchen island and wiped her hands on an apron. She was as tiny and blonde as Georgina, but quite a bit more pleasant, pulling me close and planting kisses on each of my cheeks. I tried to believe all of this friendliness was natural for Gabriel and Amy, but I couldn't shake the feeling that they were overly friendly only because they understood the situation and my place in it; they were being supportive of Alex, not of me. At least they didn't hate me or shun me. It was more than I expected, honestly. All of Georgina's friends, on the other hand, treated me with mild contempt if I breathed the same air as them.

Alex sat cross-legged with a little blonde haired, blue eyed pixie in the middle of the family room at a low circular table, madly scribbling with a crayon on some blank paper. Gabriel introduced me to his older twins, Will and Jamie, who were more interested in running around Georgina's feet than paying attention to me. He pointed to the little girl with Alex. "That's Isabel. And Carlos is sleeping in the other room."

Isabel wanted nothing to do with me, either. She was focused on Alex and only Alex. *Just like every other woman who met him*, I mused. There was, otherwise, laughter and talking and the joy of children unfettered by the sizeable elephant their older counterparts were ignoring. It actually felt like a home instead of a steel-and-concrete mausoleum where no one dared speak to each other for fear of saying something wrong, like it had felt that morning before Georgina and I left for the photoshoot.

No wonder Alex had arranged the dinner with them. If not only to piss off Georgina, his friends and their children provided us all with a happy diversion.

"Would you like some sangria?"

I blinked and looked at the small woman beside me. Alcohol was not tempting with the tequila from the previous evening still trying to make me sick, but I nodded anyway to be polite.

"It's homemade, you'll love it," Gabriel added as I walked past him toward the kitchen with Amy.

"I didn't know you'd be cooking," I said. "You should be spending time with Alex, not slaving over the meal."

Amy laughed and patted my arm. "Oh, I hardly ever get to anymore because we're always so busy and all over the place. I like cooking for my friends and family, so it's nice to find a little time to do it."

"Let's be honest," Gabriel interjected. "She just does it for Alex because she loves him more than me."

Amy waved a finger at her husband. "And don't you forget it."

I glanced at Alex, who seemed unfazed by the discussion about him. He merely lifted an eyebrow and chuckled, his attention quickly turning back to Isabel. Amy filled my empty hands with a glass and told me to sit in one of the stools surrounding the island so we could chat. I didn't argue with her. Amy wasn't the type of woman you argued with; you simply followed her commands and liked it. And even if you truly didn't, you kept your mouth shut. It must have served her well running her own restaurant kitchens.

She pulled a tray of cold tapas from the refrigerator and set it on the countertop. "Please eat something! We have so much food!"

Gabriel popped a small bite into his mouth, chewed a moment, swallowed and grinned at his wife before he leaned down to kiss her. I smiled at the interaction though it made me uncomfortable. It was so obnoxiously sweet and they were so obviously in love. They were happy and joyful. And there I sat, sipping a flavourful sangria, while a vile woman slunk her way across the room to the man I both loved and loathed.

"Would you care for anything Georgina? Alex?" Gabriel offered.

Alex waved his hand. "I'll get up for some in a minute if my darling Isabel will let me up."

Isabel ignored him. I giggled.

"Georgina?" Gabriel asked.

I detected a hint of sarcasm in his voice. We all knew Georgina didn't eat. Georgina didn't say anything and made a small sound of disapproval before falling into the seat behind Alex, close enough that she could claim her authority over him with a booted foot just touching his back, but also with him offering enough protection from the ankle biters running through the room with their toys in their hands.

"*Puta ingrata*," spat the angry Spaniard beside me.

I started at the invective and nearly spit the sangria in my mouth all over the countertop. People needed to stop making inflammatory statements while I was mid-swallow. My eyes swept to Amy, who looked at me with a mischievous gleam in her blue eyes. Never in my life was I so grateful that Georgina couldn't speak any other language than some poor French as needed for the business. Had she known Gabriel called her an "ungrateful bitch," the night would have quickly devolved into World War Three. But it was nice to share the moment with both Amy and Gabriel, even though a part of me felt like a little girl in the schoolyard spreading nasty rumours about others behind their backs.

From over the rim of my sangria goblet, I watched Alex extricate himself from his seat, cast a glare at Georgina, and walk over to us. Seven other stools surrounded the giant island, offering him ample space wherever he wanted to sit. He sat in the one next to me. Right there in front of Georgina. And I hated him for it. While I understood, on some level, he did it to counter Georgina's move, we weren't prepared for her to realise it.

I wasn't prepared for her realise it.

Alex stuffed food in his mouth and I was grateful he couldn't talk. To occupy myself, I looked at Amy. "Is there something I can help with? Please?"

Amy sensed my desperation and shot Alex a pinched glower. He merely shifted the hand beneath the counter over and placed it on my knee. I fidgeted uncomfortably though there was no way for Georgina to see it from her angle.

"Well," Amy said as she cleared her throat. "I'm mostly done getting everything ready… we'll just have to go outside for the grill—I'm making paella."

"Oh, I love paella," I chirped a little too brightly.

One of the twins tripped and fell on the other side of the room. He screamed bloody murder until Gabriel rolled his eyes and left to comfort his son. Once scooped up into his father's protective arms, the child quieted.

"I lived in Spain for about six months," I explained. "I went on a job and fell in love with it. It was amazing."

"Oh, yeah? Where did you live?"

"All over. Majorca for a little while—we did a beach shoot there and I stayed," I said. "Then I travelled to Madrid and Barcelona and Seville. Of all the travelling I did, Seville was one of my favourites. But not as much as Rome. I spent most of my time eating my way around Italy."

Amy laughed and patted her flat belly. "I did that for about three years right after culinary school. I love pasta. Pasta does not love me."

An indelicate snort across the room made the hair on the back of my neck rise. I looked up in time to watch Georgina saunter her way over to us. Alex removed his hand from my leg and shifted in his seat.

"You know, Emilia," Georgina said, butting in to the conversation as she came to a rest on the other side of kitchen island. "You might have actually made something of yourself as a model if you'd spent more time trying to find bookings instead of eating to maintain a plus size."

Except for the jabbering kids—and even they seemed to pause to look at the evil woman snaking a hand around Alex's shoulders—the room fell into a stunned silence. She had made plenty of open jabs at my physique before, but never this openly or in front of other people in such a nasty tone. Even though I was fairly happy with my body, I was mortified by the situation in front of these people. I wasn't sure why, either. They knew what Georgina was like. It shouldn't have been a surprise to any of us she would be capable saying something so cruel.

But she *had* said it—aloud—and no one but Georgina was pleased with her.

I stared at her for a long while, seeing the nearly imperceptible smirk curve her pink lips and the flash of challenge in her eyes. She was goading me to jump into the ring with her. I didn't have to.

Alex lifted a hand and batted her arm away from him. "That was completely uncalled for, Georgina."

271

Fire surged in Georgina's eyes. "It's the truth, though. The truth often hurts. If she hadn't spent so much time eating, she wouldn't weigh as much, she would be a straight size model with an actual career."

"No." Alex shoved a little harder on her arm and stood up from his seat. "No! This is ridiculous. *You* are ridiculous."

I sighed and reached for Alex, placing a hand on his arm in an attempt to stop him, not thinking how it might appear to Georgina. "Alex—"

He jerked away from me, effectively freezing the words in my throat. "If you aren't going to say something about it, I am."

Please don't, I silently pleaded.

His hatred flickered off of him in startling sparks of red hot fury. It was the first time I really witnessed his rage. Real, unadulterated rage. If I hadn't been as stunned by Georgina's boldness, I might have been frightened. His reaction wasn't all because of the comments she made and more due to the amalgamation of his continued suffering playing into the outburst, but I hated being the unwitting instigator of the argument. I hated the stigma. Georgina wouldn't be able to resist holding it over my head.

"Emilia is perfect! And if you're too spiteful to see that—" His words cut off as he searched for them. He never had trouble filling the void with his loquaciousness, but it was nice to find, in anger, he fumbled like the rest of us.

"Maybe if *you* were a little healthier, like her, you wouldn't have lost the baby." His cutting words rang throughout the silent space. By then, the kids quieted and watched the scene with wide eyes; though not understanding of the words, they certainly understood Uncle Alex's tone.

I hated it. I hated every moment of it.

Georgina was the only person, at least she presumed, to know the truth behind having "lost" the baby; bile rose up in my throat until I was nauseous. His words would do nothing to wound. They were hollow and devoid of meaning to her, but meant something far more important to him. She merely shrugged her shoulders as though it were water off a duck's back. Seeing her utter disregard for the man's emotions was something far worse than simply hearing or thinking about it after my conversation with Jack. This… this killed me. Nobody deserved it.

Alex said nothing more and left, walking out through the door to the garden, presumably to get some air. Georgina, seeing she lost her footing, spun around and exited the room. She disappeared upstairs. A few moments later, a door slammed shut.

Gabriel, Amy and I looked at each other with mouths agape. Alex and Georgina had done so well to hide their arguing around others, but not this time. This time was different. It felt different, anyway. Alex threw caution to the wind and let his emotions go, and in front of other people, no less. The illusion Georgina had constructed for her own machinations had shifted; she no longer had the perfect boyfriend who catered to her in front of others, or the misguided belief—if she was truly too stupid to realise it—she actually had a relationship with him.

"I… don't know what to do," I said.

"You don't need to do anything," Amy murmured and set a hand on my arm.

Gabriel shook his head and sighed. "I'll go see if Alex is all right."

The big man left with the two boys under his arms. Isabel returned to colouring. Amy looked at me again.

"I'm sorry, Amy," I muttered. "I've ruined dinner."

She shook her head at me. "You didn't ruin dinner. Nothing to be sorry about. And I think dinner will actually be more pleasant now, because I doubt we'll see Georgina for the rest of the night."

"But Alex will be a sulky arse," I said.

"Alex will be fine." She looked around her, searching for something in the sea of foodstuffs. "I do actually have something you could help me with, though. Do you know how to peel and devein shrimp?"

My body sagged in relief. "Oh, thank God, something to occupy me."

Amy laughed at me. "I'm a master at redirection. The kids don't know what hits them whenever I do it. Gabriel just looks at me mystified."

"I can imagine." I giggled and got up to wash my hands. Amy set a bowl of shrimp in front of me, another empty one beside it for the shells and tails, and handed me a sharp paring knife.

"Now, don't use this on Georgina," Amy warned. "Even though we've all considered it."

I smiled. "I won't. I promise."

The implement cut through the meat of the shrimp like a hot knife through butter. It would have been a fine tool to use were I in a particularly homicidal mood. Which, if I were being honest with myself, was only a hair's breadth away.

A while later, the front door opened and closed. Jack appeared in the living room and looked around; one glance was all he needed. "Aw… fuck. Where's Alex?"

"He's out back," I said, motioning with the knife in my hands.

Jack shook his head. "By the way, hello, Amy."

"Hey, Jack," she replied with a smile, though she did not stop her own preparations for cooking the paella.

We looked at each other after Jack stepped outside and degenerated into a fit of anxious, exasperated giggles. I didn't know about Amy, but for me, at least, I laughed only because my only other option was to cry. I refused to do that. I refused to give Georgina, or the thought of her, any more of my tears. She had already taken enough of them through the years.

CHAPTER 21

A CALL TO MY MOBILE drew me away from dinner that night, and though I wanted to stay and spend time with Gabriel and Amy, I also couldn't wait to get away from Alex and his sullenness. Thankfully, I had an unwitting yet helpful friend to extract me from the uncomfortable situation. When I made it into the guest house, I shut the exterior door and plopped down on the bed. I silenced the ringing before putting it to my ear.

"Hello?"

"Hey, chica," said the altogether too chipper voice on the other end. "Are you in L.A. yet?"

"I'm here. Whether I want to be or not is a completely different question."

Jordan sighed. "That doesn't sound very good at all. Where are you stayin'?"

"Right now? I'm at Alex's," I replied. "Where are you?"

"Nowhere yet. Just landed at the airport. Goin' through lines of paparazzi right now. I hate the Oscars. They just sit here and wait for us like fucking vultures."

I laughed at the annoyance in her voice. She made the big leagues with a contract with Victoria's Secret and a swimsuit cover around the time I quit modelling. Jordan had complained about the attention then. After marrying Dylan—the hottest thing to happen to country music in the past decade—the paparazzi crush in every facet of her life had become more insane. I didn't exactly feel bad for her, though. She still had some anonymity when she escaped to her husband's Tennessee ranch, not to mention a man who loved her completely and freely. She was definitely doing better than some of us.

"Be careful. They'll hear you and it'll be all over TMZ," I joked.

She groaned. "Don't remind me… hold on a minute."

Her Texas drawl came through the mobile in a muffle, but I heard her talking to someone who asked for an autograph. A few seconds later she spoke into the receiver. "Sorry about that."

"No problem."

"So anyway," she sighed. "I need to see you tomorrow for a spa day."
"Why?"

Jordan huffed into her mobile. "Don't ask me questions. I just need girl time at the spa. We're doin' the whole shebang. My treat. Wax, hair, nails, massages, facials, you know the drill. I have to get ready for the shoot with Alex."

"I don't have to do that anymore," I defended. "It's one of the reasons why I quit modelling."

"Oh, come on," Jordan said. "I know y'all haven't seen the inside of a super posh salon unless you've been there followin' Cruella around. I need a partner to help me endure the pain, and you're that person."

It was my turn to groan. "But I don't *want* to be your person."

Jordan laughed at me. "You're stuck with me anyway. I'm invoking best girlfriend code. Besides, Lindsay told me it was an order to take you out to get primped up, because you apparently have an important new boyfriend you haven't told me about."

"It's not one of those things you drop on someone over the phone."

"Tobias Sinclair is one of those things you call and tell one of your friends. Like, call the instant he asks you out to a premiere, even if it's as friends." The hurt in her voice was unmistakable. "And then I have to go and find photos of you two in a tabloid a week after the fact because Lindsay mentioned it."

"Jordan, you don't even know half the story."

"Well, I'm starting to piece it together," she returned. "It's all the more reason you and I need to go to the spa and gab."

"I know."

"Also," she took a breath, "we're going to a few red carpet events on Wednesday. You'll want to be beautified for them. I mean, not that you aren't already beautiful."

"I thought we were going out to get pissed and dance," I said. "I need that more than anything."

"I know," she confirmed. "But I've got to make a few of these appearances first… D isn't gonna get away from his stuff until Friday just in time for the actual show. So you're my date. And I'll ask you again… are you free tomorrow?"

"I guess."

She chuckled. "Don't sound so thrilled."

"Sorry." I yawned. "I'm just tired."

"Mmhmm," she hummed. "Anyway… my reservation is at the Four Seasons. I thought that's where you might be stayin' since that's Cruella's preferred chain, but I guess not."

I picked at the strands of my hair, drawing a long curl until it stretched to its full length. It really needed a cut and conditioning treatment; she was right. Though I usually kept up on my manicures, I didn't really take great care of my hair and other parts when I didn't feel like it. Besides the cost of it, the scarcity of personal time hindered trips to the salon. "I'm actually staying at Sunset Tower this time, because of the photoshoot with Alex and that's where our two other clients will be staying… the two we're dressing besides Alex and Tobias."

"Oh, well, we'll do the spa at the Four Seasons anyway," she concluded. "Tomorrow morning. Plan for ten."

"Do I really have to?"

Jordan laughed again. "Yes, you have to."

I groaned one more time for good measure, but it didn't sway

Jordan's cold heart. "I'll be there. Just nothing crazy, okay? No Brazilians."

"Honey, I wouldn't wish those on my worst enemy." She laughed. "And I'm a flippin' underwear model who does them all the time. Cruella doesn't even deserve it."

"Hold that thought," I said drily. "You'll probably think twice about that statement. She deserves a Promethean curse where she has continuous Brazilian waxes with blisters and bleeding and… and… ingrown hairs."

The muffled sounds of the airport around Jordan filled a long moment of silence on the other end of the line. Then she whistled. "Oh, hon, I think that's the worst thing you've ever said about her. I'm so proud of you."

"Thanks," I replied with a sigh. It felt good to get that bit of negativity off my chest. "So tomorrow morning?"

"Yeah. I'll see you in the morning. The luggage is just comin' down off of the carousel and I need to point it out to the driver."

"Good night, Jor."

"Night."

I waited until the line went dead before I moved the device from my ear. Tossing it aside, I stared up at the ceiling and listened to the conversation outside my abode; we'd enjoyed our meal out in the warm California dusk, but the sun had nearly set on the horizon and cast the guest house in rich violet hues. Judging from the discussion, Amy and Gabriel were preparing to get their children home to bed. I was just pulling myself up to bid my own farewells when my mobile jingled beside me. Thinking it was only Jordan having forgotten to tell me something, I picked it up in a hurry.

My face fell when I read who actually sent the message to me from a room up in a tower.

Georgina: I'm going to Vanessa's house for the night.

I waited a beat, not knowing what to reply, but I quickly typed a message back asking if she needed me to call a car. Why couldn't she trudge her arse down a flight of stairs and over to the guest house to tell me? Alex hadn't actually wounded her and she was merely proving a point.

> Georgina: Yes

She said nothing else so I began the search through my contacts for the car service we used in Los Angeles. A message popped up before I reached the "E" and Elite Limousine. I switched over to it.

> Georgina: *I want you gone by the time I return tomorrow afternoon.*

My stomach dropped to the floor like a lead weight and a tingling fuzziness set my skin on edge. My throat constricted with the sudden, uncomfortable race of my heart. I didn't know what to do. How to react. What had she meant by it? Had the argument really—

Ding.

I gulped and looked down at my mobile.

> Georgina: *Extend the hotel booking for one day.*

I breathed a partial sigh of relief. Why would I even want to continue dealing with this madness when I didn't have to? I almost wanted her to fire me so I didn't feel guilty leaving of my own volition with no safety net or plan for my future in place. Any blame, then, could be placed on her shoulders and not on mine. However, such thoughts of peace would evaporate almost instantly once I was jobless. I would, inevitably, suffer a gnawing shame knowing my responsibility in losing the job. Alex wouldn't have snipped at Georgina had I not allowed our relationship to progress the way it had.

Or maybe he would.

I sent her a message confirming the hotel extension.

> Georgina: *I won't need to see you until Tuesday for the Brit party.*

Honestly, I was surprised she hadn't told me to get out within the next few hours just to prove her point. The power she held was on a shaky footing and she, with her expertly manicured nails, usually dug her talons in for purchase in hopes of climbing back up to the top and asserting herself. I absolutely refused to let her do it again; if not for me, for Alex. As much as I didn't appreciate his methods, I couldn't deny the fact that no one deserved to suffer the way he had.

Ding.

Georgina: Have you called for a car yet?

I grumbled and tried to focus on the task at hand. My call was quick and easy and they said they'd arrive within the hour. After I alerted her to that fact, my mobile went silent. Deciding that a call to the hotel to fix my reservation could wait, I slipped it inside my pocket and went outside to rejoin the party. Alex must have been inside the house, but Jack was trying to stay out of the path of the parents collecting their children.

"Everything okay?" Gabriel inquired as I slipped beside him.

"Fine." I smiled. "It was a friend asking about my plans this week."

Amy looked up from battling the twins and stuffing their small feet in their trainers. "Anything fun?"

"Spa day tomorrow, apparently," I replied.

"Who's your friend?"

Gabriel's question didn't strike me as odd and I answered him quickly. Then I realised the shared glance over my head with Alex as he came back to the garden; it struck me that perhaps Gabriel wasn't ready to completely entrust me with Alex considering the circumstances. I understood why and wondered if they hadn't also heard about Tobias' interest in me. Tobias said he told Alex about his feelings when they met up at Starbucks the time I briefly interrupted them—and I had little doubt now about whether Alex relayed this information to them. They weren't idiots and put two and two together. What I didn't tell them was that Tobias and I had standing plans as well, made before I even left London.

But that was something I couldn't—and wouldn't—think about while I was at Alex's. Mostly because I felt terrible for hardly thinking about Tobias since he left my flat after our impromptu pizza date in my bedroom. He deserved so much more than someone preoccupied with other things... and another man. Still, I couldn't ignore the fact that when I did think of him, a stupid grin always formed on my lips.

"It'll be a busy week," I said with a small smile. "I'm sure I'll see you around at some point."

Gabriel grinned and hugged me farewell. "I hope so. Tonight was lovely, except for, well, you know…"

I nodded, but Alex interrupted us and showed the family to the front door like a good host, leaving Jack and me staring at each other.

"She's spending the night at someone's house," I said softly, slipping onto the bench seat alongside the wooden picnic table.

"She is?" He didn't believe me. "This would mark the first time she didn't make him stew in it."

"Maybe she's loosening her noose on him?"

Jack shot me a look, suspicious. "Or planning something worse."

We stared at each other, silently considering how much "worse" Georgina might create for Alex. I shuddered and shook my head. "I refuse to believe someone could be that evil."

I stood from the seat and began collecting the remaining dinnerware scattered across the table. Jack stopped me with a hand, shaking his head. "Alex and I will do it. Just get her out of here for the night and then go relax."

Not one to look a gift horse in the mouth, I nodded my head and went into the house to search for Georgina. She was hastily throwing things into one of her smaller pieces of luggage when she told me to enter the master suite.

"May I help with anything?"

Georgina shook her head. "I hope you're happy."

"I'm sorry?"

"What is it about women like you that make men like Alex want to make you one of his bloody charity projects?"

I bit my tongue and folded my hands behind my back. Without

looking at them I knew my knuckles had turned white from the strength in which I gripped the mobile between them. Her shot was well aimed. I thought from the beginning that his attraction to me was only his pity and I was nothing more than a charity project. Even now, with all I had learned, I questioned his interest in me. Was it real or a product of the situation? Had he just jumped at the first available option? Was it because any choice was better than Georgina? Any diversion would make it better?

But I knew, deep down, it wasn't pity. I didn't understand exactly what it was that drew him to me, but our conversation on the beach that morning proved to me something more informed his motives. However, her voicing my own suspicions aloud were more than a little difficult to hear.

"I knew something like this would happen," she muttered, closing the top of the case with a *clunk* and zipping it shut. "With you staying here. With you being invited to all these things."

"Something like what?" I asked softly.

Georgina turned and glared at me. "What happened earlier. It's utterly ridiculous the way he panders to people like you."

People like me? I rolled the thought over in my head. She never made any sense to me, and frankly, I couldn't have cared less about her being upset. She would be back tomorrow staking her claim on Alex to ruin a little more of his life, and I would be at the hotel hopefully finding some comfort away from them.

My mobile rang a few minutes later to alert me of the limousine's arrival. She left her bag for me to carry down after her, and I thanked the gods that we didn't run into Alex or Jack on our way out the door.

Once I saw her off, I made the quickest possible retreat to the guest house. I shut the doors and fell back into the bed, watching the ceiling fan above me spin around in the swiftly fading dusk. The rhythm of the fan blades lulled me into a mindless calm until I slipped easily into slumber, my body and mind exhausted.

I WOKE SOME TIME LATER to pitch black and warmth from a nightmare I couldn't readily remember, my skin slick with perspiration. The air in the room wasn't moving despite the fan above, turning the room into a suffocating and stuffy box. No matter how much I flipped around to find a sufficiently cool spot in the sheets, my clothing and the hot air made it impossible. With a groan, I pulled myself from the bed and walked to the set of doors facing the pool. A gust of cool but damp ocean air swirled past me when I opened them and ruffled the sheer drapes. I did the same with the doors facing the sea, creating a delectable flow of air through the small space. It immediately cooled my feverish skin.

To complete the process, I slipped out of my day clothes and put on one of my old sleep shirts beneath a dressing gown. It wasn't entirely demure, but it was enough to pop over to the main house for a cold water bottle; a look at the clock told me it was near one in the morning and the windows into the main building were dark. I wouldn't run into anyone.

The smooth ceramic tiles were cold but soothing beneath my feet as I tiptoed into the house. I closed the door behind me and crept into the kitchen for my drink. When I was slipping back out into the hallway, a faint blue glow on an opposite wall drew me down the corridor into another room. I thought I ought to turn back around and go to my bed, but curiosity got the better of me.

The large television hanging high on the wall in the family room was aglow but blank blue. Two bare masculine feet extended over the end of the sofa positioned in front of the telly and the dull snore of a deep sleep rose in the quiet. I inched over to the couch and peeked at the sleeper, finding the man of both my dreams and nightmares stretched out on the cushions, one hand resting on his chest and the other curled beneath the pillow under his head.

It struck me, for the briefest of moments, how innocently he slept. Like a child, almost, with his eyes closed and soft lashes pressed against a freckled cheek. The glowing television cast the planes of his face in harsh, mysterious illumination, but the innocence remained. Perhaps, I thought, it wasn't innocence as much as it was complete freedom from his troubles. I realised just how much his life had caught up with him. I couldn't remember the last time I saw him so untroubled. This was the Alex I wanted. Perhaps not innocent, but definitely unfettered by the weight of his choices. Something told me I would never have that person. How could he go back or disappear besides somewhere in his dreams?

With a sigh, I tiptoed back to the guest house. My bedroom still didn't feel comfortable enough when I returned, despite the cool water I sipped and even cooler breeze fanning my hair against my face, so I threw off the dressing gown and shirt. I laid on my stomach and pulled a pillow up beneath me. When sleep didn't immediately return, I flicked on a lamp and grabbed my mobile to check my emails, only to be interrupted a short few minutes later.

"Em? Are you awake?"

The low voice carried on the wind. I twisted my body toward the window and squinted at the faint silhouette of the man standing just outside the doors on the deck.

"I'm awake," I murmured. "You can come in if you want."

Alex stepped into the room and squinted his eyes in the low lamplight. A slow smile turned up the corners of his lips. "Have I wandered into a dream?"

"Perhaps." I whispered. "Are you sleepwalking?"

"Uh, no," he replied. "I woke up when you left the house."

"I thought I was quiet."

Alex shook his head. "You were. But I must have sensed your perfume and that started to wake me… you could have crawled in beside me."

I shrugged. "You looked peaceful. I didn't want to bother you."

Unmoving from his spot in the middle of the room, he waited for permission to join me in bed. It was so unlike the forceful and dominant Alex that it caught me off guard. It was nice to see a little of his vulnerability for a minute.

"Are you just going to stand there or are you going to come lie with me?"

Rather than walking around the bed and climbing in on the open side like a normal person, he strolled to my side and crawled over me. He threw one long leg over my hips to pull himself over, as though mounting a motorbike. Fingers pushed lightly into the bare skin at the small of my back just above my knickers for a bit of leverage. He completed the graceful movement and threw the other leg over.

I would have likened it to a giant kid jumping into bed, except for the fact that I was well aware of the completely sinful way his lean muscled body skimmed just so against my back. My body shuddered at the scratch of his shirt on my bare skin, a ghosting sensation which drew a small, content sigh from my lips. As he settled and stretched out beside me, he flattened the palm of his hand on my skin and slid up the curve of spine and sinew to my shoulder blade. He brushed my hair back and pressed a slow kiss to my shoulder, sweeping his soft lips further down my arm before stopping. I shivered at the sensation. My nipples constricted uncomfortably yet exquisitely against the soft bedding beneath them.

"Like a gazelle, you are," I laughed lazily.

His chuckle came out low and tired. "I prefer to be more like a lion. I rather be the hunter than the hunted."

The comment made me smile. He pushed a curly tendril behind my ear before twining his fingers deeper into my hair.

"What are you doing anyway?" he asked, nodding toward the mobile in my hands.

"Checking my emails," I answered. "I couldn't fall back asleep. The room was too stuffy and I was too hot."

"It is rather warm in here."

I glanced at him in time to see the suggestive wiggle of his expressive brows. I shook my head and tried to contain my laughter. "California must be having a heat wave."

We lapsed into silence and I tried to ignore him, but it was a Herculean feat, especially as those lovely, sure hands of his drew lazy shapes over my inflamed skin.

"Put away the work," he demanded softly. "Not in bed. Not when we're here together."

I clicked off the screen but did not put it on the table beside the bed. When he saw that I didn't take that step, he quickly snatched the mobile from me.

"Give it back to me."

My protest was weak. He held it out of my reach until I lunged for it. I didn't put much effort behind the move and fell against him laughingly, my chest partially pressed against him. He looked at me and lifted a challenging brow, daring me with his silence to try another move. I couldn't resist and easily found my strength, pressing my palms flat against his chest and pushing him back onto the bed.

He didn't seem the least bit surprised by the action, nor by the way I threw my left leg over his hips and rested my bum in the seat of his pelvis. A soft moan slipped from his lips. He was more than a little pleased with the development, if the hard length pressing through his trousers was any indication.

"You're rather easy to pin for a mighty lion," I chided softly, leaning over for the mobile. He released his grasp and watched me as I carefully relocated the thing to the bedside table. Before I turned back to him, he caught my right hand and placed a delicate but scratchy kiss on the palm. He sighed, twining his fingers with mine as I shifted back over him.

"Perhaps," he whispered, "the lion is simply learning to be mighty again."

"I don't think the lion ever lost his mightiness," I answered quietly. "He simply forgot he had it."

I leaned over him to kiss away a chuckle playing on his lips. He buried his fists into my hair and used the momentary distraction to flip our position. Strong hands pinned my wrists above my head and his mouth travelled a meandering path down the length of my neck.

"I do feel like a gazelle, though," I muttered breathlessly. "About to be devoured."

His lips curved against my collarbone. The head with the curly red mane lifted and peered down at me. Blue eyes looked at me with all sober seriousness. "You aren't the gazelle."

"Then what am I?" I giggled.

"You are a lioness," he muttered, pressing a searing kiss to my lips. "*My* lioness."

His words made my heart flutter. They were just words, but they were words I needed to hear. I gave into him fully, wrapping my legs around his waist and enjoying the feel of his weight pressing me back into the bed.

In the morning, I would tell him I was leaving for the hotel, but until that time, I made the conscious decision to enjoy him—to enjoy us—and think of nothing else. Not of duty, or work, or family, or terrible people ruining our lives.

Fortunately, Alex made doing that all too easy.

CHAPTER 22

THE EARLY MORNING SUN woke me before the alarm beeped on my mobile. A chilly breeze blew in through the windows, throwing the sheer curtains up into the air, giving me a clear view of the serene outdoors for the briefest of moments. I buried deeper into the wildly flung bedclothes when the cool air kissed my nakedness and coaxed gooseflesh to the surface, but I ended up hitting a hard, warm body stretched out behind me.

It was surprising, but lovely, that he stayed through the night. No surprises waited for me like they had when I rushed downstairs to get out of the house without having to face his mother in embarrassment. I wouldn't have to worry about the location of my knickers or the fact that Georgina ended her holiday to France earlier than expected. We could simply wake up like two normal humans after a night shared with each other. However, the universe, as it was wont to do, was ever so quick to remind me we were not two normal human beings in a normal situation which would allow us the normalcy of a paradise so complete.

Alex's strong arm curled around my torso and pulled me back against his chest, securely fitting my curves into all the bends and ridges of his muscular body as though I belonged there. His fingers tickled the skin over my ribs and slipped further north before they insinuated themselves just under the heavy globe of my left breast.

The thumb swept over the curve but stopped halfway as he pushed one of his legs between my thighs to twine an ankle around one of mine. I couldn't move from the position even if I wanted to do so. The sheer possessiveness of the action made me sigh with a contentment I did not know was possible.

It would have been so easy to forget about everything and fall into this embrace never to leave it again, but I knew, deep down, such a thing wasn't possible. Even lying there in our early morning bliss tempted fate.

He sighed, the breath ruffling the hair by my ear. The change in his breathing told me he had awoken, or was very near to it, but I dared not speak. Speaking would ruin the moment of perfect peace. The complete awareness of this oddly calming possession would evaporate as soon as I told him what could wait no longer.

His soft lips brushed the shell of my ear, my neck and the top of my shoulder. "Don't get up," he breathed. The voice was low and gravelly with sleep. "Not yet."

"I have to," I muttered. "I have things to do."

"Like?"

"I have to pack."

He hummed lowly and used his thumb to draw a lazy circle around my nipple until it puckered. "Why?"

I gulped. "I'm going to the hotel this morning."

Employing a finger in his lackadaisical ministrations, he lightly pinched the hardened flesh, enticing a small cry from me. "Not until tomorrow."

I couldn't stay in my spot. He couldn't keep doing those things to me. I had to keep my head about me, especially since we already overstayed our time together. He growled when I grabbed his hand and pulled it away from my body. I untangled myself from his grasp and scooted to the edge of the bed as gracefully as possible. The shirt he discarded when he joined me many hours before was the nearest piece of clothing, so I slipped it on over my naked torso. It barely covered my bottom, but it was enough to give me protection from his absurdly incredible touch and his wandering gaze.

When I turned to face him, he sat up in bed with dejection written on his face. "You're not going to the hotel until tomorrow."

"No," I corrected. "Today. This morning."

"No," he said flatly. Decisively. "Tomorrow."

I sighed. "Georgina said I had to be gone before she returned."

"I don't give a flying fuck about what she told you," Alex growled. "This is my fucking house, and if I want you to fucking stay one more day, you're staying."

"You can't exactly *make* me stay, either."

He looked at me with fire in his eyes, the red-sparking anger from the previous night returned. I was unsure whether it was due to me, or due to Georgina, or a combination of us both. He scrambled out of bed, fully nude and in a rage which made me take a few steps back. He didn't care about his nakedness; for my part, even though I had so many things running through my mind, I couldn't help but stare at his golden beauty. He looked like a bloody fearsome Greek statue with the early morning sunbeams washing over his skin.

"I *want* you to stay here with me."

I sighed and forced myself to meet his eyes. "What about what I want?"

"You don't want to stay?" he asked, his voice faltering. "I thought we had…"

"Thought we had… what?"

He held his arms out in incensed confusion. "I thought since you knew about everything—"

"That I'm just going to fall all over you? Let you continue to be selfish and an overbearing arsehole? This isn't a bloody relationship, Alex. This is us occasionally fucking. There's no romance or love involved."

I wished it were the truth. Unfortunately, it all meant quite a bit more to me than it ever did to him. Of course he might fancy himself in love, but put to the test, his feelings were likely based on lust. Only the lure of control kept him interested.

Alex took two steps forward.

I backed up and held my hands up to stop his advancement. "Please put some clothes on."

"*You're* wearing *my* clothes."

Disconcerted, I looked down at myself and grumbled. "Where are your bloody pants and trousers?"

We half-heartedly looked around the room from where we stood, but came up with nothing. He growled again and began tossing sheets and blankets around the room. "I don't understand why you don't want to—"

"Why?" Tears burned my eyes, but I swallowed them with the lump in my throat. "If you have to ask why then you're even more clueless than I thought."

"You don't want to stay because of Georgina?" he asked.

"Alex, I don't want to stay because of either of you," I said, my voice wavering. "Last night at dinner should have proved to you what could happen—"

"Last night!" He stepped toward me and paused to slip one leg, then the other, into his boxers. He pulled them to his hips. Running his hands through his wild hair, he turned to look at me and spoke under his breath, "Last night I fucking defended you from that conniving bitch and this is how you repay me?"

His words were a slap in the face. Whether he meant them or whether said hastily in anger, they hit their mark squarely in the centre of my chest. It chipped away at my heart as I fumbled to put it out of reach. I had to turn my emotions off.

"I don't owe you a fucking thing!"

Alex scoffed. "That's not what I—"

I waved my hands in front of me like a referee motioning an incomplete scoring attempt. "Oh my God! I can't do this anymore!"

He stared at me, eyes flashing with barely contained aggravation.

So I laid into him. I let all of the rage, guilt, confusion, empathy and pain building since Venice boil to the top in a flurry of furious words. "We can't keep doing this… this… this arguing! I can't keep doing this with all the high ups and the low lows. I'm going positively *mad* trying to keep everything straight by serving more than one master. No one person can do all this shit and expect to make it out for the fucking better. Jesus bloody Christ! Here I am serving all these different people and I can't for one fucking minute think about my own fucking self or about what *I* want or what *I* need. Don't you get that? I thought I explained that to you yesterday on the beach. Don't you see you're trying to do to me exactly what she did to you with her mind games?"

He seemed to deflate at my words, but barely enough. The muscles in his jaw clenched, released, and clenched again. He turned away. I saw the tears in his eyes. It was the last reaction I expected from him.

Alex cleared his throat. "So what was last night then? Just a good-bye fuck? A farewell because you knew what you were going to do to me in the morning?"

"I-I… No, it wasn't." I tried to find my words, but he blindsided me with his. By their rawness. He seemed genuinely hurt. But I had to stay strong. I had to do this. For the both of us. "Alex, I'm doing this because I can't keep up with our arrangement. The stress of it is too much for us… for *me*. You're barely holding it together as it is."

"N—" he began to protest but I held up a hand to stop him.

"You've got a lot of people who love you and who are very worried about you," I explained. "And I'm not helping you. I'm making you worse. Then I wake up hating myself for giving in to you and in to my own selfishness every single time you come 'round. It's not healthy for me and it's certainly not healthy for you."

Alex's fists clenched at his sides and he turned around in a few circles looking for the pyjama trousers thrown elsewhere in the room. He found them under a pillow on the other side of the bed and quickly pulled them on.

"You need to sort your life out," I said, taking a breath. "I'm only getting in the way."

When he strode back over to me, he didn't stop until we stood chest-to-chest. He held my gaze. "Emilia, shut up."

I opened my mouth to protest his rudeness, but he stopped me with strong fingers biting into my upper arms, holding me in place to prevent my escape. Then he kissed me. Roughly. My knees weakened when he stepped back and let go. I wobbled a moment and met his pained, but knowing, eyes. He proved his point.

"You still want to tell me to bugger off?" he challenged. His voice was dead. It made me sick.

"That's not my point, Alex."

"What *is* your point? Enlighten me."

"The point is I'm going to the bloody hotel this morning. You can't control what's happening any more than I can."

A brow raised in challenge. He knew his power over me and proved it with one rough kiss. His arrogance infuriated me. I wanted to slap him, but I restrained myself.

"Until the time in which you get your shit together, this isn't happening," I finished, heaving a great sigh. It would probably never happen again, anyway. Once he got rid of Georgina, he would move on to bigger and better things. And to other women.

I watched him slide the mask of indifference back into place. The heat of his anger turned into cold conceit. He breathed and shook his head. "Is that all, then?"

With a pained wince, I nodded.

Alex rolled his eyes and threw his hands up in disgust. "I'm going back to the house."

"Fine."

"Fine," he snapped and left through the open doors for his refuge.

I stood and stared at the wreck of a bed for what seemed like an age until I gave up and started getting ready. I had already wasted enough time with him.

OUR ARGUMENT and Alex's unsettling anger stayed on my mind all the way to my hotel room as I stacked my luggage in the closet. They followed me back down the lifts, and haunted me on the short walk toward the Four Seasons. The taxis looked tempting, but the traffic was characteristically bad; I figured the walk would do me good. I hoped it would clear my mind.

Naturally it didn't, but as I walked up to the front entrance, a large party happened to be exiting a group of sleek black SUVs. The disturbance was enough to draw my attention away from my head. Judging from the number of attendants, it clearly involved someone important. When I tried focusing on my own path on the pavement, however, a large man stepped in front of me. I stopped dead and looked up at him. His chrome name badge and plastic ear piece gave away his position in hotel security.

"May I help you, miss?"

I cleared my throat. "I've an appointment at the spa at ten."

He eyed me cautiously. He didn't like the fact that I arrived on foot. It was apparent to me, though, he was simply stalling for time until the party in the dark vehicles finally disappeared inside the building. I squinted in the direction of the group to see if I could figure out who deserved that level of protection; I had never been so happy to see a familiar face in a tan Stetson. I didn't contain my glee and shouted in his direction.

"Oi! Dylan!"

And that was when the security guy gave me a once over and decided I was up to no good. My behaviour seemed to confirm for him I was nothing more than a crazy fan.

"Miss, you need to leave the property," the security guard said, already beginning to shove me.

I turned back to him. "You don't understand. I'm here to meet his wife… she's my friend. I was chief bridesmaid at their wedding."

The man's eyes narrowed critically.

Movement out of the corner of my eye made me turn; Dylan heard me anyway and sauntered over in our direction.

"Now, you wouldn't be here to visit my wife, would you?" he asked with a giant grin.

"Well, I'm supposed to, that is if this fine gentleman would let me pass," I said. We both looked at the security guard, me with a little more triumph than strictly necessary.

Yes, believe it or not, Mr. Security Guard, I am someone.

"It's all right, she's with me," Dylan said, shooing the man away.

Sometimes I wished I was as important as someone like him. Or like Georgina. As sad as it was, I couldn't deny the power I felt following Georgina around. Maybe I had enjoyed the perks of her celebrity more than I cared to admit.

Dylan pulled me into his arms without warning, but his strong hug was more than welcome. He smelled spicy and felt rather solid beneath his Western-style button down. He had been like a big, dopey, ridiculously talented brother since Jordan first introduced us three years prior. Even though we weren't what one would term best mates—we usually kept up on each others' lives through Jordan—I had never met a sweeter Southern gentleman in my life.

Jordan always said one of her favourite qualities about him was that at any given moment he looked sun kissed and rugged, like he spent the day roping cattle and working with his hands, only to come back home to sing the night away. There was nothing prissy or elegantly English about him. And I thought, for a fleeting moment, how nice it was to be pulled into a comforting masculine hug without out a million thoughts of guilt flashing before my eyes. He felt safe. Secure. There was no confusion about affairs with Alex or my tepid feelings for Tobias. It just was.

"How're you doin', darlin'?" His light Tennessean twang sounded like music to my ears.

"Honestly?"

He set me back and looked in my eyes. "I don't like the sound of that. But I'm sure Jordan will fix it for you."

"She's pretty magical, but I don't think she can solve this one for me."

Dylan slid an arm around my shoulders and moved us in the direction of the front entrance where the other members of his entourage awaited him.

"Why are you here anyway? I thought—"

"We ended up rescheduling some things so I could make it out here earlier. I wanted to spend time with my honey," he explained. "And the Academy person said I had to be here for rehearsals for the song."

I grinned. "Congratulations, by the way."

Dylan laughed as we stepped inside the lobby. "I haven't won it yet. Don't jinx me."

"I won't." I shook my head. "Does she know you're here?"

"I called last night to let her know," he said. "So I'll be sleeping off months of being on the road in the hotel room while you two have your day. Then I have a photoshoot tonight as my penance for the time off the road."

"You sure you don't want to join us? I hear there's hair ripping involved. It's not to be missed."

He laughed at that. "The last thing my pea pickin' heart needs is to know two of my favourite girls are in pain. I'll pass."

"You're no fun."

Dylan chuckled and nodded his head in the direction of the lifts. The doors peeled back to reveal the gorgeous raven haired woman in question; I had long marvelled at her ability to not only turn heads when she appeared anywhere, but also to stun everyone into silence. She was perfect without makeup and without any computer program changing her. Jordan also didn't walk. She floated… right across the floor like she was the reigning empress of the world. I both loathed her and adored her for her utter effortlessness.

"Baby!"

She ran the last few feet to launch herself onto Dylan's body. He scooped all five-foot-eleven of her into his arms and twirled her around as they kissed, making quite a scene for everyone within viewing range. I shifted uncomfortably and tried not to stare at them. It was too difficult to see them together—so blissfully happy, so per-fect—while I was there as a third wheel barely holding it all together and desperately trying to forget about being in love with someone I shouldn't be.

When they finally parted, Jordan attacked me, too. God, I had missed her. She pulled back and looked me over, her eyes searching my face for something. Whatever it was, she didn't find it and offered me a careworn sigh. She grabbed my hand, patted the back of it and said, "All right, I see you need an intensive Momma Jordan session."

I rolled my eyes at her. "It's good to see you too, Jor."

She grinned her million dollar smile. "By the way—D, before you go. We're all havin' dinner tomorrow with Clémence."

"We are?"

She nodded. "Yes."

Dylan seemed less than pleased with the idea, but mostly because he didn't want to share his precious time with his wife with anyone else. "Won't seeing her later this week be enough?"

Jordan shook her head wildly. "It's just dinner. We both have to eat. Then I promise nothing else until later in the week. Okay?"

He blew air out his lips and shook his head. "Whatever you want, baby."

"Trust me, you'll want to be there. Emilia's boyfriend is invited, too, if he's in town."

"Jor, please," I mumbled, feeling the heat of a blush as it inflamed my face. "Not here in front of everyone…"

Jordan chuckled. "Oh, sorry, I didn't realise it was supposed to be a secret."

I cast her a long look. She seemed to understand, finally, that there was a story attached and it wasn't a happy story. She sighed again. "Well, whether she has a boyfriend or not, y'all are goin' to dinner with Clémence. Eight sharp tomorrow."

My shoulders slumped. Dinners with Clémence Dubois weren't just friends getting together for a drink or two; you didn't get invited to these things, you were summoned. And if summoned, you showed up regardless of your previous plans. A Clémence dinner consisted of reservations at the finest and most expensive restaurant in town followed by an even more luxurious service. She spared no expense. As such, she expected a certain level of participation from her guests, including people dressed to the nines.

After too many dinners and dinner parties of late, a dinner with Clémence really wasn't my idea of fun, despite including my good friends. It was also the absolute last place I wanted to be, besides going back to Alex's house and facing him and Georgina. I wanted to curl up in front of the hotel television with a bottle of wine drunk out of those generic glass tumblers they put in each room. The tumblers were optional, however. At this point, drinking straight from the bottle was a very real option.

So I thought of my best excuse.

"I don't have anything to wear," I said. It sounded so lame on my lips. She wouldn't let me out of going. We were denizens of the fashionable world, after all. Not having something to wear was the worst excuse. "Not for a dinner with Clémence, anyway."

"I've got you covered."

I frowned.

Jordan leaned into me and grinned conspiratorially. "Etienne had this sublime dress he made for someone who ended up not taking it and I snapped it up. It's a gift."

"Will it—"

"Of course it will." She winked. "I know your measurements. Trust me?"

"I do, it's just that…" the words trailed off as I thought about them.

Why couldn't I have this? Why couldn't I trust her to make me beautiful? If there was one person on this planet who would make me gorgeous, it was Jordan. I also knew, for a fact, Tobias was available.

Jordan smiled. "Come out with us, whether you invite Tobias or not. You need to get out."

"I do," I agreed.

"Good," she said. "We'll all go then. Got it, D?"

Dylan laughed and shook his head. "I definitely have no choice now. I'll have to vet the new boyfriend before I can allow him to date Emilia."

"Sam and Lindsay already approve," I replied. "And I still don't know if he's free…"

Jordan clapped her hands together. "Well, you call him while we're doin' our thing in the spa. Dylan, you go up to the room, baby. I'll see you later."

Without much more fanfare, my friend pulled me in the opposite direction, presumably toward the spa to prepare for our beautification ritual. For the first time since I woke to Alex's arms around me, I let myself truly smile. It felt good to be back with friends, even bossy ones. Their company couldn't have come at a better time.

CHAPTER 23

SMALL MIRACLES DID HAPPEN, apparently, and the universe gifted me with one when a full twenty-four hours elapsed without Georgina calling. Maybe it wasn't the best omen, considering how out of the ordinary it was for her to refrain from bothering me on a day off, but I enjoyed it nonetheless, and didn't even notice her absence until much later while Jordan and I were sitting around and catching up at Dylan's shoot.

We sipped wine from large goblets until our mutual buzzes made us giggly and, perhaps, a little too adventurous. Well, adventurous for me. It started by inviting Tobias over to the hotel—an invitation he eagerly accepted—and evolved into poking fun at Dylan's attempt at modelling while we waited for my companion to arrive. Which led us, finally, into a competition to out-model the other person.

I couldn't believe how relaxing it was to laugh with the people I loved and who loved me without having to worry about work or my affair. Though the thought that I could live the same sort of life back home with Lindsay and Sam did cross my mind more than once, something about the change of scenery, if only for a day, was ultimately refreshing.

When we finally returned to our wine and food, and our laughter turned to companionable silence, I hummed to myself and peered out at the glittery Hollywood dusk in wistful contemplation. A small part of me missed my life of modelling at photoshoots and wine with friends between set ups. I spent so much time fretting over the day-to-day running of Georgina's business, over the fear that I would do something wrong and lose my job, I never actually found the time to enjoy the high fashion lifestyle. Not like I once did.

Were I not bound by my obligation as a sister and caretaker—to bring money from a consistent job into the picture—I saw myself seamlessly slipping back into modelling and enjoying it. But that wasn't possible. Not now. It took a lot to develop a brand; I had hardly developed one before I quit the first time. The time needed to achieve a worthwhile career and making it lucrative were not luxuries I had. Besides, I could not know, without a shadow of doubt, that going back would make me happy and fulfilled, especially if I considered the disaster of my early twenties. Of all my options, though—even the job offer from Jack—I preferred returning to the profession I knew so well. I understood how this world operated and there was some level of peace in its familiarity.

I pushed my thoughts out of the way, though. I sighed softly and turned to look for my friends in the hope they might make me forget my crazy fantasies. Someone had to talk some sense into me before I made another rash decision about my future.

Dylan and Jordan, however, were no help. They had twisted into a knot of arms and legs and sprawled out on one of the two-person chaises adorning the balcony overlooking the city. Dylan leaned in and tenderly brushed his lips across Jordan's forehead as soon as she rested her head on his shoulder. His guitar string-roughened fingers squeezed the nape of her neck and she visibly shivered with delight. The sound she made I could only equate to the purr of a cat.

I swallowed my discomfort and averted my gaze, allowing them their tender peace amid the clamour of the photoshoot. The bottom of my wine glass seemed like the perfect place to stare while they shared their moment—a moment that I wanted. No, that I *needed*. I didn't need the drama of Alex's life interfering with mine. I already had my own. What I needed was stability. I needed a free man able to do what he wished with *who* he wished. A man who actually treated me like I deserved to be treated. I needed a man like Tobias, not Alexander.

Didn't I?

"I hope you're not looking for the secrets of the universe in there."

The hair on the back of my neck prickled at the sound of the deep voice drifting down from the space above my head. I chuckled and lifted my gaze until I met Tobias's kind smile. Silent amusement crinkled the corners of his eyes.

"I learned a long time ago that the only thing to be found at the bottom of a wine goblet is a hangover," I mused.

"Indeed."

He winked and set a hand on the back of my seat to balance himself. He bent to place a chaste kiss on my lips. I grinned against his mouth; my head wanted to float off my shoulders, but I couldn't say for sure whether it was the lightheaded and giddy appreciation of male attention or the amount of alcohol I had consumed while waiting for him. He slipped away from me, just a hair's width, and murmured, "How was your day?"

"Fantastic," I said with a smile. "Better now that you're here, though."

His lopsided grin turned my belly into a somersaulting gymnast. "I'm glad you invited me."

"Go pour yourself some wine," I whispered, pointing my thumb to the table behind me.

He waggled his brows and dipped once again for another kiss, this time longer and more deliberate. "Why would I do that when I can taste it here?"

The heat of my blush forced a shy giggle out of me. What was he doing, anyway? He had been one thing a few nights before on the floor of my bedroom as we discussed his interest in me—and shared our wine—but this was a different side of him. Playful. Flirty. More what I wanted and certainly more of what made me feel feminine and desired. And yet... and yet... what if I was imagining it? Or worse yet, if it was the alcohol talking? I could claim to consuming a bottle of wine by myself. Could I really trust what I was feeling or was it the Merlot?

He moved to the table, allowing me a moment to come back to reality. When I did, I realised he was in the middle of introducing himself to both Dylan and Jordan. They seemed at ease with him, which didn't surprise me. Tobias' calmness was a balm to the frenetic anxiety I suffered whenever Alex was in the same room.

"Thanks for inviting me over," he was saying.

Jordan playfully smacked his arm. "Consider it an inquisition. You know, best girlfriend privileges to see if I approve of you."

"Jor," I groaned and hung my head.

"What? It's my duty."

"You don't think Lindsay hasn't already done it?"

Jordan laughed. "No, because Lindsay was half in love with him before any of this ever happened. So he's not a reliable source."

"Sam likes me," Tobias defended. "Surely that accounts for something."

She squinted her eyes, assessing the man carefully from head to foot. Then she pursed her lips. "Well, if Sam likes you—"

"Only because he bought Sam pizza and watched footy with him," I added. "He's not a good judge of character either."

My mobile beeped loudly in the silence between my words and their laughter. I didn't have to look at the screen to know who had texted me. With a sigh, I fished the thing out of my pocket and unlocked it.

Jordan practically dove into my lap, grabbing for it. "Nuh-uh! No cell phone."

"I have to," I returned drily. "It's work. I am here on work, don't forget."

Jordan stuck her hip out to the side and set her hand on it in a fashion entirely too reminiscent of a mother reaching her limit with her offspring. "After what Cruella did to you last night, you don't owe her nothing, señorita."

Tobias cleared his throat and slipped into the open seat beside me. "What happened last night?"

"I don't really want to talk about it," I murmured, shoving Jordan's other hand away from me when she swiped again for the mobile. "Come on, Jordan."

I managed to pull the screen up and catch a glimpse of the words before she took it from me, but it wasn't enough time to read them. "Fine! Just tell me what it says and then you can keep it until I leave."

Jordan cleared her throat and flicked her thumb along the mobile screen. After another beat, she began speaking in the most nasally voice and with the worst English accent she could manage. Jordan's inability to hide the American twang in her voice achieved full hilarity before she even started.

"*My interview for tomorrow was changed. I will be at Alex's shoot. Please*—oh, she actually said please—"

"You didn't say 'please' with enough condescension," Tobias interjected. "She says it because it's expected, not because she means it."

I almost didn't hear Tobias' stage direction, considering the tsunami of relief that washed over me knowing I wouldn't have to face Alex in the morning. With any luck, I wouldn't actually see his infuriating face until later in the week when I accompanied Georgina to a few pre-Oscar events, which was just fine in my book. Any time I didn't have to be in his suffocating presence was a gift.

"Oh, right. Thank you, Mr. Director."

Jordan giggled and walked over to the table of refreshments, pouring a full glass of the champagne she'd been sipping with Dylan. I glanced at her husband, who watched on in rapt attention. Jordan spun around again, obviously looking for something else, but didn't find it.

She harrumphed. "Damn. Hold on a minute."

Jordan ran inside to the dispersing photographers and stylists, leaving the three of us to share in our confusion. When she re-emerged, she had wrapped a pink floral scarf around her neck and put on big black sunglasses that made her look like an insect. Both articles were adorned with the iconic interlocking Cs of Georgina's favourite brand.

I couldn't contain my laughter as she gracefully took to her make-shift stage once again. "Nice costume."

"Okay, I understand the sunglasses, but the scarf..." Tobias frowned. "Why the scarf?"

"It's Chanel," Jordan and I answered simultaneously.

Tobias squinted his eyes; I saw the wheels turning in his head as he tried to work out the meaning behind it.

I patted his arm. "It's okay. You're only a man, I'm not surprised you didn't notice."

Jordan giggled. "Tobias, honey, the devil may wear Prada, but Georgina Cavendish wears Chanel."

"*Pink* Chanel," I supplemented.

"She does?"

"Like eighty percent of the time," I confirmed and looked at Jordan. "Would you finish the text? I'd really like to know what she said."

"Okay, okay," she drawled. "No need to be testy. Hold on a minute."

Jordan sucked in her cheeks and grabbed the champagne flute from the table. A splash sloshed over the rim onto the concrete balcony. She hummed and assumed her position, flicking the mobile screen again. "Oh, good, here it is— *My interview for tomorrow was changed. I will be at Alex's shoot. Please schedule a car for us tomorrow at seven as we are going out. Together.*"

Dylan and Tobias cheered her performance. Tobias said he'd give her his Olivier. I, on the other hand, sank deeper into the cushions surrounding me. My stomach roiled. Georgina and Alex were going out? Together? To a non-red carpet event? Who engineered that and how had she suckered him into going with her? I couldn't help but feel as though the added "together" was a direct jab at me. But she didn't know about us, so how could it be a jab?

The warring questions running through my mind only ceased fire when a warm hand slipped along the exposed skin of my arm. Lifting my eyes to meet those of the man sitting beside me, he gave me a small, but heartbreaking, smile. I felt like he knew exactly what was going on—he knew my confusion and, if I were being completely honest with myself, saw the green tinge of jealousy colouring my skin.

Perhaps I was wrong. Maybe Tobias didn't see any of that. Maybe it was my own guilt eating at me, knowing in the deepest part of my soul, that I shouldn't obsess over Alex and Georgina while I had a gorgeous, wonderful man sitting right beside me. One who came all the way from his flat in Santa Monica to spend time with me. One that was completely free to do what he wanted. One who, for all intents, was completely into me.

I hated Georgina. And I hated Alex for pulling me into this situation. Most of all, I hated myself for allowing any of it to happen. I sighed and plastered on the happiest smile in my repertoire. I was a model, after all. Fooling anyone into believing in my happiness was my forte. Tobias deserved that much. Alex didn't.

Conversation blissfully drifted in another direction, but I never quite caught up with it. The effects of the alcohol I had poured down my throat did their job and numbed me from the immediacy of my troubles. Much later in the evening when Dylan tried coaxing his wife to bed, a remarkably sober Tobias took the cue and ushered me toward the door. After a quick round of half drunken and overly touchy-feely farewells, we made plans to share a car to Clémence's dinner the following evening. Tobias and I then made our way to the lifts. I leaned against his sturdy frame, clutching clothing and muscle between my fingers so the lift didn't throw me off balance on our ten-floor descent.

"I'm a little pissed, Tobias," I mumbled into the cotton of his shirt.

"Only a little?"

"Don't laugh at me."

He chuckled. "I'm not laughing at you."

The scent of patchouli and sandalwood filled my nose. I lightly smacked his well defined chest. "You smell like a hippie."

"I think that rubbed off from your day at the spa."

"I don't think so," I said.

He laughed at me again as the lift doors peeled back onto the lobby. Fortunately I wasn't inebriated enough that walking was impossible. The last thing I wanted was to make an arse of myself in front of the many shutterbugs—paparazzi and fan alike—pulling their cameras out to snap a few shots of Tobias. The same black-suited security guard from earlier in the morning appeared out of nowhere and ushered us into a Town Car with tinted windows once we were outside the front doors.

"Where are we going?" asked the driver.

"Sunset Tower, please."

Neither of us said much more to each other during the short drive through the bustling Hollywood streets to my hotel. We repeated the previous process in reverse once we arrived, until we finally came to a stop outside my room in the sedate taupe-themed corridor. My skin prickled with the excited knowledge that, for the first time since he admitted anything to me about his interest, we were truly alone. There were no friends or brothers or paparazzi bearing down on us, claiming some moment of our time or yelling at us to pay for the pizza delivery. I stared at him, waiting for him to make a move, to pin me against the wall and claim me like Alex had done too many times. I wanted him to make me forget about everything.

But he didn't.

I leaned forward and offered him a kiss, hoping to stoke his fire, but true to his nature, he moved coolly and slowly. A part of me wondered, very briefly, if he was even worth it, especially if he was incapable of showing some passion in the ways I craved it. Perhaps there was something to be said for taking time and not rushing—I was the poster child for jumping without looking—but I couldn't stand his staid and stoic demeanour. Not with a sure thing standing right in front of him.

I slipped away from him and cleared my throat. "Would you, um, like to come in?"

He gave me a sweet smile and finally kissed me, pushing me back until I pressed against the wall. The kiss broke and he smiled again. "I would love to, Em, but I won't. Not tonight."

"And why not?"

"Because." He sucked in a breath and ran a shaky hand through his black hair. "You've had too much to drink and probably aren't thinking clearly—"

"I am thinking clear—"

He pressed a finger to my lips, but quickly removed it to steal another kiss. "I don't want to do this if you aren't completely sure you want me. And right now all the wine and the night have clouded your judgment."

"But I *do* want you," I murmured.

"I don't think you know who or what you want, love."

No disdain or malice filled his words. It was nothing more than a simple statement of fact. A fact which, unfortunately, was entirely true. Even in my inebriated state, I was trying to make it work—making the round hole a little wider to fit the smaller square peg through it. In the end, though, neither were made for each other. No amount of telling myself otherwise was going to change that.

I sighed. "I do. I think I'm just... confused."

"I know," he said. "I'm not giving up yet. We'll figure it out. Not tonight, though."

"Okay."

He kissed my forehead and stepped away from me. "I'll see you tomorrow for dinner, eh?"

I nodded. "Of course. I can't wait."

"Until then," he bade. If he had a hat, he would have doffed it in an entirely too proper way. He was a gentleman, after all. "Sleep well."

"I'll try."

He retreated around the corner in the direction of the lifts while I convinced my ego he wasn't running away from me. It was useless, considering the haste in which he moved.

A gentleman though he may have been, I realised then, in that moment, I didn't want perfection. I wanted someone a little rough around the edges. Someone who toed the line between good and bad. Someone who did what his body wanted him to do, and not what his logical brain told him to do. Of course, I couldn't say the other man in my life had any of those qualities in his present state, as confused as he was, but I knew, deep down, Tobias wasn't the right one no matter how much I enjoyed spending time with him.

I sighed and shook my head as I slipped the key card into the lock and let myself in the room. The door closed behind me with a satisfying click. As Tobias had said, this wasn't the night for figuring out the meaning of life. There was always tomorrow.

CHAPTER 24

A BARRAGE OF PUSHY PHOTOGRAPHERS wielding overpriced flashing cameras met us for dinner the following evening. Paparazzi always lurked around celebrity hotspots in the hopes of catching a juicy story; I wasn't exactly surprised, but the sudden onslaught of attention did remind me I wasn't just Emilia out to dinner. I was normal Emilia out to dinner with her superstar friends and possible-maybe boyfriend Tobias Sinclair. I regretted, for just a brief moment, ever inviting him.

We were photographed together in London and in L.A. Twice in L.A., actually, after the previous evening. For people who didn't know me, they would definitely jump on the "Tobias has got a girlfriend" bandwagon. I wasn't sure I was prepared for that insanity. I didn't even know where our relationship stood, after all, but I steeled my nerves anyway and slid out of the car after Dylan.

Catching one of America's most prominent celebrity couples exiting the vehicle sent the photographers into a tizzy, but the fact that superstar Tobias Sinclair emerged behind me sent them into near hysteria.

"Sorry about all this," I whispered as he stepped beside me and placed a hand on my lower back. The warmth seemed to burn through the thin silk fabric of my wine-coloured cocktail dress.

"Well, then we might as well give them something to talk about."

He chuckled and kissed my cheek. The flashes blinded me. The shouting increased. It was almost as bad as a red carpet. Almost.

I sighed. It was the absolute last thing I wanted, but I wasn't angry. People would talk anyway; I figured we might as well give them a story, no matter how true or false, rather than leave it up to the wild speculation which followed out-of-context images. Since Tobias was the one who had to deal with the fan fall out, if there were any, I didn't try to stop him.

Once we were inside, the host immediately showed us back into one of the private dining areas, though it was hardly private. Glass wine cellar walls formed two sides of the room and flimsy partitions the others. Clémence, already arrived, somehow made the circular shape of the table seem like a rectangle, sitting in the head seat in un-paralleled poise. She looked queenly in tailored Chanel suiting with her black and silver hair slicked into a severe knot resting on her neck. She assessed each of us in that proud French way of hers with shrewd brown eyes through small, rectangular tortoise shell glasses. Then she cracked a smile and stood from her seat, first welcoming Jordan and Dylan with a hearty, "Bonsoir, mes amis!" before turning to me.

"O, mon Dieu, I have missed you!" She kissed each cheek. After a small step back, she held my hands out to the side and closely inspected my appearance from head to foot just as I expected she would. I had watched her do it to all of her clients for years, long after she moved on from a fashion agent's life. It was her own visual confirmation that the product was still in working order should she require modelling services in the future.

I received a slight nod of approval as she raised her gaze to mine again. "Ça va bien?"

"Oui, merci," I said.

It was a lie, but I was quite finished with serious conversations about the choices of my life for one day. Listening to Jordan's re-counting of her poor experience at Alex's shoot—due to his and

Georgina's constant bickering—while we were getting ready for dinner was enough to make me want to forget I had anything to do with them. I intended to have a happy evening with minimal questioning.

"Et toi?" I asked.

Clémence nodded and patted my cheek, but her attention was already on Tobias, welcoming him with the same warmth she showed me. I didn't hear what they were saying to each other as my attention went to the elegant table covered with silverware, fine china and pristine linens. Dylan and Jordan situated themselves in two open seats to the left of Clémence's place, leaving four additional settings.

"Come, sit down! I've ordered hors d'oeuvres and some terribly expensive champagne."

I breathed a sigh when I felt Tobias' hand on my back again. He motioned for me to precede him around the table to the right, positioned so we could see out the entrance in one of the partitioned walls. Diners craned their necks trying to catch a glimpse inside the room, but they wouldn't get much out of us other than Tobias helping to push my chair in like a perfect gentleman.

"Are we expecting more?" I asked as I took the folded serviette from the plate in front of me and laid it across my lap.

Clémence turned from her new conversation with Jordan. "Hmm?"

I laid my hands on the table and nodded to the remaining open chairs. "The extra settings. Are we expecting more?"

"O, oui," she spoke. "I need all my girls here while I can."

Her words struck fear in me, but it was nothing compared to the grip of icy panic which curled around my spine when Tobias tensed in his seat. I didn't need to look at the entrance to confirm who cast such a long shadow over the table; the grating quality of her whiny voice was enough to confirm the other invited guests. True, deep-seated dread, however, came in the form of the man accompanying her. He responded to one of her questions in the low honeyed purr I had come to loathe and love. Blood drained from my face and my heart jumped to my throat in an asphyxiating lump.

No.

I reached for the water goblet and took a long swallow, glancing over the clear rim at Jordan's wide eyes. She mouthed a simple *"Oh my God"* before she cleared her throat and set her serviette on the table in preparation to welcome the new additions to the party. Dylan shifted beside her—enough to tell me Jordan explained to him what was going on with me—but did not get up from his seat. A heavy tension settled on top of us all, except for the one person who remained ignorant of the situation.

Clémence tittered profusely over Georgina like she had with us, but Georgina seemed to enjoy it more than I did. And why wouldn't she? The future of *Modiste*'s editorial staff was gushing over the beautiful Murad confection in the sickening shade of candy floss pink she chose to wear for the evening.

Georgina had yet to recognise who else was in the room; she, after all, did not see things she didn't wish to see. Her companion, however, saw us. Saw me. The hair on the nape of my neck rose over my flushed skin. I felt the intensity of his hot, angry stare assessing me with displeasure. I refused to meet his gaze, unable to process whatever I might see in it. If it wasn't contempt for me, it certainly was for the person beside me.

Oh, Tobias.

I glanced at the stalwart man to my left. His small smile struggled to convince me not to worry, but I was worried all the same and in the worst possible way. Nothing he did would make the situation better. He just didn't know—couldn't grasp—what had happened since we touched down in Los Angeles, and I felt terrible for leaving him out in the cold. He deserved to know what he was getting into and he certainly didn't deserve to be put into this situation unprepared for what he would face. Why hadn't I told him everything when I had the chance?

Making matters worse was the simple fact that I did not trust myself. I did not trust Georgina. And I did not trust Alex. There was no telling what might happen as we sat at the round table as equals like knights at Arthur's court, especially since at least one of us held very severe prejudices toward me.

"I didn't see you there, Emilia," said the grating voice. Georgina regained the syrupy sweetness of the façade she adopted in public, but I did not mistake the displeasure hovering just below the saccharine overtones. "You look pretty."

I bit my tongue and turned my head to look at her. She slipped into the seat beside Tobias. "Thank you, Georgina. The Murad is lovely."

"Who are you wearing?" she asked. "Or is it off the rack?"

I cleared my throat. "Etienne Roux."

Georgina didn't pay me any more mind. She didn't care what designer I wore. She said it only to appear interested. I puffed my cheeks and shook my head. Of course it was all just part of the act.

I looked across the table at Jordan and Dylan, but I didn't get there without coming across my worst nightmare sitting in the last available seat. That he had not commandeered the seat directly beside one of his best friends was telling enough for me, but I wondered if it had more to do with the other seat being a better angle for him; it certainly enabled him to stare crossly at me all night without hurting his neck.

His thin lips pressed themselves into a grim line. I blinked a few times, taking in the deep lines carved in his face. He looked utterly wretched. Not that he wasn't as gorgeous as always, but it seemed as though everything he had suffered had finally surfaced. His duplicities dared to break free of the carefully constructed mask he wore for months. That I might have caused some of that wretchedness made me miserable, but there was no way around it. I had to put a stop to it for both of us. Someone had to be the saner and stronger person.

A waiter entered the room then to deliver bottles of champagne in preparation for the dinner service. I struggled to look away from Alex and to pull myself back to the present, but when I did, I focused on Jordan while the head waiter poured for each of us. Not one to ever be at a loss for words, I hoped she would fill the gaping maw left between all of us. She didn't.

"Why is everyone so quiet?" Clémence finally asked as she scanned the table. "Aren't we supposed to have fun?"

"I think we're all just a little exhausted," I tried to explain. "You know, between jet lag and work."

The excuse was terrible and Clémence was astute enough to see it. "I was not born yesterday, ma chérie. Something is wrong."

"No, we're really just jet lagged," said the baritone beside me.

I looked up at Tobias and smiled.

Tobias shifted and sat forward in his seat, engaged in the discussion. "I swear those transatlantic flights don't get any easier or shorter every consecutive time you do them."

"We ran into some turbulence on ours," Alex mentioned. The words might as well have been balls of fire for the way he hurled them at me. "It made for an interesting flight, didn't it, Emilia?"

I hoped the glare I shot in his direction was sufficient enough to silence him, but he didn't sway. I cleared my throat. "Yes, it was even bad enough to wake up Georgina."

Clémence laughed at the exchange.

"I don't know about Jordan's and Dylan's schedules, but we've all been really busy between fashion weeks and such," I continued, trying to change the subject. Trying to take some power away from him. But then I remembered: what power did he actually have that I hadn't given to him? That I hadn't allowed him to take? He had none. I had to show him that. Somehow.

Dylan, thankfully, used the opportunity to jump into the conversation to talk about his tour, leaving me a moment to my thoughts. I had to extricate myself from the situation, but an opportunity had not yet presented itself.

A large hand rested on my thigh where the hem of skirt ended and my bare skin began. I squeaked and fidgeted uncomfortably at the sudden intrusion. Tobias must have meant the touch to be a comfort, but it did nothing he intended. In fact, it did the opposite. It made me even more uncomfortable knowing Alex was watching us from his spot across the table like a black spectre at the feast.

And then, for some reason, I remembered the morning at the beach with Alex. What had only been a few days before felt as though ages had passed. So much had happened in so little time. But what I remembered, most acutely, was the way Alex's hand possessively dug into the same spot on my thigh to hold me. To keep me with him, as though grasping for some sort of purchase on a world spinning out of control. I liked it. I liked the possessiveness. It wasn't Tobias' place to touch or hold; Alex had somehow marked it for his own personal use.

In that moment, I truly recognised the disparity between them. Tobias would never be an adequate substitute for what I felt with Alex, despite all the turmoil Alex had caused. He would never be *better* or make my body sing in pleasure. Of course he'd probably never make my heart ache, either, but I knew it would never be enough for me if such a simple touch didn't do it. Though ever being with Alex was unlikely, I certainly couldn't stay with Tobias. That would have been the worst lie of them all. Tobias didn't deserve it.

"... and then Emilia showed up for her spa day with Jordan," Dylan explained, forcibly pulling me back to the conversation. "The security guards thought she was a crazy fan. I'm like... didn't you see the photos of the wedding in *People*? What's the point in allowing the tabs to release your personal photos if people aren't going to see them?"

"Better safe than sorry, though," Jordan supplied with a laugh. "I mean, look at her, she looks like she could do some serious damage. She's got a crazed look in her eyes."

My cheeks warmed at Jordan's teasing. She did it to lighten the mood, but taking the piss out of me was somewhat embarrassing. She had an innate ability to make me laugh, but also to get her point across.

"Emilia's pretty harmless, I think." Tobias laughed. "But it definitely is a really weird world we live in."

Dylan and Alex both nodded their heads in agreement, but Georgina was the one to jump into the conversation out of the blue. "You're not wrong. I'm just so sick of dealing with Alex's fans."

My gaze snapped to Alex. A momentary panic passed across his face, but he masked it quickly.

"How so?" Tobias asked. I wished he hadn't humoured her outburst.

"I was going through Alex's suits for the photoshoot this morning," she said, "and in the interior pockets in one there were lacy red knickers that Alex said a fan slipped to him and he didn't know what to do with them, so he stuffed them in the pocket."

My ears were burning before Georgina finished speaking. I didn't need to ask what suit coat she had found them in or what the knickers looked like or even if they were my fucking size. I didn't need that sort of confirmation; my intuition told me enough. At least I knew where my knickers went after my night at his mum's. But I still looked across the table at Alex, who didn't even have the good graces to be contrite. With a self-satisfied smirk, he leaned back in his seat.

"They're only fans, Georgina," Alex commented drolly, blue eyes flicking to me before he continued. "They don't mean anything to me."

I wanted the floor to swallow me whole. If he had intended to twist the metaphorical knife buried deep into my back, he had done it. He was clearly upset and found the most expedient way of relaying what he felt, no matter the toll it took on me. Frankly, I expected something like this to happen before long. I never planned to have it happen in front of my friends.

I was, however, never so thankful that Georgina was such an unobservant tit. She didn't appear to have any suspicions about the previous owner of said knickers. At least, I *hoped* she didn't.

"Yeah, fans can get pretty—"

Georgina cut off Jordan's words with an indelicate snort and sipped her champagne before fully interrupting. "It doesn't change the fact that they're positively mad thinking they could ever have Alex. Or that slipping him lacy lingerie would persuade him to sleep with them. It's so gauche. So beneath someone like him. He deserves someone from his level."

"Oh?" Alex asked lightly.

"Yes."

Alex chuckled in amusement. "Someone like you?"

She scoffed, and then proceeded to dig her own grave. "Of course someone like me. We're social and economic equals. We travel in the same circles. It's a match made in heaven. I just wish you'd see that. But you insist on picking up charity projects and it blindsides you from the path you should be taking. How great you *could* be."

Everyone at the table shifted around in their seats restlessly, unable to stop Georgina's tirade or the train from crashing. Even though Georgina's idea of greatness was very different than Alex's definition, he said nothing.

"By pandering to them, you give them too much hope that they could have a chance with you," Georgina finished. I prayed that it was the end of it.

"I don't think you understand what it means to be a film actor or a musician and the symbiotic relationship we have with fans," Tobias interjected. "You're being unfair to Alex, and frankly, to Dylan and me as well."

I had never heard the man raise his voice, and though he wasn't exactly yelling, his words were firm and didn't allow any room for argument. At least, I wouldn't have continued after that. But Georgina was interminable.

"It's not only his fans, though. It's everyone. Well, everyone but me," Georgina gloated. "Emilia has become his project of choice recently. She seems to enjoy it… perhaps a little too much."

The energy in the room shifted again at the mention of my name. My friends became defensive; Jordan perched at the edge of her chair as though she were preparing to throttle the woman. Dylan didn't quite know what to make of the situation, but he sat up in his seat in preparation to hold his wife back.

For myself, I felt sick. My heart beat a mile a minute and a cold, clammy sweat broke out on parts of my skin. I recognised it as sheer panic—panic over the fact that she saw more than I originally thought. The floor swallowing me whole wouldn't be enough; nothing could shield me from the mortification. Dead and gone, turned to dust, I'd still feel the shame bearing down on me in all its oppressiveness.

"But you wouldn't understand, either, Tobias," Georgina added, "since you seem rather involved in your own Emilia charity."

Tobias sucked in a breath.

I realised then that the only way I wouldn't have to listen to her tirade was to leave. I pushed my seat out and stood up, drawing a surprised gasp from Clémence. "I'm very sorry, Clémence, but I have to go. I can't sit here and take this all night."

"Oh, sit down, Emilia!" Georgina spat at me. "You like the attention. No one would be paying you any otherwise."

I wanted to punch her. Lay her out flat on the floor. My right hand curled into a fist, but to my credit, I locked my arm at my side and looked at Tobias. With a shaky voice, I said, "Tobias, do you want to…"

"Definitely," he replied without missing a beat.

He was up an instant later, warm hand once more on the small of my back. I didn't know if it was to propel me forward or to support me, but it felt nice. I needed the connection or I might have said some other terrible things to Georgina. Things I refused to say in front of others. I couldn't bear to see their faces or have anyone in the restaurant overhear it.

"Let's go," he murmured close to my ear.

We made a quick exit through the paparazzi lining the entrance and slipped into a cab the valet called for us. Tobias gave the driver an address and directions to some location; I stayed silent, staring straight ahead and willing myself not to cry or scream. My date sat just as silently, with an arm around my shoulders, not holding me to him, but letting me know he was there.

"Where are we going?" I inquired after a long time trying to calm myself.

"My flat," he answered. "I'm only a few more miles away. I thought we could grab my car and take it for a drive, get something to eat, and have a nice, long chat."

I turned to look at him. "I may not be very good company."

He shrugged his shoulders. "It's better than eating alone, and I don't think you want to be alone right now."

"No," I confirmed. "I don't."

Being alone would only leave me with the thoughts stampeding through my head and I did not want to deal with them. I wanted to shut everything off. But even then, something told me Tobias wouldn't let me off the hook.

Glancing at him, I saw confusion, anger, and annoyance playing on his expressive face. His kindness dictated he do this, but I wondered how much he wanted to be a part of it. When he realised I was watching him, his expression became impassive. "We'll talk about it."

I nodded. "We will."

"We'll sort it all out."

"I hope."

Tobias smiled. "We will."

CHAPTER 25

TOBIAS AND I looked like two escapees from some depressing school formal huddled together in the corner of a red-and-white tiled In-N-Out Burger, nursing our fountain drinks and fighting over fresh French fries. It wasn't a Michelin-rated restaurant or a fancy celebrity party, but it was a relatively quiet location just off the Pacific Coast Highway in Long Beach and far enough away from Hollywood to let us breathe a bit.

We both desperately attempted to ignore the elephant in the room for most of the meal, but our tactics and friendly banter about the food only lasted for so long. Finally conceding defeat and a full stomach, I sat back in the uncomfortable plastic swivel chair and let out a long sigh. Tobias glanced across the table at me through a tangle of floppy hair obscuring his eyes. He used his fingers to comb it quickly out of the way.

"I can't wait until we're done filming the new series," he grumbled. "I hate all the floppy hair."

"It makes you look younger," I commented, but instantly thought better of it. "Not that you're old or anything… I just…"

He gave me a stern frown, but couldn't maintain its severity. A bark of laughter left his lips, drawing some attention from a family of four eating their meals on the other side of the restaurant. "No, I know. I look like a little boy. My mum has the photos to prove it."

I leaned forward in my seat again and pinched one of his round cheeks. "It's because you're so adorable."

Tobias used the opportunity to grab my hand. I didn't try to pull back from the strong clasp and allowed him to lower it to the table. Long fingers traced a line down my thumb and back up, drawing a slight shiver from my body. A sudden sense of importance fell between us with the movement, completely changing the lighthearted moment to one of gravity.

"So," he uttered in a rush of air.

"So," I repeated. I knew he wouldn't let me beat around the bush for long. He wasn't that type of person.

Tobias released my hand as though he had forgotten he was holding it and had never intended to hold it. He crossed his arms and set his elbows on the small table. "I take it things have happened in the few days you've been here that you didn't tell me about last night."

I sighed. "I'm so sorry about tonight. I didn't know—"

"Don't. I know you didn't. And no one could have prepared for Georgina's tirade. Even Alex didn't know… didn't you see how uncomfortable he was?"

"What?" I scoffed. "He was angry, not uncomfortable. Angry at me. For an argument we had yesterday morning."

Tobias cleared his throat. "Argument?"

He tried to keep the hope out of his voice by maintaining a neutral tone, but it wasn't working and I heard a slightly raised note of optimism in his baritone.

"I told him we couldn't keep seeing each other," I recounted. "Definitely not while he was dealing with all of this shit. He's come so close to wrecking both our lives."

"How would he wreck your life?" Tobias' incredulity upset me. "Even with the way he is, he would make it better. At least you would know he wanted you for you."

"He… what?"

Tobias groaned. "For all of Alex's less than great personality tics, he's only ever wanted you for you. I don't agree with how he's handled things, and I can't be happy with how he's treated you because I *know* I could treat you better, but don't ever doubt for a minute his interest wasn't genuine interest… and I can't believe I'm saying this. I'm actually defending the bloody wanker."

I didn't know whether to laugh or cry. So I sat in silence, pondering his words.

"Look, when I made my move before you left London, we discussed it. I understood there was shit you had to work out with Alex. I'm not mad or upset. Truly. If he's what you want, then you should go for it."

"Tobias, I can't," I moaned. "No matter what he thinks about me, he treats me like a possession. He has since… since… Venice. It all changed that night at the masquerade for some reason. I don't know why, but it did. Maybe it was because he thought he could get away with treating someone like that because no one would recognise him in a mask."

Tobias nodded. "Anonymity can allow people a lot of freedom, but the complete opposite of that, what Alex and I live in our daily lives, is stifling. When he had a chance to experience it, he grabbed it and held onto it as tight as possible. But he didn't plan for the repercussions of what would happen the next day. That's his fault, but you have to understand where he's coming from, especially with the Georgina business. You are his freedom. Don't underestimate what that means to people like us. Like Alex."

I shook my head and focused on the drink in front of me, running my index finger over the rim of the plastic top. "It's very magnanimous of you to defend him when you could take the spoils of war and run."

"This isn't a war, Emilia." His voice was flat and somewhat scolding. "He's still one of my best mates though we're not really speaking right now. I love him like a brother and that's not going to change. If that means conceding defeat, if you want him, then so be it."

"Even if I did, I couldn't."

Tobias gave me a sour look. "Why not?"

"I would lose my job. And I can't do that."

"There are other jobs. Better ones."

"I know. Jack offered me a job."

Tobias sighed. "And why the fuck didn't you take it on the spot?"

"Because."

"Because why?"

"Because I'm tired of people always sorting things for me. Everyone in my life has done it to me. My grandmother decided I would focus on academics, not art. My grandmother asked this seamstress she knew if I could have a job as a teenager, so I took it because we desperately needed money. It was decided I would go to Oxford and do what she told me."

I stopped and drew in a long stream of air before continuing. "The first thing I did for *myself* was to start modelling. I made that decision myself. But I hated it. I hated the skinny culture. And then when my grandmother died and I returned to London permanently, Clémence basically sorted it all out that I would work for Georgina. I took the job because I owed a lot to Clémence and I was worried about what I was going to do. Look where the fuck that got me. I'm sick and tired of people in my life telling me what to do, or deciding what I should do, promising me the world, and then that world ending up being full of shit. Jack's deal looks good on the surface, but what shit is there behind the façade?"

He looked exasperated. In a refrain in which I had become increasingly weary, he said, "Anything's better than working for Georgina."

"I don't doubt that it would, but I can't take the income loss of finding a new position while unemployed, nor can I find time to do it while I'm working sometimes twenty hour days for her."

Tobias sighed and crossed his arms in front of his chest.

"The fact remains that she gave me a job when no one else would, with no skills, no training, no nothing," I concluded.

"She didn't give you one. Clémence basically sold you into indentured servitude, from what it sounds like."

I balked at this notion even though I certainly felt like a servant at times. "It's only gotten truly bad with the Alex stuff. With Alex supposedly breaking it off with her after the Oscars and him not in my life—"

Tobias shook his head. "Wrong! It's always been bad and it will always be bad."

I could tell he was growing antsy. Not angry necessarily, but his temper certainly went from placid to exasperated rather quickly. He had no sympathy for me. So, I stayed silent.

He leaned forward. "When are you going to start being honest with yourself, Em?"

"Huh?"

"Do you remember when you told me you were happy the night we went to the premiere together?"

Nodding, I had to look away from him.

"I'm hazarding a guess that you weren't happy. I know you weren't, because I can read people. You aren't happy now. No one on this planet could say they were truly happy in a life that included working for Georgina Cavendish. You're just *existing*."

"Tobias, please… that's not…"

He held up a hand to stop my words. "No, let me say it. I deserve a little bit of a soapbox after being dragged into this situation."

I chewed on my lip and sighed. "All right. Fine."

The man straightened in his seat. "I think you're only existing because someone or something happened in your life to make you think it's right and that's all you fucking deserve. You think you deserve this life you've created for yourself… It's like the only way you can be happy is to continue putting yourself in these hopeless situations because it makes you feel important somehow. Needed. And when you don't feel needed, you sabotage yourself until you get to a place where you can play the bloody victim again. Then you, perhaps subconsciously, want someone to tell you what to do with your life, whether it's good for you or not, but you never own up to your own responsibility in accepting their terms."

His words hurt me, but he didn't stop.

"The woman keeps you around like a pet dog to use and abuse for her whims. You and Alex both. You are miserable with her. And you've deluded yourself into thinking this is all you have left. It's not. And that's what really pisses me off about this whole situation. You just sit there and take it like a good little girl because you're too fucking scared to go, see, and do what you really want with your life."

"But Sam needs…"

Tobias scoffed. "And you use your brother as an excuse not to take your life by the balls and do something. So what? Living is a little thin for a few months while you find a new job. That's life. It happens. If you're so worried about it, there are people who would help—"

I cut him off with a hard stare. "I'm sick and tired of being a charity project!"

"You're not a charity, Emilia," he rebuffed immediately. "You're a friend. And friends loan friends money."

"Sounds like charity to me."

He huffed and sucked on his straw. Nothing but air came through the plastic. Shaking the ice in the bottom of the cup, he stood smoothly from his seat. "I'm going to get a refill. Do you want some more?"

I shook my head. He glided across the floor to the soda fountains, and I watched his precise movements as his words replayed in my head. I honestly didn't know what to feel about this development. After leaving the restaurant, this wasn't the conversation I expected to have, or the fact that, like Jordan and Lindsay, Tobias' tune was remarkably similar to what I had heard from them.

It was true that I was tired of the charity of others, of everything being figured out for me, that I couldn't even contemplate a life where I got to make decisions based on what I wanted. I jumped into my relationship with Alex on that reasoning, after all. It was a moment of want I gave into because I thought I fucking deserved it after all the self-flagellation. Even then, it turned out to bite me in the arse. Because he, ultimately, made the choice for me. Did I really let him do it so I could blame him for all my problems?

Because I liked playing the victim?

Tobias folded himself back into the seat and sat staring at me for a few minutes. Until, finally, he sighed, for the umpteenth time that evening. "What do you want out of life, Emilia?"

"What?"

"What do you want?"

I shrugged. At that point, I didn't know. "I want a job so I can pay for my flat and my brother and…"

"No!" His deep, snipping words startled me. "No. What would make *you* happy? Not what would make other people happy so that it makes you feel needed."

The awareness that I didn't know hit me hard. I had an idea, sure, but I just hadn't put enough thought into it.

"How about I give you an example of what I want and we'll go from there?"

"All right…"

Tobias took a breath. "I want a family. More than anything else in the world, I want a family to call my own. I'm tired of being lonely."

I nodded in understanding.

"I don't want a flash in the pan, instantaneous love at first sight. I want slow burning, long lasting commitment more than anything. If insatiable love comes from that friendship and commitment, then great. But what I want is a wife. Someone who is my own freedom from the crazy world. Someone who is constant. Someone who wants children with me. Someone who is my equal. I've already achieved what I wanted in my career… it's just these few little things left that I seem to have trouble with."

My mouth felt dry. So I sipped my drink, turning his words over in my head. What was he saying, anyway? It sounded like a fucking job interview, not a proposal of friendship, for dating, or for marriage.

"I want you, Emilia. I told you that the night before you left," he said. "But I'm not convinced my wanting you and you accepting me is what you want. I feel like you're entertaining me because you know I can't possibly make you happy as a lover, but you know it will make me happy so you're doing it anyway. And then I wonder if you aren't trying to get Alex out of your system and simply using me, much in the same way Alex has used you."

It made a lot of sense, but I couldn't see that. I adored his attention, too. But I never truly wanted it romantically.

He folded his hands on the table and held me with his steady gaze. "So what do *you* want?"

"I-I... I guess I want a family, too. One of my own. I want to dabble in art and maybe be a housewife because I want to provide for my family emotionally and materialistically in the way my mother and grandmother were never able to. I want to be loved unconditionally. I want someone to take care of me at times. I'm so fucking tired of taking care of everyone else and getting nothing in return."

"Okay," he asserted, drawing the last syllable out. "Maybe I'm your man... maybe I'm not. There's a hesitancy in your voice..."

I flicked my gaze up to meet his. "Tobias, I know I'm damaged. And it's going to take me some time to figure out what I want. I just don't know. I've spent so long... my whole life, really... living for other people that I just don't know."

"I understand," he replied and grabbed my hands, holding them in his own. "You need to take your time. Do some soul searching."

"It's really hard," I complained weakly.

Tobias squeezed my fingers. "Love, it always is."

A lull in our conversation followed, but it didn't last for long. Tobias was right in everything he said; he was an unwitting bystander watching all of this happen. He knew both sides of the story—Alex's and mine—and even had a vested interest in keeping me away from his friend.

But he didn't.

At that very moment, I understood what he meant. He wasn't trying to use me, or possess me, or treat me like a charity. He wanted me to know that there were people in this world that were capable of treating me like a person who could make her own decisions. Only I could own up to them; it was my responsibility to change myself and my right to choose who and what I wanted without fear of reprisal.

He deserved the same consideration.

"Tobias?" I said softly.

"Hmm?"

"I love you."

He choked on his drink. "What?"

"Maybe it was a poor choice of words," I corrected. "I do adore you, but I can't be the woman you want right now. I can't ask you to wait for me to catch up to you."

Tobias nodded his head as a small smile passed his lips. "I needed to hear you say that."

"I'm sorry. It's not fair to you that I'm playing around, hoping it can work, but knowing in my heart that I'm not ever going to be completely happy with you as my lover."

"Thank you," he breathed.

"For what?"

He swallowed and smiled sweetly. "For being honest with me and for being honest with yourself."

Tears pricked at my eyes. I barely kept them from spilling over with a clear of my throat. "We should probably be heading back…"

"Yes," he agreed. "If you want to."

We were quiet as we collected our rubbish and deposited it in the bins near the door. He held the car door as I slid into the passenger seat and then walked around to his side. Silence prevailed as the engine cranked to life and we took off down the highway.

As we were merging onto the 405 ten minutes later, I turned to look at him. "If somebody doesn't snap you up like tomorrow, I'm going to be angry."

He laughed. "I'll keep you as a reference, okay? For when I meet the future Mrs. Sinclair."

"I can write a letter of recommendation, too," I volunteered.

"I think meeting her will be fine."

"How would that go, anyway? Here's the girl I sort of had a thing for, but…"

Tobias shook his head. "When and if it happens, I'll figure it out then."

I chuckled and turned to watch the passing night in the window beside me. Traffic was terrible, as per usual, but it was nice not to worry about where we stood. Now I knew, and it was because I put my foot down. I prayed that I could translate this newfound resolve into the other parts of my life.

"Just tell me one thing," Tobias said, interrupting my thoughts.

"What?"

He glanced at me. "Do you love him?"

I spluttered. "How can you even ask me that?"

"Because I think you're in love with him."

"I'm not in love with Alex. He's toxic."

Tobias turned again and held my gaze for a little longer before he absolutely had to watch the motorway. "Emilia, I'm no expert on matters of the heart, obviously, but you forget that I knew you well before Alex cornered you in Venice. You could barely hold it together around him between blushes and such."

"Any love I might have had was infatuation only," I said firmly. "It's like he was grooming me… preparing me to be his mistress."

"I can see how you might feel that way. But you know, for every action there is an equal and opposite reaction. Georgina was so extreme, he lost track of himself. Give him a chance to prove himself worthy."

I shook my head. "I can't deal with him right now. Whenever he's around, he consumes me like a fast burning fire. He leaves nothing but charred debris behind. If I'm trying to better myself, I can't do that with him…"

"Still, consider it," Tobias said. "Because it would be a bloody shame if neither one of us convinced you to love us."

Tobias' words made a bittersweet smile stretch my lips. He didn't say anything else, and I was thankful for that. I certainly didn't need to be considering Alex in such a way.

While we made our way down Sunset, I reached into my clutch for my mobile. I had felt it buzzing sporadically since leaving the dinner party, but had ignored it in favour of spending time with Tobias. There were exactly three texts and one voicemail from a number I didn't recognise. One text was from Georgina, saying she needed me the following day for something at the beach house. The next was from Clémence, asking me about doing lunch before she went back to New York. The third was from Jordan, freaking out that I hadn't returned her previous calls.

I looked up just as Tobias pulled to a stop outside Sunset Tower. I exhaled deeply as a doorman appeared on my side.

"I'll see you around," I said.

"I plan on it," he responded. "When we get back to London, we'll do something. I've been invited to Family Football Day at Sam's club."

"Oh, please don't come to that. I'll just embarrass myself in front of you," I half-pleaded.

Tobias grinned. "That's supposed to make me not want to go? Ha! Goodnight, Emilia."

"Goodnight, Tobias." I leaned over and gave him a chaste peck on the cheek, transferring what was left of my lipstick to his skin. Reaching up, I rubbed it away. "Go find Ms. Right, will ya?"

"Tonight I begin my quest."

I laughed at him.

"I feel like I need my sunglasses for this, riding off into the night," he joked. "Full tank of petrol…"

The door beside me finally opened and the doorman welcomed me back to the hotel; I said my final farewell to my driver and then a thank you to the doorman. As I stepped into the elevator, I dialled Jordan's mobile number. She picked it up in one ring.

"Oh, thank God you're all right! I've been callin' and callin'! Where the hell have you been and what makes you think you can just ignore me like that? We were worried sick about you!" She said all of this in a barely decipherable rush.

"I'm sorry, Jordan," I said evenly. "I didn't want to talk. Besides, I was with Tobias. That's pretty safe."

Jordan made a sound of disapproval. "Well, shit happened after you left and I've been tryin' to get a hold of you to tell you what's going on…"

"I don't really want to know."

The elevator reached my level and the doors opened, leaving me a long view of the main hallway. I took the path and turned right down the side corridor leading to my room.

"Trust me, you do," she assured me, a little darkly. "Clémence fired Georgina."

"Georgina doesn't work for Clémence."

Jordan cackled evilly. "She was about to."

"Huh?"

"Clémence is taking over as editor-in-chief at *Modiste*. Georgina was gonna be the new creative director," she said. "That's what tonight was going to be about… Georgina accepting the job and celebrating."

Gobsmacked wasn't an appropriate enough word to describe how I felt hearing the news, especially seeing as it would affect me in so many ways. I slipped my key card into the door and waited for the quiet *snick* from the automated lock.

"Did you know all this before you invited me?" I turned the knob and pushed the heavy thing open with my shoulder.

"No, not at all. I didn't even know Georgina would be there, remember? She said she and Alex were going out in that text and I heard nothing about it at the shoot this morning."

I stepped inside the modest sized room. I had left one of the lights on in a far corner—as I always did for my safety when I planned to return to a hotel room at night. But that didn't mean an intruder wouldn't frighten me, like the one sitting on the end of my king-sized bed did. He stared at me with a stony, impassive expression on his bearded face until the door shut heavily behind me.

"Jordan," I squeaked, "I have to go."

"Why?"

"I just have to go," I breathed out. "Alex is here."

ALEXANDER UNMASKED

WHEN I WAS SIXTEEN, my mother dragged us all around the Continent on a summer holiday that I didn't want to go on. At the time, my only concerns were my mates and what trouble I could get into with the female sex during my time off my studies. Going to an all male boarding school certainly put a damper on girlfriend finding during normal school terms, and I wanted no part of my mother's plan to give us culture and the opportunity to experience other places in the summertime. That was, of course, until I found out there were even more beautiful women on the Continent.

As I stood in the middle of a dressing room being fitted for the costume I would don at the masquerade ball later in the evening, I realised not much had changed in nineteen years. Only this time, it wasn't an unwillingness to be seen or spend time with my mum. Rather, it was more the complete hatred of an utterly ridiculous woman who liked to think she was my girlfriend. She dragged me all over Europe in the span of a month between spring fashion weeks. My attitude didn't improve upon arriving in Venice. As beautiful as the city was, I just couldn't make myself enjoy it. Not with her around. Not with her dictating my every move. A few short weeks later and I would be free of her, if Jack's plan worked, but even that knowledge didn't make it easier for me to fake a grin and bear it.

The only moments alleviating my pain were when Emilia popped over to our hotel suite to execute her duties as Georgina's assistant before leaving to experience the city on her own. More than anything, I wanted to accompany her—to listen to her talk in her nearly perfect Italian as we investigated the city together and marvelled at extravagant Renaissance art. I wanted to watch her smile and laugh and dance in the middle of St. Mark's Square with the rest of the revellers enjoying the festivities of Carnevale.

I was, however, thankful for the brief reprieve from Georgina. What made it even sweeter was the fact that she allowed me out with Emilia—a surprise all on its own. Georgina seemed totally unconcerned about my interest in her assistant. Even though she had been reticent to invite Emilia to the ball that night at my request, she was more concerned about herself than my infatuation with another woman.

We spent nearly two hours—two peaceful, Georgina-free hours—in the costume shop, poring over rows and rows of gaudy fancy dress. I was tired. Emilia was tired. It was obvious to me that neither one of us wanted to keep going and taking the time of the busy shop assistants. But Georgina kept sending negative texts in reply to the test photos Emilia sent her.

After watching Emilia check the time on her mobile ten times in the span of two minutes, I looked at her as we stood in the mirror admiring the overly decorated coat she slipped on my shoulders.

"Got a hot date?" I asked.

Her cheeks turned pink and she shook her head. "No. Just a walking tour in and around the piazza that I scheduled for this afternoon."

"Sounds like fun," I murmured, turning to assess the lay of the eighteenth century coat on my back. I moved my arms and stretched my shoulders. It was too tight. The tailoring would be too extensive to change this late. "This isn't going to work. Shoulders aren't wide enough."

Emilia slipped her mobile back into her pocket and stepped

forward to help me out of the garment. She called to the assistant helping us before disappearing out into the shop with the coat. I stood in the silence of the room, looking at my tired eyes in the full length mirror, thinking I really needed some decent sleep in a bed by myself. It was difficult enough sharing a bed with Georgina when we were fucking each other, but doing so when I could barely stand her was cruel punishment and sleep was elusive.

"I think I found it!" came a joyful shout from somewhere in the massive shop.

My personal assistant for the morning appeared in the doorway carrying a suit made of red and gold brocade. It looked luxurious and comfortable—more so than the rest of the overly ornate costumes looked and felt. Simplistic in its design and decoration, it was more like me. I hated to be festooned with jewels and gobs of fabric, even in my modern day suiting.

"It should look wonderful with your colouring," Emilia said. "It's so hard to find colours that go well with the auburn hair."

"Is that what the problem's been?" I asked with some amount of amusement in my voice.

She shrugged at me and thrust the costume out to the shop assistant when he appeared to help. "Who knows what's going through Georgina's mind... I'm just going to be out there looking at the masks."

I glanced at the small Italian man who eyed the costume in his hands. After a heavy sigh and a shake of his head, he began the process of handing me pieces. I started first by removing the previous set of breeches and putting the new pair on, listening to the muffled conversation taking place somewhere else in the shop about masks and wigs.

Emilia waltzed back into the fitting room as I was pulling on the coat, though she was more concerned with the items in her hands than with me. On her head, she wore a feathery tricorne hat made from black leather and lined in gold stitching. The sight made me chuckle lowly, though I thought the hat looked abnormally fetching on her. I thought she might make a rather attractive—and buxom—Anne Bonny.

"So?" I piped up, drawing her attention from a black ribbon connected to the gilded mask in her hands.

She looked up and froze, eyes travelling the length of my body in a slow, wholly feminine assessment. I watched in the mirror from my place on the low pedestal, waiting for her to say something, but liking—no, *adoring*—the feel of her gaze burning into me. There were times over the last few months when I caught her looking, but she always turned away quickly and blushed when she realised it.

This open perusal was completely different.

Whether for her job or not, she lingered far longer than was necessary, first on my arse and, as I turned back to her, my groin. The frank nature in which she remained transfixed on the area required me to think of the most repellent thing imaginable in an attempt to maintain some modesty. However, when a small flash of pink tongue subconsciously flicked out of her mouth and wetted her lips, my knees went weak. In that instant, I knew there wasn't anything I wouldn't give to have her pretty little mouth somewhere on my body, whether it was wrapped around my cock or not.

Shocked hazel eyes shot up to mine a moment later—not at my reaction to her, but to *her* reaction to me. I gave her what I hoped translated into a pleased smile and not a pained one; repellent image in my head or not, my body refused to recognise it. All it saw was a gorgeous Amazon standing in the entrance to the dressing room appraising me with a critical but heated stare.

"What do you think?" I asked again in a desperate attempt to ignore my physical discomfort.

She cleared her throat and stepped closer to me. "I think you don't have to try on any more."

"You don't need to send a photo to Georgina for approval?"

Emilia shook her head. "Ah, no. There's really no other choice, is there?"

"Well, there was the dark blue one with the crystals." I pointed to the long-tailed coat hanging on a hook across the room. We left it there because it had been a possibility if we could find no other costume to fit.

She glanced in that direction and pursed her lips, hemming and hawing at the other option for a few moments. "It doesn't really go with Georgina's costume… she's more Marie Antoinette, not Sarah from *Labyrinth*."

I grinned at her reference. "But I could rock at being Bowie for the night."

"Nobody can rock the Bowie unless they are, in fact, David Bowie," she quipped, her humour restored and her previous embarrassment forgotten. "But, to be fair, you could probably give the man a run for his money. Crazy Jareth makeup, hair, and all."

Laughter bubbled up in my chest.

"Stay with the red and gold," she said. "It makes you look regal."

I laughed and ran the soft fabric of one sleeve hem between my fingers. "You think so?"

I saw her soft blush again. She held out the white wig in her hand. "Here, put this on."

"It's not really…" I muttered, struggling with the thing.

She rolled her eyes. "Oh my God, step down off the platform. Let me do it."

Doing as she said, I stepped off the platform and presented my head to her. She reached up to arrange my longer hair beneath the wig, making the task seem all too easy even though all I could focus on was her intoxicating perfume and the heat of her body so close to mine. When she was done, she motioned for me to turn toward the mirror.

"It looks good," I said, "but weird with my Shakespeare beard."
"Your what?"

I pointed to my face. "My Shakespeare beard."

"You call that your 'Shakespeare beard?'"

"Why not? I usually only have it when I'm doing a play."

She shook her head and laughed. "You didn't have a full one for *Macbeth*."

"We weren't going for that regal look. We were going for rugged and scruffy," I argued. "Did you see the play?"

I already knew she hadn't; I would have noticed her sitting in the audience if she had been there.

Emilia shrugged her shoulders. "I was supposed to."

Her words made me pause. "Supposed to?"

"My friend got tickets to one of the shows," she elaborated. "But something with Georgina came up and I couldn't go. I was so angry. I'd been looking forward to it for ages."

My stomach dropped uneasily. It likely didn't mean as much to her as it did to me, but I felt ill as the full knowledge of what might have been back then invaded my consciousness. To think, had Georgina not required her to work, we might have met on a cold winter's night and the whole trajectory of my life over the last two years would have been completely different. Georgina would never have become a factor in my life beyond that of a girlfriend's boss.

What would my life have been like? Could I have been *happy*? At least, happier than I was?

"So you never saw it?" I asked, finally, in an attempt to keep my wandering mind from going down the path that never was.

She smiled. "I watched a bootleg. Don't turn me in, okay?"

I clicked my tongue against my teeth and shook my head. "Naughty."

"To be fair, I would have paid through the nose to see it," she defended. "I was a little bit of a fan."

"Was?"

Emilia blushed again. "*Am* a fan? It's different now… now that I know you."

I turned back to the mirror and smoothed a hand over my bristly chin. "I should still shave the beard, though. I don't really need it now since I'm done with Petruchio."

"Oh, don't do that," she replied. "I like the beard. The mask should cover it."

I looked down at the gilt mask in her hands. Much larger than the one delivered to the hotel suite for Georgina's costume, it would cover my whole face with its gold protruding chin and large nose.

She motioned to my face. "May I?"

I smiled. Didn't she know I would do anything to have her close to me?

She lifted the mask and pressed it against my face. "Hold it there for me, just over the bridge of the nose."

I accidentally brushed my fingers over hers in the exchange. She hurriedly pulled her hand away like I had burned her with my touch. I couldn't deny the thrilling sensation that passed through my own arm at the connection. Neither could I ignore that her hands had a slight tremor as she drew the black ribbons behind my wigged head and secured the mask. It was a relief to know I wasn't the only one who felt something beyond what was strictly acceptable between me and my girlfriend's employee.

The mask itself was not as heavy as I expected, but still an odd addition to my body. I especially liked the fact that it covered my entire face and only highlighted my eyes in gilt frames. Anonymity had become increasingly difficult over the years, and even at exclusive events like the masquerade, people still had a tendency to become bothersome. With this costume, I could drop my fake smile for one night and allow the physical mask to hide my emotions from the world; my anonymity would allow me the freedom to be myself, if only for a little while, so I could enjoy the evening in whomever's presence I wished.

"Do you like it?" she inquired, her voice careful as though she expected me to say that I didn't. "There are others…"

"I love it," I replied.

She grinned. "Good. You can take it off to eat and drink, of course, but it's designed so you don't have to."

"I don't intend to remove it at all tonight."

One dark, finely shaped brow arched at me in confusion, but she giggled anyway. "All right then."

"Signor? Signorina?"

We both turned toward the entrance where our shop assistant stood. I hadn't noticed him slip out after he helped me change; Emilia and her thorough consideration had been my only concern.

"Will this be it?" he asked.

Emilia replied that it would be my costume.

"And the hat?"

"The—oh!" she exclaimed, reaching up to remove the tricorne from her head.

I stopped her movement, my hand on her arm. "No hat…"

"But…"

"No," I pressed. "Besides, it looks better on you."

"I'll take your word for it," she replied with a sigh. She wasted no time in asking the shop assistant to help me undress and then excused herself from the room.

When I looked at the little Italian man again, I realised he was watching her retreat with an interest that unsettled me. That wasn't his. That was *mine*, whether she knew it or not. I cleared my throat and he turned to me.

"She is very beautiful, no?" asked the man in conversation as he took the mask and wig and set it aside.

"She is," I replied. "Very."

Our conversation quickly lapsed after that, for which I was grateful. I couldn't risk her overhearing me. When I finished, I made my way out into the extensive shop, but didn't find her. The clerk behind the front till informed me that she took a call outside the shop. Glancing toward the windows in the front, I saw her frowning into the mobile as she talked to whoever was on the other side. I paid for my costume and gathered the bags, stepping out of the atelier in time to hear her bid farewell to the caller.

"Anything wrong?"

She startled and looked up at me. "No. Just an issue with the car for tonight. It's all straightened out... ready?"

Emilia held her hands out to take the garment bags from me, but I pulled them away from her. "I'll take this back to the hotel," I told her. "I'm sure you're anxious to get to your tour."

"I am. Thank you, Alex."

"No, thank you."

Emilia's smile was all I needed as she waved at me and turned to leave. I watched her until she disappeared into the massive crowd congregating in the street.

Instinct told me she would get me into a lot of trouble, but I was powerless to resist my urges. Fortunately, I had a mask to wear and a costume to match it, allowing me the opportunity to taste that which would have been otherwise forbidden.

CHAPTER 26

SEVERAL THINGS PASSED THROUGH my mind when I found Alex
in my hotel room waiting for me to arrive, but none of them formed
into easily accessible words. I was positively knackered and angry
after my evening, and seeing him only made me angrier and no less
confused. Then there was Jordan, still speaking rapidly in my ear,
asking me questions I had no hope of answering for her.

"Jordan, I'll call you back," I repeated.

"I don't feel right about this, Em," she replied, worried. "What if
he—"

I sighed. "He's not going to hurt me."

My gaze slipped to his face, looking for some form of confirmation that he wouldn't stoop to that level. Even though I knew him—at
least liked to believe I knew him—who was to say he wouldn't? So
many things about him had surprised me.

The man, for his part, gave me a nearly imperceptible nod.
Physically, he might not hurt me. He had, however, already done
a fair job of inflicting enough pain with what he said at dinner. I
hoped he didn't plan to continue down that path.

"I'll call you later. I promise."

I didn't wait for her to respond and ended the call, looking at the
screen on my mobile until it shut off, and then glanced at the man
and his impassive stare. His suit coat and tie were missing, but the

white dress shirt had been rolled to his elbows and unbuttoned at his neck. He seemed relaxed, but not. The energy in the room wasn't the type that inspired me to let down my guard; his unwavering eye contact made me fidget restlessly.

"How did you get in here?"

He silently held up a small plastic key card.

"I didn't—"

Alex stopped my words. "The room is under Georgina's name. They know I'm Georgina's boyfriend. They gave me a key."

"I hope no one saw you! They know Georgina's not staying here…"

"Oh, I'm sure the clerk who helped me is halfway to TMZ right now."

His flippant remark made me want to strangle him. Maybe I wouldn't have to worry about Alex harming me, after all. Rather, it might end up the other way around. I thought he had better have a care for his person, because my fingers itched to cause damage, though even I knew I wouldn't actually touch him. Touching him was bad. Touching him would lead to other things that neither of us needed to face.

"Are you trying to get caught? First with the knickers, now this?" I asked. "Are you trying to ruin both our lives?"

A chuckle full of regret passed his lips. He stood on long legs and rested his hands on slender hips. "Funny thing, that. My life is already fairly mired in shit, so I thought, why not add a little more to it?"

"Some of us aren't in the same boat," I defended, though even to me they sounded like nothing more than empty words. If I learned anything in the time I spent with Tobias, my own life—the one I mistakenly thought I should live—had reached its own point of no return.

He ignored my words and took a few steps toward me; I held up my hands to stop him with enough distance between us. I couldn't be that close to him. Despite everything, my resolve threatened to slip if I let him near me again.

"Why are you here?" My voice wavered at the question.

He cleared his throat. "I came to see you."

"I thought I made myself clear yesterday."

"Crystal," he replied darkly.

"And you're ignoring it."

He stepped forward again. "No, I'm fully aware that my very face offends you on the deepest, most fundamental of levels. But I had to know…"

"Know… what?"

"I had to know why."

Why? He must have seen the confusion on my face and quickly filled the space between us with words.

"Why Tobias?" The rich honey of his voice broke and my eyes snapped to his face. He swallowed. "Why would you choose him over me? What does he have that I don't?"

"You're kidding, right?" I asked in disbelief and pushed past him into the room. I didn't want to have this conversation. Frankly, I didn't want to see him. Period. Yet there he stood in the middle of my room and, while I allowed him to continue speaking to me, I didn't want to hear it. He had no right to have these feelings about my relationship with Tobias, whether he knew about where his friend and I stood or not.

"No, I'm not kidding," he said.

I dropped my clutch and mobile on the desk and leaned my hip against it. "You came all the way over here, risking exposing us both because you feel… what? Cuckolded? No, that's not the right term…"

Alex's brows furrowed in irritation.

"Displaced?" I tried again. "Gosh, it's right there on the tip of my tongue…"

"Stop." The command came from him with no little amount of force. I blinked back at him. "What is it about him—"

I shook my head. "Fuck off, Alex. You're only here because your pride's wounded. Because someone beat you at your own game. Because there's a stronger challenger for your lioness."

The soubriquet he used two nights before to claim me as his own hit him squarely where I wanted it. I would have been lying if I said I hadn't enjoyed, in some sick, twisted part of my brain, seeing the flinch that resulted from my words.

"This isn't a fucking game!" His hand, palm flat, connected with the desk with a crack that resounded in the otherwise quiet room. "You've never been a game!"

"It sure as hell felt like I was one."

He lifted his hands to his head and raked his fingers through his hair, setting the curls askew. "*You've* made it a fucking game!"

"*Me*?"

He took in a ragged breath. The blotchy redness covering his furious face did not abate even though he tried to calm himself. When he released the breath he held, his words followed. "Yes, *you*. With all of these damn rules about what you can and cannot do, what I can and cannot do, playing me back and forth with new conditions and stipulations. And here I am following you around, trying to convince you to give me a fucking chance, because I think you'll understand the situation. That you can look past all the shit and still see me for me, and see me trying to survive until it's all over with Georgina."

"Oh my God." I rolled my eyes at him and bent down to remove my shoes. "If you wanted me to see that, you should have told me from the very beginning what was happening. I might've had—"

"Would it have mattered to you? I mean, seriously… Would. It. Have. Mattered?"

I swallowed and turned away from him.

He drew in a heaving breath. "You're the one who has constantly perverted my intentions. I understand the situation is a bad one and in the beginning you didn't know any better. I even understand the fact that I should have approached you differently than I did. I own to that. But it almost seems like you *wanted* to make something more out of it than was actually there. You wallow in self-pity and some sort of manufactured guilt over my interest in you because you don't want to face the fact that you want me too. When it's all said and done, you were all too ready to join me down this path."

A moment of silence spread between us and all I heard was the television in the room beside us playing some sort of music. It was muffled enough that I didn't know what it was, but it made me aware of the fact that the hotel walls were thin. I took two cleansing sighs, attempting to rein in my emotions so as to avoid shouting and giving my neighbour something to talk about. Not that it really mattered if what Alex said about the desk clerk was true.

His lips pressed into a dour line. "Look me in the eyes and tell me you didn't want to be with me from the moment we met."

I raised my chin until I met his eyes and opened my mouth to say that I hadn't. I was completely sure of my ability to lie to him. To say that I never wanted him. To say I wasn't in love with him. But when I began to say the words, nothing but a choking croak came from my throat. I wanted to slap him for the self-satisfied smirk that crossed his face.

"See? You can't even say it," he spat. "It's like you can't take one fucking thing and enjoy it. Or maybe it's because you can't be happy unless you're neck deep in drama? Even if something good is staring at you from across a fucking ballroom in the middle of Venice, you jump to the worst possible scenario and belittle it before you even give it a chance."

Had I wanted to, I couldn't have said anything, so flabbergasted was I by his words. I supposed he deserved the chance to present his argument. I hadn't let him do much talking the previous morning, but that didn't make listening to him any easier.

He sighed and shook his head. "You just don't want to be happy, do you?"

"Happy?" I couldn't believe him. "*Happy*? How could I have ever been happy with you while you were, for all I knew, going to marry the slag while still sticking your nose where it shouldn't have been?"

Perhaps my words were a little below the belt, but it was true.

"But now you know the truth and you're still not willing to give me a chance," he said. "I thought our conversation on the beach... it gave me hope that maybe..."

And that was where he broke. I didn't expect it, but I heard his voice crack again. I huffed.

"Alex, we've been round and round about this," I stated with forced calmness. "I don't know what else to say. You have some things to sort out and I'm only going to get in the way. I have to do some things, as well. Clearly, after the way dinner went, that much is a given. We both need a clear head when dealing with her. You know what she's like. What she can do if we aren't on top of it."

The look of fear and the curl of his lip told me that he knew exactly what I meant about Georgina. Of course he did. We were the only two people on Earth who had any real conceptualisation of how vindictive the woman was; what happened at dinner was just an appetiser for the others in our party. And, perhaps, I knew even more about it considering what I knew about her alleged pregnancy.

"Then when?" he demanded, tearing me from my thoughts. "Will there ever be a time that you could see yourself being happy with me?"

I looked up at him, holding his gaze in the low light from the lamp in the corner of the room. Tears bit at my eyes, threatening to spill over onto my cheeks. "I don't know."

A low, feral growl came from him. "What do you mean you don't know?"

"At the risk of sounding cliché, you and me, we're like a combustible mixture of materials waiting to explode," I said. "I don't want it blowing up in my face. I'm trying to figure out my own life right now and I don't want to get burned. Considering how this whole thing began..."

He shook his head. "It could also be the most beautiful, brilliant firework we've ever seen. Knowing what I know about those few times we were together—"

"I wish I shared your optimism."

Alex grunted a small, rueful chuckle. "Even my optimism is waning. But you did give me hope that things could and were changing for me."

His words cut straight through me in an entirely different way, stabbing the glass case I had built around my heart. I could almost feel the cracks webbing out from one tiny chip.

"Alex, I can't be that person right now, and I can't guarantee that I will ever be right for you."

He backed away from me. "Will you continue seeing Tobias?"

I hung my head in irritation, the relative calm at the end of our argument shattered. "We're not seeing each other. And, if it matters to you, he has only ever had your best interests at heart."

Alex didn't believe me. I saw that much in his eyes when I finally met his steady gaze. "Oh, he has, has he?"

"Don't be like that," I snapped. "That's something else you need to sort out."

He clearly didn't like my opinion on that subject.

I pushed past him and moved to the bathroom. "I'd like to point out that you were the one who put him into that situation."

"So much for loyalty," Alex muttered.

"Loyalty?" I called.

"He obviously told you about the favour I asked of him. It was meant to stay between us."

I poked my head out of the bathroom. "He was honest with me. It's more than I can say for you."

"You're no paragon of honesty, either," he remarked.

I ignored him and turned on the water from the cold tap, hovering over the sink bowl to splash it on my face. His large presence filled the space of the tiny bathroom and he leaned against the doorjamb in that maddening nonchalant way. Even at his angriest, he still looked as though he had it all together.

He watched me as I washed my face of the thick makeup Jordan slathered on it earlier. I wished he would just go. Was he trying to intimidate me? We had nothing more to say to each other; he was just prolonging the inevitable. Or did he hope, if he waited long enough, I might change my mind?

When I came up for air and grabbed a hand towel to dry my face, I noticed a small grin playing on his lips. "Now you're smiling?" I didn't care that I sounded incredulous.

"I'm thinking," he said.

I didn't ask him what was on his mind and tried to go back to the main room. But that was a mistake. The space left open between him and the open doorjamb was small. I thought he would be a gentleman and let me pass. He didn't. A hand circled around my arm to stop me. When I turned to look up at him, he pressed against me until my back hit the unforgiving wooden frame.

"Don't you want to know what I'm thinking about?"

"Not really." I shook my head. "Why are you making this harder than it already is? Why don't you just go?"

He elaborated anyway since I was a fairly captive audience. "I'm thinking about the night of my birthday in Paris, when I brought you the cold medicine. You had been doing something in the bathroom right before you answered the door because you had a hand towel with you."

The memory came, fully formed, into my mind. Of course I remembered it. Even though I was as sick as a dog and nobody else cared that I was convalescing in my room, he ordered me soup and brought me much needed medication as well as some company. I thought, at the time, about how much I wished I had a man who did that for me all the time; Alex had been nothing more than Prince Charming. A fantasy. That Alexander Thorne didn't exist anymore.

"See? That's what I'm trying to say. Is that Prince Charming the real you or an act? Or is this miserable, arrogant man the real you?" I asked. "I can never know…"

"The real me is all of that, and more," he replied. "I'm miserable because of choices I've made, and perhaps I've let a little too much go to my head and it's made me arrogant. But don't ever, for a minute, think I don't care very deeply for you or that I don't want to treat you like a princess."

"I don't want to be treated like a princess."

He pressed closer, his long, lean body holding me securely in place. I couldn't run; even if I could convince my brain I needed to go, my legs wouldn't have responded. Par for the course, my legs turned to jelly in our close proximity.

"I tried for so long to leave you out of this mess. I could have made my move shortly after we first met, but I didn't. I could have done it the night of the Christmas party. Or when you were out here with us for the Golden Globes and SAGs. I *could* have done it all then, if I only had the worst intentions at heart," he said. "But I didn't."

His thigh pressed between my legs and a hand buried itself in my hair, popping the tiny pins holding the hairdo in place. A few hit my shoulders before they fell silently to the ground.

He continued. "I made the mistake of thinking that one masked night could give me the satisfaction I needed until I was done with this Georgina business."

The warmth of his body seared through the thin layer of his shirt and my slinky dress. I swore I almost felt his heart beating alongside mine, but I was too distracted to focus on it as his head dipped down.

"But I was wrong… oh, so wrong," he purred. "The way you kissed m—"

My hands shot up between us, pressing flat against his muscled chest to hold him an infinitesimal distance from me. "*You* kissed *me*!"

"You kissed back," he replied matter-of-factly. His mouth froze a hairsbreadth from mine, beckoning me to move. Calling for me to close the distance. Soft, warm puffs of breath through his barely parted lips ruffled some of the hair that fell across face. My only reaction was to stick my tongue out to wet my own lips. He didn't restrain himself when he saw the opportunity, covering my mouth with his.

He was quick, though, in his touch. Teasing. When he pulled away, I needed more. I had always known, of course, but I couldn't let myself fall completely to my whims. Not after I promised Tobias I would take some time for myself and figure out what I wanted out of life.

"I was terrified by how much I wanted you and what I wanted to do to you," he breathed against my mouth, tender lips brushing mine as he formed the words in his impassioned speech. "I ran away. I tried to get you out of my system, and it didn't work. I just couldn't get you off my mind. What I didn't realise at the time was that it would be so difficult to maintain an act like that in public."

He breathed in, then sighed.

"I'm not a cheater, Emilia. I don't go around having affairs willy-nilly. I pursued you because, in my mind, my previous relationship was over. I pursued you because I wanted you. Because I had, in my own way, fallen in love with you before anything in Venice ever happened."

I expected him to kiss me again—fully—at this pause, but he stepped back and out into the entryway, leaving me cold and wanting with his last words echoing in my head. Words were one thing. Deeds were something else entirely. I wasn't prepared to trust him.

He placed a hand on the door handle and looked back at me, expecting me to stop him. I could not, however, do that. When he didn't receive the response he wanted, he turned the handle and walked out into the hallway.

He waited once more, but I couldn't convince myself to move beyond the doorway. I watched him turn and followed his stalking frame half way down the hall until something spurred me forward.

"Alex! Wait…"

I moved swiftly down the corridor until I was close enough to him to wrap my fingers in the open button placket of his undone shirt collar. Hope crossed his face, but I dashed it when I realized what I was going to do to him.

No. No kissing. No impulsiveness. I promised Tobias. I promised myself. I let go of his shirt and stepped back, holding out my hand.

"Please give me the key to my room."

Like a small boy relinquishing his favourite toy, he dug into a pocket and produced the plastic key card. "Here."

"Thank you."

He sighed. "Goodnight, bellissima."

"Good*bye*, Alex."

His eyes closed.

"Goodbye," he said in a soft rumble. There was a finality about it that made my heart ache, but I knew in the depths of my soul that this was right. We both needed time and space, each for wildly different reasons.

Alex turned on his heels and left me standing in the middle of the hallway until he turned a corner and disappeared into the bay of lifts. I exhaled, feeling strangely lighter—as though a huge weight had been lifted from my shoulders—but also sick to my stomach. After the day and night I had, I knew it could be any combination of emotions or thoughts racing through me causing the upset. I didn't dwell on it. I had no brainpower left to compute what I felt, even if I wanted.

When I returned to my room, I sent Jordan a text telling her I was fine, Alex was gone, but that I needed to sleep. She threatened me with an early morning call if she let me off the hook for the night. I agreed.

I slipped out of my dress, leaving it in a pool on the floor, and crawled straightaway into bed without bothering with nightclothes. My body relaxed into the cloud-like mattress and I pulled the comforter up to my nose. The last thing I remembered as I drifted off to sleep was the fact that, in the morning, I had a meeting with Georgina.

And I knew, perhaps for the first time in my life, exactly what I wanted—no, *needed*—to do. There was only one way to proceed after the last forty-eight hours. Though I was terrified of my future, I found a great deal of peace in knowing my own mind. It was that peace which allowed me to slip easily into a truly deep slumber for the first time in a long time.

CHAPTER 27

THE NEXT MORNING, I woke with a clear head, ready to face a life free of doing what people told me to do or listening to a nagging conscience always telling me I could do better. For the first time in my life, I felt like I was enough. And because I was enough, it was time to redesign the tattered remnants of my life, one stitch at a time, into becoming the person I wanted to be. Of course I had absolutely no idea how to begin a project so completely alien to me, and I was more than monumentally terrified at the prospect of travelling on an uncharted path, but I figured a good breakfast was a decent place to start.

Room service delivered the meal after my shower and I sat down at my laptop to type the letter I had dreamt about from the moment I signed my employment contracts with Georgina. With shaking fingers—a mixture of fear and anticipation—I committed all the words to paper. A knock at the door interrupted my train of thought, and I got up to see who was waiting for me on the other side.

Thankfully, there was no man involved. Jordan hid underneath a baseball cap and the huge black sunglasses from her Georgina act. She carried with her two large Starbucks coffees and stopped knocking for a moment to look anxiously over her shoulder, as though she expected someone to pop out and harass her. Jordan pulled off her sunglasses and slipped them into the neck of her shirt.

My friend shot me a look of annoyance as soon as I opened the door. "It's awfully hard to talk in the morning when you aren't answerin' your damn cell phone."

She pushed straight into my room without a formal invite and took the second seat at the small table where I was enjoying my breakfast. Her right leg bounced up and down, in what I could only surmise was a product of too much caffeine. She drank the most potent coffee, black with a shot or two of espresso on the side, and in such huge quantities it always made me wonder how she didn't float off into space.

"Good morning to you, too," I muttered as I shut the door and followed the path to my seat. "To what do I owe this early morning visit?"

Jordan grabbed a piece of cantaloupe from my plate and popped it into her mouth. She silently chewed the melon as though gathering her thoughts. After a moment, she drew in a long breath and pulled her mobile out of her pocket. She held it out for me to read the screen.

My reasonably peaceful morning full of sweet fruit, Danishes, and a relieving sense of finality as I typed my resignation letter instantly evaporated into thin air. The reality of the situation came slamming back into me, hitting me square in the chest, with the force of a runaway lorry. I slumped into the vacant chair, took the mobile from her hands and stared at an old modelling photo of mine sandwiched between two other photos: one of Tobias kissing my cheek at the restaurant and the other one—grainy, poorly lit, but clearly of Alex and me—in Venice.

In the gondola.

In flagrante delicto.

With the headline: *Cheating Shocker! Sexiest Man Alive Caught with Girlfriend's Assistant!*

How had they found a photo of us together?

My face was indistinguishable in the poor quality of the zoomed photo, but the captions attributed the woman in the photo to me. No one would know it was actually me without an outside source giving the news agency the full story. No hotel clerk running to TMZ the night before would know about it. And yet, there was my face, plastered across the front page of Perez Hilton.

Ignoring the uncomfortable roiling in my stomach, I quickly scanned the article. I didn't have to do much thinking as to who might have leaked the information. That part was fairly obvious. And even though I should have been livid—at Georgina, at Alex, at *myself* for letting it happen—my only thought was about how it would affect Alex and Tobias. Tobias certainly shouldn't have had to deal with that kind of press. And Alex, well, Alex may have deserved some small portion of the heartache, but not to the extent the story would explode on the week of the Academy Awards. The narrative would no longer be about his perfect performance, but rather focus on his mucked up love life.

The purpose of Alex sticking it out with Georgina until after the show was to protect him from facing the madness that was about to ensue. No one wanted to deal with those questions—and, without doubt, there would be millions of them—while attempting to focus on one of the highlights of his career. If he and Jack had waited to announce the breakup until after the awards, Alex could retreat to London and ride out the storm in the comfort of his home, surrounded by friends and family. Now he had to face it head on. Everything he had suffered through to lessen the impact of his break up with her was for nothing.

I let out a breath, willing myself to remain calm. I placed the mobile on the table in front of me with a shaky hand. Jordan looked at me expectantly, or maybe waited for me to break down, but whatever her intent, her eyes didn't leave my face.

"I'm fine."

"You're not fine," she said. "No one in their right mind would be fine. You know what this means for you, don't you? What shit the press is going to do to your name? You saw what they were like at my wedding. The only thing they love more than an engagement is a really juicy breakup complete with lyin' and cheatin'."

"I honestly don't give a fuck," I replied. "I'm actually kind of glad it's out there in the open. I'm so sick of keeping secrets."

Jordan set her coffee cup down and brushed her hands free of any food debris—she had moved onto the half-finished Danish on the small china plate. For a moment, I hated her. Hated that she could eat pretty much anything she wanted and still stay thin. But that was only projecting my hatred onto someone whom I loved dearly. My real hatred was meant for other people and other things.

"Well, there's a huge mob of paparazzi downstairs. You're gonna have to deal with it," she told me. "I ordered a car to be delivered in an hour so we can get you moved out of here to another hotel."

I reached for the other cup of coffee she had offered to me by placing it in front of my computer. The liquid seared my tongue and the back of my throat. It didn't help my queasy belly like I thought it would. Grimacing and coughing, I looked at her. "I'm not going to another hotel. I'm going home."

"Don't go home! That means she's won," Jordan said. "She'll be this smug little bitch at all the parties this week and I'll be tempted to haul off and punch her. I'm too pretty to go to jail for assault."

"I'm going down to the business centre to print my resignation letter." I pointed to my computer screen. "Then I'm going to sign it, gather my things and go over to Alex's and give it to her."

Jordan groaned. "She's going to think she's won."

"How? She'll have to do all the work this week herself. She hasn't truly worked a day in her life; she doesn't know what and where and how to get stuff. She can barely send a fucking email," I said. "If she makes it out of Hell Week unscathed, I'll be extremely surprised."

My friend looked at me as though I had gone mad. Which, for all intents and purposes, I *had*. I had gone mental a long time ago, thinking this hell of a life was one I was destined to live because of my past mistakes and choices. This was the first time I planned to do what I wanted and didn't care about the repercussions on my own life. Maybe my courage would falter on that long, lonely flight home to London, but standing up to Alex taught me I could do it. I could resist the temptation to live for someone else. And that maybe, just maybe, I'd be better off for it.

"I still have something up my sleeve if she tries to make this worse," I muttered. I didn't want to stoop to Georgina's level, but I wasn't beyond my own form of blackmail. Not when my life and the lives of those I loved could be affected by the fallout.

"What happened to you last night after you left dinner?" Jordan asked, her tone mystified. "Did Tobias implant a Pod Person in you or something? Are you an alien wearing an Emilia suit?"

I shrugged and shut the lid on my laptop. "I've had enough of everybody's shit. I'm done. So completely done. I'm done with Georgina. And Alex. And Clémence. And myself."

A slow but tight smile spread across my friend's face. "Honey, you know I'll support whatever you want to do. I just think you should stay the week and go to all these fabulous parties with me and show her that what she did didn't faze you... this runnin' and hidin'..."

"I don't want to make it bigger than it already is," I insisted. "Especially if Alex or Tobias are at any of the parties. Just think about that."

Jordan shook her head. "I think you should stay."

"For what? For you? So *you* feel better about it?"

"No, of course not, I..." she started, but let the words trail off. "No, you're right."

"Who knows what this will mean to me if I have to find a new job back in London. Why make it worse? You read the headline—I'm a slut who makes a habit of sleeping around with eligible British actors."

"You never slept with Tobias, did you? I mean, I know you said you hadn't..."

"I'm offended you would even feel the need to know."

Jordan pursed her lips together. "I'm sorry. I didn't mean it to sound like that."

I waved her off. "Can I use the car you ordered to go to Alex's?"

"Yeah, of course."

With another sigh, I turned my mind to gathering an outfit for the day. It was all I could do to push the thoughts of the article away. I chose comfort over style considering I planned to be on a flight home in a few hours, and dressed in such an obligated, deliberate manner I might as well have been preparing for a war—a war I didn't want to fight, though it needed to be done. There was no telling what I would walk into when I reached Alex's house, so I prepared for nothing short of World War Three.

"Would you do me a favour, Jor?"

She cleared her throat. "Yeah. What?"

"Find me a ticket home to Heathrow. British Airways. Later today if possible."

In a matter of seconds, I heard her twangy drawl and took the opportunity to lock myself in the bathroom. I intended to put on a little war paint in the form of mascara and lip balm, but instead stood and stared at my face in the mirror. I just couldn't be bothered to care—to truly care—about the photos of us or what it might do to my life. I knew, perhaps, that a complete absence of emotion was too far over onto the other side of the spectrum of my life, but at that moment, my options were either caring too much or caring too little. I did not have the comfort of a middle ground like normal people. That would only come with time.

Conceding that makeup would not help hide my apathy, I stuffed everything in my toiletry bags. Jordan handed me a scrap of paper with the ticket details on it as soon as I stepped out of the bathroom. "You leave at six tonight."

"Did you get my card from my handbag?"

She shook her head and didn't answer me.

"Jordan… I didn't…" I stopped when her hands covered her ears. I grunted and shook my head. "You didn't have to."

"I wanted to," she replied with a grin. "First class British Airways all the way home. Because you deserve some luxury."

"A private jet would be nicer."

She laughed. "Don't get cheeky."

"Worth a try, right?"

I pushed past her to finish packing. For once, I was thankful I hadn't completely emptied the bags when I first arrived at the hotel; it made packing the few things I had removed much easier to replace.

Jordan didn't say much as she helped me pack, and a half hour later, I was wheeling my bag through the lobby with her at my side. The photographers and reporters descended on us like a swarm of bees; between clicking camera shutters and shouted questions the sound they made was more deafening than any hive drone. Hotel security barely held them back as I ducked my head and hid my face in a jumper. I sat in the dark windowed SUV, a loud *whoosh* of air leaving my body. This wasn't my life. This was someone else's life.

Jordan slipped into the seat beside me, but not before flipping off a particularly insistent photographer shoving his camera inside the vehicle. When the door finally shut, she turned to look at me. "You okay?"

"Not really," I admitted. "I never wanted this to happen."

"No one ever does," Jordan replied and leaned forward to speak to the driver. "You can go. Four Seasons, please."

It took some doing to convince her not to accompany me all the way to Alex's. I didn't relish more witnesses—no matter how close we were—to the product of my inability to stand up for myself. She relented begrudgingly, but understood that I needed to do it alone.

"I meant to say earlier," Jordan added in the quiet of the vehicle as we drove along Sunset toward her hotel, "that Clémence intended for you to come to New York and work at the magazine as *her* assistant. She might still offer you the job."

I folded my hands in my lap. "I wouldn't accept it. Even if I hadn't realised I have to stop letting everyone else dictate my life. London is home and I hate New York, probably more than I hate the superficiality of Hollywood. And I'd have to uproot Sam as well. It just wouldn't happen."

Jordan nodded. "I figured that's what you'd say."

"Clémence has been good to me," I added, "and I appreciated it even when I didn't really... but I'm done with living by someone else's rules. I need to make my own way."

"I think Clémence would be happy for you," Jordan noted. "She said she'll give you a call soon."

I sighed and looked out the window as we were pulling up to the Four Seasons. Frankly, I didn't want to hear from Clémence even if she was still on my side. I was done with the fashion and celebrity world for a while and I certainly didn't relish returning any time soon.

The vehicle rolled to a slow stop and Jordan paused with her hand on the door. She looked back at me.

"What?" I asked.

A second later her strong arms wrapped around my neck. She concluded her encompassing embrace with a small chuckle. "I'm so proud of you, my beautiful friend." She sat back and pressed my cheeks between her hands. "If you need anything at all in the coming months, you know you can call me and I'll be on the first flight out, all right?"

"I think I'll be fine," I said, smiling at her. "Sam and Lindsay will keep me flying straight."

"Even so, sometimes you need girl time, right?"

I laughed at her. "You're still my friend. Just because I'm officially leaving this life behind doesn't mean that's going to stop... quit acting like this is it."

"I'm just so happy for you." She sighed wistfully. "You need to be happy, and that's all that matters. Maybe I'll see if D can't get some time on the European leg of his tour and we'll come visit you guys. Won't that be fun? The two Southerners in cowboy boots walkin' around Soho with you?"

"You'll be the highlight of the day."

Jordan giggled and kissed my forehead. "I love you, Em."

"I love you, too, Jordan," I said. "I'm sorry we didn't get to spend more time together."

She shrugged and slung her purse over her shoulder. "Babe, you know me. As long as it's ten minutes on a layover in the same city, I'm a happy girl."

"Thank you for everything."

"Any time," Jordan replied with a wave. "Now, if you don't mind, I'm gettin' out of this car, and you're going to Alex's to do whatever it is you need to do."

She hopped out of the car and blew a playful kiss at me before disappearing into the building. I looked at the suited driver who had stayed silent for the whole conversation. His eyes met mine in the rear view mirror. "Where to?"

"Malibu."

I dug out a pen and tore a piece of paper from a notebook, scribbling down Alex's address. He took the paper and plugged the information into his GPS. Soon we were on the motorway. There would be no turning back after this. I made my choice. For that moment, at least, I felt confident in my decisions, even though they might falter when I faced my monsters.

CHAPTER 28

CLUTCHING MY BAGS CLOSER to my body as though they were shields, I pushed open the front door and let myself into the beach house, prepared for anything. The hinges creaked ominously in the quiet foyer, giving the space a creepiness it should not have had with all the bright light coming in through the surrounding windows.

I stood in the middle of the room listening to my surroundings as I shut the door behind me. Listening for what, exactly, I could not say, but I instantly noticed the strange hush. I expected something… *more*. More rushed. More violent.

Fights had not erupted and arguments were not being shouted. Nobody jumped out of the corner to scare me like some fun house actor at a carnival. None of Alex's "people" madly dashed in and out of the house trying to create and implement a mollifying battle strategy for the tabloids. Nothing. Nothing but complete and utter silence. It all seemed rather placid, as though I stepped into an alternate reality where everything was right with the world and my photo was not on the front page of every online tabloid in the English speaking world. As though I wasn't being hailed as the next Whore of Babylon.

When I received no acknowledgement of my arrival, I retreated to the kitchen to go through my handbag and extricate the tablet and other artefacts of my daily business supplies not belonging to me. Georgina had said to be at the house by ten in her message the previous evening; she was nowhere to be found. I thought about going upstairs to call for her, but decided against it. It was better not to wake a sleeping dragon needlessly.

I considered leaving everything, sneaking out, and sending her a text about it later. Simple. Painless. Easy. But I changed my mind quickly. I couldn't leave like that. That was the coward's way out. And I was done being a coward. Nothing worth doing was ever easy, and the old adage applied to my situation more than I ever thought it would.

So I sat in the pleasant breakfast nook, at the comfortable little glass top table with four chairs, shutting down and deleting the traces of my life with Georgina and keeping the bits of information I might need in the future—especially if there ever came I time where I had to fight fire with fire.

In the middle of updating my contacts on my personal mobile, I heard the telltale signs of life leave the bedroom upstairs. The clacking of her high-heeled feet struck the wood floors with a light staccato rhythm, then descended the staircase, and continued through to the living room. Georgina appeared in the kitchen entrance, looking unfazed by the disaster she had wrought. She wore a bubblegum pink sundress and strappy wedges. There was a time I would have admired her coolness and ability to handle a stressful situation with such reserve. But nearly two and a half years as her assistant and a handful of weeks as her boyfriend's mistress taught me otherwise. This wasn't quiet resilience. This was cool, manipulative calculation. She knew she was in control and made certain she was never out of it.

She cast an icy, but laughing, gaze at me and managed some sort of smile that made my skin crawl. "Did you have a nice night after you left? I am sure Tobias was more than accommodating."

"Tobias was lovely, thank you," I replied.

Georgina sniffed at my innocuous answer, but walked across the floor to me anyway, intent on getting a rise out of me. From her pocket, she withdrew a handful of red lace I recognised instantly. However, the mortification from the previous evening wasn't there. My detachment from my emotions frightened me, but I supposed it was probably better that way. She would be the first person to exploit a weakness in my emotional state if she found one. Sure, I was still angry about it, but she couldn't play on the anger if I didn't show it to her.

"I believe these are yours."

Georgina dropped the knickers in front of me. The soft cloth made no sound as it fell lightly on the table. I stared at the crumbled heap. Insignificant as the garment was, it possessed no little amount of force in its mere existence. It was the evidence of Alex's infidelity and my shame.

I marvelled for a moment at how such a silent thing could pack such a whopping punch to my gut. For one irrational moment, I considered denying I had anything to do with them. But that argument was useless. Everyone knew who they belonged to and I refused to lie. I refused to stoop to her level.

"Did you really expect me to believe some fan gave them to him and he forgot them?" Georgina said in the middle of an amused laugh. "Jack follows him around like a puppy. He would have taken them, wouldn't he?"

I tried to focus on what I was doing, ignoring the stain of crimson sitting right in front of me.

She continued without being provoked, adding another derisive chuckle for good measure. "I mean, really, did you think I wouldn't see it? What other woman of his acquaintance wears such a... *large* size?"

Finding the courage to lift my eyes, I watched her drift across the room to grab a porcelain teacup. She then stared at the electric kettle on the countertop, pushing buttons here and there, but not finding the correct one to turn it on. Her indelicate grunt of annoyance made me roll my eyes. She stared at it again before turning to me, forgetting her tea.

"How stupid did you think I was? Did you think I wouldn't notice how he acted around you? How you two danced at the masquerade? Or the hushed conversations afterward? He could barely wait to get away from Greece to get home to you."

I didn't say anything. I *couldn't* say anything. My lips felt like someone glued them together, my tongue a leaden weight inside my mouth.

"How did it feel to be his whore?" she asked. "Did you like it? Did it make you feel dirty? Or, perhaps, you felt loved? A shame, really, if you did. Those things never last, after all."

I clenched my mobile in my hands. I wanted to jump up and strangle her myself. Jordan's words about being too pretty to go to jail echoed in my head. A bubble of laughter wiggled its way out of my mouth. I clamped my lips shut when Georgina spun on me.

She sneered. "What was it like knowing you could never have all of him because he was mine all along?"

One of her delicate, blonde brows arched in challenge. Yet to find any of my own words to volley back at her, she returned to the kettle and tapped at the buttons again.

"In what world did you ever think you could have someone like him? He and I… we're from the same sort of people." The ire in her voice grew as she mashed buttons, picked up the kettle, and set it down. "You'd never fit in with his crowd, whether his mother deigned to have lunch with you or not. You'd stick out like a sore thumb amongst them."

My face grew hot at her words. How did she know about my lunch with Mary? Did she have someone follow us?

"Oh, yes, I know about that," she answered my unasked question with a smirk. "I know *all* about that. Just like the gondola, and dinner at his mother's, and the afternoon he spent with you at the studio, and the night you spent with him at Mary's. Amazing how little it cost me to have that paparazzo follow you around. They'll literally do anything for a quid or two."

Georgina glanced, only momentarily, in my direction to see my reaction. I was so gobsmacked by her words, I barely understood them. She waited a beat, until she was sure her words hit home, before she continued to twist her tiny knife. "How was that in the morning, by the way? How was his mum with you? Never did like that cow much. Always had the idea that Alex could do better than me, so I know she must have thought even less of a chav like you."

"Shut up! Just… shut up!" The words were out of my mouth before I could push myself up from my seat. Clenching my fists at my sides, I attempted counting to ten before continuing. It was useless. "You have no right to say anything like that—"

She sniffed and shook her head. "I have every right after the way I've been treated."

"After the way *you've* been treated?"

Georgina pointed to the kettle and moved away from it, unconcerned about the fury in my tone. "How do you turn this thing on?"

A bark of laughter escaped me, but did nothing to minimise its impact in the silence between us. Georgina's murderous glare turned to me a split second later. I thought she might slap me, but that would have taken too much effort. Instead, she stood still and stared.

I cleared my throat. "Do you really think I'm going to boil your bloody tea water after the way *you've* treated *me* in the last forty-eight hours?"

"It's your job," she replied.

I carefully marched my way to the kitchen island, clenching the plain white envelope in my hand. "Not any longer."

Her face contorted into a look of disgust as I pushed the thing across the smooth granite countertop. "Oh, this is brilliant! Just brilliant. Quitting on me this week of all weeks?"

I backed away. "I'm leaving later this evening."

"I absolutely forbid you leaving," Georgina shrieked. "We have a week of styling appointments and meetings! I need you here!"

"I don't give a fuck about what you need. I'm done."

She huffed. "If you leave, I'll make your life even more of a hell than it already is. I have photos from all over the place. Don't think I won't give them to the appropriate sources like I did last night."

"Do whatever the fuck you want with them," I told her. "I don't care anymore."

Georgina clicked her tongue against her teeth and shook her head as though she were suddenly more disappointed in me than angry. It mesmerised me the way she could so suddenly flip her mind games around. One minute she was worried she genuinely needed me to work the following week, and in the next she flipped the switch back to calm, cool control with a threat. Her typical tactics weren't working this time; she was losing her footing. A moment of relief flooded me at the realisation.

She sighed and shrugged. "I'm sorry it has to end like this. We could still work it out, you know. We don't have to like each other to work together."

"We never liked each other, Georgina... and what work have you actually done in the years I've worked for you?" I asked. "Huh? Oh, that's right, you've done nothing. I've done everything. And you've reaped all the benefits. So fuck you, Georgina. Do it yourself for a change."

I collected my things from the table and stuffed them into my bag. Nodding at the tablet I worked on earlier, I said, "There's the iPad. I've changed all the passwords to generic ones, written on the note stuck to it."

She scoffed at me. Again. And again. As though making those sounds were going to change my mind. "I can't believe you're doing this. What am I going to do this week?"

"Your job." I rummaged through my tote and located my key ring. "Here's the studio key. If you need any help or have any questions, don't call me."

Georgina refused to open her hand to take the key, so I set it on the counter next to my unopened resignation letter. "You won't find a job anywhere in London. Everyone in the world will know what you did."

"They already do." I shrugged. "What do I have to lose when I've already lost everything?"

Well, everything but the people I loved.

"So you're just going to leave like that?" Her voice followed me as I slung my bags over my shoulder.

I paused mid-stride and spun around to look at her. "Yes, I'm leaving."

"You're an ungrateful little bitch," she spat. "I gave you a job when no one else would hire you."

"And I'm thankful for that, but this is something I should have done long ago. Like the day after I started working for you."

Georgina chuckled, though she seemed to be vibrating from anger. She lifted a shaky hand and drew her skeletal fingers through golden wisps of hair. "If you leave now, you leave without him."

"True," I acknowledged. "But at least I had him. And you know what? He chose me over you. I had him because he wanted me. Not because I blackmailed him into being with me. Not like you. How does that make you feel, Georgina, knowing that the only reason he stayed with you was because you threatened him?"

Georgina advanced on me quickly, with an angry, insinuating finger pointing at my chest. I towered over her, even though her wedges gave her a few extra inches. For the first time since I met her, I felt powerful. Strong. Larger than life. It was an exhilarating feeling. The imbalance of power, now shifted, made her take a step back to regroup her thoughts. The fury in her blue-grey eyes gave me sick pleasure.

She squared her shoulders and lifted her chin, her voice low and dangerous. "I'll ruin both your lives. The things I could do to Alex's image… and I can drag you down with him and blame you for all of it."

"If you say anything to anyone about the miscarriage you supposedly had with Alex's child," I said, "I'll tell the press everything I know. I'm sure they'd just love to know about that tawdry little affair you had back in 2013. You know, that one with the ectopic pregnancy that led to a complete hysterectomy? I'm sure Morgan King would love to know what her husband was up to back then."

The blood drained from her face and she deflated at my words. She had truly loved Morgan's husband, Scott. Well, loved as much as she was capable of loving. She had been the mistress then, completely besotted with him. The last thing she wanted was for me to divulge that secret, or the one she had been holding over Alex's head for months.

Thinking I won and she would leave me alone, I repositioned the bag on my shoulder. I turned around with a parting shot on my lips. It died instantly when I saw the two men standing in the doorway. I noticed Jack first, but only because I didn't want to acknowledge the other man beside him, murderous rage unconcealed on his face.

I couldn't move as Alex's cold gaze assessed me before turning to Georgina. And back again. A shiver skittered up my spine in the heavy stillness that followed.

"I thought you were at breakfast." Georgina's words cracked from fear. She coughed lightly to cover it.

Alex's voice, just above a rumbling whisper, but hard and as deadly as any other cutting word I had ever heard from him, broke through the heaviness. "Get out of my house."

"Alex, be reasonable," Georgina said, trying to keep the cool in her voice but failing to hide the tremor. "I have no other place—"

"Get your things. Get. Out. Of. My. House."

Georgina, seeing that he would not be moved, let loose a strangled cry and fled to the room upstairs. The master bedroom door slammed shut with such force it shook the window panes all around the substantial house. I crossed my arms over my chest as protection from the wrath he quickly turned on me.

"You too."

"I never intended to stay."

But even though I had every intention of leaving, it still killed me to hear the words said with such frostiness; no two words could have injured me more.

"Alex, hold on a minute—" Jack began, I hoped in my defence.

He held his hands up to silence his friend. Knowing I wouldn't get anywhere with him, I pulled together what remained of my courage and pushed past the men. At least I attempted to. Strong fingers cruelly clamped down on my upper arm to stop my retreat.

Daring a glimpse at him, I noticed that the sharp features of his face seemed severe at this angle. Sinister. But not. His rage was unmistakable, but underneath the veneer of hate was a swirling mass of pain and regret, like a wounded lion dazed and confused pacing around its cage. My belly twisted into an unforgiving knot as his eyes locked with mine.

"How long have you known?"

"Only a few days," I said. "I had no clue... but connected the dots when Jack told me about Georgina's miscarriage—or supposed one."

"And you didn't tell me as soon as you found out?" His voice shook with rage. "How could you... how could you look me in the eyes and make love to me when there was something like that you were keeping from me?"

"Alex—"

"No! It's no wonder you kept pulling away because you knew you were lying to me! And you couldn't stand it."

"I wasn't lying to you."

"You just didn't tell me? Right, because omission is always better."

I looked to Jack and opened my mouth to tell Alex what we decided for him, but I couldn't find the words to do it. He needed someone to trust, because I certainly wasn't that person, no matter how blameless I might have been in this. He needed someone he could go to for comfort in the coming days. I refused to be the person to ruin all of his close connections in the span of five minutes.

"How was I going to tell you?" I deadpanned. "I didn't want to hurt you more when you had so much going on. It just wasn't a good time. It was only to protect you. Don't you see that?"

He shook his head. "Why would you care about protecting me? You couldn't give a fuck—"

"Because I was in love you! That's why!"

Alex's immediate laughter was surprising and terrifying in its shaking fury. He let go of me and stepped away, but turned back around, holding his hands out. "You're no better than she is, you know? Playing these fucking mind games. One minute you can't stand to be in the same room as me and then you fucking love me? Bollocks!"

"Oh, fuck you, Alex," I said. "It wasn't like that at all and if you won't see that—"

Jack whistled loudly. He stepped between us and held his arms out to keep us apart. "Alex, if you want to be angry, be angry at me. I told her to wait. She wanted to tell you right away."

Alex didn't deflate. It looked, instead, as though he wanted to punch something.

Jack's voice rose like that of a tired, annoyed teacher. "Frankly, the both of you are going to need each other now more than ever to get through this whole fucking scandal."

I looked at Jack. "I'm done with this utter shit. So, so done."

Both men stared at me with blinking eyes.

"I'm going home."

Jack blinked. "To the hotel?"

"No," I replied, readjusting the strap on my shoulder. "I'm going home to London. If you need me, you know how to get in touch."

Alex shook his head and made a low groaning sound in his throat. He turned to leave through the back door, presumably to get some air. Jack and I stared at the empty space where he had paced like a caged animal and then looked at each other.

"I'll handle him and the press," Jack assured me. "If anyone contacts you for an interview, give them my information."

"I'm not the celebrity… and I certainly don't have money to pay you for your services," I said. "If I ignore it—"

Jack shook his head. "I'm doing it gratis, Emilia, because we're friends, and in the end it helps Alex. And if you think this is going to go away any time soon—you're mistaken. People will latch onto it. Maybe they'll forget it for a bit. But then the next time he's in a relationship, they'll bring it back out. And it will be horrible for him. And they'll drag your name through the mud again. I'm going to do my best to minimise everything."

"I trust your good judgment." I gave him a nod. Frankly, I just wanted to get out of the house. I never wanted to see it again. "But I really do have to go. The car's waiting for me."

"I know. I saw it when we came in."

I turned an ankle and took a step but paused and glanced at the long-suffering publicist. "Tell him I'm sorry for me?"

"Are you kidding?" Jack laughed. "I'm going to be grovelling myself. You do your own apologising."

I sighed.

Jack rolled his eyes. "When you're ready of course."

"If ever."

"London's a small town," Jack said with a chuckle at his joke. "I'm sure you'll run into each other sooner than you think. Then you can say whatever you need to him. Distance and time can heal a lot of things."

"What are you? Some strange publicist bodhisattva?"

He shrugged his shoulders. "I've thought about adding it to my business cards."

"Well, go work your magic on him," I bade. "He needs it more than I do at the moment."

Jack bowed his head. "When you're right, you're right."

I waited until he retreated out the door leading to the garden before I left through the front. Stepping out onto the entry steps, I took in a cleansing breath of sea air. I didn't feel any better for how the situation ended—I would have preferred a smoother exit—but it was over.

I was a free woman.

And in a matter of hours, I would be on a flight headed for London, which was exactly where I wanted to be, watching telly snuggled between the only two men in the world that I knew loved me unconditionally.

CHAPTER 29

MY MOBILE JINGLED until I was awake to answer, though I contemplated throwing it against the wall to silence it forever. After a momentary, irrational fear that it was Georgina calling me to do her bidding, I relaxed back into the soft mattress and felt around on my bedside table for the device. She would never call me again, thankfully. Squinting without my glasses, I could just make out the contact name on the front screen and groaned into my pillow.

"Do you know what time it is?" I asked by way of greeting, my voice hoarse from sleep.

"It's probably about ten there, right?" said the serious voice on the other end.

I groaned again and burrowed deeper into my pillows. "What do you need, Jack?"

The sound of his long-suffering sigh on the other end made me laugh.

"Did I wake you? I thought it would be early enough."

"My sleep is all fucked up with the jet lag and time difference," I complained. "And since I don't have to work, I've not tried to regulate it. Quite useful, though, when you get a sudden urge to clean the flat top-to-bottom at three in the morning. I made three cakes and a batch of scones afterward. Not sure Lindsay and Sam were too thrilled with my banging around, though."

He chuckled. "You're plucky. Are you feeling better?"

"Define 'better,'" I said. "If by better you mean that at least Mary doesn't hate me, then sure. Or that the calls from reporters looking to interview me have slowed down to like five a day, then yes. It's better. If you mean better like my life is back to normal and I don't hate myself for everything that's happened, then no."

"I'll take the former," he replied. "I'll take anything, honestly. From you and from Alex."

The mention of his name did a strange thing to me. All at once my body tensed in anxiety and tingled with need. My heart swelled with a mixture of hate and love. Most of all, my eyes misted over as they were wont to do anytime I thought about him. I had to swallow my emotion. The constant urge to bawl my eyes out was, perhaps, the strangest thing to overcome me since setting foot back on my native soil.

Lindsay told me what I was feeling was normal, that I was grieving for the death of my old self—the old self that took a beating and kept going right back into the fight expecting a different outcome but finding none. More so, I was grieving the loss of a man I had loved but never really had.

What I truly felt, however, was a relief so profound that I didn't know what to do. There were a million different paths for me to take, yet I couldn't choose. There were even more worries ahead of me, but my freedom from Georgina and, sadly, from Alex, made me feel completely empty. I had no purpose. It was as though everything I ever was and ever identified with had been ripped from me and there were huge gaping holes waiting to be filled with something else.

But I didn't know what else. Something better, hopefully. There wasn't a manual that went along with existential crises. The fear of not being able to find myself was the impetus for my tears, not complete grief, and the mention of Alex's name only drew those thoughts back from their shadowy hiding spots in my mind. To say I was grieving diminished real grief, in my opinion. All I knew was that the emptiness made me feel strange, and somehow meant I was going to cry when any memory of the old life came back to haunt me.

"Emilia?" The faintness of Jack's worry came through in his voice.

"Yeah, sorry," I said. "Did you need something?"

"I wanted to make sure you would be watching tonight."

The words took time to filter through my sleep-fogged brain. But when they did, I let out a long, annoyed laugh. "The last thing I want to do is watch the Oscars and remember what I left behind."

"I just think you should," Jack urged. "Morgan was ever so thankful you called in that favour to get the dress for her when Georgina flaked. I can confirm she's never looked better."

"I'm glad I could help."

Jack chuckled. "You did more than help. You set her up with jewellery and hair and makeup, too. All this from London."

"Well, I know people," I commented.

"Long story short, she looks beautiful, and I think you need to watch the red carpet, at least," he said. "When we get back, Morgan's business manager will write a check for your services."

"Jack, no…"

He jumped in before I could continue. "It's only right. You did the job. You styled her."

"It took me all of ten minutes to call the right people," I said. "I did it because you've been helping with the whole gossip article fallout."

"Just stop arguing," he scolded me in exasperation. "The studio already paid the fees and I'll be damned if Georgina sees a penny for the work she didn't do."

With a heaving sigh, I closed my eyes and tried to block out the thoughts of the last woman I wanted on my mind. "Whatever. We'll figure it out when you're back in town. I'm going back to sleep."

"If you can't sleep, consider watching tonight, okay?"

There was something more he wasn't telling me, but I didn't have the brain power to be suspicious. "I will."

"Thank you, Em," he said. "Sleep well."

"I'm trying to, but you called me," I shot back drily.

Jack laughed. "Goodbye."

When the line went dead, I lay in silence, trying desperately to fall asleep. I didn't want to get up and further torture myself with a viewing of something which would upset me more. But, as I laid there, making out the faint grey shapes of the things in my dark room, I didn't grow sleepier. My eyes were wide open as Jack's insistence that I watch the show began to eat away at me. What was so important that I needed to see it?

I conceded defeat when I heard rustling in the kitchen and popcorn popping. Lindsay was preparing for his own Oscars viewing party. The intoxicating smell was what convinced me to get up; my stomach quickly reminded me I hadn't eaten since Lindsay forced me to have an egg at breakfast. Throwing the covers off my body, I plodded my way toward the kitchen. Sam was already in front of the telly watching the presenters discuss the fashion they expected to see on the red carpet.

Lindsay saw me first. "Glad you could come out from your burrow for a bit."

Making a rude gesture at him, I dropped into the middle seat on the sofa facing the television. Sam looked at me askance but didn't say anything. He merely shifted in his seat and threw his arms around me.

"I missed you," he mumbled.

I chuckled and hugged him until he let me go. "I was only in the other room."

"And we've seen you maybe twice since you came home," Lindsay called from the kitchen. "Not that I don't understand why, but it's like we've been living with a recluse."

The large man joined us with a bowl of popped kernels and two bottles of ale. He held one out in front of me. "You're going to need this."

I glanced up at him as I took the bottle and sipped it. "I need a few drams of Scotch. Not some piddly ale."

"Da just gave me a bottle of the 30-year, if you want some," he offered.

"I'm not wasting a 30-year on popcorn or an empty stomach." I scrunched up my face at the thought. "The ale's fine for now. We'll talk later, though."

Lindsay merely laughed and wedged himself into the last seat on the couch so that we were all cheek-to-cheek. When he was settled, he put the bowl of popcorn in my lap. At my teasing annoyance, he merely shook his head. "You sat in the middle. You get that duty."

The presenters came back on the screen with an interview of Meryl Streep, but I only half listened to the conversation as my attention was on the split screen watching the limo arrivals.

I popped two kernels in my mouth. "So you saw your Da?"

Lindsay nodded his head. "He was down for some meeting with his distributors. We had lunch."

"I didn't know you two were speaking."

Lindsay cast me a look of disappointment he masked quickly. "There's a lot of things I haven't told you since you've been dealing with all of this."

The silence that followed between us hit me like a ton of bricks. I hadn't been the best of friends to him recently, wrapped up as I was in my own drama. Frankly, I deserved to be dropped on the kerb and left to find new friends. But my stalwart mate hadn't let me fend for myself.

A slow grin spread across Lindsay's face. "Don't apologise. I get it. We're good."

"I'll do better. I promise."

"That's all I can ask for," Lindsay said. "Now, can we please focus on the telly? I'm expecting the object of my wet dreams to pop up here any second."

"The object of your wet dreams?"

Lindsay nodded. "Yes. It's a bloody shame he only likes girls, though."

"Are we talking about who I think we're talking about?" I asked, arching an eyebrow.

"Who do you think we're talking about?"

I punched his arm, but that was the end of our argument as a particularly attractive Sean O'Connor floated across the screen.

"Now there's an Irishman I wouldn't mind getting alone," Lindsay mentioned.

"And you wonder why I never invited you to any red carpet events."

He scoffed in mock affront. "Just because I'm saying it now doesn't mean I'd say it to his face."

Sam and I both looked at him; I couldn't recall a time when Lindsay had ever kept his opinions to himself. Why would he start? Lindsay waved us off and made a short grunting sound in the back of his throat. The cameras changed back to the presenters.

The three of us sat silently for some time watching the screen, jockeying for precedence in liberating popcorn from the bowl. Sam gave up after awhile but then hurriedly grabbed two handfuls, stuffing one, then the other, in his mouth. He smiled around the half-chewed food.

I bumped his shoulder with a playful laugh. "Didn't anyone ever tell you to keep your mouth closed when you eat?"

His kernel grin widened. "Nope."

I couldn't focus on the telly after that, no matter how hard I tried. For the first time since I came home, I realised I felt somewhat like a normal person again. I felt warm and full—perhaps somewhat due to the alcohol I had consumed—but it was a pleasant feeling. When I arrived home, I had been exhausted, angry and hurt, which resulted in snapping at Lindsay and Sam in turn. They did their best to stay away from me for the week. A part of me wished I saw how much I actually needed their company from the beginning rather than neglecting our relationships for the sake of wallowing in my own depression. It would have made the feeling of emptiness less of an issue.

"Oh, look, there he is!" Lindsay called, making me jump in my seat. My thoughts vanished.

Tobias adjusted the tailored tuxedo coat on his shoulders after stepping out of the sleek black limo. He looked good. Too good. But I knew he would, because I found the tuxedo for him.

What I didn't expect to see was a second person crawling out of the back of the limo, long limbed and equally as gorgeous in his pristine suit. He had shaved the beard and had his hair cut back into a short, fashionable trim. To be honest, he looked like a new man standing there buttoning the jacket over his waistcoat. I couldn't say he looked particularly excited to face another round of interviews, but he seemed more at ease. A smile and wave toward the screaming crowd in the stands watching the procession on the red carpet was all he needed to do to confirm that.

I sucked in a shaky breath. Did Jack know they were coming together? Where was Jack anyway? He was with Morgan, so who was governing Alex's interaction on the carpet? Tobias' publicist slipped out on the other side of the vehicle, and I figured that she was in charge of them both if they arrived together—Jack sent me information earlier in the week saying he was working directly with her regarding the issues surrounding the article.

Jack's insistence that I watch made some sense now, if not a whole lot. Both of them arriving together was a brilliant public relations move after the article and with all the rumours flying—if they went together, it showed a level of solidarity that might convince people I hadn't been between them. But it also said a lot that Georgina wasn't present. In a rather poetic way, Alex broke free of that burden and took a step to repairing his own life, first and foremost by pushing aside whatever beef had built up between Tobias and him and, ultimately, rising above it.

At least I hoped they had their row and shook hands so they could get back to being friends again. I hoped it wasn't a completely staged, fake pleasantness on each of their faces as they stood together for photos, arms around each other's shoulders.

Tobias said something the camera did not pick up and Alex chuckled. My experience with the man told me it wasn't a forced laugh. The last few months had been nothing but light laughs and half smiles that never reached his eyes. My shoulders sagged and I couldn't help the relieved smile pulling at my own lips. Though his pure happiness was fleeting, he seemed to be in a decent humour again. I was glad to see his genuine smile.

I realised, only belatedly as I thought on it, that it was the first one I had seen from him in ages. Since Christmas, by my estimation.

Soon the red carpet handlers pushed both men deep into the herd for photographs and interviews until the camera lost sight of them. I breathed a sigh of relief and managed a glance at Lindsay. He was watching me for my reaction.

"You handled that well."

"Did I?"

I didn't feel like it.

Lindsay chuckled. "You didn't throw a shoe at the television and you smiled."

I shrugged. "I'm just glad those two have worked it out. I think Alex's going to need a lot of 'guy' time coming up."

"You think he's sworn off women completely? Hmmm?" Lindsay pursed his lips together in thought, but burst out in laughter anyway.

I ignored his hopeful comment, and fixed my eyes on the screen. The ale did its job and I was starting to feel sleepy again, especially as the telecast extended into a long hour of interviews and chatting with actors I didn't particularly care to see. My eyelids began drooping around the time that Morgan finally appeared. She looked very good—perfect—in her Elie Saab couture, but Jack hadn't really wanted me to watch for her. It was obvious what he had wanted me to see.

Lindsay and I chatted a little more about the hideous green cake topper worn by a young actress I didn't know and awed over another's sapphire blue Tony Ward. I froze, however, when the presenter announced his next interview. Tobias and Alex appeared on the screen again, smiling and more at ease than earlier.

"We're here with two people who don't really need an introduction," said the presenter. "Tobias Sinclair and Alexander Thorne. Nice to see you both!"

Both acknowledged the presenter with a few short words and by shaking his hand.

"Tobias, you are of course here to present an award this year, after winning last year for *The Sailor's Son,*" the presenter said. "How does it feel to have a bit of a rest?"

Tobias laughed. "It's spectacular, actually. All I have to do is show up and say my lines and hand out an award. It's brilliant. Not like Alex who has to sit and stew for most of the night."

"It's not that terrible," Alex replied with a small laugh. "At least I hope…"

The presenter chuckled and looked at the camera. "Of course, Alexander is nominated this year for his role as Guy Fawkes in the film *Gunpowder*. How does it feel?"

An audible sigh escaped Alex's lungs. "It feels a little crazy, you know? This is like *the* top. I'm in awe of being here. If you'd told young actor me that I would arrive here so quickly and with all of these very talented people that I can call my friends and colleagues, I would have laughed in your face."

"Yes. Definitely," the presenter agreed. "You're nominated in the same category as some Hollywood heavyweights this year, some who've won quite a few awards in the past. Does that make the evening any more difficult?"

Alex shrugged and smiled, glancing at Tobias, though Tobias' attention was on something off to the side of the screen. "I'm just so proud of the film and the people in the cast and crew. And my category this year is so full of talent. I'm happy just to be nominated, winning would be icing on the cake. But if I lose, I'd cheerfully lose to one of them."

"If you win tonight, how do you plan to celebrate?" the presenter asked.

"Whether I win or not, I plan to go to a few parties," he explained with a laugh, "but then I'm headed out for a holiday somewhere tropical and alone. You know, a little breather before I begin filming my next project. Hopefully I don't have terrible tan lines. The make-up girls will hate the amount of foundation they have to paint on me."

That elicited a laugh from everyone in front of the camera. Alex visibly eased, sticking his hands in his pockets as the camera took in a full body shot.

"Are there any plans after that? More theatre perhaps?"

Alex shook his head. "Not right at the moment. After I'm done filming this one, I plan to take a very long, extended holiday to get things in order and really take my time picking something I love."

"You've certainly earned a bit of a breather, mate," Tobias said. Both he and Alex exchanged knowing glances.

"One of the strange things about this life is that if you aren't careful, as your success grows, your personal life tends to go a shambles," Alex elaborated quickly, looking directly at the camera. "You get really single minded and forget about what else is important in life. So you've got to take some time for yourself and balance everything out or it all goes haywire."

"Too true, too true," the presenter said without delving deeper. I silently thanked the gods that he got the one presenter who wasn't into the juicy story. Or, perhaps, they had been warned previous to the actual interview not to push for more. "Quickly, before you go, I have to ask who you're wearing."

"I'm in Burberry," Tobias replied.

"Armani," Alex added.

The presenter smiled. "Thank you both for your time. As always, it was a pleasure to talk with you. Have a great show and good luck!"

A minute later, they were gone from the screen and the cameras were on someone else I didn't immediately recognise. I released the breath I was holding for much of the short interview, relieved that the minor assault on my fragile heart was over.

Whatever Jack had truly meant by asking me to watch the show, I was glad I watched it. Though it wasn't as good as talking to either Tobias or Alex, I knew there would be a time in the future when everything would be laid bare between us. I didn't know when and if that time would equate to two ships passing in the night, coming to terms with each other, and going on our own separate paths, or if it involved each other. After the way we ended things in Los Angeles, I was fairly certain it was the first option, but it needed to happen. We would need the closure to move on with our respective lives. But right now, it was just too raw a topic. What had happened was closure enough for me while I sorted through my own life.

Though, if I were honest with myself, a part of me still wished that my new life included Alexander Thorne, the *real* Alexander Thorne. The difficult part would be convincing myself that if it didn't end up including him, that I was strong enough to live my life happily without him in it. It would end up being the truest test of my growth, but I was strangely ready for whatever the world threw at me.

I stood up from my seat to looks of confusion from both Lindsay and Sam.

"Where are you going? We haven't even seen Jordan and Dylan yet," Lindsay said.

"To bed," I replied. "I saw what I needed to see."

"Aren't you tired of sleeping?" Sam asked.

I chuckled at him and ruffled his hair. "Not yet. I'll see you in the morning."

"You're such a spoilsport," Lindsay replied.

I shook my head at him. "No, I just need my beauty sleep. I've got things to do in the morning."

"Like?"

"I don't know yet, I thought I'd wing it and see how I feel. Maybe check in at a university or two."

"Who are you and what have you done to Emilia?" Lindsay teased, though he smiled.

With a laugh, I left them to their television watching and closed myself in my room. I yawned as I got into bed and pulled the covers up to my chin. Tomorrow was a brand new day.

I couldn't wait for its possibilities.

EPILOGUE

THE DAY FELT LIKE A RACE AGAINST TIME from the moment I woke up and realised I forgot to set my alarm. The trains ran behind, my lectures ran over. And then, to make matters worse, my weekly tutorial got onto the subject of the Italian Renaissance... which devolved into my learned tutor giving me the most dry, long winded speech on Caravaggio I had ever heard.

I would have rather poked my eyes out with forks than listen to him, but I stayed silent; he was important to my future and he promised to give me the name of another professor who had a few reference materials in her collection for an essay on a Renaissance triptych by Hieronymus Bosch. But he held Dr. Jones' name ransom until he talked himself out, and though I attempted to stop by Dr. Jones' office, her curt secretary told me she was gone for the evening, thereby pushing me even further behind, and all for naught.

The only thing, as a matter of fact, that managed to remain on schedule was the heavy downpour forecasters predicted all week. And, as my luck had gone all day, it started smack dab in the middle of my walk from the Tube to my flat. I had never been so glad to reach the safety of my own home, but dreaded the knowledge I would have to leave it again for a work function as quickly as I could dress.

It was of absolutely no surprise to me then when, even within the perceived safety of my flat, my curling wand decided to stop working right when I needed it most. I conceded defeat and managed to tame the mess of frizzy curls on my head into a simple knotted twist held securely with a jewelled clasp.

Fortunately, my dress still looked amazing, the zipper didn't break, and my makeup had been in sufficient order. If one of those things weren't in order, I would have locked myself in my room and refused to leave it until my fortune changed. And I would have done it in stretchy trousers and fuzzy jumper, too. Not a semi-formal cocktail gown and heels.

Wrapping a scarf around my neck as I exited my room, I dared a glance at the small clock on the mantle over the fireplace. 8:33 and I still wasn't out the door. "Oh my God, I'm so late."

Lindsay looked up from the magazine in his hands. "You're fine. No one gets to those things on time anyway."

"Still, it doesn't look good considering it's my department hosting the thing," I replied.

"You'll be fine." Supremely unconcerned by my rushing around, he returned to reading. "You look spectacular, by the way."

I grinned and smoothed a hand down the front of my cocktail dress. "Do I?"

Going dress shopping had been an event, especially when I found out I dropped a full dress size and still had to have the smaller size taken in a bit. Playing more football with Sam—among other things—had helped more than I noticed.

He nodded but didn't look at me. "The gold really suits your skin tone."

I chuckled and bent down to slip on my stilettos, cursing as I did it. As I stood to my full, wobbly height, I couldn't help but shake my head. "You know, I got out of high fashion so I didn't have to wear these things. And now all I do is wear heels to work."

"The only reason you got out of high fashion?" Lindsay asked dubiously.

Walking by him to the coat rack, I made sure to smack his shoulder. "Ow! What was that for?"

"You know what for." I grabbed one of the warm coats and wrapped it around my body. "All right. Please make sure Sam eats something when he gets back. He's been really bad about it the last few weeks."

Lindsay's eyes flicked up again. He lazily flipped a page and chuckled. "You'll be a lot later if you run down the overprotective sister list for the billionth time."

I chuckled and grabbed my clutch. "You're right, of course."

"I always am."

"Your confidence is mind-boggling."

Lindsay shrugged at me and reached for his cup of tea. "Have a good time."

"I'll try."

The air outside was blustery and damp—a perfectly respectable early November evening for any Londoner. A fine mist replaced the deluge earlier and made it much easier to hail a taxi. I sat in the back of the vehicle in silence, tapping my toe anxiously and wishing the driver would put a little speed into the ride, but he was nothing if not observant of all posted speed signs. By the time we pulled to a stop in front of the huge museum, I was more than a little ready to jump free of the vehicle.

Practically tossing my fare at the man, I stepped out with the aid of a valet standing at the end of a red carpet. I thanked the valet and looked toward the assembled crowd of paparazzi held behind a velvet rope like mindless lemmings. My instantaneous reaction to hide upon seeing them weighed heavily on my mind, but there was little chance any of them would recognise me. My story was old. Practically eight months old. Even though I looked more like I had in my modelling years, they wouldn't care. What good was I to their gossip columns now?

I held my head high and followed the latecomers up the stairs, stopping briefly at the cloakroom just inside the doors. The security crew manning the front of the building stopped to check my name against the guest list, but my boss, Peter, happened by and motioned to the guards to let me pass. A black plastic half mask had been pushed to the top of his short salt-and-pepper hair. He grabbed two filled flutes of champagne from the bar and met me in the middle with long strides.

"I didn't think you were going to make it!" he exclaimed over the deafening dissonance of music, laughter, and chatter within the cavernous space. I almost didn't understand his words with the thickness of his German-accented English.

"Sorry, everything was running behind," I explained. "But I'm here now."

Peter grinned, offering me one of the flutes. "We need to get you a mask, too. They're walking around with ones to hand out to people who did not bring one."

"I'll find one."

I hoped my dismissive tone didn't anger him, but the last thing I planned to do in the course of the evening was don another mask. As a matter of fact, I was quite finished with masquerades in general, and had tried to convince my department to change the theme of the theatre costume exhibition opening. Since Peter had hired me as his assistant, I thought I had some sway.

They overruled me. Quite vociferously, at that. I had enjoyed the egalitarianism that came with the democratic nature of my new world in the arts, but it was no easier to accept my lot as low woman on the totem pole. Of course, they didn't know about the last year of my life; I didn't have that to back up my motion to change the theme. However, that didn't mean I had to like it or participate in all the trappings of a masquerade-themed party.

Besides, there were plenty of people within eyesight not wearing masks.

"Everything's gone off perfectly, by the way," he said. "I really appreciate the expertise in event planning you brought to the table to make this happen."

The heat of a blush coloured my face and a stupid grin followed. I still wasn't comfortable with praise from the person I was working for, but it was, nonetheless, nice to hear. Especially from someone I respected greatly as a curator and supervisor. "It's my pleasure, Peter."

He smiled, but was distracted by an older woman—probably a wealthy benefactor I did not know—and lifted his glass to me. "Go mingle. Have fun! You deserve it after all your hard work."

I sipped my champagne after a ceremonial clink. He excused himself. As I sipped, I let my eyes wander through the assembled crowd while they milled around the rotunda chatting and dancing, or followed their friends into the corridors and exhibits opened to them. There were so many people—amongst them, many of note in the arts and entertainment industry—that I felt like I was back in high fashion, after all. But I knew that after this night of glamour, my days would go back to normal between university and working part time at the museum. I quite liked pushing paper at a desk for Peter, with defined hours. There was a level of comfort in that knowledge and it allowed me to enjoy the moment. This wasn't my life now.

My champagne, unfortunately, disappeared all too quickly. When I noticed it, I made a beeline for the middle of the rotunda and the circular bar set up beneath the gorgeous Chihuly sculpture hanging from the dome. I ordered a vodka martini and leaned my back against the bar, my elbows resting on the top, to face out into the crowd.

A group of laughing women moved around the dance floor, trying to find partners to dance but ended up with each other. I watched them for a little bit as they attempted a foxtrot to the Duke Ellington cover played by the big band on the other side of the floor. They failed miserably. Didn't anyone know how to dance?

I didn't notice the bar beside me filling up with people. When I turned to collect my tart drink, I bumped into the tall, solid person standing beside me. A strong hand steadied me, clutching the bare skin of my shoulder with warm fingers. I shivered and glanced at the hand before I looked at the body connected to it.

And I knew.

It was probably a matter of seconds, but it felt like an eternity, when all I could do was stare at his chest covered in bespoke suit. McQueen. Slim cut. Bowtie. Hidden buttons on the crisp white shirt. Sucking in a breath as though it would give me the confidence I suddenly needed, I allowed my gaze to travel northward. Angular jaw, straight nose, short auburn curls, blue eyes. At least they were blue in the low light of the makeshift dancehall. To complete his look, he wore one of those cheap black half-masks.

I tried blinking away my déjà vu, but it was useless. He was still standing there with the same intensity I saw in his eyes that night in Venice so many months before. Except it was different now. I didn't feel like the deer caught in the headlamps. Though he surprised me, I stood my ground. And, unlike the last time, I knew everything he was and everything he wasn't; there were no fancy illusions playing into the sudden gravitational pull I felt toward his orbit.

He reached up to pull the mask off, gave it a cursory assessment and set it gingerly on the bar. When he turned back, a small grin played at his lips.

"I've been looking for you all night," he said.

The lump in my throat made it difficult to breathe or talk. As a result, he filled the space with more of his own words. "Jack said you'd be here—that you work in the fashion and textiles department."

"I-I do," I managed to utter. "But Jack told me you were busy filming in California and wouldn't be able to attend."

He shrugged. "I was busy. I made time."

"Peter—the curator—will be happy," I told him. "He wanted you here since we added the Fawkes costume to the display. I told him I knew someone... I'm glad you could make it."

When I realised I was rambling, and my words weren't important to the situation, I clamped my lips shut and looked at him again. All the wretchedness, all the pain I had seen on his face the last time we were in the same room with each other seemed to have faded. Perhaps he looked a little older now, a few more frown lines etching his skin, but he seemed better. Lighter. Tamed. He still managed that damnable intensity in his stare and in his posture, though.

He shook his head as though slightly bewildered by my words. "I'm not here because they wanted me here or because it would be a good thing for my image. I'm here for you. Because you wanted me to be here."

I sucked down half of my drink to busy my mouth. What could I say to that? My knees were weak just thinking about it.

"I have a flight back to the States in the morning."

"Oh, how long are you there for?"

Why did it matter anyway?

He shrugged.

"So you're here just for the night?" I asked, the words quiet and all too hopeful on my lips.

Whether he intended to or not, he took a step closer. I felt the heat of his body and smell the faintness of his light cologne. God, he smelled good. I hadn't noticed how much I missed that part of him.

"Just tonight," he said.

"Oh."

I sipped my drink this time. It gave me the courage I needed to hold his gaze. After shifting around clumsily and self-consciously, I finally set the glass down with a decisive clunk that made him look at it. If I only had him for one night, I wasn't going to waste it talking. And frankly, the talking could come later, if it was meant to be.

At that point, I didn't care. I wanted to have him, unimpeded by a fake girlfriend, a job, or shame, for one night. Just to see what it was like to have him freely.

Finally, when he looked back at me with the faintest smile on his lips, I motioned with my thumb to the dance floor. "So, um, would you care to dance? I mean, since you're here and—"

His full, bright smile was instantaneous. He chuckled lightly, but it turned into a soft hum of pleasure. "I thought you would never ask, bellissima."

"Okay, great."

He grabbed my right hand with his much larger left and made to move, but stopped suddenly and looked back at me.

"What is it?"

"I wanted to make sure Cinderella had her shoes on this time."

His jest was exactly what I needed. What we needed. It broke what remained of the clumsiness between us.

My face warmed. "No, I'm trying to be proper."

He shook his head and pulled me to his side, leaning down a fraction, whispering low and purring into my ear. "I rather like it when you're improper, though."

The heat on my face shot straight to my belly and lower, gripping and coiling. His lips were so close I felt them as they formed the words. He finished his sentence with a tender kiss on my temple. Sweet. Loving. Not at all like before. But his intent was unmistakable. I thought, for the briefest of moments, that there might be more for us. Maybe we could make it work.

I looked at him again, seeing the same hopeful glimmer in his smile. It said... *maybe*.

"Let's go, bellissima," he said with a squeeze of my hand. "If I have one night, I intend to use it to its full extent."

My nervous giggle disappeared into a breathless sigh as he whisked me out onto the dance floor and into his arms, his mask left forgotten at the bar.

ACKNOWLEDGEMENTS

There are countless people I need to thank for helping me reach this goal of publishing, but the following are at the top of the list:

Thank yous go out to my Mom for reading to me as a kid and encouraging my love for the written word. Also for not explicitly telling me to get a "real job" when I said I wanted to be a writer, but instead warned me to have a backup plan. Thank you for being who you are even when we don't agree.

To the rest of my family for always being there and being who you are... also when we don't agree.

Also to Joy, who didn't really help me write the book, but deserves a second mention because she had to live with me during this process.

Great big thank yous to my editors and hand holders Rebecca Coffman, Stephanie Jiang, and Susan Gorman. You girls have been so much help and put up with my procrastination like pros.

Finally, I am grateful to anyone who had any part in giving me the confidence to publish this in a legitimate format. You know who you are. You have no idea how much you changed my life for the better, but you have.

ABOUT THE AUTHOR

THERESA BUTLER developed a need for expressing herself in many different formats in her early grade school years and writing seemed like the perfect outlet. Unfortunately, it took many years of her adult life to realize her heart truly belonged in a book, not in a science lab.

By day, Theresa works as an executive assistant for a family real estate company, but soon hopes to make writing and publishing a full time career. She is also the owner of Butler Did It Publishing, her own indie imprint.

Theresa can be found hanging out in the cool comfort of the desert home she shares with her best friend, a chatty-but-reclusive feline roommate, and a lovable-but-not-so-bright dog. Otherwise, you can find her at your nearest renaissance festival, historical reenactment or geeky con pretending to live in the past.

WWW.THERESABUTLERAUTHOR.COM

For deleted scenes and an additional "epilogue" with your favourite *Masquerade* characters, visit

WWW.THERESABUTLERAUTHOR.COM

beginning November 14, 2015.

The password is "venice."